THE
NIGHT
CIRCUS

The circus arrives without warning.

No announcements precede it, no paper notices on downtown posts and billboards, no mentions or advertisements in local newspapers. It is simply there, when yesterday it was not.

The towering tents are striped in white and black, no golds and crimsons to be seen. No color at all, save for the neighboring trees and the grass of the surrounding fields. Black-and-white stripes on grey sky; countless tents of varying shapes and sizes, with an elaborate wrought-iron fence encasing them in a colorless world. Even what little ground is visible from outside is black or white, painted or powdered, or treated with some other circus trick.

But it is not open for business. Not just yet.

Within hours everyone in town has heard about it. By afternoon the news has spread several towns over. Word of mouth is a more effective method of advertisement than typeset words and exclamation points on paper pamphlets or posters. It is impressive and unusual news, the sudden appearance of a mysterious circus. People marvel at the staggering height of the tallest tents. They stare at the clock that sits just inside the gates that no one can properly describe.

And the black sign painted in white letters that hangs upon the gates, the one that reads:

Opens at Nightfall
Closes at Dawn

"What kind of circus is only open at night?" people ask. No one has a proper answer, yet as dusk approaches there is a substantial crowd of spectators gathering outside the gates.

You are amongst them, of course. Your curiosity got the better of you, as curiosity is wont to do. You stand in the fading light, the scarf around your neck pulled up against the chilly evening breeze, waiting to see for yourself exactly what kind of circus only opens once the sun sets.

The ticket booth clearly visible behind the gates is closed and barred. The tents are still, save for when they ripple ever so slightly in the wind. The only movement within the circus is the clock that ticks by the passing minutes, if such a wonder of sculpture can even be called a clock.

The circus looks abandoned and empty. But you think perhaps you can smell caramel wafting through the evening breeze, beneath the crisp scent of the autumn leaves. A subtle sweetness at the edges of the cold.

The sun disappears completely beyond the horizon, and the remaining luminosity shifts from dusk to twilight. The people around you are growing restless from waiting, a sea of shuffling feet, murmuring about abandoning the endeavor in search of someplace warmer to pass the evening. You yourself are debating departing when it happens.

First, there is a popping sound. It is barely audible over the wind and conversation. A soft noise like a kettle about to boil for tea. Then comes the light.

All over the tents, small lights begin to flicker, as though the entirety of the circus is covered in particularly bright fireflies. The waiting crowd quiets as it watches this display of illumination. Someone near you gasps. A small child claps his hands with glee at the sight.

When the tents are all aglow, sparkling against the night sky, the sign appears.

Stretched across the top of the gates, hidden in curls of iron, more firefly-like lights flicker to life. They pop as they brighten, some accompanied by a shower of glowing white sparks and a bit of smoke. The people nearest to the gates take a few steps back.

At first, it is only a random pattern of lights. But as more of them ignite, it becomes clear that they are aligned in scripted letters. First a *C* is distinguishable, followed by more letters. A *q*, oddly, and several *e*'s. When the final bulb pops alight, and the smoke and sparks dissipate, it is finally legible, this elaborate incandescent sign. Leaning to your left to gain a better view, you can see that it reads:

Le Cirque des Rêves

Some in the crowd smile knowingly, while others frown and look questioningly at their neighbors. A child near you tugs on her mother's sleeve, begging to know what it says.

"The Circus of Dreams," comes the reply. The girl smiles delightedly.

Then the iron gates shudder and unlock, seemingly by their own volition. They swing outward, inviting the crowd inside.

Now the circus is open.

Now you may enter.

Part I

PRIMORDIUM

The whole of Le Cirque des Rêves is formed by series
of circles. Perhaps it is a tribute to the origin of the word
"circus," deriving from the Greek *kirkos* meaning circle,
or ring. There are many such nods to the phenomenon
of the circus in a historical sense, though it is hardly a
traditional circus. Rather than a single tent with rings
enclosed within, this circus contains clusters of tents like
pyramids, some large and others quite small. They are set
within circular paths, contained within a circular fence.
Looping and continuous.

—FRIEDRICK THIESSEN, 1892

A dreamer is one who can only find his way by moonlight, and his punishment is that he sees the dawn before
the rest of the world.

—OSCAR WILDE, 1888

Unexpected Post

The man billed as Prospero the Enchanter receives a fair amount of correspondence via the theater office, but this is the first envelope addressed to him that contains a suicide note, and it is also the first to arrive carefully pinned to the coat of a five-year-old girl.

The lawyer who escorts her to the theater refuses to explain despite the manager's protestations, abandoning her as quickly as he can with no more than a shrug and the tip of a hat.

The theater manager does not need to read the envelope to know who the girl is for. The bright eyes peering out from under a cloud of unruly brown curls are smaller, wider versions of the magician's own.

He takes her by the hand, her small fingers hanging limp within his. She refuses to remove her coat despite the warmth of the theater, giving only an adamant shake of her head when he asks her why.

The manager takes the girl to his office, not knowing what else to do with her. She sits quietly on an uncomfortable chair beneath a line of framed posters advertising past productions, surrounded by boxes of tickets and receipts. The manager brings her a cup of tea with an extra lump of sugar, but it remains on the desk, untouched, and grows cold.

The girl does not move, does not fidget in her seat. She stays perfectly still with her hands folded in her lap. Her gaze is fixed downward, focused on her boots that do not quite touch the floor. There is a small scuff on one toe, but the laces are knotted in perfect bows.

The sealed envelope hangs from the second topmost button of her coat, until Prospero arrives.

She hears him before the door opens, his footsteps heavy and echoing in the hall, unlike the measured pace of the manager who has come and gone several times, quiet as a cat.

"There is also a . . . package for you, sir," the manager says as he opens the door, ushering the magician into the cramped office before slipping off to attend to other theater matters, having no desire to witness what might become of this encounter.

The magician scans the office, a stack of letters in one hand, a black velvet cape lined with shockingly white silk cascading behind him, expecting a paper-wrapped box or crate. Only when the girl looks up at him with his own eyes does he realize what the theater manager was referring to.

Prospero the Enchanter's immediate reaction upon meeting his daughter is a simple declaration of: "Well, fuck."

The girl returns her attention to her boots.

The magician closes the door behind him, dropping the stack of letters on the desk next to the teacup as he looks at the girl.

He rips the envelope from her coat, leaving the pin clinging steadfastly to its button.

While the writing on the front bears his stage name and the theater address, the letter inside greets him with his given name, Hector Bowen.

He skims over the contents, any emotional impact desired by the author failing miserably and finally. He pauses at the only fact he deems relevant: that this girl now left in his custody is, obviously, his own daughter and that her name is Celia.

"She should have named you Miranda," the man called Prospero the Enchanter says to the girl with a chuckle. "I suppose she was not clever enough to think of it."

The girl looks up at him again. Dark eyes narrow beneath her curls.

The teacup on the desk begins to shake. Ripples disrupt the calm surface as cracks tremble across the glaze, and then it collapses in shards of flowered porcelain. Cold tea pools in the saucer and drips onto the floor, leaving sticky trails along the polished wood.

The magician's smile vanishes. He glances back at the desk with a frown, and the spilled tea begins seeping back up from the floor. The cracked and broken pieces stand and re-form themselves around the liquid until the cup sits complete once more, soft swirls of steam rising into the air.

The girl stares at the teacup, her eyes wide.

Hector Bowen takes his daughter's face in his gloved hand,

scrutinizing her expression for a moment before releasing her, his fingers leaving long red marks across her cheeks.

"You might be interesting," he says.

The girl does not reply.

He makes several attempts to rename her in the following weeks, but she refuses to respond to anything but Celia.

*

SEVERAL MONTHS LATER, once he decides she is ready, the magician writes a letter of his own. He includes no address, but it reaches its destination across the ocean nonetheless.

A Gentlemen's Wager

Tonight is the final performance of a very limited engagement. Prospero the Enchanter has not graced the London stage in some time, and the booking is for a single week of performances, with no matinees.

Tickets, though exorbitantly priced, sold out quite quickly, and the theater is so packed, many of the women keep their fans at hand to flutter against their décolletage, warding off the heavy heat that permeates the air despite the autumnal chill outside.

At one point in the evening, each of those fans suddenly becomes a small bird, until flocks of them loop the theater to uproarious applause. When each bird returns, falling into neatly folded fans on their respective owners' laps, the applause only grows, though some are too stunned to clap, turning fans of feathers and lace over in their hands in wonder, no longer at all concerned about the heat.

The man in the grey suit sitting in the stage-left box does not applaud. Not for this, nor for a single trick throughout the evening. He watches the man upon the stage with a steady, scrutinizing gaze that never wavers through the entire duration of the performance. Not once does he raise his gloved hands to clap. He does not even lift an eyebrow at feats that elicit applause or gasps, or the occasional shriek of surprise, from the rest of the rapt audience.

After the performance has concluded, the man in the grey suit navigates the crush of patrons in the theater lobby with ease. He slips through a curtained door leading to the backstage dressing rooms unnoticed. Stagehands and dressers never so much as glance at him.

He raps on the door at the end of the hall with the silver tip of his cane.

The door swings open of its own accord, revealing a cluttered dressing room lined with mirrors, each reflecting a different view of Prospero.

His tailcoat has been tossed lazily over a velvet armchair, and his waistcoat hangs unbuttoned over his lace-edged shirt. The top hat which featured prominently in his performance sits on a hatstand nearby.

The man appeared younger on the stage, his age buried under the glare of the footlights and layers of makeup. The face in the mirrors is lined, the hair significantly greying. But there is something youthful in the grin that appears as he catches sight of the man standing in the doorway.

"You hated it, didn't you?" he asks without turning away from the mirror, addressing the ghostly grey reflection. He wipes a thick residue of powder from his face with a handkerchief that might once have been white.

"It is a pleasure to see you too, Hector," the man in the grey suit says, closing the door quietly behind him.

"You despised every minute, I can tell," Hector Bowen says with a laugh. "I was watching you, don't try to deny it."

He turns and extends a hand the man in the grey suit does not accept. In response, Hector shrugs and waves his fingers dramatically in the direction of the opposite wall. The velvet armchair slides forward from a corner packed with trunks and scarves while the tailcoat floats up from it like a shadow, obediently hanging itself in a wardrobe.

"Sit, please," Hector says. "It's not as comfortable as the ones upstairs, I'm afraid."

"I cannot say I approve of such exhibitions," the man in the grey suit says, taking off his gloves and dusting the chair with them before he sits. "Passing off manipulations as tricks and illusion. Charging admission."

Hector tosses the powder-covered handkerchief onto a table littered with brushes and tins of greasepaint.

"Not a single person in that audience believes for a second that what I do up there is real," he says, gesturing in the general direction of the stage. "That's the beauty of it. Have you seen the contraptions these *magicians* build to accomplish the most mundane feats? They are a bunch of fish covered in feathers trying to convince the public they can fly, and I am simply a bird in their midst. The audience cannot tell the difference beyond knowing that I am better at it."

"That does not make it any less frivolous an endeavor."

"These people line up to be mystified," Hector says. "I can mystify them easier than most. Seems a waste to let the opportunity pass by. Pays better than you might think, as well. Can I get you a drink? There are bottles hidden around here somewhere, though I'm not entirely sure there are glasses." He attempts to sort through the contents of a table, pushing aside piles of newspapers and a birdless birdcage.

"No, thank you," the man in the grey suit says, shifting in his chair and resting his hands on the handle of his cane. "I found your performance curious, and the reaction of your audience somewhat perplexing. You were lacking in precision."

"Can't be too good if I want them to believe I'm as fake as the rest of them," Hector says with a laugh. "I thank you for coming and suffering through my show. I'm surprised you even turned up, I was beginning to give up hope. I've had that box reserved for you the entire week."

"I do not often decline invitations. Your letter said you had a proposition for me."

"I do, indeed!" Hector says, striking his hands together in a single sharp clap. "I was hoping you might be up for a game. It has been far too long since we've played. Though first, you must meet my new project."

"I was under the impression that you had given up on teaching."

"I had, but this was a singular opportunity I could not resist." Hector walks over to a door mostly hidden by a long, standing mirror. "Celia, dearest," he calls into the adjoining room before returning to his chair.

A moment later a small girl appears in the doorway, dressed too nicely for the chaotic shabbiness of the surroundings. All ribbons and lace, perfect as a shop-fresh doll save for a few unruly curls escaping her braids. She hesitates, hovering on the threshold, when she sees that her father is not alone.

"It's all right, dearest. Come in, come in," Hector says, beckoning her forward with a wave of his hand. "This is an associate of mine, no need to be shy."

She takes a few steps closer and executes a perfect curtsey, the lace-trimmed hem of her dress sweeping over the worn floorboards.

"This is my daughter, Celia," Hector says to the man in the grey suit, placing his hand on the girl's head. "Celia, this is Alexander."

"Pleased to meet you," she says. Her voice is barely more than a whisper, and pitched lower than might be expected from a girl her size.

The man in the grey suit gives her a polite nod.

"I would like you to show this gentleman what you can do," Hector says. He pulls a silver pocket watch on a long chain from his waistcoat and puts it on the table. "Go ahead."

The girl's eyes widen.

"You said I was not to do that in front of anyone," she says. "You made me promise."

"This gentleman is not just anyone," Hector replies with a laugh.

"You said no exceptions," Celia protests.

Her father's smile fades. He takes her by the shoulders and looks her sternly in the eye.

"This is a very special case," he says. "Please show this man what you can do, just like in your lessons." He pushes her toward the table with the watch.

The girl nods gravely and shifts her attention to the watch, her hands clasped behind her back.

After a moment, the watch begins to rotate slowly, turning in circles on the surface of the table, trailing its chain behind in a spiral.

Then the watch lifts from the table, floating into the air and hovering as though it were suspended in water.

Hector looks to the man in the grey suit for a reaction.

"Impressive," the man says. "But quite basic."

Celia's brow furrows over her dark eyes and the watch shatters, gears spilling out into the air.

"Celia," her father says.

She blushes at the sharpness of his tone and mumbles an apology. The gears float back to the watch, settling into place until the watch is complete again, hands ticking the seconds forward as though nothing had happened.

"Now that is a bit more impressive," the man in the grey suit admits. "But she has a temper."

"She's young," Hector says, patting the top of Celia's head and ignoring her frown. "This is with not even a year of study, by the time she's grown she will be incomparable."

"I could take any child off the street and teach them as much. Incomparable is a matter of your personal opinion, and easily disproved."

"Ha!" Hector exclaims. "Then you are willing to play."

The man in the grey suit hesitates only a moment before he nods.

"Something a bit more complex than last time, and yes, I may be interested," he says. "Possibly."

"Of course it will be more complex!" Hector says. "I have a natural talent to play with. I'm not wagering *that* for anything simple."

"Natural talent is a questionable phenomenon. Inclination perhaps, but innate ability is extremely rare."

"She's my own child, of course she has innate ability."

"You admit she has had lessons," the man in the grey suit says. "How can you be certain?"

"Celia, when did you start your lessons?" Hector asks, without looking at her.

"March," she answers.

"What year, dearest?" Hector adds.

"This year," she says, as though this is a particularly stupid question.

"Eight months of lessons," Hector clarifies. "At barely six years of age. If I recall correctly, you sometimes start your own students a bit younger than that. Celia is clearly more advanced than she would be if she did not have natural ability. She could levitate that watch on her first try."

The man in the grey suit turns his attention to Celia.

"You broke that by accident, did you not?" he asks, nodding at the watch sitting on the table.

Celia frowns and gives him the tiniest of nods.

"She has remarkable control for one so young," he remarks to Hector. "But such a temper is always an unfortunate variable. It can lead to impulsive behavior."

"She'll either grow out of it or learn to control it. It's a minor issue."

The man in the grey suit keeps his eyes on the girl, but addresses Hector when he speaks. To Celia's ears, the sounds no longer resolve into words, and she frowns as her father's responses take on the same muddled quality.

"You would wager your own child?"

"She won't lose," Hector says. "I suggest you find a student you can tolerate parting with, if you do not already have one to spare."

"I assume her mother has no opinion on the matter?"

"You assume correctly."

The man in the grey suit considers the girl for some time before he speaks again, and still, she does not comprehend the words.

"I understand your confidence in her ability, though I encourage you to at least consider the possibility that she could be lost, should the competition not play out in her favor. I will find a player to truly challenge her. Otherwise there is no reason for me to agree to participate. Her victory cannot be guaranteed."

"That is a risk I am willing to take," Hector says without even glancing at his daughter. "If you would like to make it official here and now, go right ahead."

The man in the grey suit looks back at Celia, and when he speaks she understands the words once more.

"Very well," he says with a nod.

"He made me not hear right," Celia whispers when her father turns to her.

"I know, dearest, and it wasn't very polite," Hector says as he guides her closer to the chair, where the man scrutinizes her with eyes that are almost as light and grey as his suit.

"Have you always been able to do such things?" he asks her, looking back at the watch again.

Celia nods.

"My . . . my momma said I was the devil's child," she says quietly.

The man in the grey suit leans forward and whispers something in her ear, too low for her father to overhear. A small smile brightens her face.

"Hold out your right hand," he says, leaning back in his chair. Celia immediately puts out her hand, palm up, unsure of what to expect. But the man in the grey suit does not place anything in her open palm. Instead, he turns her hand over and removes a silver ring from his pinkie. He slides it onto her ring finger, though it is too loose for her slim fingers, keeping his other hand around her wrist.

She is opening her mouth to state the obvious fact that the ring, though very pretty, does not fit, when she realizes that it is shrinking on her hand.

Her momentary glee at the adjustment is crushed by the pain that follows as the ring continues to close around her finger, the metal burning into her skin. She tries to pull away but the man in the grey suit keeps his hand firmly around her wrist.

The ring thins and fades, leaving only a bright red scar around Celia's finger.

The man in the grey suit releases her wrist and she steps back, retreating into a corner and staring at her hand.

"Good girl," her father says.

"I will require some time to prepare a player of my own," the man in the grey suit says.

"Of course," Hector says. "Take all the time you need." He pulls a gold band from his own hand and puts it on the table. "For when you find yours."

"You prefer not to do the honors yourself?"

"I trust you."

The man in the grey suit nods and pulls a handkerchief from his coat, picking up the ring without touching it and placing it in his pocket.

"I do hope you are not doing this because my player won the last challenge."

"Of course not," Hector says. "I am doing this because I have a player that can beat anyone you choose to put against her, and because times have changed enough to make it interesting. Besides, I believe the overall record leans in my favor."

The man in the grey suit does not contest this point, he only watches Celia with the same scrutinizing gaze. She attempts to step out of his line of sight but the room is too small.

"I suppose you already have a venue in mind?" he asks.

"Not precisely," Hector says. "I thought it might be more fun to leave a bit of leeway as far as venue is concerned. An element of surprise, if you will. I am acquainted with a theatrical producer here in London who should be game for staging the unusual. I shall drop a few hints when the time comes, and I am certain he will come up with something appropriate. Better to have it on neutral ground, though I thought you might appreciate starting things on your side of the pond."

"This gentleman's name?"

"Lefèvre. Chandresh Christophe Lefèvre. They say he's the illegitimate son of an Indian prince or something like that. Mother was some tramp of a ballerina. I have his card somewhere in this mess. You'll like him, he's quite forward-thinking. Wealthy, eccentric. A bit obsessive, somewhat unpredictable, but I suppose that is part and parcel of having an artistic temperament." The pile of papers on a nearby desk shifts and shuffles until a single business card finds its way to the surface and sails across the room. Hector catches it in his hand and reads it before handing it to the man in the grey suit. "He throws wonderful parties."

The man in the grey suit puts it in his pocket without so much as glancing at it.

"I have not heard of him," he says. "And I am not fond of public settings for such matters. I will take it under consideration."

"Nonsense, the public setting is half the fun! It brings in so many restrictions, so many challenging parameters to work around."

The man in the grey suit considers this for a moment before he nods.

"Do we have a disclosure clause? It would be fair, given my awareness of your choice of player."

"Let's have no clauses at all beyond the basic rules of interference and see what happens," Hector says. "I want to push boundaries with this one. No time limits, either. I'll even give you first move."

"Very well. We have an agreement. I shall be in touch." The man in the grey suit stands, brushing invisible dust from his sleeve. "It was a pleasure to meet you, Miss Celia."

Celia bobs another perfect curtsey, all the while regarding him with wary eyes.

The man in the grey suit tips his hat to Prospero and slips out the door and then out of the theater, moving like a shadow onto the busy street.

*

IN HIS DRESSING ROOM, Hector Bowen chuckles to himself while his daughter stands quietly in a corner, looking at the scar on her hand. The pain fades as quickly as the ring itself, but the raw red mark remains.

Hector takes the silver pocket watch from the table, comparing the time to the clock on the wall. He winds the watch slowly, regarding the hands intently as they swirl around the face.

"Celia," he says without looking up at her, "why do we wind our watch?"

"Because everything requires energy," she recites obediently, eyes still focused on her hand. "We must put effort and energy into anything we wish to change."

"Very good." He shakes the watch gently and replaces it in his pocket.

"Why did you call that man Alexander?" Celia asks.

"That's a silly question."

"It's not his name."

"Now, how might you know that?" Hector asks his daughter, lifting her chin to face him and weighing the look in her dark eyes with his own.

Celia stares back at him, unsure how to explain. She plays over in her mind the impression of the man in his grey suit with his pale eyes and harsh features, trying to figure out why the name does not fit on him properly.

"It's not a real name," she says. "Not one that he's carried with him always. It's one he wears like his hat. So he can take it off if he wants. Like Prospero is for you."

"You are even more clever than I could have hoped," Hector says, not bothering to refute or confirm her musings about his colleague's nomenclature. He takes his top hat from its stand and puts it on her head, where it slides down and obscures her questioning eyes in a cage of black silk.

Shades of Grey

The building is as grey as the pavement below and the sky above, appearing as impermanent as the clouds, as though it could vanish into the air without notice. Nondescript grey stone renders it indistinguishable from the surrounding buildings save for a tarnished sign hanging by the door. Even the headmistress inside is clad in a deep charcoal.

Yet the man in the grey suit looks out of place.

The cut of his suit is too sharp. The handle of his cane too well polished beneath his pristine gloves.

He gives his name but the headmistress forgets it almost instantly and is too embarrassed to ask him to repeat it. Later, when he signs the required paperwork, his signature is completely illegible, and that particular form is lost within weeks of being filed.

He presents unusual criteria in what he is looking for. The headmistress is confused, but after a few questions and clarifications she brings him three children: two boys and one girl. The man requests to interview them privately and the headmistress reluctantly agrees.

The first boy is spoken to for only a few minutes before he is dismissed. When he passes through the hallway, the other two children look to him for some indication of what to expect, but he only shakes his head.

The girl is kept longer, but she too is dismissed, her forehead wrinkled in confusion.

The other boy is then brought into the room to speak with the man in the grey suit. He is directed to sit in a chair across from a desk, while the man stands nearby.

This boy does not fidget as much as the first boy did. He sits quietly and patiently, his grey-green eyes taking in every detail of the room and the man subtly, aware but not outright staring. His dark hair is badly cut, as though the barber was distracted during the process, but some attempt has been made to flatten it. His clothes are ragged but well kept, though his pants are too short and may have once been blue or brown or green but have faded too much to be certain.

"How long have you been here?" the man asks after silently examining the boy's shabby appearance for a few moments.

"Always," the boy says.

"How old are you?"

"I'll be nine in May."

"You look younger than that."

"It's not a lie."

"I did not mean to suggest that it was."

The man in the grey suit stares at the boy without comment for some time.

The boy stares back.

"You can read, I presume?" the man asks.

The boy nods.

"I like to read," he says. "There aren't enough books here. I've read all of them already."

"Good."

Without warning, the man in the grey suit tosses his cane at the boy. The boy catches it in one hand easily without flinching, though his eyes narrow in confusion as he looks from the cane to the man and back.

The man nods to himself and reclaims his cane, pulling a pale handkerchief from his pocket to wipe the boy's fingerprints from the surface.

"Very well," the man says. "You will be coming to study with me. I assure you I have a great many books. I will make the necessary arrangements, and then we shall be on our way."

"Do I have a choice?"

"Do you wish to remain here?"

The boy considers this for a moment.

"No," he says.

"Very well."

"Don't you want to know my name?" the boy asks.

"Names are not of nearly as much import as people like to suppose," the man in the grey suit says. "A label assigned to identify you either by this institution or your departed parents is neither of interest nor value to me. If you find you are in need of a name at any point, you may choose one for yourself. For now it will not be necessary."

The boy is sent to pack his small bag of negligible possessions. The man in the grey suit signs papers and responds to the headmistress's questions with answers she does not entirely follow, but she does not protest the transaction.

When the boy is ready, the man in the grey suit takes him from the grey stone building, and he does not return.

Magic Lessons
1875–1880

Celia grows up in a series of theaters. Most often in New York, but there are long stretches in other cities. Boston. Chicago. San Francisco. Occasional excursions to Milan or Paris or London. They blend together in a haze of must and velvet and sawdust to the point where she sometimes does not recall what country she is in, not that it matters.

Her father brings her everywhere while she is small, parading her like a well-loved small dog in expensive gowns, for his colleagues and acquaintances to fawn over in pubs after performances.

When he decides she is too tall to be an adorable accessory, he begins abandoning her in dressing rooms or hotels.

She wonders each night if perhaps he will not return, but he always stumbles in at unseemly hours, sometimes petting her gently on the head while she pretends to be asleep, other times ignoring her entirely.

Her lessons have become less formal. When before he would sit her down at marked, though irregular, times, now he tests her constantly, but never in public.

Even tasks as simple as tying her boots he forbids her to do by hand. She stares at her feet, silently willing the laces to tie and untie in messy bows, scowling when they tangle into knots.

Her father is not forthcoming when she asks questions. She has gathered that the man in the grey suit whom her father called Alexander also has a student, and there will be some sort of game.

"Like chess?" she asks once.

"No," her father says. "Not like chess."

*

THE BOY GROWS UP in a town house in London. He sees no one, not even when his meals are delivered to his rooms, appearing by the door on covered trays and disappearing in the same manner. Once a month, a man who does not speak is brought in to cut his hair. Once a year, the same man takes measurements for new clothing.

The boy spends most of his time reading. And writing, of course. He copies down sections of books, writes out words and symbols he does not understand at first but that become intimately familiar beneath his ink-stained fingers, formed again and again in increasingly steady lines. He reads histories and mythologies and novels. He slowly learns other languages, though he has difficulty speaking them.

There are occasional excursions to museums and libraries, during off-hours when there are few, if any, other visitors. The boy adores these trips, both for the contents of the buildings and the deviation from his set routine. But they are rare, and he is never permitted to leave the house unescorted.

The man in the grey suit visits him in his rooms every day, most often accompanied by a new pile of books, spending exactly one hour lecturing about things the boy is unsure he will ever truly understand.

Only once does the boy inquire as to when he will actually be allowed to do something, the kinds of things that the man in the grey suit demonstrates very rarely himself during these strictly scheduled lessons.

"When you are ready" is the only answer he receives.

He is not deemed ready for some time.

*

THE DOVES THAT APPEAR ONSTAGE and occasionally in the audience during Prospero's performances are kept in elaborate cages, delivered to each theater along with the rest of his luggage and supplies.

A slamming door sends a stack of trunks and cases tumbling in his dressing room, toppling a cage full of doves.

The trunks right themselves instantly, but Hector picks up the cage to inspect the damage.

While most of the doves are only dazed from the fall, one clearly has a broken wing. Hector carefully removes the bird, the damaged bars repairing as he sets the cage down.

"Can you fix it?" Celia asks.

Her father looks at the injured dove and then back at his daughter, waiting for her to ask a different question.

"Can I fix it?" she asks after a moment.

"Go ahead and try," her father says, handing it to her.

Celia gently strokes the trembling dove, staring intently at its broken wing.

The bird makes a painful, strangled sound much different than its normal coo.

"I can't do it," Celia says with tears in her eyes, lifting the bird up to her father.

Hector takes the dove and swiftly twists its neck, ignoring his daughter's cry of protest.

"Living things have different rules," he says. "You should practice with something more basic." He picks up Celia's only doll from a nearby chair and drops it to the floor, the porcelain head cracking open.

When Celia returns to her father the next day with the perfectly repaired doll he only nods his approval before waving her away, returning to his preperformance preparations.

"You could have fixed the bird," Celia says.

"Then you wouldn't have learned anything," Hector says. "You need to understand your limitations so you can overcome them. You do want to win, don't you?"

Celia nods, looking down at her doll. It bears no evidence that it had ever been damaged, not a single crack along the vacant, smiling face.

She throws it under a chair and does not take it with her when they depart the theater.

*

THE MAN IN THE GREY SUIT takes the boy for a week in France that is not precisely a holiday. The trip is unannounced, the boy's small suitcase packed without his knowledge.

The boy assumes they are there for some manner of lesson, but no particular area of study is specified. After the first day, he wonders if they are visiting only for the food, entranced by the luscious crackle of fresh-baked bread in *boulangeries* and the sheer variety of cheeses.

There are off-hour trips to silent museums, where the boy tries and fails to walk through galleries as quietly as his instructor does, cringing when each footfall echoes. Though he requests a sketchbook, his instructor insists it will be better for him to capture the images in his memory.

One evening, the boy is sent to the theater.

He expects a play or perhaps a ballet, but the performance is something he finds unusual.

The man on the stage, a slick-haired, bearded fellow whose white gloves move like birds against the black of his suit, performs simple tricks and sleight-of-hand misdirections. Birds disappear from cages with false bottoms, handkerchiefs slip from pockets to be concealed again in cuffs.

The boy watches both the magician and his modest audience curiously. The spectators seem impressed by the deceptions, often applauding them politely.

When he questions his instructor after the show, he is told the matter will not be discussed until they return to London at the end of the week.

The next evening, the boy is brought to a larger theater and again left alone for the performance. The sheer size of the crowd makes him nervous, he has never been in a space so full of people before.

The man on this stage appears older than the magician from the previous night. He wears a nicer suit. His movements are more precise. Every exhibition is not only unusual but captivating.

The applause is more than polite.

And this magician does not hide handkerchiefs within his lace shirt cuffs. The birds that appear from all manner of locations have no cages at all. These are feats that the boy has seen only in his lessons. Manipulations and illusions he has been expressly informed again and again must be kept secret.

The boy applauds as well when Prospero the Enchanter takes his final bow.

Again, his instructor refuses to answer any of his questions until they return to London.

Once in the town house, falling back into a routine that now feels as though it had never been disrupted, the man in the grey suit first asks the boy to tell him the difference between the two performances.

"The first man was using mechanical contraptions and mirrors, making the audience look different places when he did not wish them to see something, to create a false impression. The second man, the one named for the duke from *The Tempest*, he was pretending to do similar things, but he did not use mirrors or tricks. He did things the way you do."

"Very good."

"Do you know that man?" the boy asks.

"I have known that man for a very long time," his instructor says.

"Does he teach those things as well, the way you teach me?"

His instructor nods, but does not elaborate.

"How can the people watching not see the difference?" the boy asks. To him it is clear, though he cannot properly articulate why. It was something he felt in the air as much as observed with his eyes.

"People see what they wish to see. And in most cases, what they are told that they see."

They do not discuss the matter further.

While there are other not-quite holidays, though they are rare, the boy is not taken to see any other magicians.

*

PROSPERO THE ENCHANTER uses a pocket knife to slit his daughter's fingertips open, one by one, watching wordlessly as she cries until calm enough to heal them, drips of blood slowly creeping backward.

The skin melds together, swirls of fingerprint ridges finding one another again, closing solidly once more.

Celia's shoulders fall, releasing the tension that has knotted in them, her relief palpable as she draws herself safely together.

Her father gives her only moments to rest before slicing each of her newly healed fingers again.

*

THE MAN IN THE GREY SUIT takes a handkerchief from his pocket and drops it on the table, where it lands with a muffled thump, something heavier than silk hidden in the folds. He pulls the square of silk upward, letting the contents, a solitary gold ring, roll out onto the table. It is slightly tarnished and engraved with something that the boy thinks might be words in Latin, but the script is looping and flourished and he cannot make them out.

The man in the grey suit replaces the now empty handkerchief in his pocket.

"Today we are going to learn about binding," he says.

When they reach the point of the lesson that includes the practical demonstration, he instructs the boy to place the ring on his own hand. He never touches the boy, regardless of the circumstances.

The boy tries in vain to pry the ring from his finger as it dissolves into his skin.

"Bindings are permanent, my boy," the man in the grey suit says.

"What am I bound to?" the boy asks, frowning at the scar where the ring had been moments before.

"An obligation you already had, and a person you will not meet for some time. The details are not important at this point. This is merely a necessary technicality."

The boy only nods and does not question further, but that night, when he is alone again and unable to sleep, he spends hours staring at his hand in the moonlight, wondering who the person he is bound to might be.

*

THOUSANDS OF MILES AWAY, in a crowded theater that thunders with applause for the man onstage, hidden in the shadows formed between disused pieces of scenery backstage, Celia Bowen curls herself into a ball and cries.

Le Bateleur

Just before the boy turns nineteen, the man in the grey suit removes him from the town house without notice, setting him up in a modestly sized flat with a view of the British Museum.

At first he assumes that it is only a temporary matter. There have been, of late, journeys of weeks or even months, to France and Germany and Greece, filled with more studying than sightseeing. But this is not one of those not-quite holidays spent in luxurious hotels.

It is a modest flat with basic furnishings, so similar to his former rooms that he finds it difficult to feel anything resembling homesickness, save for the library, though he still possesses an impressive number of books.

There is a wardrobe full of well-cut but nondescript black suits. Crisp white shirts. A row of custom-fitted bowler hats.

He inquires as to when what is referred to only as his *challenge* will begin. The man in the grey suit will not say, though the move clearly marks the end of formal lessons.

Instead, he continues his studies independently. He keeps notebooks full of symbols and glyphs, working through his old notes and finding new elements to consider. He carries smaller volumes with him at all times, transcribing them into larger ones once they are filled.

He begins each notebook the same way, with a detailed drawing of a tree inscribed with black ink inside the front cover. From there the black branches stretch onto the subsequent pages, tying together lines that form letters and symbols, each page almost completely covered in ink. All of it, runes and words and glyphs, twisted together and grounded to the initial tree.

There is a forest of such trees, carefully filed on his bookshelves.

He practices the things he has been taught, though it is difficult to gauge the effectiveness of his illusions on his own. He spends a great deal of time regarding reflections in mirrors.

Unscheduled and no longer under lock and key, he takes long walks around the city. The sheer volume of people is nerve-racking, but the joy in being able to leave his flat whenever he chooses outweighs his fear of accidentally bumping into passersby as he attempts to traverse the streets.

He sits in parks and cafés, observing people who pay him little notice as he blends into crowds of young men in interchangeable suits and bowler hats.

One afternoon, he returns to his old town house, thinking perhaps it would not be an imposition to call on his instructor for something as simple as tea, but the building is abandoned, the windows boarded.

As he walks back to his flat, he places a hand on his pocket and realizes that his notebook is missing.

He swears aloud, attracting a glare from a passing woman who steps aside as he stops short on the crowded pavement.

He retraces his steps, growing more anxious with each turn.

A light rain begins to fall, not much more than mist, but several umbrellas spring up amongst the crowd. He pulls the brim of his bowler hat down to better shield his eyes as he searches the dampening pavement for any sign of his notebook.

He stops at a corner beneath the awning of a café, watching the lamps flickering on up and down the street, wondering if he should wait until the crowd thins or the rain lets up. Then he notices that there is a girl standing some paces away, also sheltered beneath the awning, and she is poring over the pages of a notebook that he is quite certain is his own.

She is perhaps eighteen, perhaps a bit younger. Her eyes are light, and her hair is an indeterminate color that cannot seem to decide if it is blond or brown. She wears a dress that would have been quite fashionable two years ago and is damp from the rain.

He steps closer, but she does not notice, she stays completely absorbed in the book. She has even removed one of her gloves to better handle the delicate pages. He can now see that it is, indeed, his own journal, open to a page with a card pasted onto it, printed with winged creatures crawling over a spoked wheel. His handwriting covers the card and the paper around it, incorporating it into solid text.

He watches her expression as she flips through the pages, a mixture of confusion and curiosity.

"I believe you have my book," he says after a moment. The girl jumps in surprise and nearly drops the notebook but manages to catch it, though in the process her glove flutters to the pavement. He bends down to retrieve it, and when he straightens and offers it to her, she seems surprised to see that he is smiling at her.

"I'm sorry," she says, accepting her glove and quickly pushing the journal at him. "You dropped it in the park and I was trying to give it back but I lost track of you and then I . . . I'm sorry." She stops, flustered.

"That's quite all right," he says, relieved to have it back in his possession. "I was afraid it was lost for good, which would have been unfortunate. I owe you my deepest gratitude, Miss . . . ?"

"Martin," she supplies, and it sounds like a lie. "Isobel Martin." A questioning look follows, waiting for his own name.

"Marco," he says. "Marco Alisdair." The name tastes strange on his tongue, the opportunities to speak it aloud falling few and far between. He has written this variant of his given name combined with a form of his instructor's alias so many times that it seems like his own, but adding sound to symbol is a different process entirely.

The ease at which Isobel accepts it makes it feel more real.

"Pleased to meet you, Mr. Alisdair," she says.

He should thank her and take his book and go, it is the sensible thing to do. But he is not particularly inclined to return to his empty flat.

"Might I buy you a drink as a token of my thanks, Miss Martin?" he asks, after slipping the notebook into his pocket.

Isobel hesitates, likely knowing better than to accept invitations for drinks from strange men on darkened street corners, but to his surprise, she nods.

"That would be lovely, thank you," she says.

"Very well," Marco says. "But there are better cafés than this particular one"—he gestures at the window next to them—"within a reasonable distance, if you don't mind a damp walk. I'm afraid I don't have an umbrella with me."

"I don't mind," Isobel says. Marco offers her his arm, which she takes, and they set off down the street in the softly falling rain.

They walk only a block or two and then down a rather narrow alley, and Marco can feel her tense in the darkness, but she relaxes when he stops at a well-lit doorway next to a stained-glass window. He holds the door open for her as they enter a tiny café, one that has quickly become his favorite over the past few months, one of the few places in London where he feels truly at ease.

Candles flicker in glass holders on every available surface, and the walls are painted a rich, bold red. There are only a few patrons scattered about the intimate space and plenty of empty tables. They sit at a small table near the window. Marco waves at the woman behind the bar, who then brings them two glasses of Bordeaux, leaving the bottle on the table next to a small vase holding a yellow rose.

As the rain patters gently against the windows, they converse politely about insubstantial things. Marco volunteers very little information about himself, and Isobel responds in kind.

When he asks if she is hungry she gives a polite non-answer that betrays that she is famished. He catches the attention of the woman behind the bar again, who returns a few minutes later with a platter of cheese and fruit and slices of baguette.

"However did you find a place like this?" Isobel asks.

"Trial and error," he says. "And a great many glasses of horrible wine."

Isobel laughs.

"I'm sorry," she says. "Though at least it worked out well in the end. This place is lovely. It's like an oasis."

"An oasis with very good wine," Marco agrees, tipping his glass toward her.

"It reminds me of France," Isobel says.

"Are you from France?" he asks.

"No," Isobel says. "But I lived there for a while."

"As did I," Marco says. "Though that was some time ago. And you are correct, this place is very French, I think that's part of the charm. So many places here don't bother to be charming."

"You're charming," Isobel says, and immediately blushes, looking like she would pull the words back into her mouth if she could.

"Thank you," Marco replies, unsure what else to say.

"I'm sorry," Isobel says, clearly flustered. "I didn't mean to . . ." She begins to trail off, but perhaps emboldened by a glass and a half of wine, she continues. "There are charms in your book," she says. She looks to him for a reaction but he says nothing and she looks away. "Charms," she continues to fill the silence. "Talismans, symbols . . . I don't know what all of them mean but they are charms, are they not?"

She takes a nervous sip of her wine before daring to look back at him.

Marco chooses his words carefully, wary about the direction the conversation is taking.

"And what does a young lady who once lived in France know of charms and talismans?" he asks.

"Only things I've read in books," she says. "I don't remember what all of them mean. I only know the astrological symbols and some of the alchemical ones, and I don't know them particularly well, either." She pauses, as though she cannot decide whether or not she wants to elaborate, but then she adds, "*La Roue de Fortune*, the Wheel of Fortune. The card in your book. I know that card. I have a deck, myself."

While earlier Marco had determined her to be little more than mildly intriguing and fairly pretty, this revelation is something more. He leans into the table, regarding her with considerably increased interest than he had moments before.

"Do you mean you read the tarot, Miss Martin?" he asks.

Isobel nods.

"I do, at least, I try," she says. "Only for myself, though, which I suppose is not really reading. It's . . . it's just something I picked up a few years ago."

"Do you have your deck with you?" Marco asks. Isobel nods again. "I would very much like to see it, if you don't mind," he adds, when she makes no move to take it from her bag. Isobel glances around the café at the other patrons. Marco gives a dismissive wave. "Don't worry yourself about them," he says, "it takes a great deal more than a deck of cards to frighten this lot. But if you would rather not, I understand."

"No, no, I don't mind," Isobel says, picking up her bag and carefully pulling out a deck of cards wrapped in a scrap of black silk. She removes the cards from their covering and places them atop the table.

"May I?" Marco asks as he moves to pick them up.

"By all means," Isobel answers, surprised.

"Some readers do not like other people touching their cards," Marco explains, recalling details from his divination lessons as he gently lifts the deck. "And I would not want to be presumptuous." He turns over the top card, *Le Bateleur*. The Magician. Marco cannot help but smile at the card before replacing it in the pile.

"Do you read?" Isobel asks him.

"Oh no," he says. "I am familiar with the cards, but they do not speak to me, not in ways enough to properly read." He looks up from the cards at Isobel, still not certain what to make of her. "They speak to you, though, do they not?"

"I have never thought of it that way, but I suppose they do," she says. She sits quietly, watching him flip through the deck. He treats it with the same care she showed with his journal, holding the cards delicately by their edges. When he has looked through the entire deck, he places them back on the table.

"They are very old," he says. "Much older than you, I would venture to guess. Might I inquire as to how they came into your possession?"

"I found them in a jewelry box in an antiques shop in Paris, years ago," Isobel says. "The woman there wouldn't even sell them to me, she just told me to take them away, get them out of her shop. Devil cards, she called them. *Cartes du Diable*."

"People are naïve about such things," Marco says, a phrase oft repeated by his instructor as both admonishment and warning. "And they would rather write them off as evil than attempt to understand them. An unfortunate truth, but a truth nonetheless."

"What is your notebook for?" Isobel asks. "I don't mean to pry, I just found it interesting. I hope you will forgive me for looking through it."

"Well, we are even on that matter, now that you have allowed me to look through your cards," he says. "But I am afraid it is rather complex, and not the easiest of matters to explain, or believe."

"I can believe quite a lot of things," Isobel says. Marco says nothing, but watches her as intently as he had regarded her cards. Isobel holds his gaze and does not look away.

It is too tempting. To have found someone who might even begin to understand the world he has lived in almost his entire life. He knows he should let it go, but he cannot.

"I could show you, if you wish," he says after a moment.

"I would like that," Isobel says.

They finish their wine and Marco settles their bill with the woman behind the bar. He places his bowler hat on his head and takes Isobel's arm as they leave the warmth of the café, stepping out once again into the rain.

Marco stops abruptly in the middle of the next block, just outside a large gated courtyard. It is set back from the street, a cobblestone alcove formed by grey stone walls.

"This will do," he says. He leads Isobel off of the pavement and into the space between the wall and the gate, positioning her so her back is against the cold wet stone, and stands directly in front of her, so close that she can see each drop of rain on the brim of his bowler hat.

"Do for what?" she asks, apprehension creeping into her voice. The rain is still falling around them and there is nowhere to go. Marco simply raises a gloved hand to quiet her, concentrating on the rain and the wall behind her head.

He has never had someone to try this particular feat on before, and he is uncertain he will even be able to manage it.

"Do you trust me, Miss Martin?" he asks, watching her with the same intense stare from the café, only this time his eyes are barely inches from her own.

"Yes," she says, without hesitation.

"Good," Marco says, and with a swift movement he lifts his hand and places it firmly over Isobel's eyes.

*

STARTLED, ISOBEL FREEZES. Her vision is obscured completely, she can see nothing and feels only the damp leather against her skin. She shivers, and is not entirely sure it is due to the cold or the rain. A voice close to her ear whispers words she has to strain to hear and that she does not understand. And then she can no longer hear the rain, and the stone wall behind her feels rough when moments before it had been smooth. The darkness is somehow brighter, and then Marco lowers his hand.

Blinking as her eyes adjust to the light, Isobel first sees Marco in front of her, but something is different. There are no drops of rain on the brim of his hat. There are no drops of rain at all; instead, there is sunlight casting a soft glow around him. But that is not what makes Isobel gasp.

What elicits the gasp is the fact that they are standing in a forest, her back pressed up against a huge, ancient tree trunk. The trees are bare and black, their branches stretching into the bright blue expanse of sky above them. The ground is covered in a light dusting of snow that sparkles and shines in the sunlight. It is a perfect winter day and there is not a building in sight for miles, only an expanse of snow and wood. A bird calls in a nearby tree, and one in the distance answers it.

Isobel is baffled. It is real. She can feel the sun against her skin and the bark of the tree beneath her fingers. The cold of the snow is palpable, though she realizes her dress is no longer wet from the rain. Even the air she is breathing into her lungs is unmistakably crisp country air, with not a hint of London smog. It cannot be, but it is real.

"This is impossible," she says, turning back to Marco. He smiles, his bright green eyes dazzling in the winter sun.

"Nothing is impossible," he says. Isobel laughs, the high-pitched delighted laugh of a child.

A million questions rush through her head and she cannot properly articulate any of them. And then a clear image of a card springs suddenly into her mind, *Le Bateleur*. "You're a magician," she says.

"I don't think anyone has actually called me that before," Marco responds. Isobel laughs again, and she is still laughing when he leans closer and kisses her.

The pair of birds circle overhead as a light wind blows through the branches of the trees around them.

To passersby on the darkened London street, they look like nothing out of the ordinary, only young lovers kissing in the rain.

False Pretenses

Prospero the Enchanter gives no formal reason for his retirement from the stage. His tours have been so sporadic in recent years that the lack of performances passes mostly without notice.

But Hector Bowen still tours, in a manner of speaking, even if Prospero the Enchanter does not.

He travels from city to city, hiring out his sixteen-year-old daughter as a spiritual medium.

"I hate this, Papa," Celia protests frequently.

"If you can think of a better way to bide your time before your challenge begins—and don't you dare say reading—then you are welcome to it, provided it makes as much money as this does. Besides, it is good practice for you to perform in front of an audience."

"These people are insufferable," Celia says, though it is not exactly what she means. They make her uncomfortable. The way they look at her, the pleading glances and tear-streaked stares. They see her as a thing, a bridge to their lost loved ones that they so desperately cling to.

They talk about her as though she is not even in the room, as if she is as insubstantial as their beloved spirits. She must force herself not to cringe when they inevitably embrace her, thanking her through their sobs.

"These people mean nothing," her father says. "They cannot even begin to grasp what it is they think they see and hear, and it is easier for them to believe they are receiving miraculous transmissions from the afterlife. Why not take advantage of that, especially when they are so willing to part with their money for something so simple?"

Celia maintains that no amount of money is worth such an excruciating experience, but Hector is insistent, and so they continue to travel, levitating tables and producing phantom knocking on all manner of well-papered walls.

She remains baffled by the way their clients crave the communication, the reassurance. Not once has she ever wished to contact her departed mother, and she doubts her mother would want to speak with her if she could, especially through such complicated methods.

This is all a lie, she wants to say to them. *The dead are not hovering nearby to knock politely at teacups and tabletops and whisper through billowing curtains.*

She occasionally breaks their valuables, placing the blame on restless spirits.

Her father picks different names for her as they change locales, but he uses Miranda often, presumably because he knows how much it annoys her.

After months of it she is exhausted from the travel and the strain and the fact that her father barely lets her eat, as he claims looking like a waif makes her seem more convincing, closer to the other side.

Only after she genuinely faints during a session, rather than perfectly executing the choreographed dramatic swoon, does he relent to a respite at their home in New York.

At tea one afternoon, in between glares at the amount of jam and clotted cream she is slathering on her scones, he mentions that he has contracted her services for the weekend to a weeping widow across town, who has agreed to pay twice her normal rate.

"I said you could have a rest," her father says when Celia refuses, not even looking up from the pile of papers he has spread across the dining table. "You've had three days, that should suffice. You look fine. You're going to be even prettier than your mother someday."

"I'm surprised you remember what my mother looked like," Celia says.

"Do *you*?" her father asks, glancing up at her and continuing when she only frowns in response. "I may only have spent a matter of weeks in her company, but I remember her with more clarity than you do, and you had her for five years. Time is a peculiar thing. You'll learn that eventually."

He returns his attention to his papers.

"What about this challenge you're supposedly training me for?" Celia asks. "Or is that just another way for you to make money?"

"Celia, dearest," Hector says. "You have great things ahead of you, but we have relinquished control of when they will begin. Our side does not have the first move. We will simply be notified when it is time to put you on the board, as it were."

"Then why does it matter what I do in the meantime?"

"You need the practice."

Celia tilts her head, staring at him as she puts her hands on the table. All of the papers fold themselves into elaborate shapes: pyramids and helixes and paper birds with rustling wings.

Her father looks up, annoyed. He lifts a heavy glass paperweight and brings it down on her hand, hard enough to break her wrist with a sharp crack.

The papers unfold and flutter back to the surface of the table.

"You need the practice," he repeats. "Your control is still lacking."

Celia leaves the room without a word, holding her wrist and biting back tears.

"And for Christ's sake, stop *crying*," her father calls after her.

It takes her the better part of an hour to set and heal the shards of bone.

*

ISOBEL SITS IN A RARELY OCCUPIED ARMCHAIR in the corner of Marco's flat, a rainbow of silk ribbon twisted around her fingers as she attempts in vain to form it into a single elaborate braid.

"This seems so silly," she remarks, frowning at the tangle of ribbon.

"It's a simple charm," Marco says from his desk where he sits surrounded by open books. "A ribbon for each element, bound with knots and intent. It's like your cards, only influencing the subject instead of simply divining its meaning. But it won't work if you don't believe it will, you know that."

"Perhaps I am not in the proper mood to believe it," Isobel says, loosening the knots and putting the ribbons aside, letting them cascade over the arm of the chair. "I'll try again tomorrow."

"Help me, then," Marco says, looking up from his books. "Think of something. An object. A significant object that I cannot possibly know about."

Isobel sighs but she obediently closes her eyes, concentrating.

"It's a ring," Marco says after a moment, picking the image out of her mind as easily as if she had drawn him a picture. "A gold ring with a sapphire flanked by two diamonds."

Isobel's eyes snap open.

"How did you know that?" she asks.

"Is it an engagement ring?" he counters with a grin.

She clasps her hand to her mouth before she nods.

"You sold it," Marco says, picking up the fragments of memory attached to the ring itself. "In Barcelona. You fled an arranged marriage, that's why you're in London. Why did you not tell me?"

"It is not exactly a topic of proper conversation," Isobel says. "And you hardly tell me anything about yourself, you could have fled an arranged marriage of your own."

They stare at each other for a moment, while Marco tries to come up with an appropriate response, but then Isobel laughs.

"He probably looked for the ring longer than he looked for me," she says, glancing down at her bare hand. "It was such a lovely thing, I almost didn't want to part with it but I had no money and nothing else to sell."

Marco starts to say he can tell she received quite a good price for the ring, but then there is a knock on the door of the flat.

"Is it the landlord?" Isobel whispers, but Marco puts a finger to his lips and shakes his head.

Only one person ever knocks upon that door unannounced.

Marco waves Isobel into the adjoining study before he answers.

The man in the grey suit does not enter the flat. He has never entered the space since he orchestrated the transition, pushing his student out into the world.

"You will be applying for a position to work for this man," he says without greeting, taking a faded business card from his pocket. "You will likely need a name."

"I have a name," Marco says.

The man in the grey suit does not inquire as to what it might be.

"Your interview is scheduled for tomorrow afternoon," he says. "I have handled a number of business matters for Monsieur Lefèvre of late and I have put in a strong recommendation, but you should do whatever is needed to secure the position."

"Is this the beginning of the challenge?" Marco asks.

"This is a preliminary maneuver, to place you in an advantageous position."

"Then when does the challenge start?" Marco asks, though he has asked the question dozens of times before and never received a firm answer.

"That will be clear at the time," the man in the grey suit says. "When it does begin, it would be wise to focus your attention on the competition itself"—his eyes move pointedly to the closed door to the study—"without any distractions."

He turns and exits down the hall, leaving Marco standing in the doorway, reading and rereading the name and address on the faded card.

*

HECTOR BOWEN EVENTUALLY relents to his daughter's insistence that they remain in New York, but he does so for his own purposes.

While he makes occasional comments that she should be practicing more, for the most part he ignores her, spending his time alone in the upstairs parlor.

Celia is quite pleased with the arrangement, and spends most of her time reading. She sneaks out to bookstores, surprised when her father does not inquire as to where the piles of freshly bound volumes came from.

And she does practice, often, breaking all manner of things around the house in order to put them back together again. Making books fly around her room like birds, calculating how far they can travel before she must adjust her technique.

She becomes quite adept at manipulating fabric, altering her gowns as expertly as a master tailor to accommodate the weight she has regained, her body feeling like her own again.

She has to remind her father to come out of the parlor for meals, though lately he has refused more and more often, barely leaving the room at all.

Today he will not even respond to her insistent knocking. Irritated, and knowing he has charmed the locks so she cannot unlatch them without his own keys, she kicks the door with her boot and to her surprise, it swings open.

Her father stands by a window, intently watching his arm as he holds it out in front of him, the sunlight filtering in through the frosted glass and falling over his sleeve.

His hand fades completely and then returns. He stretches his fingers, frowning at the audible creaking of the joints.

"What are you doing, Papa?" Celia asks, curiosity trumping her annoyance. It is not something she has seen him do before, either onstage or in the privacy of her lessons.

"Nothing to concern yourself with," her father says, pulling the frilled cuff of his shirt down over his hand.

The door slams shut in her face.

Target Practice

The dartboard hangs precariously on a wall in the study, between tall bookcases and ornately framed oil paintings. It is almost camouflaged in the shadows despite its bold pattern, but the knife reaches its target each and every time it is thrown, very near the bull's-eye that is obscured by the newspaper clipping pinned to the board.

The clipping is a theatrical review, an article carefully removed from the London *Times*. It is a positive review; some might call it glowing. Nevertheless, it has been put in this position of execution, and the silver-handled knife is being thrown at it. The knife slices through the paper and sinks into the cork of the dartboard. It is retrieved and removed only to have the process repeated again.

The knife is being thrown gracefully, from the handle so it rotates over and over perfectly until the tip of the blade finds its mark, by Chandresh Christophe Lefèvre, whose name is printed in clear typeset letters in the last line of the aforementioned newspaper clipping.

The sentence that holds his name is the particular one that has incensed M. Lefèvre to the point of knife throwing. A single sentence, that reads thusly: "M. Chandresh Christophe Lefèvre continues to push the boundaries of the modern stage, dazzling his audiences with spectacle that is almost transcendent."

Most theatrical producers would likely be flattered by such a remark. They would clip the article for a scrapbook of reviews, quote it for references and referrals.

But not this particular theatrical producer. No, M. Chandresh Christophe Lefèvre instead focuses on that penultimate word. Almost. *Almost.*

The knife flies again across the room, over furniture of velvet and intricately carved wood, passing perilously close to a crystal decanter of brandy. It somersaults swiftly, handle over blade, and finds itself buried in the dartboard once again. This time it pierces the now nearly shredded paper in between the words "audiences" and "spectacle," obscuring the "with" completely.

Chandresh follows in the wake of the knife, pulling the blade from the board carefully but with a fair amount of force. He walks back across the room, knife in one hand, a glass of brandy in the other, and turns swiftly on his heel, letting the knife fly once more, aiming for that horrible word. Almost.

Clearly he must be doing something wrong. If his productions are merely almost transcendent, when the possibility of true transcendence exists somewhere nearby, waiting to be attained, then there is something else that must be done.

He has been pondering this ever since the review was placed on his desk, neatly clipped and labeled by his assistant. Additional copies have been filed elsewhere for posterity and safekeeping, as the desk copies often meet such gruesome fates while Chandresh agonizes over every word.

Chandresh relishes reactions. Genuine reactions, not mere polite applause. He often values the reactions over the show itself. A show without an audience is nothing, after all. In the response of the audience, that is where the power of performance lives.

He was raised in the theater, sitting in boxes at the ballet. Being a restless child, he quickly grew bored with the familiarity of the dances and chose instead to watch the audiences. To see when they smiled and gasped, when the women sighed and when the men began to nod off.

So perhaps it is not terribly surprising that now, many years later, he still has more interest in the audience than in the performance itself. Though the performance must be spectacular in order to coerce the best reactions.

And because he is incapable of observing the faces of every audience member at every performance of every show (shows that range from compelling drama to exotic dancing girls and a few that creatively combine the two), he relies on the reviews.

Though there has not been a review in some time that vexes him the way that this particular one does. And certainly not one in years that provoked knife throwing.

The knife flies once again, this time piercing the word "stage."

Chandresh goes to retrieve it, sipping his brandy on the way. He regards the nearly decimated article curiously for a moment, peering at the almost illegible words. Then he bellows for Marco.

With your ticket in hand, you follow a continuous line of patrons into the circus, watching the rhythmic motion of the black-and-white clock as you wait.

Beyond the ticket booth the only way forward is through a heavy striped curtain. One by one each person passes through it, vanishing from sight.

When it is your turn, you pull back the fabric and step forward, only to be engulfed by darkness as the curtain closes again.

It takes your eyes a few moments to adjust, and then tiny dots of light begin appearing like stars, lining the dark walls in front of you.

And while moments before you were so close to your fellow circusgoers that you could have touched them, now you are alone as you feel your way tentatively forward through a mazelike tunnel.

The tunnel twists and turns, the tiny lights providing the only illumination. You have no way of discerning how far you have gone or which direction you are moving in.

Finally you reach another curtain. Fabric that feels as soft as velvet beneath your hands parts easily when you touch it.

The light on the other side is blinding.

Truth or Dare

They sit in the oak tree in the afternoon sun, the five of them. His sister Caroline on the highest branch, because she always climbs the highest. Her best friend Millie perches below. The Mackenzie brothers, throwing acorns at the squirrels, are somewhat lower than that, but not low enough to be considered anything but high. He is always on the low branches. Not for fear of heights but for where he ranks in the group, when he is even allowed to be a part of it. Being Caroline's younger brother is both a blessing and a curse that way. Bailey is sometimes allowed to join them, but always kept in his place.

"Truth or dare," Caroline calls from the upper branches. She receives no reply, so she drops an acorn directly on her brother's head. "Truth. Or. Dare. Bailey," she repeats.

Bailey rubs his head through his hat. Maybe the acorn makes him choose the way he does. "Truth" is a resigned response, a yielding to Caroline's abusive, nut-throwing version of the game. "Dare" is marginally more defiant. Even if he is humoring her, at least he isn't a coward.

It seems like the right thing to say, and he feels rather proud of himself when it takes Caroline a moment to respond. She sits on her branch some fifteen feet above him, swinging her leg and looking off over the field while she formulates the dare. The Mackenzie brothers continue to torment the squirrels. Then Caroline smiles, and clears her throat to make her proclamation.

"Bailey's dare," she starts, making it his own and no one else's, binding him to it. He begins to feel uneasy before she even says what the dare actually consists of. She pauses dramatically before declaring: "Bailey's dare is to break into the Night Circus."

Millie gasps. The Mackenzie brothers stop their acorn throwing and look up at her, squirrels abruptly forgotten. A huge smile spreads across

Caroline's face as she stares down at Bailey. "And bring something back as proof," she adds, unable to keep the hint of triumph out of her voice.

It is an impossible dare, and all of them know it.

Bailey looks out across the field to where the circus tents sit like mountains in the middle of the valley. It is so still in the daytime, with no lights and no music and no crowds of people. Just a bunch of striped tents, looking more yellow and grey than black and white in the afternoon sun. It looks odd, and perhaps a bit mysterious, but not extraordinary. Not in the middle of the day. And not terribly scary, Bailey thinks.

"I'll do it," he says. He jumps down from his low branch and starts across the field, not waiting to hear their replies, not wanting Caroline to retract the dare. He is certain she expected him to say no. An acorn whizzes by his ear, but nothing else.

And for reasons Bailey cannot quite put words to, he is walking toward the circus with a considerable amount of determination.

It looks just as it did the first time he saw it, when he was not quite six years old.

It materialized in the same spot then, and now it looks like it never left. As though it were merely invisible for the five-year period when the field sat empty.

At the age of not quite six, he was not allowed to visit the circus. His parents deemed him too young, so he could only stare from afar, enchanted, at the tents and the lights.

He had hoped it would stay long enough for him to age properly into old enough, but it vanished without notice after two weeks, leaving too-young Bailey heartbroken.

But now it has returned.

It arrived only a few days ago and is still a novelty. Had it been present for longer, Caroline likely would have chosen a different dare, but the circus is currently the talk of the town, and Caroline likes to keep her dares *en vogue*.

The night before had been Bailey's first proper introduction to the circus.

It was like nothing he had ever seen. The lights, the costumes, it was all so different. As though he had escaped his everyday life and wandered into another world.

He had expected it to be a show. Something to sit in a chair and watch.

He realized quickly how wrong he was.

It was something to be explored.

He investigated it as best he could, though he felt woefully unprepared. He did not know what tents to choose out of dozens of options, each with tantalizing signs hinting at the contents. And every turn he took through the twisting striped pathways led to more tents, more signs, more mysteries.

He found a tent full of acrobats and stayed amongst them as they twirled and spun until his neck ached from staring up. He wandered through a tent full of mirrors and saw hundreds and thousands of Baileys staring, wide-eyed, back at him, each in matching grey caps.

Even the food was amazing. Apples dipped in caramel so dark they appeared almost blackened but remained light and crisp and sweet. Chocolate bats with impossibly delicate wings. The most delicious cider Bailey had ever tasted.

Everything was magical. And it seemed to go on forever. None of the pathways ended, they curved into others or circled back to the courtyard.

He could not properly describe it afterward. He could only nod when his mother asked if he had enjoyed himself.

They did not stay as long as he would have liked. Bailey would have stayed all night if his parents had let him, there were still so many more tents to explore. But he was ushered home to bed after only a few hours, consoled with promises that he could go back the next weekend, though he anxiously recalls how quickly it disappeared before. He ached to go back almost the moment he walked away.

He wonders if he accepted the dare, in part, to return to the circus sooner.

It takes Bailey the better part of ten minutes to walk all the way across the field, and the closer he gets, the larger and more intimidating the tents look, and the more his conviction fades.

He is already trying to come up with something he can use as proof without having to go in, when he reaches the gates.

The gates are easily three times his height, the letters atop it spelling out LE CIRQUE DES RÊVES are almost indiscernible in the daylight, each one perhaps the size of a rather large pumpkin. The curls of iron around the letters do remind him of pumpkin vines. There is a complicated-looking lock holding the gates shut, and a small sign that reads:

Gates Open at Nightfall & Close at Dawn

in swirly lettering, and under that, in tiny plain letters:

Trespassers Will Be Exsanguinated

Bailey doesn't know what "exsanguinated" means, but he doesn't much like the sound of it. The circus feels strange in the daytime, too quiet. There is no music, no noise. Just the calls of nearby birds and the rustling of the leaves in the trees. There doesn't even appear to be anyone there, as though the whole place is deserted. It smells like it does at night, but fainter, of caramel and popcorn and smoke from the bonfire.

Bailey looks back across the field. The others are still in the tree, though they look tiny from so far away. They are undoubtedly watching, so he decides to walk around to the other side of the fence. He is no longer entirely certain he wants to do this, and if and when he does, he doesn't particularly want to be watched.

Most of the fence past the gates borders the edges of tents, so there isn't really anywhere to enter. Bailey keeps walking.

A few minutes after he loses sight of the oak tree, he finds a part of the fence that is not right up against a tent but borders a small passageway, like an alley between them, wrapping around the side of one tent and disappearing around a corner. It is as good a place as any to try to get in.

Bailey finds that he does, actually, want to go inside. Not just because of the dare but because he is curious. Dreadfully, hopelessly curious. And beyond proving himself to Caroline and her gang, beneath the curiosity, there is that need to return tugging at him.

The iron bars are thick and smooth, and Bailey knows without trying that he will not be able to climb over. Besides the fact that there are no good footholds past the first few feet, the top of the fence curls outward in swirls that are something like spikes. They are not overly intimidating, but they are definitely not welcoming.

But the fence was apparently not built with the express purpose of keeping ten-year-old boys out, for while the bars are solid, they are spread almost a foot apart. And Bailey, being somewhat small, can squeeze through comparatively easily.

He does hesitate, just for a moment, but he knows he will hate himself later if he doesn't at least try, no matter what might happen after.

He had thought it would feel different, the way it had at night, but as he pulls himself through the fence and stands in the passage between the tents, he feels exactly as he had on the outside. If the magic is still there in the daytime, he cannot feel it.

And it seems to be completely abandoned, with no sign of any workers or performers.

It is quieter inside; he cannot hear the birds. The leaves that rustled around his feet on the outside have not followed him past the fence, though there is room enough for the breeze to carry them through the bars.

Bailey wonders which way he should go, and what might count as proof for his dare. There doesn't seem to be anything to take, only bare ground and the smooth striped sides of tents. The tents look surprisingly old and worn in the light, and he wonders how long the circus has been traveling, and where it goes when it leaves. He thinks there must be a circus train, though there is not one at the nearest station, and as far as he can tell, no one ever sees such a train come or go.

Bailey turns right at the end of the passage, and finds himself in a row of tents, each with a door and a sign advertising its contents. FLIGHTS OF FANCY, reads one; ETHEREAL ENIGMAS, another. Bailey holds his breath as he passes the one marked FEARSOME BEASTS & STRANGE CREATURES, but he hears nothing from inside. He finds nothing to take with him, as he is unwilling to steal a sign, and the only other things out in plain sight are scraps of paper and the occasional smushed piece of popcorn.

The afternoon sun casts long shadows across the tents, stretching over the dry ground. The ground has been painted or powdered white in some areas, black in others. Bailey can see the brown dirt beneath that has been kicked up by so many feet walking over it. He wonders if they repaint it every night as he turns another corner, and because he is looking at the ground, he nearly runs into the girl.

She is standing in the middle of the path between the tents, just standing there as though she is waiting for him. She looks to be about his own age, and she wears what can only be called a costume, as they certainly aren't normal clothes. White boots with lots of buttons, white stockings, and a white dress made from bits of every fabric imaginable, scraps of lace and silk and cotton all combined into one, with a short white military jacket over it, and white gloves. Every inch from her neck down is covered in white, which makes her red hair exceptionally shocking.

"You're not supposed to be here," the red-haired girl says quietly. She does not sound upset or even surprised. Bailey blinks at her a few times before he manages to respond.

"I . . . uh, I know," he says, and it sounds to him like the stupidest thing in the world to say, but the girl only looks at him. "I'm sorry?" he adds, which sounds even stupider.

"You should probably leave before anyone else sees you," the girl says, glancing over her shoulder, but Bailey cannot tell what she is looking for. "Which way did you come in?"

"Back, uh . . ." Bailey turns around but cannot tell which way he came, the path turns in on itself and he cannot see any of the signs to know which ones he had passed. "I'm not sure," he says.

"That's all right, come with me." The girl takes his hand in her white-gloved one and pulls him down one of the passageways. She does not say anything more as they walk through the tents, though she makes him stop when they reach a corner and they do not move for almost a minute. When he opens his mouth to ask what they are waiting for she simply holds her finger to her lips to quiet him and then continues walking a few seconds later.

"You can fit through the fence?" the girl asks, and Bailey nods. The girl takes a sharp turn behind one of the tents, down a passageway Bailey had not even noticed, and there is the fence again, and the field outside.

"Go out this way," the girl says. "You should be fine."

She helps Bailey squeeze through the bars, which are a bit tighter in this part of the fence. When he is on the other side, he turns around to face her.

"Thank you," he says. He cannot think of anything else to say.

"You're welcome," the girl says. "But you should be more careful. You're not supposed to come in here during the day, it's trespassing."

"I know, I'm sorry," Bailey says. "What does exsanguinated mean?"

The girl smiles.

"It means draining all your blood," she says. "But they don't actually do that, I don't think."

She turns and starts back down the passageway.

"Wait," Bailey says, though he doesn't know what he is asking her to wait for. The girl returns to the fence. She does not respond, just waits to hear what he has to say. "I . . . I'm supposed to bring something back," he says, and regrets it instantly. The girl's brow furrows as she stares at him through the bars.

"Bring something back?" she repeats.

"Yeah," Bailey says, looking down at his scuffed brown shoes, and at her white boots on the other side of the fence. "It was a dare," he adds, hoping she will understand.

The girl smiles. She bites her lip for a second and looks thoughtful, and then she pulls off one of her white gloves and hands it to him through the bars. Bailey hesitates.

"It's okay, take it," she says. "I have a whole box of them."

Bailey takes the white glove from her and puts it in his pocket.

"Thank you," he says again.

"You're welcome, Bailey," the girl says, and this time when she turns away he does not say anything, and she disappears behind the corner of a striped tent.

Bailey stands there for a long while before he walks back across the field. There is no one left in the oak tree when he reaches it, only a great deal of acorns on the ground, and the sun is starting to set.

He is halfway home when he realizes he never told the girl his name.

Associates and Conspirators

Midnight Dinners are a tradition at *la maison* Lefèvre. They were originally concocted by Chandresh on a whim, brought about by a combination of chronic insomnia and keeping theatrical hours, along with an innate dislike of proper dinner-party etiquette. There are places to get a meal after hours, but none of these places particularly suit Chandresh's tastes.

So he began throwing elaborate, multicourse dinners, with the first course to be served at midnight. Always precisely at midnight, at the moment the grandfather clock in the foyer begins to chime, the first plates are placed on the table. Chandresh feels it adds a sense of ceremony. The earliest Midnight Dinners were small, intimate gatherings of friends and colleagues. Over time they have become more frequent and more extravagant, eventually turning into something of an underground sensation. An invitation to a Midnight Dinner is coveted in certain circles.

They are selective, these dinners. Though occasionally there may be as many as thirty people, there are often as few as five. Twelve to fifteen guests is somewhat standard. The cuisine is exquisite regardless of the number of guests.

Chandresh never provides menus for these events. Some similar dinners, if there were dinners that could be considered similar, might have calligraphed menus on sturdy paper describing each course in great detail, or perhaps just listing an intriguing title or name.

But the Midnight Dinners have an air of nocturnal mystery already, and Chandresh finds that providing no menu, no map of the culinary route, adds to the experience. Dish after dish is brought to the table, some easily identifiable as quail or rabbit or lamb, served on banana leaves or baked in apples or garnished with brandy-soaked cherries.

Other courses are more enigmatic, concealed in sweet sauces or spiced soups; unidentifiable meats hidden in pastries and glazes.

Should a diner inquire as to the nature of a particular dish, question the origin of a bite or a seasoning, a flavor she cannot put her finger on (for even those with the most refined of palates can never identify each and every flavor), she will not be met with a satisfying answer.

Chandresh will remark that "the recipes belong to the chefs themselves and I am not one to deny them their privacy." The curious guest will return to the mysterious plate in front of her, perhaps remarking that, whatever the secrets, the dish is quite impressive, and continuing to wonder where the peculiar flavor might originate as she savors each bite with profound thoughtfulness.

Conversation at these dinners is largely reserved for the time between courses.

In truth, Chandresh prefers not to know all the ingredients, not to understand each technique. He claims such ignorance gives each dish life, makes it more than the sum of its parts.

("Ah," remarked one guest when the topic arose. "You prefer not to see the gears of the clock, as to better tell the time.")

The desserts are always astonishing. Confections deliriously executed in chocolate and butterscotch, berries bursting with creams and liqueurs. Cakes layered to impossible heights, pastries lighter than air. Figs that drip with honey, sugar blown into curls and flowers. Often diners remark that they are too pretty, too impressive to eat, but they always find a way to manage.

Chandresh never reveals the identity of his chefs. One rumor supposes that he has culinary geniuses from around the world kidnapped and imprisoned in his kitchens, where they are forced by questionable means to cater to his every whim. Another implies that the food is not cooked on the premises and instead is imported from the best restaurants in London, paid extra to stay open for the late hour. This rumor often results in debates on methods of keeping hot food hot and cold food cold, which never come to any satisfying conclusions and tend to make the debaters rather hungry.

Regardless of its origin, the food is always delectable. The decor in the dining room (or rooms, depending on the size of the event) is as extraordinary as it is in the rest of the house, in sumptuous reds and golds with art and artifacts from across the globe displayed on every available surface. Everything is lit with glowing chandeliers and copious candles, so that the light is not bright but deep and warm and bubbling.

There is often entertainment of some sort or another: dancers, conjurers, exotic musicians. The more intimate gatherings are typically accompanied by Chandresh's personal pianist, a beautiful young woman who plays continuously throughout the entire evening and never speaks a word to anyone.

They are dinner parties like any other, though the ambiance and the late hour makes them something else, something unusual and curious. Chandresh has an inherent flair for the unusual and curious; he understands the power of atmosphere.

On this particular night, the Midnight Dinner is a comparatively intimate one, with only five invited guests. And tonight's dinner is not merely a social gathering.

The first to arrive (after the pianist, already playing) is Mme. Ana Padva, a retired Romanian prima ballerina who had been dear friends with Chandresh's mother. He called her Tante Padva as a child, and continues to do so to this day. She is a stately woman, the grace of a dancer still visible through her advanced age, along with her impeccable sense of style. Her sense of style is the primary reason she is invited this evening. She is a fiend for aesthetics with an eye for fashion that is both unique and coveted, and provides her with a sizable income since her retirement from the ballet.

The woman is a magician with clothing, the papers say. A miracle worker. Mme. Padva dismisses these comments, though she does joke that with enough silk and an industrial-strength corset she could make Chandresh himself pass for the most fashionable of ladies.

On this evening, Mme. Padva wears a dress of black silk, hand embroidered with intricate patterns of cherry blossoms, something like a kimono reincarnated as a gown. Her silver hair is piled atop her head and held in place with a small jeweled black cage. A choker of perfectly cut scarlet rubies circles her neck, putting forth a vague impression of her throat having been slit. The overall effect is slightly morbid and incredibly elegant.

Mr. Ethan W. Barris is an engineer and architect of some renown, and the second of the guests to arrive. He looks as though he has wandered into the wrong building and would be more at home in an office or a bank with his timid manner and silver spectacles, his hair carefully combed to disguise the fact that it is beginning to thin. He met Chandresh only once before, at a symposium on ancient Greek architecture. The dinner invitation came as a surprise; Mr. Barris is not the type of man who receives invitations to unusual late-night social functions, or usual social functions for that matter, but he deemed it too impolite to decline. Besides, he has long desired a peek inside the Lefèvre town house, which is something of a legend amongst his colleagues who work in interior design.

Within moments of his arrival, he finds himself with a glass of sparkling wine in hand, exchanging pleasantries with a former prima ballerina. He decides then that he rather enjoys unusual late-night social functions, and should endeavor to attend them more frequently.

The Burgess sisters arrive together. Tara and Lainie do a little bit of everything. Sometimes dancers, sometimes actresses. Once they were librarians, but that is a subject they will only discuss if heavily intoxicated. They have, of late, made something of a business of consulting. On any matter. They offer advice on subjects ranging from relationships and finance to travel and shoes. Their secret (which they will also discuss if properly intoxicated) is their highly developed skill of observation. They see every detail, notice the tiniest nuances. And if ever Tara were to miss something, Lainie would catch her oversight (and vice versa).

They find they enjoy resolving other people's issues via suggestion more than doing all the work themselves. It is more satisfying, they say.

They look similar: both have the same waves of chestnut hair and large, bright hazel eyes that make them appear younger than they actually are, not that either will admit their age or disclose which one of them is older. They wear fashionable gowns that do not match exactly but coordinate beautifully, one complementing the other.

Mme. Padva greets them with the practiced disinterest she reserves for pretty young things, but warms when they enthusiastically compliment her hair and jewels and dress. Mr. Barris finds himself somewhat smitten with both of them, though it might be the wine. He has a fair amount of difficulty understanding their heavy Scottish accents, if they are Scottish at all. He is not entirely sure.

The last guest arrives shortly before dinner, just as the rest of the guests are being seated and the wine is being poured. He is a tall man of indeterminate age with indistinct features. He wears a spotless grey suit with tails and gives his top hat and cane at the door, and a card with the name "Mr. A. H——." He nods politely at the other guests as he sits, but says nothing.

Chandresh joins them at this point, followed closely by his assistant, Marco, a handsome young man with striking green eyes who quickly attracts the attention of both Burgess sisters.

"I have invited you all here for a reason," Chandresh says, "as I'm sure you have surmised by now. However, it is a business matter, and I find those to be best discussed on a full stomach, so we shall save the official discourse for after dessert." He waves vaguely at one of the waiters and as the clock in the hall begins to chime a low, heavy sound that reverberates throughout the house twelve times, the first course is brought out.

The conversation is as pleasant and flowing as the wine over the subsequent courses. The ladies are more talkative than the men. In fact, the man in the grey suit barely says a word. And though few of them have met before, by the time the *plats principaux* are cleared, an observer would have thought that they had known each other for ages.

When dessert is finished a few minutes before two o'clock in the morning, Chandresh stands and clears his throat.

"If you would all be so kind as to join me in the study for coffee and brandy, we may get down to business," he says. He nods at Marco, who slips away, rejoining them upstairs in the study with several large notebooks and rolls of paper in hand. Coffees and brandies are poured and the guests settle on various couches and armchairs around the crackling fireplace. After lighting a cigar, Chandresh begins his speech, punctuating it with purposefully placed puffs of smoke.

"Your company has been requested this evening because I have a project I am beginning, an endeavor, you might say. I do believe it is an endeavor that will appeal to all of you, and that you may each, in your unique ways, aid in the planning. Your assistance, which is entirely voluntary, will be both appreciated and well compensated," he says.

"Stop beating around the bush and tell us what your new game is, Chandresh darling," Mme. Padva says, swirling her brandy. "Some of us aren't getting any younger." One of the Burgess sisters stifles a giggle.

"But of course, Tante Padva." Chandresh bows in her direction. "My new game, as you so appropriately call it, is a circus."

"A circus?" says Lainie Burgess with a smile. "How marvelous!"

"Like a carnival?" Mr. Barris asks, sounding mildly confused.

"More than a carnival," Chandresh says. "More than a circus, really, like no circus anyone has ever seen. Not a single large tent but a multitude of tents, each with a particular exhibition. No elephants or clowns. No, something more refined than that. Nothing commonplace. This will be different, this will be an utterly unique experience, a feast for the senses. Theatrics sans theater, an immersive entertainment. We will destroy the presumptions and preconceived notions of what a circus is and make it something else entirely, something new." He gestures at Marco who spreads out the rolls of paper on the table, holding down the corners with an assortment of paperweights and oddities (a monkey skull, a butterfly suspended in glass).

The plans are predominantly sketches surrounded by notes. They show only fragments of ideas: a ring of tents, a central promenade. Lists of possible attractions or acts are scrawled down the sides, some crossed out or circled. Fortune-teller. Acrobats. Conjurer. Contortionists. Dancers. Fire artists.

The Burgess sisters and Mr. Barris pore over the sketches, reading each note as Chandresh continues. Mme. Padva smiles but remains seated, sipping her brandy. Mr. A. H— does not move, his expression inscrutable and unchanged.

"It is merely in conceptual stages, and that is why I ask you all here now, for the inception and development. What it needs is style, panache. Ingenuity in its engineering and structure. To be infused with the mesmerizing, and perhaps a touch of mystery. I believe you are the proper group for this undertaking. If any of you disagree, you are welcome to leave but I respectfully request you speak of this to no one. I prefer that these plans be kept undisclosed entirely, at least for now. Very sensitive at this point, after all." He takes a long draw off his cigar, blowing out the smoke slowly before he concludes. "If we do things properly, it will undoubtedly take on a life of its own."

There is silence when he finishes. Only the crackle of the fire fills the room for several moments as the guests look from one to the other, each waiting for someone to respond.

"Might I have a pencil?" Mr. Barris asks. Marco hands him one, and Mr. Barris begins drawing, taking the rudimentary sketch of the circus's layout and developing it into a complex design.

Chandresh's guests remain there until just before dawn, and when they do finally depart there are three times the number of diagrams and plans and notes than there had been when they arrived, strewn and pinned around the study like maps to an unknown treasure.

Condolences

The announcement in the paper states that Hector Bowen, better known as Prospero the Enchanter, entertainer and stage magician of great renown, died of heart failure in his home on the fifteenth of March.

It goes on about his work and his legacy for some time. The age listed is erroneous, a detail few readers perceive. A short paragraph at the end of the obituary mentions that he is survived by a daughter of seventeen years of age, a Miss Celia Bowen. This number is more accurate. There is also a notice that though the funeral services will be private, condolences may be sent via the address of one of the local theaters.

The cards and letters are collected, placed in bags, and brought by messenger to the Bowens' private residence, a town house that is already overflowing with appropriately somber floral arrangements. The scent of lilies is stifling and when Celia can no longer tolerate it, she transforms all of the flowers into roses.

Celia leaves the condolences piled on the dining-room table until they begin to overflow into the lounge. She does not want to deal with them, but she cannot bring herself to toss them away unread.

When she is unable to avoid the matter further, she makes a pot of tea and begins to tackle the mountains of paper. She opens each piece of mail one by one and sorts them into piles.

There are postmarks from around the globe. There are long, earnest letters filled with genuine despair. There are empty well-wishes and hollow praises of her father's talents. Many of them comment that the senders were unaware that the great Prospero had a daughter. Others remember her fondly, describing a delightful, tiny girl that Celia herself does not recall being. A few include disturbingly worded marriage proposals.

Those in particular Celia crumples into balls, placing the crushed missives on her open palm one by one and concentrating until they burst into flame, leaving nothing but cinders on her hand that she brushes away into nothingness.

"I am already *married*," she remarks to the empty air, twisting the ring on her right hand that covers an old, distinctive scar.

Amongst the letters and cards there is a plain grey envelope.

Celia pulls it from the pile, slicing it open with a silver letter opener, ready to throw it on the pile with the rest.

But this envelope, unlike the others, is addressed to her father proper, though the postmark is after his date of death. The card inside is not a note of sympathy nor a condolence for her loss.

It contains no greeting. No signature. The handwritten words across the paper read:

Your move.

and nothing more.

Celia turns the card over but the reverse is blank. Not even a stationer's imprint marring the surface. There is no return address upon the envelope.

She reads the two words on the grey paper several times.

She cannot tell if the feeling creeping up her spine is excitement or dread.

Abandoning the remaining condolences, Celia takes the card in hand and leaves the room, ascending a winding stair that leads to the upstairs parlor. She pulls a ring of keys from her pocket and impatiently unlocks three separate locks in order to access the room that is drenched in bright afternoon sun.

"What is this about?" Celia says, holding the card out in front of her as she enters.

The figure hovering by the window turns. Where the sunlight hits him he is all but invisible. Part of a shoulder appears to be missing, the top of his head vanishes in a flutter of sun-caught dust. The rest of him is transparent, like a reflection in glass.

What is left of Hector Bowen reads the note and laughs delightedly.

The Contortionist's Tattoo

Approximately once a month there are not-quite regularly scheduled Midnight Dinners that are most often referred to by the guests as Circus Dinners. They are a nocturnal amalgam of social event and business meeting.

Mme. Padva is always in attendance, and one or both Burgess sisters are a staple. Mr. Barris joins them as often as his schedule will allow, as he travels quite a bit and is not as flexible as he would prefer.

Mr. A. H— appears rarely. Tara remarks that they seem to have more productive post-dinner meetings when he is there, though he offers only occasional suggestions as to how the circus itself should be regulated.

On this particular evening, only the ladies are present.

"Where is our Mr. Barris this evening?" Mme. Padva inquires after the Burgess sisters arrive on their own, since he commonly accompanies them.

"He's in Germany," Lainie and Tara chorus in perfect unison, making Chandresh laugh as he hands them their glasses of wine.

"He's tracking down a clockmaker," Lainie continues solo. "Something about commissioning a piece for the circus, he was quite enthused about it before he left."

Tonight's dinner has no scheduled entertainment, not even the standard piano accompaniment, but entertainment arrives unannounced at the door nonetheless.

She gives her name as Tsukiko, though she does not clarify if it is her first or last name.

She is small, but not tiny. Long midnight-black hair is artfully knotted in elaborate braids upon her head. She wears a dark coat that is too large for her, but she carries herself in such a way that it seems to hang like a cloak and the effect is rather elegant.

Marco leaves her in the foyer, waiting patiently beneath the looming gold elephant-headed statue, while he attempts to explain the situation to Chandresh, which of course results in the entire dinner company filing out into the hall to see what the fuss is about.

"What brings you here at this hour?" Chandresh asks, perplexed. Stranger things have happened at *la maison* Lefèvre than unexpected entertainment, and the pianist does sometimes send a replacement when she is unavailable for a dinner.

"I have always been nocturnal" is Tsukiko's only response, and she does not elaborate as to what twists of fate brought her to this spot at this time, but the smile that accompanies her cryptic sentiment is warm and contagious. The Burgess sisters beg Chandresh to let her stay.

"We are about to sit down to dinner," Chandresh says with a frown, "but you are welcome to join us in the dining room, to do . . . whatever it is you do."

Tsukiko bows, and the smile appears again.

While the rest of them file into the dining room, Marco takes her coat, hesitating when he sees what lies beneath it.

She wears a thin wisp of a gown that would likely be considered scandalous in other company, but this gathering is not easily scandalized. It is more a delicate swathe of red silk held in place by a tightly laced corset than a proper dress.

And it is not the relative insubstantiality of her clothing that causes Marco to stare, but the tattoo that snakes across her skin.

At first, it is difficult to discern what it is, the shower of black marks that curls around her shoulder and neck, ending just above her cleavage in the front and disappearing behind the laces of her corset in the back. It is impossible to tell how far beyond that the tattoo travels.

And upon a closer look it can be discerned that the swirl of the tattoo is more than simple black marks. It is a flowing waterfall of alchemical and astrological symbols, ancient marks for planets and elements all emblazoned in black ink upon her fair skin. Mercury. Lead. Antimony. A crescent moon sits at the nape of her neck; an Egyptian ankh near her collarbone. There are other symbols as well: Norse runes, Chinese characters. There are countless tattoos, and yet they meld and flow into one design gracefully adorning her like an elegant, unusual piece of jewelry.

Tsukiko catches Marco staring, and though he does not inquire about it, she says quietly, "It is part of who I was, who I am, and who I will be."

And then she smiles and walks into the dining room, leaving Marco alone in the hall, just as the clock begins chiming midnight and the first course is served.

She slips off her shoes by the doorway and walks barefoot to an area near the piano that is catching the best light from the candelabras and the chandeliers.

At first she simply stands relaxed and calm, while the diners regard her curiously, and then it becomes immediately clear what her style of entertainment is.

Tsukiko is a contortionist.

Traditionally, contortionists are either front bending or back bending, depending on the flexibility of their respective spines, and their tricks and performances are based upon this distinction. Tsukiko, however, is one of the rare contortionists whose flexibility is equal in both directions.

She moves with the grace of a trained ballerina, a detail Mme. Padva notes and mentions in a whisper to the Burgess sisters even before the more impressive feats of agility begin.

"Could you do such things when you were a dancer?" Tara asks her, as Tsukiko pulls a leg up impossibly far over her head.

"I would have had a much busier social calendar if I could," Mme. Padva replies with a shake of her head.

Tsukiko is a consummate performer. She adds the perfect flourishes, holds positions and pauses for the ideal amounts of time. Although she twists her body into unimaginable and painful-looking positions, her beatific smile remains in place.

Her modest audience forgets their conversation and their dinner as they watch.

Lainie remarks to her sister after the fact that she was certain there was music, though there is no sound at all save for the rustle of silk against skin and the crackle from the fireplace.

"This is what I've been talking about," Chandresh says, hitting the table with his fist, suddenly breaking the charmed silence. Tara nearly drops the fork that she has been holding idly in her hand, catching it before it clatters onto her plate of half-eaten vermouth-poached oysters, but Tsukiko continues her graceful motions unfazed, though her smile increases noticeably.

"This?" Mme. Padva asks.

"This!" Chandresh repeats, waving at Tsukiko. "This is the precise flavor that the circus should be. Unusual yet beautiful. Provocative while remaining elegant. This is kismet, her coming here tonight. We simply have to have her, I will not accept anything less. Marco, get this lady a chair."

A place is set for Tsukiko; her smile is bemused as she joins them at the table.

The conversation that follows involves more creative coercion than outright job offer, and there are several deviations into the subjects of the ballet, modern fashion, and Japanese mythology.

After five courses and a great deal of wine, Tsukiko allows herself to be persuaded to accept an invitation to perform in a not yet existent circus.

"Well then," Chandresh says. "We are set as far as contortionists go. That's a start."

"Shouldn't there be more than one?" Lainie asks. "An entire tent, like the one for the acrobats?"

"Nonsense," Chandresh replies. "Better to have a single perfect diamond than a sack of flawed stones. We'll make a showcase of her, put her in the courtyard or something."

The matter is considered settled for the moment, and throughout dessert and after-dinner drinks, the only subject discussed is the circus itself.

*

TSUKIKO LEAVES A CARD providing information as to how to contact her with Marco as she departs, and she soon becomes a fixture at the Circus Dinners, often performing before or after dinner, so as to not distract the guests during the meal.

She remains Chandresh's favorite, oft-referenced criterion for what the circus should be.

Horology

Herr Friedrick Thiessen receives an unexpected visitor in his Munich workshop, an Englishman by the name of Mr. Ethan Barris. Mr. Barris admits that he has been attempting to track him down for some time after admiring several Thiessen-crafted cuckoo clocks, and was pointed in the right direction by a local shopkeeper.

Mr. Barris inquires as to whether Herr Thiessen would be interested in making a special commissioned piece. Herr Thiessen has a constant stream of custom work and tells Mr. Barris as much, indicating a shelf of variants on the traditional cuckoo clock that range from simple to ornate.

"I'm not certain you understand, Herr Thiessen," Mr. Barris says. "This would be a showcase piece, a curiosity. Your clocks are impressive, but what I am requesting would be something truly outstanding, *das Meisterwerk*. And money is absolutely no object."

Intrigued now, Herr Thiessen asks for specifications and details. He is given very little. Some constraints as to size (but still rather large), and it is to be painted solely in black and white and shades of grey. Beyond that, the construction and embellishment is up to him. Artistic license, Mr. Barris says. "Dreamlike" is the only descriptive word he uses specifically.

Herr Thiessen agrees, and the men shake hands. Mr. Barris says he will be in touch, and a few days later an envelope is delivered containing an excessive amount of money, a requested date of completion some months away, and an address in London for the completed clock to be shipped to.

It takes the better part of those months for Herr Thiessen to complete the clock. He works on little else, though the sum of money involved makes that arrangement more than manageable. Weeks are spent on the design and mechanics. He hires an assistant to complete some of the basic woodwork, but he takes care of all the details himself. Herr Thiessen loves details, and he loves a challenge. He balances the entire design on that one specific word Mr. Barris used. *Dreamlike.*

The finished clock is resplendent. At first glance it is simply a clock, a rather large black clock with a white face and a silver pendulum. Well crafted, obviously, with intricately carved woodwork edges and a perfectly painted face, but just a clock.

But that is before it is wound. Before it begins to tick, the pendulum swinging steadily and evenly. Then, then it becomes something else.

The changes are slow. First, the color changes in the face, shifts from white to grey, and then there are clouds that float across it, disappearing when they reach the opposite side.

Meanwhile, bits of the body of the clock expand and contract, like pieces of a puzzle. As though the clock is falling apart, slowly and gracefully.

All of this takes hours.

The face of the clock becomes a darker grey, and then black, with twinkling stars where the numbers had been previously. The body of the clock, which has been methodically turning itself inside out and expanding, is now entirely subtle shades of white and grey. And it is not just pieces, it is figures and objects, perfectly carved flowers and planets and tiny books with actual paper pages that turn. There is a silver dragon that curls around part of the now visible clockwork, a tiny princess in a carved tower who paces in distress, awaiting an absent prince. Teapots that pour into teacups and minuscule curls of steam that rise from them as the seconds tick. Wrapped presents open. Small cats chase small dogs. An entire game of chess is played.

At the center, where a cuckoo bird would live in a more traditional timepiece, is the juggler. Dressed in harlequin style with a grey mask, he juggles shiny silver balls that correspond to each hour. As the clock chimes, another ball joins the rest until at midnight he juggles twelve balls in a complex pattern.

After midnight the clock begins once more to fold in upon itself. The face lightens and the clouds return. The number of juggled balls decreases until the juggler himself vanishes.

By noon it is a clock again, and no longer a dream.

A few weeks after it is shipped, he receives a letter from Mr. Barris, offering his sincere thanks and marveling at the ingenuity of it. "It is perfection," he writes. The letter is accompanied by another exorbitant amount of money, enough for Herr Thiessen to retire comfortably if he wished. He does not, and continues to make his clocks in his Munich workshop.

He thinks no more of it, other than a passing thought of how the clock itself might be doing, and where it might be (though he assumes, incorrectly, that it remains in London), particularly when he is working on a clock that reminds him of the *Wunschtraum* clock, which was how he referred to it during the more troublesome parts of its construction, uncertain whether or not it was a dream that could be realized.

He does not hear from Mr. Barris beyond that single letter.

Auditory

There is an unprecedented gathering of illusionists in the lobby of the theater. A gaggle of pristine suits and strategically placed silk handkerchiefs. Some have trunks and capes, others carry birdcages or silver-topped canes. They do not speak to each other as they wait to be called in, one at a time, referenced not by name (given or stage) but by a number written on a small slip of paper given to them upon arrival. Instead of chitchatting or gossiping or sharing tricks of the trade, they shift in their seats and cast rather conspicuous glances at the girl.

A few mistook her for an assistant when they arrived, but she sits waiting in her chair with her own numbered slip of paper (23).

She has no trunk, no cape, no birdcage or cane. She is dressed in a deep-green gown with a black puffed-sleeve jacket buttoned over it. A pile of brown curls is pinned neatly upon her head under a tiny and feathered but otherwise unremarkable black hat. Her face maintains a semblance of girlishness, in the length of her eyelashes and the slight pout of her lips, despite the fact that she is clearly too old to be properly called a girl. But it is difficult to discern her age and no one dares inquire. The others think of her as the girl regardless, and refer to her as such when they discuss the affair after the fact. She acknowledges no one despite the barely concealed glances and occasional outright stare.

One by one, each illusionist's number is called by a man with a list and a notebook who escorts them through a gilded door on the side of the lobby, and, one by one, each returns to the lobby and exits the theater. Some last only minutes, while others remain in the theater for quite some time. Those with higher numbers shift impatiently in their seats as they wait for the man with the notebook to reappear and politely call out the number on their respective slips of paper.

The last illusionist to enter the gilded door (a rotund fellow with a top hat and flashy cape) returns to the lobby rather quickly and visibly agitated, flouncing through the exit back onto the street, letting the theater doors slam shut behind him. The sound is still echoing through the lobby when the man with the notebook reappears, nods absently at the room, and clears his throat.

"Number twenty-three," Marco says, checking the number on his list.

All the eyes in the room turn as the girl rises from her seat and steps forward.

Marco watches her approach, confused at first but then the confusion is replaced by something else entirely.

He could tell from across the room that she was lovely, but when she is near enough to look him in the eyes the loveliness—the shape of her face, the contrast of her hair against her skin—evolves into something more.

She is radiant. For a moment, while they look at each other, he cannot remember what he is meant to be doing, or why she is handing him a piece of paper with the number twenty-three written on it in his own handwriting.

"This way, please," he manages to say as he takes her number and holds the door open for her. She bobs the slightest of curtseys in acknowledgment and the lobby is abuzz with whispers before the door has fully closed behind them.

*

THE THEATER IS MASSIVE AND ORNATE, with rows upon rows of plush red velvet seats. Orchestra, mezzanine, and balcony spreading out from the empty stage in a cascade of crimson. It is empty save for two people seated approximately ten rows back from the stage. Chandresh Christophe Lefèvre sits with his feet propped up on the seat in front of him. Mme. Ana Padva sits on his right, pulling a watch from her bag while she stifles a yawn.

Marco emerges from the wing of the stage with the girl in the green dress trailing close behind him. He gestures for her to move to the center of the stage, unable to take his eyes from her as he announces her to the mostly empty theater.

"Number twenty-three," he says, before descending a small set of stairs near the proscenium and hovering by the edge of the front row, pen poised over his open notebook.

Mme. Padva looks up and smiles, tucking her watch back into her bag.

"What's this, then?" Chandresh asks, not directing the question at anyone in particular. The girl does not respond.

"This is number twenty-three," Marco repeats, checking his notes to make certain the number is accurate.

"We're auditioning illusionists, my dear girl," Chandresh says, rather loudly, his voice echoing through the cavernous space. "Magicians, conjurers, etcetera. No need for lovely assistants at this time."

"I am an illusionist, sir," the girl says. Her voice is calm and low. "I am here for your auditions."

"I see," Chandresh says, frowning as he looks the girl over slowly from head to toe. She stands perfectly still in the center of the stage, patiently, as though she has expected such a reaction.

"Is there something wrong with that?" Mme. Padva asks.

"I am not entirely sure it is appropriate," Chandresh says, eyeing the girl thoughtfully.

"After all of your pontificating about the contortionist?"

Chandresh pauses, still looking at the girl on the stage who, while comparatively elegant, does not appear particularly unusual.

"That's a different matter" is all he can manage as to his reasoning.

"Really, Chandresh," Mme. Padva says. "We should at least let her show off her skills before arguing over the appropriateness of a female illusionist."

"But she has so much more sleeve to hide things up," he protests.

In response, the girl unbuttons her puffed-sleeve jacket and drops it unceremoniously on the stage by her feet. Her green gown is both sleeveless and strapless, leaving her shoulders and arms completely bare save for a long silver chain with what appears to be a silver locket around her neck. She then removes her gloves and tosses them one by one on the crumpled jacket as well. Mme. Padva gives Chandresh a pointed look that is met with a sigh.

"Very well," Chandresh says. "On with it." He gestures vaguely at Marco.

"Yes, sir," Marco says, turning to address the girl. "We have a few preliminary questions before the practical demonstration. Your name, miss?"

"Celia Bowen."

Marco records this in his notebook.

"And your stage name?" he asks.

"I don't have a stage name," Celia says. Marco notes this as well.

"Where have you performed professionally?"

"I have never performed professionally before."

At this Chandresh moves to interrupt but Mme. Padva stops him.

"Then with whom have you studied?" Marco asks.

"With my father, Hector Bowen," Celia answers. She pauses for a moment before adding, "Though perhaps he is better known as Prospero the Enchanter."

Marco drops his pen.

"Prospero the Enchanter?" Chandresh removes his feet from the chair in front of him and leans forward, staring at Celia as though he is seeing a completely different person. "Your father is Prospero the Enchanter?"

"Was," Celia clarifies. "He . . . passed last year."

"I'm sorry for your loss, dear," Mme. Padva says. "But who, pray tell, is Prospero the Enchanter?"

"Only the greatest illusionist of his generation," Chandresh says. "Used to book him whenever I could get my hands on him, years ago now. Absolutely brilliant, completely mesmerized every audience. Never seen anyone to match him, never."

"He would have been pleased to hear that, sir," Celia says, her eyes briefly glancing over to the shadowed curtains at the side of the stage.

"I told him as much, though I haven't seen him in ages. Got very drunk with him in a pub some years back and he went on about pushing the boundaries of what theater can be, inventing something more extraordinary. He probably would have loved this entire endeavor. Damned shame." He sighs heavily, shaking his head. "Well, on with it then," he says, leaning back in his seat and regarding Celia with a considerable amount of interest.

Marco, pen in hand once more, returns to his list of questions.

"A-are you capable of performing without a stage?"

"Yes," Celia says.

"Can your illusions be viewed from all angles?"

Celia smiles. "You are looking for someone who can perform in the midst of a crowd?" she asks Chandresh. He nods. "I see," Celia says. Then, so swiftly she appears not even to move, she picks up her jacket from the stage and flings it out over the seats where, instead of tumbling down, it swoops up, folding into itself. In the blink of an eye folds of silk are glossy black feathers, large beating wings, and it is impossible to pinpoint the moment when it is fully raven and no longer cloth. The raven swoops over the red velvet seats and up into the balcony where it flies in curious circles.

"Impressive," Mme. Padva says.

"Unless she had him concealed in those gigantic sleeves," Chandresh mutters. On the stage, Celia crosses closer to Marco.

"May I borrow that for a moment?" she asks him, indicating his notebook. He hesitates before handing it to her. "Thank you," she says, returning to the center of the stage.

She barely glances at the list of questions in precise handwriting before tossing the notebook straight up into the air where it turns end over end and the blur of fluttering paper becomes a white dove flapping its wings and taking flight in a loop around the theater. The raven caws at it from its perch in the balcony.

"Ha!" Chandresh exclaims, both at the dove and the expression on Marco's face.

The dove swoops back down to Celia, settling gently on her outstretched hand. She strokes its wings and then releases it back into the air. It lifts up only a few feet above her head before wings are paper once again and it topples quickly down. Celia catches it with one hand and gives it back to Marco, whose complexion is now a few shades paler.

"Thank you," Celia says with a smile. Marco nods absently, not meeting her eyes, and quickly retreats to his corner.

"Marvelous, simply marvelous," Chandresh says. "This could work. This could most definitely work." He rises from his seat and moves down the aisle, stopping to pace thoughtfully in front of the orchestra pit by the footlights.

"There is the matter of costuming her," Mme. Padva calls toward him from her seat. "I had only considered formal suits. A similar sort of gown might do just as well, I suppose."

"What manner of costume do you require?" Celia asks.

"We have a color scheme to work with, dear," Mme. Padva says. "Or lack thereof, rather. Nothing but black and white. Though on you a full black gown might be a bit too funereal."

"I see," says Celia.

Mme. Padva stands and moves down the aisle to where Chandresh is pacing. She whispers something in his ear and he turns to consult with her, taking his eyes off of Celia for a moment.

No one is watching her except Marco as she stands perfectly still on the stage, waiting patiently. And then, very slowly, her gown begins to change.

Starting at the neckline and seeping down like ink, the green silk is turning a murky, midnight black.

Marco gasps. Chandresh and Mme. Padva turn at the sound just in time to witness the creeping black fade into snow-bright white at the bottom of the skirt, until all evidence that the gown was ever green is gone.

"Well, that makes my job much easier," Mme. Padva says, though she cannot conceal the delight in her eyes. "Though I think perhaps your hair is too light a shade."

Celia shakes her head and her brown curls deepen in hue to a near black, as glossy and ebony as the wings of her raven.

"Marvelous," Chandresh says, almost to himself.

Celia simply smiles.

Chandresh leaps up to the stage, taking the small flight of stairs in only two steps. He inspects Celia's gown from every angle.

"May I?" he asks before carefully touching the fabric of her skirt. Celia nods. The silk is undeniably black and white, the transition between the two a soft fade of grey, distinct fibers visible in the weave.

"What happened to your father, if you don't mind my prying?" Chandresh asks, his attention still on her gown.

"I do not mind," Celia says. "One of his tricks did not go entirely as planned."

"That's a damned shame," he says, stepping back. "Miss Bowen, might you be interested in a somewhat unique employment opportunity?"

He snaps his fingers and Marco approaches with his notebook, halting a few paces away from Celia, his stare moving from her gown to her hair and back, spending a considerable amount of time in between.

Before she can respond, a caw echoes through the theater from the raven still perched on the balcony, watching the scene in front of him curiously.

"Just a moment," Celia says. She lifts her hand in a delicate gesture at the raven. In response it caws again and spreads its large wings, taking flight and swooping toward the stage, gaining speed as it approaches. Descending quickly it dives, flying directly at Celia and not wavering or slowing as it reaches the stage, but approaching at full speed. Chandresh jumps back with a start, almost falling over Marco as the raven crashes into Celia in a flurry of feathers.

And then it is gone. Not a single feather remains and Celia is once again wearing a puffed-sleeve black jacket, already buttoned over her black-and-white gown.

In the front of the orchestra, Mme. Padva claps.

Celia bows, taking the opportunity to retrieve her gloves from the floor.

"She's perfect," Chandresh remarks, pulling a cigar from his pocket. "Absolutely perfect."

"Yes, sir," says Marco behind him, the notebook in his hand shaking slightly.

*

THE ILLUSIONISTS WAITING IN THE LOBBY grumble when they are thanked for their time and politely dismissed.

Stratagem

LONDON, APRIL 1886

She's too good to keep out in the crowd," Chandresh says. "She simply must have her own tent. We'll put the seats in a ring or something, keep the audience right in the middle of the action."

"Yes, sir," Marco says, fiddling with his notebook, running his fingers over the pages that had been wings only minutes before.

"Whatever is the matter with you?" Chandresh asks. "You're white as a sheet." His voice echoes through the empty theater as they stand alone on the stage, Mme. Padva having whisked Miss Bowen off, peppering her with questions about gowns and hairstyles.

"I am fine, sir," Marco says.

"You look awful," Chandresh says, puffing on his cigar. "Go home."

Marco looks up at him, surprised. "Sir, there is paperwork that needs to be done," he protests.

"Do it tomorrow, plenty of time for such things. Tante Padva and I will take Miss Bowen back to the house for tea and we can sort out the particulars and paperwork later. Get some rest or have yourself a drink or whatever it is you do." Chandresh waves a hand at him absently, the smoke from his cigar trailing in bobbing waves.

"If you insist, sir."

"I do insist! And get rid of the rest of those fellows in the lobby. No need to see a bunch of suits with capes when we've already found something far more interesting. Quite attractive, too, I should think, if one's predilections run in that direction."

"Indeed, sir," Marco says, a blush creeping into his pallor. "Until tomorrow then." He nods his head in something almost like a bow before turning gracefully on his heel and heading out to the lobby.

"Didn't take you to be the easily spooked type, Marco," Chandresh calls after him, but Marco does not turn.

Marco politely dismisses the illusionists in the lobby, explaining that the position has been filled and thanking them for their time. None of them notice that his hands are shaking, or that he is clutching the pen in his hand so tightly that his knuckles are white. Nor do they notice when it snaps in two within his fist, black ink seeping down his wrist.

After the illusionists have departed, Marco gathers his things, wiping his ink-covered hand on his black coat. He puts on his bowler hat before he exits the theater.

With every step, he grows more visibly distressed. People move out of his way on the crowded pavement.

When he reaches his flat, Marco drops his bag to the floor, leaning against the door with a heavy sigh.

"What's wrong?" Isobel asks from a chair next to the empty fireplace. She conceals the length of hair she has been braiding in her pocket, scowling as she knows she will have to rebraid the entire piece because her concentration was broken. It is the part she still has the most difficulty with, the concentration and focus.

For now, she abandons it and watches Marco as he crosses the room to reach the bookcases lining the wall.

"I know who my opponent is," Marco says, pulling armfuls of books down from their shelves and spreading them out haphazardly over tables, leaving several in messy piles on the floor. Those remaining on the shelves collapse, a few volumes falling, but Marco does not seem to notice.

"Is it that Japanese woman you were so curious about?" Isobel asks, watching as Marco's impeccable filing system falls into chaos. The flat has always been kept in perfect order, and she finds the sudden upheaval disquieting.

"No," Marco says as he flips through pages. "It's Prospero's daughter."

Isobel picks up a potted violet that has toppled in the wake of the falling books and places it back upon its shelf.

"Prospero?" she asks. "The magician, the one you saw in Paris?"

Marco nods.

"I didn't know he had a daughter," she says.

"I was unaware of that fact, myself," Marco says, discarding one book and picking up another. "Chandresh just hired her to be the illusionist for the circus."

"Really?" Isobel asks. Marco does not respond. "So she'll be doing what you said he did, actual magic disguised as stage illusions. Did she do that at the audition?"

"Yes, she did," Marco says, without looking up from his books.

"She must be very good."

"She's too good," Marco says, pulling another shelf worth of books from their resting places and moving them to the table, the violet an innocent victim once more. "This could be extremely problematic," he says, almost to himself. A pile of notebooks slips from the table to the floor in a flurry of fluttering pages and a sound like the wings of birds.

Isobel retrieves the violet again, placing it across the room.

"Does she know who you are?" she asks.

"I do not believe so," Marco says.

"Does this mean the circus is part of the challenge?" Isobel asks.

Marco stops flipping through pages and looks up at her.

"It must," he says before he returns his attention to the book. "That's likely why I was sent to work for Chandresh, so I would already be involved. The circus is the venue."

"Is that good?" Isobel asks, but Marco does not answer, lost in the flood of paper and ink again.

With one hand he fidgets with the cloth of the other sleeve. A splatter of black ink stains the white cuff. "She changed the fabric," he mutters to himself. "How did she change the fabric?"

Isobel moves a pile of abandoned books to the desk, where her Marseilles deck rests. She looks up at Marco, who is now deeply engrossed in a particular volume. She quietly spreads the cards out in a long line across the desk.

Keeping her eyes on Marco, she draws a single card. She flips it over on the desk and looks down to see what her cards have to say about the matter.

A man stands between two women, a cherub with bow and arrow hovering over their heads. *L'Amoureux*. The Lovers.

"Is she pretty?" Isobel asks.

Marco does not answer.

She pulls another card from the line and lays it atop the first. *La Maison Dieu.*

She frowns at the picture of the crumbling tower and the falling figure. She returns both cards to the deck, pushing it back into an orderly stack.

"Is she stronger than you?" Isobel asks.

Again Marco fails to answer, flipping through the pages of a note-book.

For years, he has felt reasonably well prepared. Practicing with Isobel has proved an advantage, enabling him to improve aspects of his illusions to the point where even with her familiarity she cannot always discern what is real.

But faced with his opponent, his feelings about the challenge have suddenly changed, replaced by nerves and confusion.

He had half expected he would simply know what to do when the time came.

And he had entertained the thought that the time might never come, that the promise of the game was something to motivate his studies and nothing more.

"So the competition will begin when the circus opens, then?" Isobel asks him. He had almost forgotten she was there.

"I suppose that would be logical," Marco says. "I don't understand how we are meant to compete when the circus is going to travel, and I must remain in London. I shall have to do everything remotely."

"I could go," Isobel says.

"What?" Marco asks, looking up at her again.

"You said the circus still needs a fortune-teller, didn't you? I could read my cards. I haven't read for anyone but myself, but I am getting better at it. I could write you letters when the circus is away. It would give me someplace to go, if you're not supposed to have me here while you play your game."

"I'm not sure that's a good idea," Marco says, though he cannot articulate why. He had never considered the possibility of involving Isobel in his life outside the bounds of the flat. He had been keeping her separate from Chandresh and the circus, both to have something of his own and because it seemed appropriate, especially given his instructor's vague advice about the matter.

"Please," Isobel says. "This way I can help you."

Marco hesitates, glancing down at his books. His thoughts remain preoccupied with the image of the girl from the theater.

"It will help you be closer to the circus," Isobel continues, "and it will give me something to do for the duration of your challenge. When it's done I can come back to London."

"I'm not even certain how the challenge is going to work," Marco says.

"But you're certain that I can't stay here during it?" she asks.

Marco sighs. They have discussed it before, not in any great detail, but enough to establish that when the game began, she would have to leave.

"I am already so busy working for Chandresh, and I will need to focus on the competition without . . . distraction," he says, using his instructor's choice of word, from an order disguised as a suggestion. He is not certain which option bothers him more: involving Isobel in the game or relinquishing the one relationship in his life that has not been dictated for him.

"This way I wouldn't be a distraction, I'd be helping," Isobel says. "And if you're not supposed to have help, well, I'd only be writing you letters, what's wrong with that? It seems like a perfect solution to me."

"I could arrange for you to meet with Chandresh," Marco suggests.

"You could . . . convince him to hire me, couldn't you?" Isobel asks. "If he needs convincing?"

Marco nods, still not entirely certain about the idea but almost desperate for some kind of strategy. A tactic to use in dealing with his newly revealed opponent.

He turns her name over and over in his mind.

"What is Prospero's daughter named?" Isobel asks, as though she can tell what he is thinking.

"Bowen," Marco says. "Her name is Celia Bowen."

"It's a pretty name," Isobel says. "Is something wrong with your hand?"

Marco looks down, surprised to find that he has been holding his right hand in his left, unconsciously stroking the empty space where a ring was once burned into his skin.

"No," he says, picking up a notebook to occupy his hands. "It's nothing."

Isobel seems satisfied with the response, lifting a pile of fallen books from the floor and stacking them on the desk.

Marco is relieved that she does not have the skill to pull the memory of the ring from his mind.

You step into a bright, open courtyard surrounded by striped tents.

Curving pathways along the perimeter lead away from the courtyard, turning into unseen mysteries dotted with twinkling lights.

There are vendors traversing the crowd around you, selling refreshments and oddities, creations flavored with vanilla and honey, chocolate and cinnamon.

A contortionist in a sparkling black costume twists on a platform nearby, bending her body into impossible shapes.

A juggler tosses globes of black and white and silver high into the air, where they seem to hover before falling again into his hands, his attentive spectators applauding.

All bathed in glowing light.

The light emanates from a large bonfire in the center of the courtyard.

As you walk closer, you can see that it sits in a wide black iron cauldron, balanced on a number of clawed feet. Where the rim of a cauldron would be, it breaks into long strips of curling iron, as though it has been melted and pulled apart like taffy. The curling iron continues up until it curls back into itself, weaving in and out amongst the other curls, giving it the cage-like effect. The flames are visible in the gaps between and rising slightly above. They are obscured only at the bottom, so it is impossible to tell what is burning, if it is wood or coal or something else entirely.

The flames are not yellow or orange, but white as snow as they dance.

Hidden Things

The arguments over Bailey's future began early and occur frequently, though at this point they often devolve into repetitive phrases and tense silences.

He blames Caroline for starting it, even though the raising of the issue was the fault of his maternal grandmother. Bailey is much more fond of his grandmother than of his sister, so he leaves the blame squarely on Caroline. Had she not given in, he would not have to fight as hard.

It was one of their grandmother's requests disguised as a suggestion, one which seemed innocuous enough, that Caroline attend Radcliffe College.

Caroline seemed intrigued by the idea through the entire length of tea in the cushioned, flower-wallpapered calm of their grandmother's Cambridge parlor.

But any resolve she might have had about the matter disappeared as soon as they were back in Concord and their father's word came down.

"Absolutely not."

Caroline accepted this with little more than a fleeting pout, deciding that it would probably be too much work, and she did not particularly care for the city, anyway. Besides, Millie was engaged and there was a wedding to plan, a subject Caroline found far more interesting than her own education.

And that was that.

Then came the response from Cambridge, the grandmotherly decree that this was acceptable, but Bailey would be going to Harvard, of course.

This one was not a request disguised as anything. This was pure demand. Finance-based protestations were crushed before they could be raised, by the clear statement that his tuition would be taken care of.

The arguments started before Bailey's opinion was even asked.

"I would like to go," he said, when there came a pause long enough to fit the words in.

"You are taking over the farm" was his father's response.

The easy thing to do would be to let the issue drop and raise it again later, especially considering Bailey is not quite sixteen and there is a substantial interim before either option will occur.

Instead, and he is not entirely certain why, he keeps the subject alive, bringing it up as often as possible. Pointing out that he could always go and return to the farm after the fact, that four years is not a terribly long time.

These statements are met with lectures at first, but they soon become loudly voiced decrees and slammed doors. His mother stays out of the arguments as much as she can, but when pressed she agrees with her husband, while at the same time quietly asserting that it should really be Bailey's decision.

Bailey is not even certain he wants to go to Harvard. He does like the city more than Caroline, and it seems to him to be the option that holds the most mystery, the most possibility.

Whereas the farm holds only sheep and apples and predictability.

He can already envision how it will play out. Every day. Every season. When the apples will fall and when the sheep will need shearing and when the frost will come.

Always the same, year after year.

He mentions something about the endless repetition to his mother, hoping it might turn into a more measured conversation about whether or not he will be allowed to leave, but she only says that she finds the cyclical nature of the farm comforting, and asks if he has finished all of his chores.

The invitations to tea in Cambridge now arrive addressed only to Bailey, leaving his sister off entirely. Caroline mutters something about not having time for such things anyway, and Bailey attends alone, grateful to be able to enjoy the trip without Caroline's constant talking.

"I do not particularly care whether or not you attend Harvard," his grandmother says one afternoon, though Bailey has not mentioned it. He generally attempts to avoid the subject, thinking he knows perfectly well where she stands.

He adds another spoon of sugar to his tea and waits for her to elaborate.

"I believe it would offer you more opportunity," she continues. "And that is something that I would like you to have, even if your parents are not enthused about the idea. Do you know why I gave my daughter permission to marry your father?"

"No," Bailey says. It is not a topic that has ever been discussed in his presence, though Caroline once told him in secret she heard it was something of a scandal. Even almost twenty years later, his father never sets foot in his grandmother's house, nor does she ever come out to Concord.

"Because she would have run off with him regardless," she says. "That was what she wished. It would not have been my choice for her, but a child should not have their choices dictated for them. I have listened to you read books aloud to my cats. When you were five years old you turned a laundry tub into a pirate ship and launched an attack against the hydrangeas in my garden. Do not try to convince me that you would choose that farm."

"I have a responsibility," Bailey says, repeating the word he has begun to hate.

His grandmother makes a noise that may be a laugh or a cough or a combination of the two.

"Follow your dreams, Bailey," she says. "Be they Harvard or something else entirely. No matter what that father of yours says, or how loudly he might say it. He forgets that he was someone's dream once, himself."

Bailey nods, and his grandmother sits back in her chair and complains about the neighbors for some time, not mentioning his father or his dreams again. Though before Bailey leaves she adds, "Do not forget what I said."

"I won't," he assures her.

He does not tell her that he has only one dream, and it is just as improbable as a career in garden piracy.

But he valiantly continues to debate with his father on a regular basis.

"Doesn't my opinion matter?" he asks one evening, before the conversation escalates to door slamming.

"No, it does not," his father answers.

"Maybe you should let this go, Bailey," his mother says quietly after his father leaves the room.

Bailey begins spending a great deal of time outside of the house.

School does not take up as many hours as he would like. At first he works more, in the far rows of the orchards, choosing the farthest points from wherever his father happens to be.

Then he resorts to taking long walks, through fields and woods and cemeteries.

He wanders past graves belonging to philosophers and poets, authors whose books he knows from his grandmother's library. And there are countless other headstones engraved with names he does not recognize, and more that have been so worn by time and wind that they are illegible, their owners long forgotten.

He walks with no particular destination in mind, but the place he ends up most frequently is the very same oak tree he so often sat in with Caroline and her friends.

It is more manageable now that he is taller, and he climbs to the topmost branches with ease. It is shaded enough to feel secluded but bright enough to read when he brings books along, which soon becomes part of his routine.

He reads histories and mythologies and fairy tales, wondering why it seems that only girls are ever swept away from their mundane lives on farms by knights or princes or wolves. It strikes him as unfair to not have the same fanciful opportunity himself. And he is not in the position to do any rescuing of his own.

During the hours spent watching the sheep as they wander aimlessly around their fields, he even wishes that someone would come and take him away, but wishes on sheep appear to work no better than wishes on stars.

He tells himself that it is not a bad life. That there is nothing wrong with being a farmer.

But still, the discontent remains. Even the ground beneath his feet feels unsatisfying to his boots.

So he continues to escape to his tree.

To make the tree his own, he even goes so far as to move the old wooden box in which he keeps his most valued possessions from its standard hiding spot beneath a loose floorboard under his bed to a nook in the oak tree, a substantial indentation that is not quite a hole but secure enough to serve the purpose.

The box is fairly small, with tarnished brass hinges and clasps. It is wrapped in a scrap of burlap that does a fairly good job of keeping it protected from the elements, and it sits securely enough that it has not been dislodged by even the most resourceful squirrels.

Its contents include a chipped arrowhead he found in a field when he was five. A stone with a hole straight through it that is supposedly lucky. A black feather. A shiny rock that his mother said was some sort of quartz. A coin that was his first never-spent pocket money. The brown leather collar that belonged to the family dog who died when Bailey was nine. A solitary white glove that has gone rather grey from a combination of age and being kept in a small box with rocks.

And several yellowed and folded pages filled with handwritten text.

After the circus departed, he wrote down every detail he could remember about it so it would not fade in his memory. The chocolate-covered popcorn. The tent full of people on raised circular platforms, performing tricks with bright white fire. The magical, transforming clock that sat across from the ticket booth, doing so much more than simply telling the time.

While he catalogued each element of the circus in shaky handwriting, he could not manage to record his encounter with the red-haired girl. He never told anyone about her. He looked for her at the circus during his two subsequent visits during proper nighttime hours, but he had not been able to find her.

Then the circus was gone, vanished as suddenly as it had appeared, like a fleeting dream.

And it has not returned.

The only proof he has now that the girl even existed, and was not a figment of his imagination, is the glove.

But he doesn't open the box anymore. It sits, firmly closed, in the tree.

He thinks maybe he should throw it away, but he cannot bring himself to do it.

Perhaps he will leave it in the tree and let the bark grow over it, sealing it inside.

*

IT IS A GREY SATURDAY MORNING, and Bailey is up earlier than the rest of the family, which is not unusual. He performs his chores as quickly as possible, packs an apple in his bag along with his book, and heads off to his tree. Halfway there he thinks perhaps he should have worn his scarf, but the day is bound to get warmer as it goes along. Concentrating on that comforting fact, he climbs up past the bottom branches he was relegated to years ago, past the branches claimed by his sister and her friends. This is Millie's branch, he thinks as his foot touches it. A feeling of satisfaction comes when he climbs above Caroline's branch, even after all this time. Surrounded by leaves that rustle in the breeze, Bailey settles into his favorite spot, his boots resting close to his almost forgotten box of treasures.

When he finally looks up from his book, Bailey is so shocked by the sight of the black-and-white striped tents in the field that he nearly falls out of the tree.

Part II

ILLUMINATION

There is so much that glows in the circus, from flames to lanterns to stars. I have heard the expression "trick of the light" applied to sights within Le Cirque des Rêves so frequently that I sometimes suspect the entirety of the circus is itself a complex illusion of illumination.

—FRIEDRICK THIESSEN, 1894

Opening Night I: Inception

LONDON, OCTOBER 13 AND 14, 1886

Opening day, or opening night, rather, is spectacular. Every last detail is planned, and a massive crowd gathers outside the gates long before sundown. When they are finally allowed to enter, they do so wide-eyed, and as they move from tent to tent, their eyes only get wider.

Every element of the circus blends together in a wonderful coalescence. Acts that have been training in separate countries on separate continents now perform in adjacent tents, each part melding seamlessly into a whole. Each costume, each gesture, each sign on each tent is more perfect than the last.

The air itself is ideal, clear and crisp and cool, permeated with scents and sounds that entice and enchant one patron after another.

At midnight, the bonfire is ceremoniously lit, having spent the earlier part of the evening standing empty, appearing to be a simple sculpture of twisted iron. Twelve of the fire performers quietly enter the courtyard with small platforms that they set up along the perimeter like numbers on a clock. Precisely one minute before the hour, they each ascend their respective platforms and pull from their backs shimmering black bows and arrows. At thirty seconds before midnight, they light the tips of their arrows with small dancing yellow flames. Those in the crowd who had not noticed them previously now watch in wonder. At ten seconds before the hour, they raise their bows and aim the flaming arrows at the waiting well of curling iron. As the clock begins to chime near the gates, the first archer lets his arrow fly, soaring over the crowd and hitting its mark in a shower of sparks.

The bonfire ignites in an eruption of yellow flame.

Then the second chime follows, the second archer sends his arrow into the yellow flames, and they become a clear sky-blue.

A third chime with a third arrow, and the flames are a warm bright pink.

Flames the color of a ripe pumpkin follow the fourth arrow.

A fifth, and the flames are scarlet-red.

A sixth brings a deeper, sparkling crimson.

Seven, and the fire is soaked in a color like an incandescent wine.

Eight, and the flames are shimmering violet.

Nine, and violet shifts to indigo.

A tenth chime, a tenth arrow, and the bonfire turns deepest midnight blue.

On the penultimate chime, the dancing flames change from blue to black, and for that moment, it is difficult to discern the fire from its cauldron.

And on the final strike, the dark flames are replaced with a blinding white, a shower of sparks falling like snowflakes around it. Huge curls of dense white smoke swirl up into the night sky.

The reaction from the crowd is uproarious. The spectators who had been considering taking their leave decide to stay just a bit longer and comment enthusiastically about the lighting of the fire. Those who do not witness it themselves hardly believe the stories told minutes or hours later.

People roam from tent to tent, wandering down paths that loop over each other, never seeming to end. Some enter each tent they pass, while others are more selective, choosing tents to enter after careful consideration of signs. Some find a particular tent so fascinating that they are unable to exit it, opting instead to stay there the duration of their visit. Patrons make suggestions to other patrons they pass on the concourses, pointing out remarkable tents they have visited already. Their advice is always taken with pleasure, though often the advisees are distracted by other tents before they locate the recommended ones.

It is difficult to usher the remaining patrons out as the dawn creeps up, and they are only consoled by assurances that they may return when the sun sets again.

All told, opening night is an undeniable success.

There is only one minor mishap of sorts, one unexpected occurrence. It passes unnoticed by any of the patrons, and many of the performers are not aware of it until after the fact.

Just before sunset, while the last-minute preparations are being made (costumes adjusted, caramel melted), the wife of the wild-cat tamer unexpectedly goes into labor. She is, when not in a delicate state, her husband's assistant. Their act has been subtly modified for her absence, but the cats themselves seem agitated.

She is expecting twins, though they are not due for a few more weeks. People joke afterward that perhaps they did not want to miss opening night.

A doctor is brought to the circus before it opens to the public and escorted discreetly backstage for the delivery (an easier feat to accomplish than moving her to a hospital).

Six minutes before midnight, Winston Aidan Murray is born.

Seven minutes after midnight, his sister, Penelope Aislin Murray, follows.

When the news is relayed to Chandresh Christophe Lefèvre, he is mildly disappointed that the twins are not identical. He had thought up various roles in the circus for identical twins to perform once the children were old enough. Fraternal twins, on the other hand, lack the amount of theatricality he had expected, but he has Marco arrange the delivery of two enormous bouquets of red roses anyway.

They are tiny things, each with a rather surprising amount of bright red hair. They barely cry, staying awake and alert, with matching pairs of wide blue eyes. They are wrapped in spare bits of silk and satin, white for her and black for him.

A steady stream of circus performers comes to see them in between acts, taking turns holding them and inevitably remarking on their exquisite timing. They will fit right in, everyone says, save for their hair. Someone suggests hats until they are old enough for hair dye. Someone else remarks that it would be a travesty to dye over such a color, a shocking red much brighter than their mother's auburn.

"It is an auspicious color," Tsukiko comments, but she refuses to elaborate on her meaning. She kisses each twin on the forehead and later makes strings of folded paper cranes to hang above their cradle.

Close to dawn, when the circus is emptying, they are taken for a walk around the tents and into the courtyard. The purpose is ostensibly to lull them to sleep, but they stay awake, watching the lights and the costumes and the stripes on the tents around them, strangely alert for being only a few hours old.

Not until the sun has risen do they finally close their eyes, side by side in the black wrought-iron cradle lined with striped blankets that already awaits them, despite their early arrival. It was delivered as a gift a few weeks earlier, though it had no card or note. The Murrays assumed it was a gift from Chandresh, though when they thanked him for it he claimed he had no idea what they were talking about.

The twins quite like it, regardless of its dubious origins.

No one recalls afterward exactly who it was that dubbed them Poppet and Widget. As with the cradle, no one takes credit for it.

But the nicknames stick, as nicknames do.

Opening Night II: Sparks

Marco spends the first several hours of opening night taking surreptitious glances at his watch, waiting impatiently for the hands to reach midnight.

The unexpected early arrival of the Murray twins has complicated his schedule already, but if the lighting of the bonfire proceeds as planned, that should be enough.

It is the best solution he can come up with, knowing that in a few weeks the circus will be hundreds of miles away, leaving him alone in London.

And while Isobel may prove helpful, he needs a stronger tie.

Ever since he discovered the venue for the challenge, he has been slowly taking on more responsibility for the circus. Doing all that Chandresh asked of him and more, to the point where he was given free rein with everything from approving the design of the gates to ordering the canvas for the tents.

It worries him, the scope of the binding. He has never attempted anything on this scale, but there seems no good reason not to start off the game as strongly as possible.

The bonfire will provide him with a connection to the circus, even though he is not entirely certain how well it will work. And with so many people involved, it seems sensible to add an element of safety to the venue.

It has taken months of preparation.

Chandresh was more than willing to let him organize the lighting, having already deemed him invaluable to the circus planning with only mild coercion. A wave of a hand, and the details were all up to him.

And most important, Chandresh agreed to let it be a secret. The lighting itself took on the air of a Midnight Dinner, with no questions permitted as to the ingredients or menu.

No answers provided as to what the arrows are tipped with to create such an astounding effect. How the flames are made to shift from one vibrant hue to another.

Those who did inquire, during preparations and rehearsals, were told that to reveal the methods would ruin the effect.

Though, of course, Marco has been unable to rehearse the most important part.

It is easy enough for him to slip away from Chandresh in the crowded courtyard just before midnight.

He makes his way toward the twisted iron, moving as close as he can to the empty cauldron. He takes a large, leather-bound notebook from his coat, a perfect copy of one that has been safely locked in his office. No one in the milling crowd notices as he tosses it into the bottom of the cauldron. It lands with a thud that is muffled by the ambient noise.

The cover flips open, exposing the elaborate ink tree to the star-speckled night sky.

He stays close to the edge of the twisted metal while the archers take their places.

His attention remains focused on the flames despite the press of patrons around him as the fire is amplified through a rainbow of hues.

When the last arrow lands, he closes his eyes. The white flames burn red through his eyelids.

*

CELIA EXPECTED TO FEEL like a poor imitation of her father during her first performances, but to her relief the experience is vastly different from the one she watched so many times in theater after theater.

The space is small and intimate. The audiences are modest enough that they remain individual people rather than blending into an anonymous crowd.

She finds she is able to make each performance unique, letting the response of the audience inform what she chooses to do next.

While she enjoys it more than she thought she would, she is grateful that she has stretches of time to herself in between. As it nears midnight, she decides to see if she can find a place to discreetly watch the lighting of the bonfire.

But as she makes her way through the area that is already being referred to as backstage despite the lack of stage, she is quickly swept up in the somewhat ordered chaos surrounding the impending birth of the Murray twins.

Several of the performers and staff have gathered, waiting anxiously. The doctor who has been brought in seems to find the entire situation strange. The contortionist comes and goes. Aidan Murray paces like one of his cats.

Celia endeavors to be as helpful as she can, which consists mainly of fetching cups of tea and finding new and creative ways to assure people that everything will be fine.

It reminds her so much of consoling her old spiritualist clients that she is surprised when she is thanked by name.

The soft cry that sounds minutes before midnight comes as a relief, met by sighs and cheers.

And then something else immediately follows.

Celia feels it before she hears the applause echoing from the courtyard, the shift that suddenly spreads through the circus like a wave.

It courses through her body, sending an involuntary shiver down her spine, almost knocking her off of her feet.

"Are you all right?" a voice behind her says, and she turns to find Tsukiko laying a warm hand on her arm to steady her. The too-knowing gleam that Celia is beginning to find familiar shines in the contortionist's smiling eyes.

"I'm fine, thank you," Celia says, struggling to catch her breath.

"You are a sensitive person," Tsukiko says. "It is not unusual for sensitive people to be affected by such events."

Another cry echoes from the adjoining chamber, joining the first in a gentle chorus.

"They have remarkable timing," Tsukiko says, turning her attention to the newborn twins.

Celia can only nod.

"It is a shame you missed the lighting," Tsukiko continues. "It was remarkable as well."

While the Murray twins' cries subside, Celia tries to shake the feeling that remains tingling over her skin.

She is still unsure who her opponent is, but whatever move has just been made, it has rattled her.

She feels the entirety of the circus radiating around her, as though a net has been thrown over it, trapping everything within the iron fence, fluttering like a butterfly.

She wonders how she is supposed to retaliate.

Opening Night III: Smoke and Mirrors

Chandresh Christophe Lefèvre enters not a single tent on opening night. Instead, he wanders through pathways and concourses and walks in loops around the courtyard with Marco in tow, who is taking notes whenever Chandresh finds something to comment upon.

Chandresh watches the crowd, discerning how people decide which tents to enter. He identifies signage that needs to be adjusted or elevated to be easier to read, doors that are not visible enough and others that are too predominant, drawing too little attention or too much of a crowd.

But these are minute details, really, extra oil for inaudible squeaking. It could not be better. The people are delighted. The line for tickets snakes around the outside of the fence. The entire circus glistens with excitement.

A few minutes before midnight, Chandresh positions himself by the edge of the courtyard for the lighting of the bonfire. He chooses a spot where he can view both the bonfire and a good portion of the crowd.

"Everything is ready for the lighting, correct?" he asks.

No one answers him.

He turns to his left and his right, finding only giddy patrons streaming past.

"Marco?" he says, but Marco is nowhere to be found.

One of the Burgess sisters spots Chandresh and approaches him, carefully navigating her way through the crowded courtyard.

"Hello, Chandresh," she says when she reaches him. "Is something wrong?"

"I seem to have misplaced Marco," he says. "Strange. But nothing to worry about, Lainie, dear."

"Tara," she corrects.

"You look alike," Chandresh says, puffing on his cigar. "It's confusing. You should stay together as a set to avoid such faux pas."

"Really, Chandresh, we're not even twins."

"Which of you is older, then?"

"That's a secret," Tara says, smiling. "May we declare the evening a success yet?"

"So far it is satisfactory, but the night is relatively young, my dear. How is Mrs. Murray?"

"She is doing fine, I believe, though it's been an hour or so since I heard any news. It will make for a memorable birthday for the twins, I should think."

"They might be useful if they're as indistinguishable as you and your sister. We could put them in matching costumes."

Tara laughs. "You might wait until they can walk, at least."

Around the unlit cauldron that will hold the bonfire, twelve archers are taking their positions. Tara and Chandresh halt their conversation to watch. Tara observes the archers while Chandresh watches the crowd as their attention is drawn to the display. They turn from crowd to audience as though choreographed along with the archers. Everything proceeding precisely as planned.

The archers let their arrows fly, one by one, sending the flames through a rainbow of conflagration. The entire circus is doused in color as the clock tolls, twelve deep chimes reverberating through the circus.

On the twelfth knell, the bonfire blazes, white and hot. Everything in the courtyard shudders for a moment, scarves fluttering despite the lack of any breeze, the fabric of the tents quivering.

The audience bursts into applause. Tara claps along, while beside her Chandresh stumbles, dropping his cigar to the ground.

"Chandresh, are you all right?" Tara asks.

"I feel rather dizzy," he says. Tara takes Chandresh by the arm to steady him, pulling him closer to the side of the nearest tent, out of the way of the crowd that has started moving again, spilling out in all directions.

"Did you feel that?" he asks her. His legs are shaking and Tara struggles to support him as they are jostled by passersby.

"Feel what?" she asks, but Chandresh does not reply, still clearly unsteady. "Why did no one think to put benches in the courtyard?" Tara mutters to herself.

"Is there a problem, Miss Burgess?" a voice asks behind her. She turns to find Marco hovering behind her, notebook in hand and looking quite concerned.

"Oh, Marco, there you are," Tara says. "Something is wrong with Chandresh."

They are beginning to attract stares from the crowd. Marco takes Chandresh's arm and pulls him into a quieter corner, standing with his back to the courtyard to provide a modicum of privacy.

"Has he been like this long?" Marco asks Tara as he steadies Chandresh.

"No, it came on quite suddenly," she replies. "I worry he might faint."

"I'm sure it's nothing," Marco tells her. "The heat, perhaps. I can handle this, Miss Burgess. It's nothing to concern yourself with."

Tara furrows her brow, reluctant to leave.

"It's nothing," Marco repeats emphatically.

Chandresh looks at the ground as though he has lost something, not seeming to register the conversation at all.

"If you insist," Tara relents.

"He's in perfectly good hands, Miss Burgess," Marco says, and then he turns before she can say another word, and he and Chandresh walk off into the crowd.

"There you are," Lainie says, appearing at her sister's shoulder. "I've been looking everywhere for you. Did you see the lighting? Wasn't it spectacular?"

"Indeed," Tara says, still scanning the crowd.

"Whatever is the matter?" Lainie asks. "Did something happen?"

"How much do you know about Chandresh's assistant?" Tara asks in response.

"Marco? Not very much," Lainie says. "He's worked for Chandresh for a few years, specializes in accounting. Before that he was a scholar of some sort, I believe. I'm not entirely sure what he studied. Or where, for that matter. He's not particularly talkative. Why do you ask? Seeking another dark and handsome conquest?"

Tara laughs, despite her distraction.

"No, nothing like that. Only curiosity." She takes her sister by the arm. "Let us go and seek out other mysteries to explore for the moment."

Arm in arm they navigate the crowd, circling around the glowing bonfire that many patrons are still gazing at, mesmerized by the dancing white flames.

In this tent, suspended high above you, there are people.
Acrobats, trapeze artists, aerialists. Illuminated by dozens
of round glowing lamps hanging from the top of the tent
like planets or stars.

There are no nets.

You watch the performance from this precarious vantage
point, directly below the performers with nothing in between.

There are girls in feathered costumes who spin at various
heights, suspended by ribbons that they can manipulate.
Marionettes that control their own strings.

Normal chairs with legs and backs act as trapezes.

Round spheres that resemble birdcages rise and descend
while one or more aerialists move from within the sphere to
without, standing on the top or hanging from the bars on the
bottom.

In the center of the tent there is a man in a tuxedo, suspended by one leg that is tied with a silver cord, hands clasped
behind his back.

He begins to move, extremely slowly. His arms reach out
from his sides, first one and then the other, until they hang
below his head.

He starts to spin. Faster and faster, until he is only a blur
at the end of a rope.

He stops, suddenly, and he falls.

The audience dives out of the way below him, clearing a
space of bare, hard ground below.

You cannot bear to watch. You cannot look away.

Then he stops at eye level with the crowd. Suspended by

the silver rope that now seems endlessly long. Top hat undisturbed on his head, arms calmly by his sides.

As the crowd regains its composure, he lifts a gloved hand and removes his hat.

Bending at the waist, he takes a dramatic, inverted bow.

Oneiromancy

Bailey spends the entire day willing the sun to set, but it defies him and keeps its usual pace across the sky, a pace that Bailey has never really thought about before but today finds excruciatingly slow. He almost wishes it were a school day so he would have something to help pass the hours. He wonders if he should take a nap, but he is far too excited about the sudden appearance of the circus to possibly sleep.

Dinner passes the same way it has for months, stretches of silence broken by his mother's attempts at polite conversation and Caroline's occasional sighs.

His mother mentions the circus, or more specifically, the influx of people it will bring.

Bailey expects the silence to fall again, but instead Caroline turns to him.

"Didn't we dare you to sneak into the circus the last time it was here, Bailey?" Her tone is curious and light, as though she truly does not remember whether or not such a thing occurred.

"What, during the day?" his mother asks. Caroline nods, vaguely.

"Yes," Bailey says quietly, willing the uncomfortable silence to return.

"Bailey," his mother says, managing to turn his name into a disappointment-laced admonishment. Bailey is not certain how it is his fault, being the daree and not the darer, but Caroline responds before he can protest.

"Oh, he didn't do it," she says, as though she now recalls the incident clearly.

Bailey only shrugs.

"Well, I would hope not," his mother says.

The silence resumes, and Bailey stares out the window, wondering what exactly constitutes nightfall. He thinks perhaps it would be best to get to the gates as soon as it could even remotely be considered dusk and wait if necessary. His feet feel itchy beneath the table, and he wonders how soon he will be able to escape.

It takes ages to clear the table, an eternity to help his mother with the dishes. Caroline disappears to her room and his father pulls out the newspaper.

"Where are you going?" his mother asks as he puts on his scarf.

"I'm going to the circus," Bailey says.

"Don't be too late," she says. "You have work to do."

"I won't," Bailey says, relieved that she has neglected to specify a time, leaving "too late" up to interpretation.

"Take your sister," she adds.

Only because there is no way to leave the house without his mother watching to see whether or not he stops at Caroline's room, Bailey knocks at the half-closed door.

"Go away," his sister says.

"I'm going to the circus, if you would care to join me," Bailey says, his voice dull. He already knows what her answer will be.

"No," she says, as predictable as the dinnertime silence. "How childish," she adds, shooting him a disdainful glare.

Bailey leaves without another word, letting the wind slam the front door behind him.

The sun is just beginning to set, and there are more people out than usual at this time of day, all walking in the same direction.

As he walks, his excitement begins to wane. Perhaps it is childish. Perhaps it will not be the same.

When he reaches the field there is already a crowd gathered, and he is relieved that there are plenty of patrons his own age or much older, and only a few have children with them. A pair of girls around his age giggles as he passes them, trying to catch his eye. He cannot tell if it is meant to be flattering or not.

Bailey finds a spot to stand within the crowd. He waits, watching the closed iron gates, wondering if the circus will be different than he remembers.

And he wonders, in the back of his mind, if the red-haired girl in white is somewhere inside.

The low orange rays from the sun make everything, including the circus, look as though it is aflame before the light disappears completely. It is quicker than Bailey expected, the moment that shifts from fire to twilight, and then the circus lights begin flickering on, all over the tents. The crowd "ooohs" and "ahhs" appropriately, but a few in the front gasp in surprise when the massive sign above the gates begins to sputter and spark. Bailey can't help but smile when it is fully lit, shining like a beacon: Le Cirque des Rêves.

While the day of waiting was tediously slow, the line to enter the circus moves remarkably fast, and soon Bailey is standing at the ticket booth, purchasing a single admission.

The winding path speckled with stars seems endless as he feels his way through the dark turns, anxiously anticipating the brightness at the end.

The first thing he thinks when he reaches the illuminated courtyard is that it smells the same, of smoke and caramel and something else that he cannot place.

He is not sure where to start. There are so many tents, so many choices. He thinks perhaps he should walk around a bit first, before deciding which tents to enter.

He thinks, also, that by simply wandering the circus he might improve his chances of happening upon the red-haired girl. Though he refuses to admit to himself that he is looking for her. Silly to look for a girl he only met once under extremely strange circumstances several years ago. There's no reason to believe that she'd even remember him, or recognize him, and he is not entirely sure he would recognize her, either, for that matter.

He decides to walk into the circus, through the courtyard with the bonfire and out the other side, and then attempt to work his way back. It is as good a plan as any, and the crowd might not be as thick on the far side.

But first, he thinks, he should get a mulled cider. It does not take him long to find the proper vendor in the courtyard. He pays for his cup, the steaming concoction contained in black-and-white marbled swirls, and wonders for a moment before his first sip if it won't taste as good as he remembers. He has recalled that taste countless times in his head, and despite the wealth of apples in the area, no cider with or without spices has ever tasted as good. He hesitates before taking the tiniest of sips. It tastes even better than he remembers.

He picks a path to take and along it, between the entrances to the surrounding tents, there is a small group gathered around a raised platform. A woman stands on the platform in a very fitted costume covered in black-and-silver swirls. She is twisting and bending in such a way that it seems both horrible and elegant. Bailey stops to join the spectators, even though it is almost painful to watch.

The contortionist lifts a small silver metal hoop from the ground, brandishing it with a few simple but impressive movements. She passes it to a man in the front of the crowd, in order to establish that it is solid. When he hands it back to her, she passes her entire body through it, extending her limbs in fluid, dance-like motions.

After discarding the hoop, she places a small box in the center of the platform.

The box looks no more than a foot wide or high, though in reality it is slightly larger than that. While the act of a fully grown (if below-average-size) woman condensing herself into such a confined space would be impressive regardless of the details of the box, it is made even more impressive in this case by the fact that this box is made of glass, completely transparent.

The edges are metal, oxidized to a blackish tinge, but the side panels and the lid are clear glass, so she is visible the entire time as she bends and twists and folds herself into the tiny space. She does it slowly, making each minute movement part of the show, until her body and head are completely within the box and only her hand remains without, sticking out the top. The view from Bailey's perspective looks impossible, a bit of leg here, the curve of a shoulder there, part of her other arm underneath a foot.

Only one hand remains, it waves cheerfully before pulling the lid closed. It latches automatically, and the box is undeniably closed, with the contortionist clearly visible inside.

And then the glass box with the woman trapped inside slowly fills with white smoke. It curls through the tiny cracks and spaces not occupied by limbs or torso, and seeps between her fingers as they press against the glass.

The smoke thickens, obscuring the contortionist completely. There is only white smoke visible inside the box, and it continues to ripple and undulate against the glass.

Suddenly, with a popping noise, the box breaks. The glass panels fall to the sides and the lid collapses downward. Curls of smoke rise into the night air. The box, or, rather, the small pile of glass upon the platform that had once been a box, is empty. The contortionist is gone.

The crowd waits for several moments, but nothing happens. The last wisps of smoke dissipate, the crowd begins to disperse.

Bailey takes a closer look as he walks by, wondering if the contortionist is somehow concealed in the platform, but it is solid wood and open underneath. She has vanished completely despite the plain evidence that there was nowhere for her to go.

Bailey continues down the winding path. He finishes his cider and finds a bin to discard his cup, though as soon as he places it within the shadowed container it seems to vanish.

He walks on, reading signs, trying to decide which tent to enter. Some are large and decorated with flourishes and long descriptions of their contents.

But the one that catches his eye is smaller, as is the tent on which it hangs. Looping white letters on a black background.

Feats of Illustrious Illusion

The entrance is open, and a line of patrons files into the illusionist's tent. Bailey joins them.

Inside it is lit by a line of black iron sconces along the rounded wall and contains nothing but a ring of plain wooden chairs. There are only about twenty of them, in two staggered rows so that the view from each seat is comparable. Bailey chooses a seat in the inside row, across from the entrance.

The rest of the seats fill quickly, save for two: the one to his immediate left and another across the circle.

Bailey notices two things at once.

First, that he can no longer see where the entrance had been. The space where the audience had entered now appears to be solid wall, seamlessly blending with the rest of the tent.

Second, there is now a dark-haired woman in a black coat sitting to his left. He is certain that she was not there before the door disappeared.

Then his attention is removed from both these events as the empty chair across the circle bursts into flame.

The panic is instant. Those occupying the chairs closest to the flaming chair abandon their seats and rush for the door, only to find that there is no longer a door to be found, only a solid wall.

The flames grow steadily higher, staying close to the chair, licking around the wood, though it does not appear to be burning.

Bailey looks again at the woman to his left, and she winks at him before standing and walking to the center of the circle. Amidst the panic, she calmly unbuttons her coat and removes it, tossing it with a delicate gesture toward the burning chair.

What had been a heavy wool coat becomes a long piece of black silk that ripples like water over the chair. The flames vanish. Only a few lingering wisps of smoke remain, along with the sharp smell of charred wood that is slowly changing to the comforting scent of a fireplace, tinged with something like cinnamon or clove.

The woman, standing in the center of the circle of chairs, pulls back the black silk with a flourish, revealing a still-intact chair on which now perch several snow-white doves.

Another flourish, and the black silk folds and curves in on itself, becoming a black top hat. The woman places it on her head, topping off an ensemble that looks like a ball gown fashioned out of the night sky: black silk dotted with sparkling white crystals. She acknowledges her audience with a subtle bow.

The illusionist has made her entrance.

A few people, including Bailey, manage to applaud, while those who had abandoned their seats return to them, looking both disturbed and curious.

The performance is continuous. The displays Bailey has difficulty thinking of as tricks meld one into the other. The doves vanish frequently, only to reappear on hats or under chairs. There is also a black raven, far too large to have been cleverly concealed. It is only after the performance has gone on for some time that Bailey slowly realizes that because of the circle of chairs, the shape and closeness of the space, there is no room for mirrors or tricks of the light. Everything is immediate and palpable. She even transforms one audience member's pocket watch from metal to sand and back again. At one point all the chairs float some distance off the ground, and while the movement is steady and secure, Bailey's toes barely graze the floor and he clutches the sides of his chair nervously.

At the end of the act, the illusionist takes a bow with a pivoting turn, acknowledging the entire circle as the audience applauds. As she completes the rotation, she is no longer there. Only a few sparkling shimmers remain, echoes of the crystals in her gown.

The door reappears in the side of the tent and the small audience makes their way out. Bailey lags behind, glancing back as he leaves at the spot where the illusionist had been.

Outside, though it was not there before, is another raised platform, much like the one the contortionist stood on. But the figure on this platform does not move. Bailey almost thinks it is a statue, dressed in a white gown edged in matching fur that cascades beyond the platform to the ground. Her hair and skin, even her eyelashes, are an icy white.

But she moves. Very, very slowly. So slowly that Bailey cannot pinpoint exact motions, only slight changes. Soft flakes of iridescent snow float to the ground, falling from her like leaves from a tree.

Bailey walks around, looking at her from every angle. Her eyes follow him, though the snow-flecked lashes do not blink.

There is a small silver plaque on the platform, partially obscured by the cascading gown.

It reads IN MEMORIAM, but it does not specify who it is for.

Rules of the Game
1887–1889

There are fewer Circus Dinners now that the circus itself is up and running properly, gaining its self-sufficiency, as Chandresh phrased it at one dinner not long after opening night. The original conspirators still gather for dinner occasionally, particularly when the circus is performing nearby, but this has become more and more infrequent.

Mr. A. H— does not appear, despite his standing invitation.

And as these meetings were the only opportunity Marco was given to see his instructor, the continued absence frustrates him.

After a year without a sign, without any word or a single glimpse of the grey top hat, Marco decides to call on him.

He does not know his instructor's current residence. He assumes, rightly, that it is likely a temporary place and by the time he tracked down the proper location his instructor would have moved to a new, equally temporary residence.

Instead, Marco carves a series of symbols into the frost on the window of his flat that faces out to the street, using the columns of the museum beyond as a guide. Most of the symbols are indistinguishable unless the light hits them at precise angles, but they are collectively set into the shape of a large *A*.

The next day there is a knock at the door.

As always, the man in the grey suit refuses to enter the flat. He only stands in the hall and fixes Marco with a cool grey stare.

"What is it that you want?" he asks.

"I would like to know if I am doing well," Marco says.

His instructor looks at him for a moment, his expression as inscrutable as ever.

"Your work has been sufficient," he says.

"Is this how the challenge is going to proceed?" Marco asks. "Each of us manipulating the circus? How long will it go on?"

"You have been given a venue to work within," his instructor says. "You present your skills to the best of your ability and your opponent does the same. You do not interfere with each other's work. It shall continue in this manner until there is a victor. It is not that complex."

"I'm not certain I understand the rules," Marco says.

"You don't need to understand the rules. You need to follow them. As I said, your work has been sufficient."

He starts to leave, but then hesitates.

"Do not do that again," he says, pointing over Marco's shoulder at the frost-covered window.

Then he turns and walks away.

The symbols on the window melt into meaningless streaks.

*

IT IS THE MIDDLE OF THE DAY and the circus sleeps quietly, but Celia Bowen stands in front of the Carousel, watching as black and white and silver creatures file past, suspended on coordinating ribbons, riderless.

"I don't like this thing," a voice behind her says.

Hector Bowen is no more than an apparition in the dimly lit tent. His dark suit vanishes into the shadows. The shifting light catches and releases the brightness of his shirt, the grey of his hair, illuminating the disapproving glare on his face as he watches the Carousel over his daughter's shoulder.

"Whyever not?" Celia responds without turning. "It's extremely popular. And it was a great deal of work; that should count for something, Papa."

His derisive scoff is only an echo of what it once was, and Celia is relieved that he cannot see her smile at the softness of the sound.

"You would not be so reckless were I not . . ." His voice trails off with a wave of a transparent hand next to her arm.

"Don't be cross with me about that," Celia says. "You did it to yourself, it's not my fault you cannot undo it. And I am hardly being reckless."

"How much did you tell this architect of yours?" her father asks.

"I told him as much as I thought he needed to know," Celia says as he drifts past her, moving to inspect the Carousel. "He's fond of pushing boundaries, and I offered to help him push them further. Is Mr. Barris my opponent? That would be quite devious of him, building me a carousel to avoid suspicion."

"He is not your opponent," Hector says with a dismissive gesture, the lace cuff of his shirt fluttering like a moth. "Though such a thing could very well be considered cheating."

"How is utilizing an engineer to execute an idea not working within the venue, Papa? I discussed it with him, he handled the design and construction, and I . . . embellished it. Would you like to ride it? It goes quite a bit farther than around and around."

"Obviously," Hector says, looking down at the darkened tunnel that the line of creatures disappears into. "I still don't like it."

Celia sighs, walking to the edge of the Carousel to pet the head of an oversized raven as it passes by.

"There are already countless elements in this circus that are collaborative," she says. "Why can I not use that to my advantage? You keep insisting that I have to do more than just my performances, but I need to create opportunities in order to manage that. Mr. Barris is quite helpful in that capacity."

"Working with others will only drag you down. These people are not your friends, they are inconsequential. And one of them is your opponent, don't forget that."

"You know who it is, don't you?" Celia asks.

"I have my suspicions."

"But you won't tell me what those are."

"The identity of your opponent does not matter."

"It matters to me."

Hector frowns, watching as she absently toys with the ring on her right hand.

"It shouldn't," he says.

"But my opponent knows who I am, yes?"

"Indeed, unless your opponent happens to be profoundly stupid. And it is unlike Alexander to choose a profoundly stupid student. But it doesn't matter. It is better for you to do your own work without influence from your opponent, and without any of this *collaborating* as you call it."

He waves an arm at the Carousel and the ribbons shudder, as though the softest of breezes has wandered into the tent.

"How is it better?" Celia asks. "How is anything better than anything else here? How is one tent comparable to another? How can any of this possibly be judged?"

"That is not your concern."

"How can I excel at a game when you refuse to tell me the rules?"

The suspended creatures turn their heads in the direction of the ghost in their midst. Gryphons and foxes and wyverns stare at him with glossy black eyes.

"Stop that," Hector snaps at his daughter. The creatures return to their forward-facing gazes, but one of the wolves growls as it settles back into its frozen state. "You are not taking this as seriously as you should."

"It's a circus," Celia says. "It's difficult to take it seriously."

"The circus is only a venue."

"Then this is not a game or a challenge, it's an exhibition."

"It's more than that."

"How?" Celia demands, but her father only shakes his head.

"I have told you all the rules you need to know. You push the bounds of what your skills can do using this circus as a showplace. You prove yourself better and stronger. You do everything you can to outshine your opponent."

"And when do you determine which of us is shinier?"

"I do not determine anything," Hector says. "Stop asking questions. Do more. And stop collaborating."

Before she can respond, he vanishes, leaving her standing alone in the sparkling light from the Carousel.

*

AT FIRST, the letters Marco receives from Isobel arrive frequently, but as the circus travels to far-flung cities and countries, weeks and sometimes months stretch wordlessly between each missive.

When a new letter finally arrives, he does not even take off his coat before ripping open the envelope.

He skims the opening pages that are filled with polite inquiries into his own days in London, remarks about how she misses the city, misses him.

The goings-on of the circus are dutifully reported, but with such matter-of-fact precision that he cannot picture it in the richness of detail that he desires. She glazes over things she considers mundane, the traveling and the train, though Marco is certain they cannot be moving solely by train.

The distance of the circus feels more pronounced despite the tenuous contact through paper and ink.

And there is so little about *her*. Isobel does not even inscribe her name upon the pages, referring to her in passing only as the illusionist, a precaution he advised himself and now regrets.

He wants to know everything about her.

How she spends her time when not performing.

How she interacts with her audiences.

How she takes her tea.

He cannot bring himself to ask Isobel these things.

When he writes her in return, he requests that she continue to write as often as possible. He emphasizes how much her letters mean to him.

He takes the pages inscribed with her handwriting, descriptions of striped tents and star-speckled skies, and folds them into birds, letting them fly around the empty flat.

*

IT IS SO RARE to have a new tent appear that Celia considers canceling her performances entirely in order to spend the evening investigating it.

Instead she waits, executing her standard number of shows, finishing the last a few hours before dawn. Only then does she navigate her way through nearly empty pathways to find the latest addition to the circus.

The sign proclaims something called the Ice Garden, and Celia smiles at the addendum below which contains an apology for any thermal inconvenience.

Despite the name, she is not prepared for what awaits her inside the tent.

It is exactly what the sign described. But it is so much more than that.

There are no stripes visible on the walls, everything is sparkling and white. She cannot tell how far it stretches, the size of the tent obscured by cascading willows and twisting vines.

The air itself is magical. Crisp and sweet in her lungs as she breathes, sending a shiver down to her toes that is caused by more than the fore-warned drop in temperature.

There are no patrons in the tent as she explores, circling alone around trellises covered in pale roses and a softly bubbling, elaborately carved fountain.

And everything, save for occasional lengths of white silk ribbon strung like garlands, is made of ice.

Curious, Celia picks a frosted peony from its branch, the stem breaking easily.

But the layered petals shatter, falling from her fingers to the ground, disappearing in the blades of ivory grass below.

When she looks back at the branch, an identical bloom has already appeared.

Celia cannot imagine how much power and skill it would take not only to construct such a thing but to maintain it as well.

And she longs to know how her opponent came up with the idea. Aware that each perfectly structured topiary, every detail down to the stones that line the paths like pearls, must have been planned.

It would be so taxing to manage something similar, she feels fatigued even considering it. She almost wishes her father were there, as she is beginning to understand why he had always been so adamant about building up her strength and control.

Though she is not entirely certain she wants to thank him for it.

And she likes having the space to herself, the stillness and the calm sweetened with the subdued scent of frozen flowers.

Celia remains in the Ice Garden long after the sun rises outside, and the gates have been closed for the day.

*

THE CIRCUS ARRIVES NEAR LONDON for the first visit in some time, and the afternoon before it opens there is a knock on the door of Marco's flat.

He opens the door only partway, holding it in place when he finds Isobel in the hallway.

"You changed your locks," she says.

"Why did you not tell me you were coming?" Marco asks.

"I thought you might like the surprise," Isobel says.

Marco refuses to let her enter the flat, but he leaves her waiting in the hall for only moments before returning, bowler hat in hand.

The afternoon is crisp but bright and he takes her to tea.

"What is that?" Marco asks, glancing down at Isobel's wrist as they walk.

"Nothing," she says, pulling the cuff of her sleeve down to obscure his view of the bracelet, a carefully woven braid of her hair entwined with his.

He does not inquire further.

Though Isobel never takes the bracelet off, it is gone when she returns to the circus that evening. Vanished from her skin as though it had never been there.

Tasting

Herr Friedrick Thiessen is on holiday in France. He often goes on holiday in France in the autumn, as he is a great lover of wine. He picks a region and roams the countryside for a week or perhaps two, visiting vineyards and collecting bottles of pleasing vintage to be shipped back to Munich.

Herr Thiessen is friendly with several French winemakers and has made clocks for many of them. He visits one such winemaker on this particular trip, to pay his respects and sample the latest bottles. Over a glass of burgundy, the winemaker suggests that Friedrick might enjoy the circus that is in town, set up in a field a few miles away. A rather unusual circus, only open at night.

But it is the clock, the elaborate black-and-white clock situated just inside the gates, that the winemaker thinks might particularly interest Herr Thiessen.

"Reminds me of your work," the winemaker says, gesturing with his glass to the clock on the wall above the bar, shaped like a cascading bunch of grapes that tumble into a wine bottle that fills with wine as the hands on its label (an exact replica of the vineyard's label) tick by the seconds.

Herr Thiessen is intrigued, and after an early dinner, he puts on his hat and gloves and begins walking in the general direction his wine-maker friend had indicated. It is not difficult to locate his destination, as several townspeople are walking in the same direction, and once they pass out of town and into the fields, the circus cannot be missed.

It glows. That is Herr Friedrick Thiessen's first impression of Le Cirque des Rêves, seen from half a mile away and before he even knows its name. He walks toward it on this chilly evening through the French countryside like a moth to a flame.

There is a considerable crowd outside when Herr Thiessen finally reaches the gates, and despite the crowd, he would have spotted his clock instantly, even without having been informed of its placement. It looms across from the ticket booth, just inside the large iron gates. It is about to strike seven o'clock, and he stands back to watch it, letting the line for tickets pass in front of him as the harlequin juggler pulls out a seventh ball from thin air, as the dragon's tale twitches and the clock chimes seven quiet chimes, barely audible over the din of the circus.

Herr Thiessen is pleased. The clock appears to be in perfect working order and has obviously been well taken care of, despite being left out in the elements. He wonders if it might need a stronger varnish, and wishes he had been informed that it would be used out of doors when he was constructing it, though it looks none the worse for wear. He keeps his eyes on it as he waits in line, wondering if he should try to contact Mr. Barris about the matter, if he still has the London address in his files back in Munich.

When it is his turn, he gives the posted amount of francs to the ticket seller, a young woman in a black dress and long white gloves, looking more prepared for an elegant evening at the opera than for a night selling tickets at a circus. As she pulls out a ticket he inquires, first in French and then in English when she does not catch his meaning, if she might know whom he could contact about the clock. She does not reply but her eyes light up when he identifies himself as the person responsible for its construction. She returns his francs with his ticket despite his protestations, and after rummaging through a small box, she produces a business card which she hands him as well.

Herr Thiessen thanks her, moving out of line and off to the side, inspecting the card. It is a high-quality card on heavy stock. A black background embossed with silver.

Le Cirque des Rêves
Chandresh Christophe Lefèvre, Proprietor

The back has an address in London. Herr Thiessen places it in his coat pocket along with his ticket and his saved francs, and takes his first steps into the circus.

He begins by simply wandering, casually investigating the odd home of his *Wunschtraum* clock. Perhaps because of the months he spent absorbed in working on the clock itself, the circus feels familiar, comfortable. The monochromatic color scheme, the endless circles of the pathways like clockworks. Herr Thiessen is amazed at how well his clock fits the circus, and how well the circus fits his clock.

He enters only a fraction of the tents that first night, stopping to watch fire-breathers and sword dancers, sampling a very fine eiswein in a tent marked DRINKERY, MATURE VISITORS ONLY. When he inquires about it, the bartender (the only person in the circus that Friedrick encounters who speaks when spoken to, albeit minimally) informs him that it is a Canadian wine and notes the vintage for him.

By the time Herr Thiessen departs the circus, motivated solely by exhaustion, he is completely and utterly besotted. He attends twice more before returning to Munich, paying his admission in full both times.

He writes a letter to M. Lefèvre upon his return, to thank him for giving his clock such a wondrous home and for the experience of the circus itself. He goes on at length about the mastery of it, and says he gathered there is no rhyme or reason to its itinerary, but expresses his hope that it will come to Germany.

Some weeks later, he receives a letter from M. Lefèvre's assistant, stating that M. Lefèvre greatly appreciates Herr Thiessen's compliments, especially coming from such a talented artist. The letter speaks highly of the clock, and mentions that should there be any kind of problem with it, Herr Thiessen will be contacted immediately.

The letter mentions nothing of the current location of the circus or anything about it coming to Germany, much to Herr Thiessen's disappointment.

He thinks about the circus frequently, often as he works, and it begins to have an influence upon his work. Many of his new clocks are done in black and white, some with stripes and many with scenes from the circus: tiny acrobats, miniature snow leopards, a fortune-teller who lays out minuscule tarot cards on the hour.

Though he fears he never does the circus justice in these clockwork tributes.

Chaperoned

While the Murray twins are more or less allowed to run rampant around the hidden corners of what is often referred to as backstage—a sprawling mansion's worth of space dispersed into nooks and passageways where the occupants of the circus live their lives when they are not performing—if they wish to be out and about in the circus proper during performance hours they must have a chaperone. They protest this rule loudly and often, but their father insists that these rules will stay in place until they are eight years old, at the very least.

Widget asks often if the eight years counts if it is a combined total, in which case they already meet the criteria.

They are repeatedly reminded that they must have some sort of structure to their nocturnal schedule, being the only children in a rather unconventional household.

For now they have a rotating company of chaperones, and tonight the illusionist is on twin-supervising duty. She is not often assigned this role, though the twins are quite fond of her. But this evening she has enough time to spare between performances to escort them for a while.

None of the patrons recognize Celia without her top hat and black-and-white gown, even those who watched her perform earlier in the evening. If passersby pay her any notice it is only to wonder how the children at her heels ended up with such red hair when her own is so dark. Beyond that she appears to be just a young woman in a blue coat, wandering the circus as any other patron might.

They start in the Ice Garden, though the twins grow impatient with the leisurely pace that Celia prefers to take around the frozen trees. Before they have traveled halfway through the space they are begging to ride the Carousel instead.

They argue over who will get to ride the gryphon but Widget relents when Celia tells them the story of the nine-tailed fox just behind it, which suddenly sounds much more appealing. As soon as they disembark, a second ride is requested. For the subsequent trip through the loops of silver clockwork and tunnels they end up on a serpent and a rabbit with no complaints to be heard.

After the Carousel rides, Widget wants something to eat, so they head for the courtyard. When Celia procures him a black-and-white-striped paper bag of popcorn, he insists he wants caramel as well, and will not eat it plain.

The vendor dipping apples on sticks into dark, sticky caramel obliges him, drizzling it over the top. Several patrons nearby request the same.

Poppet claims she isn't hungry. She seems distracted, so as they walk down a quieter passage away from the courtyard, Celia asks if anything is bothering her.

"I don't want the nice lady to die," Poppet says, tugging gently at Celia's skirt.

Celia stops walking, putting out a hand to keep Widget, who is oblivious to anything other than his popcorn, from continuing along in front of her.

"What do you mean, dearest?" she asks Poppet.

"They're going to put her in the ground," Poppet explains. "I think that's sad."

"What nice lady?" Celia asks.

Poppet scrunches up her face while she thinks.

"I don't know," she says. "They look the same."

"Poppet, sweetheart," Celia says, pulling the twins aside into an alcove and bending down to talk to her face-to-face. "Where is this lady in the ground? Where did you see her, I mean?"

"In the stars," Poppet says. She stands on tiptoes as she points upward.

Celia glances up at the star-filled sky, watching the moon disappear behind a cloud before returning her attention to Poppet.

"Do you often see things in the stars?" she asks.

"Only sometimes," Poppet says. "Widge sees things on people."

Celia turns to Widget, who is eating his caramel-drizzled popcorn in messy handfuls.

"You see things on people?" she asks him.

"Fumtimes," he mumbles through a mouthful.

"What kind of things?" Celia asks.

Widget shrugs his shoulders.

"Places they've been," he says. "Stuff they've done."

He shoves another handful of sticky popcorn into his mouth.

"Interesting," Celia says. The twins have told her a great many odd things before, but this seems like more than childish fancies. "Can you see anything on me?" she asks Widget.

Widget squints at her while he chews his popcorn.

"Rooms that smell like powder and old clothes," he says. "A lady that cries all the time. A ghost man with a frilly shirt that follows you around and—"

Widget stops suddenly, frowning.

"You made it go away," he says. "There's nothing there anymore. How did you do that?"

"Some things are not for you to see," Celia says.

Widget pushes his lower lip out in an impressive pout, but it only lasts as long as it takes him to bring another fistful of popcorn to his mouth.

Celia looks from the twins back in the direction of the courtyard, where the light from the bonfire gleams along the edges of the tents, casting dancing shadows of patrons across the striped fabric.

The bonfire never goes out. The flames never falter.

Even when the circus moves it is not extinguished, moved intact from location to location. Smoldering the entire length of each train journey, safely contained in its iron cauldron.

It has burned steadily since the ceremonious lighting on opening night.

And at the same moment, Celia remains certain, something was put in motion that impacted the entire circus and everyone within it once that fire was lit.

Including the newborn twins.

Widget born just before midnight, at the end of an old day. Poppet following moments later in a new day only just begun.

"Poppet," Celia says, turning her attention back to the little girl who has been playing with the cuff of her jacket, "if you see things in the stars that you think might be important, I want you to tell me about them, do you understand?"

Poppet nods solemnly, clouds of red hair bobbing in waves. She leans in to ask Celia a question, her eyes dreadfully serious.

"May I have a caramel apple?" she asks.

"I'm out of popcorn," Widget complains, holding out his empty bag.

Celia takes the bag from him and folds it up into ever-smaller squares while the twins watch, until it disappears completely. When they clap, Widget's hands are no longer covered in caramel, though he does not notice.

Celia considers the twins for a moment, while Widget tries to figure out where the popcorn bag has gone and Poppet casts thoughtful glances up at the sky.

It is not a good idea. She knows it is not a good idea but it would be better to keep them close, to watch them more carefully given the circumstances and their apparent talents.

"Would the two of you like to learn how to do things like that?" Celia asks them.

Widget nods immediately, with such enthusiasm that his hat slips forward over his eyes. Poppet hesitates but then she nods as well.

"Then when you are a little bit older I shall give you lessons, but it will have to be our secret," Celia says. "Can you two keep a secret?"

The twins nod in unison. Widget has to straighten his hat again.

They follow Celia happily as she leads them back to the courtyard.

Wishes and Desires

PARIS, MAY 1891

When the beaded curtain parts with a sound like rain, it is Marco who enters the fortune-teller's chamber, and Isobel immediately flips her veil from her face, the impossibly thin black silk floating back over her head like mist.

"What are you doing here?" she asks.

"Why didn't you tell me about this?" Ignoring her question, he holds out an open notebook, and in the flickering light Isobel can discern a bare black tree. It is not like the trees that are inscribed in so many of his books, this one is covered in dripping white candles. Surrounding the main drawing are detailed sketches of twisting branches, capturing several different angles.

"That's the Wishing Tree," Isobel says. "It's new."

"I know it's new," Marco says. "Why didn't you tell me about it?"

"I haven't had time to write you," Isobel says. "And I wasn't even sure whether or not it was something you had done yourself. It seemed like something you might have made. It's lovely, the way wishes are added to it, by lighting candles with ones that are already lit and adding them to the branches. New wishes ignited by old wishes."

"It's hers," Marco says simply, pulling the notebook back.

"How can you be certain?" Isobel asks.

Marco pauses, looking down at the sketch, annoyed that he could not properly capture the beauty of the thing in hastily rendered drawings.

"I can feel it," he says. "It is like knowing that a storm is coming, the shift in the air around it. As soon as I walked into the tent I could sense it, and it is stronger closer to the tree itself. I am not certain it would be perceptible if one were unfamiliar with such sensation."

"Do you think she can feel what you do in the same way?" Isobel asks.

Marco has not considered this before, though it seems it would be true. He finds the idea strangely pleasing.

"I do not know" is all he says to Isobel.

Isobel pushes the veil that is slipping over her face back behind her head again.

"Well," she says, "now you know about it, and you can do whatever you want to it."

"It doesn't work that way," Marco says. "I cannot use anything she does for my own purposes. The sides need to remain separate. If we were playing a game of chess, I could not simply remove her pieces from the board. My only option is to retaliate with my own pieces when she moves hers."

"But there can't possibly be an endgame, then," Isobel says. "How can you checkmate a circus? It doesn't make any sense."

"It's not like chess," Marco says, struggling to explain something that he has finally begun to understand even though he cannot properly articulate it. He glances at her table where a few cards remain laid faceup, one in particular catching his attention.

"It's like this," he says, pointing out the woman with her scales and sword, *La Justice* inscribed below her feet. "It's a set of scales: one side is mine, the other is hers."

A set of silver scales appears on the table between the cards, balancing precariously, each side piled with diamonds that sparkle in the candlelight.

"So the object is to tip the scales in your favor?" Isobel asks.

Marco nods, turning through the pages of his notebook. He keeps flipping back to the page with the tree.

"But if you both keep adding to your sides of the scale, increasing the weight on each side in turn," Isobel says, watching the gently swaying scale, "won't it break?"

"I do not believe it is an exact comparison," Marco says, and the scales vanish.

Isobel frowns at the empty space.

"How long is this going to go on?" she asks.

"I have no idea," Marco says. "Do you want to leave?" he adds, looking up at her. Unsure of what response he wants to the question.

"No," Isobel says. "I . . . I don't want to leave. I like it here, I do. But I would also like to understand. Maybe if I understood better I could be more helpful."

"You are helpful," Marco says. "Perhaps the only advantage I have is that she does not know who I am. She only has the circus to react to and I have you to watch her."

"But I haven't seen any reaction," Isobel protests. "She keeps to herself. She reads more than anyone I have ever met. The Murray twins adore her. She has been nothing but kind to me. I have never seen her do a single thing out of the ordinary beyond when she performs. You say she is making all these moves and yet I never see her do anything. How do you know that tree is not Ethan Barris's work?"

"Mr. Barris creates impressive mechanics, but this is not his doing. Though she's embellished his carousel, I'm certain of that. I doubt even an engineer of Mr. Barris's talent can make a painted wooden gryphon *breathe*. That tree is rooted in the ground, it is a living tree even if it does not have leaves."

Marco turns his attention back to his sketch, tracing the lines of the tree with his fingertips.

"Did you make a wish?" Isobel asks quietly.

Marco closes his notebook without answering the question.

"Does she still perform on the quarter hour?" he asks, drawing a watch from his pocket.

"Yes, but . . . you're going to sit there and watch her show?" Isobel asks. "There's barely room for twenty people in her tent, she'll notice you. Won't she think it strange that you're here?"

"She won't even recognize me," Marco says. The watch vanishes from his hand. "Whenever there is a new tent, I would appreciate it if you would let me know."

He turns and walks away, moving so quickly that the candle flames shiver with the motion of the air.

"I miss you," Isobel says as he leaves, but the sentiment is crushed by the clatter of the beaded curtain falling closed behind him.

She tugs the black mist of her veil back down over her face.

*

AFTER THE LAST of her querents has departed in the early hours of the morning, Isobel takes her Marseilles deck from her pocket. She carries it with her always though she has a separate deck for circus readings, a custom-made version in black and white and shades of grey.

From the Marseilles deck she draws a single card. She knows which it will be before she turns it over. The angel emblazoned on the front is only a confirmation of what she already suspects.

She does not return it to the deck.

Atmosphere

The circus has arrived near London, the train creeping in just after nightfall without drawing any notice. The train cars collapse, doors and halls sliding apart, silently forming chains of windowless rooms. Canvas stripes unfurl around them, uncoiled ropes snapping taut and platforms assembling themselves amongst carefully draped curtains.

(The company assumes there is a crew that accomplishes this feat while they unpack their trunks, though some aspects of the transition are clearly automated. This was once the case, but now there is no crew, no unseen stagehands moving bits of scenery to their proper places. They are no longer necessary.)

The tents sit quiet and dark, as the circus will not be open to the public until the following evening.

While most of the performers are spending the night in the city visiting old friends and favorite pubs, Celia Bowen sits alone in her backstage suite.

Her rooms are modest in comparison to others hidden behind the circus tents, but they are filled with books and well-worn furniture. Mismatched candles burn merrily on every available surface, illuminating the sleeping doves in their cages hanging amongst sweeping curtains of richly colored tapestries. A cozy sanctuary, comfortable and quiet.

The knock on the door comes as a surprise.

"Is this how you intend to spend your entire night?" Tsukiko asks, glancing at the book in Celia's hand.

"I take it you came to suggest an alternative?" Celia asks. The contortionist does not often visit solely for the sake of visiting.

"I have a social engagement, and I thought you might join me," Tsukiko says. "You spend too much time in solitude."

Celia attempts to protest, but Tsukiko is insistent, taking out one of Celia's finest gowns, one of few with any color, a deep blue velvet embellished with pale gold.

"Where are we going?" Celia asks, but Tsukiko refuses to say. It is too late an hour for their destination to be the theater or the ballet.

Celia laughs when they arrive at *la maison* Lefèvre.

"You could have told me," she says to Tsukiko.

"Then it would not have been a surprise," Tsukiko responds.

Celia has attended only a single function at *la maison* Lefèvre, and that was more pre-circus-opening reception than proper Midnight Dinner. But despite visiting the house on only a handful of occasions between her audition and the opening of the circus, she finds she is already acquainted with each of the guests.

Her arrival with Tsukiko is a surprise to the rest of them, but she is greeted warmly by Chandresh and swept into the parlor with a glass of champagne in her hand before she can apologize for her unexpected presence.

"See that they set an additional place for dinner," Chandresh says to Marco, before taking her on a cursory spin around the room to make sure she has met everyone. Celia finds it odd that he does not seem to remember.

Mme. Padva is gracious as always, her gown the warm copper of autumn leaves glowing in the candlelight. The Burgess sisters and Mr. Barris have apparently already been making light of the fact that the three of them have all worn various shades of blue, an unplanned detail, and Celia's gown is cited as proof that it must simply be in fashion.

There is some mention of another guest that may or may not be attending, but Celia does not catch his name.

She feels slightly out of place in this gathering of people who have known each other for so long. But Tsukiko makes a point of including her in the conversation, and Mr. Barris pays such attention to her every word when she does speak, that Lainie begins to tease him about it.

While Celia knows Mr. Barris quite well, having met with him several times and exchanged dozens of letters, he does an impressive job of pretending they are mere acquaintances.

"You should have been an actor," she whispers to him when she is certain no one will overhear.

"I know," he replies, sounding genuinely sad. "Such a shame that I missed my true calling."

Celia has never spoken with either of the Burgess sisters at much length—Lainie is more talkative than Tara—and tonight she learns in greater detail the touches that they have put on the circus. While Mme. Padva's costumes and Mr. Barris's feats of engineering are obvious, the mark of the Burgess sisters is more subtle, though it permeates almost every aspect of the circus.

The scents, the music, the quality of the light. Even the weight of the velvet curtains at the entrance. They have arranged each element to appear effortless.

"We like to hit all of the senses," Lainie says.

"Some more than others," Tara adds.

"True," her sister agrees. "Scent is often underestimated, when it can be the most evocative."

"They are brilliant with atmosphere," Chandresh remarks to Celia as he joins their conversation, switching her empty glass of champagne with a freshly poured replacement. "Both of them, absolutely brilliant."

"The trick is to make it seem as though none of it is purposeful," Lainie whispers. "To make the artificial feel natural."

"To tie all the elements together," Tara finishes.

It seems to Celia that they provide a similar service within the present company. Celia doubts that these gatherings would have continued so long after the circus began without the Burgess sisters' infectious bubbling laughter. They ask the perfect questions to keep the conversation flowing, warding off any lulls.

And Mr. Barris provides an ideal contrast, serious and attentive, keeping the dynamic of the group in balance.

A movement in the hall catches Celia's eye, and while anyone else might have credited a number of candles or mirrors for the reflection, she knows the cause immediately.

She steps out into the hall unnoticed, slipping out of sight into the shadowed library across from the parlor. It is lit only by a panel of stained glass stretching in a glowing sunset along one wall, sending its warm hue cascading over the closest shelves and letting the rest of the room fall into shadow.

"Can I not have one evening to enjoy myself without you following me?" Celia whispers into the darkness.

"I do not think social engagements of this sort are a proper use of your time," her father replies, the sunset light catching part of his face and the front of his shirt in a distorted column of red.

"You do not get to dictate how I spend every moment of my time, Papa."

"You are losing your focus," Hector replies.

"I cannot lose my focus," Celia says. "Between new tents and embellishments, I actively control a significant part of the circus. Which is closed at the moment, if you hadn't noticed. And the better I know these people, the better I can manipulate what they've already done. They created it, after all."

"I suppose that is a valid point," Hector says. Celia suspects he is scowling despite the admission, though it is too dark to tell. "But you'd do well to remember that you have no reason to trust anyone in that room."

"Leave me alone, Papa," Celia says, and sighs.

"Miss Bowen?" a voice says behind her and she turns, surprised to find Chandresh's assistant standing in the doorway, watching her. "Dinner is about to begin, if you would care to join the rest of the guests in the dining room."

"My apologies," Celia says, her eyes darting back to the shadows, but her father has vanished. "I was distracted by the size of the library. I did not think anyone would notice I was missing."

"I am certain that they would," Marco says. "Though I have been distracted by the library, myself, many times."

The charming smile that accompanies the statement catches Celia off guard, as she has rarely seen anything but varying degrees of reserved attentiveness or occasional nervousness on his countenance.

"Thank you for coming to fetch me," she says, hoping that dinner guests talking to themselves while supposedly perusing books without the aid of proper lighting is not an unusual occurrence at *la maison* Lefèvre.

"They likely suspect you vanished into thin air," Marco responds as they walk through the hall. "I thought perhaps that was not the case."

He holds each door open for her as he escorts her to the dining room.

Celia is seated between Chandresh and Tsukiko.

"This is preferable to spending the evening alone, is it not?" Tsukiko asks, smiling when Celia admits that it is true.

As the courses progress, when she is not distracted by the astounding quality of the food, Celia makes a game of deciphering the relationships between the guests. Reading the way they interact, intuiting the emotions hidden beneath the laughter and conversation, catching the places that gazes linger.

Chandresh's glances at his handsome assistant grow more obvious with each glass of wine, and Celia suspects Mr. Alisdair is well aware of it, though Marco remains a quiet presence at the edge of the room.

It takes her three courses to determine which of the Burgess sisters Mr. Barris favors, but by the time the artfully arranged plates of what appear to be whole pigeons spiced with cinnamon arrive, she is certain, though she cannot tell if Lainie herself knows.

Mme. Padva is called "Tante" by the entire company, though she feels more like a matriarch than merely an aunt. When Celia addresses her as "Madame," everyone turns to look at her in surprise.

"So proper for a circus girl," Mme. Padva says with a gleam in her eye. "We shall have to loosen those corset laces if we intend to keep you as intimate dinner company."

"I expected the corset unlacing would take place *after* dinner," Celia says mildly, earning a chorus of laughter.

"We shall be keeping Miss Bowen as intimate company regardless of the state of her corset," Chandresh says. "Make a note of that," he adds, waving a hand at Marco.

"Miss Bowen's corset is duly noted, sir," Marco replies, and the laughter bubbles over the table again.

Marco catches Celia's glance with a hint of the smile from earlier before he turns away, fading into the background again almost as easily as her father vanishes into shadows.

The next course arrives and Celia returns to listening and observing, in between trying to figure out if the meat disguised in feather-light pastry and delicate wine sauce is actually lamb or something more exotic.

There is something about Tara's behavior that Celia finds bothersome. Something almost haunted in her expression that comes and goes. One moment she is actively engaged in the conversation, her laugh echoing her sister's, and the next she seems distant, staring through the dripping candles.

It is only when the echoed laugh sounds almost like a sob for a moment that Celia realizes that Tara reminds her of her mother.

The dessert course halts the conversation entirely. Globes of thinly blown sugar sit on each plate and must be broken open in order to access the clouds of cream within.

After the cacophony of shattering sugar, it does not take long for the diners to realize that, though the globes appeared identical, each of them has been presented with an entirely unique flavor.

There is much sharing of spoons. And while some are easily guessed as ginger with peach or curried coconut, others remain delicious mysteries.

Celia's is clearly honey, but with a blend of spices beneath the sweetness that no one is able to place.

After dinner, the conversation continues over coffee and brandy in the parlor, until an hour most of the guests deem extremely late but Tsukiko points out that it is comparatively early for the circus girls.

When they do begin to say their goodbyes, Celia is embraced no differently than anyone else, and given several invitations to meet for tea while the circus remains in London.

"Thank you," she says to Tsukiko as they leave. "I enjoyed that more than I had expected to."

"The finest of pleasures are always the unexpected ones," Tsukiko replies.

*

MARCO WATCHES FROM THE WINDOW as the guests depart, catching a last glimpse of Celia before she disappears into the night.

He does a round through the parlor and dining room, and then downstairs to the kitchens to make certain everything is in order. The rest of the staff has already departed. He extinguishes the last of the lights before ascending several flights to check on Chandresh.

"Brilliant dinner tonight, don't you think?" Chandresh asks when Marco reaches the suite that comprises the entire fifth story, each room lit by a multitude of Moroccan lanterns that cast fractured shadows over the opulent furniture.

"Indeed, sir," Marco says.

"Nothing on the agenda for tomorrow, though. Or later today, whatever time it is."

"There is the meeting in the afternoon regarding next season's ballet schedule."

"Ah, I had forgotten," Chandresh says. "Cancel that, would you?"

"Of course, sir," Marco says, taking a notebook from his pocket and marking down the request.

"Oh, and order a dozen cases of whatever that brandy was that Ethan brought. Marvelous stuff, that."

Marco nods, adding it to his notes.

"You're not leaving, are you?" Chandresh asks.

"No, sir," Marco says. "I had thought it too late to be going home."

"*Home*," Chandresh repeats, as though the word sounds foreign. "This is your home as much as that flat you insist on keeping is. More so, even."

"I shall endeavor to remember that, sir," Marco says.

"Miss Bowen is a lovely woman, don't you think?" Chandresh remarks suddenly, turning to gauge the reaction to the question.

Caught by surprise, Marco only manages to stammer something he hopes resembles his standard impartial agreement.

"We must invite her to dinner whenever the circus is in town, so we might get to know her better," Chandresh says pointedly, emphasizing the statement with a satisfied grin.

"Yes, sir," Marco says, struggling to keep his expression impassive. "Will that be all for tonight?"

Chandresh laughs as he waves him away.

Before he retires to his own rooms, a suite three times the size of his flat, Marco quietly returns to the library.

He stands for some time in the spot where he found Celia hours before, scrutinizing the familiar bookshelves and the wall of stained glass.

He cannot guess what she might have been doing.

And he does not notice the eyes staring at him from the shadows.

Rêveurs
1891–1892

Herr Friedrick Thiessen receives the card in the mail, a plain envelope amongst his invoices and business correspondence. The envelope holds no letter or note, simply a card that is black on one side and white on the other. "Le Cirque des Rêves" is printed on the front in silver ink. On the back, handwritten in black ink on white, it reads:

Twenty-nine September
Just outside Dresden, Saxony

Herr Thiessen can barely contain his glee. He makes arrangements with his clients, finishes his clocks in progress in record time, and secures a short-term flat rental in Dresden.

He arrives in Dresden on September 28, and spends the day wandering the outskirts of the city, wondering where the circus might set up. There is no indication of its impending arrival, only a slight electricity in the air, though Herr Thiessen is unsure if anyone, save himself, can sense it. He feels honored at having been given advance notice.

On September 29, he sleeps in, anticipating the late night ahead. When he leaves his flat in the early afternoon to find something to eat, the streets are already buzzing with the news: a strange circus has appeared overnight, just west of the city. A gargantuan thing, with striped tents, they are saying when he reaches the pub. Never seen anything like it. Herr Thiessen stays silent on the matter, enjoying the excitement and curiosity around him.

Shortly before sunset Herr Thiessen heads west, finding the circus easily as there is a large crowd assembled outside already. While he waits with the crowd, he wonders how the circus manages to set up so quickly.

He is certain that the field it sits in now, as though it has always been there, had been empty the day before when he walked around the city. The circus has simply materialized. Like magic, he overhears someone remark, and Herr Thiessen has to agree.

When the gates open at last, Herr Friedrick Thiessen feels as though he is returning home after an extended absence.

He spends almost every night there, and during the day he sits in his rented flat or at the pub with a glass of wine and a journal and he writes about it. Pages and pages of observations, recounting his experiences, mostly so he will not forget them but also to capture something of the circus on paper, something he can hold on to.

He occasionally converses about the circus with his fellow pub dwellers. One of these is a man who edits the city paper, and after some persuading and several glasses of wine, he manages to get Friedrick to show him the journal. After a shot or two of bourbon, he convinces Friedrick to allow excerpts of it to be published in the newspaper.

The circus departs Dresden in late October, but the newspaper editor keeps his word.

The article is well received, and followed by another, and then another.

Herr Thiessen continues to write, and over the following months some of the articles are reprinted in other German papers, and eventually they are translated and printed in Sweden and Denmark and France. One article finds its way into a London paper, printed under the title "Nights at the Circus."

It is these articles that make Herr Friedrick Thiessen the unofficial leader, the figurehead, of those most ardent followers of the circus.

Some are introduced to Le Cirque des Rêves through his writing, while others feel an instant connection with him as they read his words, an affinity for this man who experiences the circus as they do, as something wondrous and inimitable.

Some seek him out, and the meetings and dinners that follow herald the formation of a kind of club, a society of lovers of the circus.

The title of *rêveurs* begins as a joke, but it sticks, secure in its appropriateness.

Herr Thiessen enjoys this immensely, being surrounded by kindred spirits from all over Europe, and occasionally even farther, who will discuss the circus endlessly. He transcribes the stories of other *rêveurs* to include in his writings. He constructs small keepsake clocks for them depicting their favorite acts or performances. (One of these is a marvel of tiny flying acrobats on ribbons, made for a young woman who spends most of her hours at the circus in that massive tent, staring upward.)

He even, somewhat unintentionally, starts a fashion trend amongst the *rêveurs*. He comments at a dinner in Munich—where many of the dinners are held near his home, though they are also held in London and Paris and countless other cities as well—that when he attends the circus he prefers to wear a black coat, to better blend in with his surroundings and feel a part of the circus. But with it, he wears a scarf in a brilliant scarlet, to distinguish himself from it as well, as a reminder that he is at heart a spectator, an observer.

Word spreads quickly in such select circles, and so begins a tradition of *rêveurs* attending Le Cirque des Rêves decked in black or white or grey with a single shock of red: a scarf or hat, or, if the weather is warm, a red rose tucked into a lapel or behind an ear. It is also quite helpful for spotting other *rêveurs*, a simple signal for those in the know.

There are those who have the means, and even some who do not but creatively manage anyway, to follow the circus from location to location. There is no set itinerary that is public knowledge. The circus moves from place to place every few weeks, with the occasional extended break, and no one truly knows where it might appear until the tents are already erected in a field in a city or the countryside, or somewhere in between.

But there are those few people, select *rêveurs* who are familiar with the circus and its ways, who have made polite acquaintance of the proper individuals and are notified of impending locations, and they in turn notify others, in other countries, in other cities.

The most common method is subtle, and works both in person and by post.

They send cards. Small, rectangular cards, much like postcards, that vary but are always black on one side and white on the other. Some use actual postcards, others choose to make their own. The cards state simply:

and list a location. Sometimes there is a date, but not always. The circus functions in approximations more than exacting details. But the notification and location is often enough.

Most *rêveurs* have a home base and prefer not to travel terribly far. *Rêveurs* who call Canada home may be hesitant to travel to Russia but easily make extended visits to Boston or Chicago, while those in Morocco may travel to many destinations in Europe but perhaps not all the way to China or Japan.

Some, though, follow the circus wherever it may lead, through money or luck or extensive favors from other *rêveurs*. But they are all *rêveurs*, each in their own way, even those who only have the means to visit the circus when it comes to them, rather than the other way around. They smile when they spot each other. They meet up at local pubs to have drinks and chat while they wait impatiently for the sun to set.

It is these aficionados, these *rêveurs*, who see the details in the bigger picture of the circus. They see the nuance of the costumes, the intricacy of the signs. They buy sugar flowers and do not eat them, wrapping them in paper instead and carefully bringing them home. They are enthusiasts, devotees. Addicts. Something about the circus stirs their souls, and they ache for it when it is absent.

They seek each other out, these people of such specific like mind. They tell of how they found the circus, how those first few steps were like magic. Like stepping into a fairy tale under a curtain of stars. They pontificate upon the fluffiness of the popcorn, the sweetness of the chocolate. They spend hours discussing the quality of the light, the heat of the bonfire. They sit over their drinks smiling like children and they relish being surrounded by kindred spirits, if only for an evening. When they depart, they shake hands and embrace like old friends, even if they have only just met, and as they go their separate ways they feel less alone than they had before.

The circus knows of them, and appreciates them. Often someone approaching the ticket booth in a black coat with a red scarf will be waved in without paying admission, or given a mug of cider or bag of popcorn gratis. Performers spotting them in the audience will bring out their best tricks. Some of the *rêveurs* wander the circus continuously, methodically visiting every tent, watching each performance. Others have their favorite spots which they rarely leave, choosing to pass the entire night in the Menagerie or the Hall of Mirrors. They are the ones who stay the latest, through the small hours when most visitors have gone to seek their beds.

Often, just before dawn, there is no color to be seen in Le Cirque des Rêves save for their small splashes of scarlet.

*

HERR THIESSEN RECEIVES DOZENS OF LETTERS from other *rêveurs*, and he responds to each. While some remain single letters, content with their onetime replies, others evolve into longer exchanges, collections of ongoing conversations.

Today he is replying to a letter he finds particularly intriguing. The author writes about the circus with stunning specificity. And the letter is more personal than most, delving into thoughts on his own writings, observations about his *Wunschtraum* clock containing a level of detail that would require observing it for hours on end. He reads the letter three times before he sits at his desk to compose his reply.

The postmark is from New York, but he does not recognize the signature as belonging to any of the *rêveurs* he has met in passing in that or any other city.

Dear Miss Bowen, he begins.

He hopes that he will receive another letter in turn.

Collaborations

Marco arrives at Mr. Barris's London office only a few minutes before his scheduled appointment, surprised to find the normally well-ordered space in near bedlam, full of half-packed crates and stacks of boxes. The desk is nowhere to be seen, buried beneath the chaos.

"Is it that late already?" Mr. Barris asks when Marco knocks on the open door, unable to step inside due to a lack of available floor. "I should have left the clock out, it's in one of those crates." He waves at a line of large wooden crates along the wall, though if one of them is ticking it is impossible to tell. "And I meant to clear a path, as well," he adds, pushing boxes aside and picking up piles of rolled blueprints.

"Sorry to intrude," Marco says. "I wanted to speak with you before you left the city. I would have waited until you were settled again, but I thought it best to discuss the matter in person."

"Of course," Mr. Barris says. "I wanted to give you the spare copies of the circus plans. They are around here somewhere." He sifts through the pile of blueprints, checking labels and dates.

The office door closes quietly, untouched.

"May I ask you a question, Mr. Barris?" Marco inquires.

"Certainly," Mr. Barris says, still sorting through rolls of paper.

"How much do you know?"

Mr. Barris puts down the blueprint in his hand and turns, pushing his spectacles up on the bridge of his nose to better regard Marco's expression.

"How much do I know about what?" he asks after the pause has gone on too long.

"How much has Miss Bowen told you?" Marco asks in response.

Mr. Barris looks at him curiously for a moment before he speaks.

"You're her opponent," he says, a smile spreading across his face when Marco nods. "I never would have guessed."

"She told you about the competition," Marco says.

"Only in the most basic of terms," Mr. Barris says. "She came to me several years ago and asked what I might say if she were to tell me that everything she does is real. I told her that I would have to take her at her word or think her a liar, and I would never dream such a lovely lady to be a liar. And then she asked what I might design if I did not have such constraints as gravity to concern myself with. That was the beginning of the Carousel, but I imagine you knew that already."

"I assumed as much," Marco says. "Though I was not certain to what degree you were knowingly involved."

"I am in the position to be quite useful, as I see it. I believe stage magicians employ engineers to make their tricks appear to be something they are not. In this case, I provide the opposite service, helping actual magic appear to be clever construction. Miss Bowen refers to it as grounding, making the unbelievable believable."

"Did she have anything to do with the Stargazer?" Marco asks.

"No, the Stargazer is purely mechanical," Mr. Barris says. "I can show you the structural plans if I can locate them in this mess. It was inspired by a trip to the Columbian Exposition in Chicago earlier this year. Miss Bowen insisted there was no way to improve it, though I think she may have something to do with keeping it running properly."

"Then you are a magician in your own right, sir," Marco says.

"Perhaps we simply do similar things in different ways," Mr. Barris says. "I had thought, knowing Miss Bowen had an opponent lurking somewhere, that whomever you might be, you were not in need of any assistance. The paper animals are astonishing, for example."

"Thank you," Marco says. "I have improvised quite a bit trying to come up with tents that did not require blueprints."

"Is that why you're here?" Mr. Barris asks. "For something of the blueprint variety?"

"Primarily, I wanted to be certain about your awareness of the game," Marco says. "I could make you forget this entire conversation, you know."

"Oh, there is no need for such precaution," Mr. Barris says with a vehement shake of his head. "I assure you, I am capable of remaining neutral. I am not fond of taking sides. I will assist either you or Miss Bowen as much or as little as you would each prefer and I shall reveal nothing to the other that you or she tell me in confidence. I will not say a word to anyone else about the matter. You can trust me."

Marco rights a toppling pile of boxes while he considers the matter.

"All right," he says. "Though I must admit, Mr. Barris, I am surprised at how accepting you are of all this."

Mr. Barris chuckles in response.

"I admit that of the lot of us, I seem the least likely," he says. "The world is a more interesting place than I had ever imagined when I came to that first Midnight Dinner. Is that because Miss Bowen can animate a solid wooden creature on a carousel or because you could manipulate my memory, or because the circus itself pushed the boundaries of what I dreamed was possible, even before I entertained the thought of actual magic? I cannot say. But I would not trade it for anything."

"And you will keep my identity from Miss Bowen?"

"I shall not tell her," Mr. Barris says. "You have my word."

"In that case," Marco says, "I would appreciate your assistance with something."

*

WHEN THE LETTER ARRIVES, Mr. Barris fears for a moment that Miss Bowen will be upset with the turn of events, or inquire as to who her opponent is, as she will have easily figured out that he is now aware of that fact himself.

But when he opens the envelope, the enclosed note reads only: *May I make additions to it?*

He writes back to inform her that it has been specifically designed to be manipulated by either side, so she may add whatever she wishes.

*

CELIA WALKS THROUGH a hallway full of snow, sparkling flakes of it catching in her hair and clinging to the hem of her gown. She holds out her hand, smiling as the crystals dissolve over her skin.

The hall is lined with doors, and she chooses the one at the very end, trailing a melting breath of snow behind her as she walks into a room where she must duck to avoid colliding with the cascade of books suspended from the ceiling, pages tumbling open in frozen waves.

She reaches a hand out to brush over the paper, the entire room swaying gently as the motion passes from page to page.

It takes her quite a while to locate another door, hidden in a shadowed corner, and she laughs when her boots sink into the powder-soft sand that fills the room beyond.

Celia stands on a shimmering white desert with a sparkling night sky stretching in every direction. The sense of space is so vast that she must put her hand out in front of her to find the wall hidden in the stars and it is still a surprise when her fingers hit the solid surface.

She feels her way around the star-speckled walls, searching the perimeter for another way out.

"This is abhorrent," her father's voice says, though she cannot see him in the dim light. "You are meant to be working separately, not in this . . . this debauched juxtaposition. I have warned you about collaborating, it is not the proper way to exhibit your skills."

Celia sighs.

"I think it's quite clever," she says. "What better way to compete than within the same tent? And you cannot rightfully call it a collaboration. How can I collaborate with someone whose identity I don't even know?"

She only catches a glimpse of his face as he glares at her and then she turns away, returning her attention to the wall.

"Which is superior, then?" she asks. "A room full of trees or a room filled with sand? Do you even know which ones are mine? This is getting tiring, Papa. My opponent clearly possesses comparable skills. How will you ever determine a winner?"

"That is not your concern," her father's voice hisses, closer to her ear than she would like. "You are a disappointment, I expected better from you. You need to do more."

"Doing more is exhausting," Celia protests. "I can only control so much."

"It's not enough," her father says.

"When will it be enough?" Celia asks, but there is no reply, and she stands alone amongst the stars.

She sinks to the ground, picking up a handful of pearl-white sand and letting it fall slowly through her fingers.

*

ALONE IN HIS FLAT, Marco constructs tiny rooms from scraps of paper. Hallways and doors crafted from pages of books and bits of blueprints, pieces of wallpaper and fragments of letters.

He composes chambers that lead into others that Celia has created. Stairs that wind around her halls.

Leaving spaces open for her to respond.

The Ticking of the Clock

The office is large but looks smaller than it is due to the volume of its contents. While a great deal of its walls are composed of frosted glass, most of it is obscured by cabinets and shelves. The drafting table by the windows is all but hidden in the meticulously ordered chaos of papers and diagrams and blueprints. The bespectacled man seated behind it is almost invisible, blending in with his surroundings. The sound of his pencil scratching against paper is as methodical and precise as the ticking of the clock in the corner.

There is a knock on the frosted-glass door and the scratching pencil halts, though the ticking clock pays no heed.

"A Miss Burgess to see you, sir," an assistant calls from the open door. "She says not to bother you if you are otherwise occupied."

"Not a bother at all," Mr. Barris says, placing his pencil down and rising from his seat. "Please, send her in."

The assistant moves from the doorway and is replaced by a young woman in a stylish lace-trimmed dress.

"Hello, Ethan," Tara Burgess says. "My apologies for dropping by unannounced."

"No apologies necessary, my dear Tara. You look lovely, as always," Mr. Barris says, kissing her on both cheeks.

"And you haven't aged a day," Tara says, pointedly. His smile wavers and he looks away, moving to close the door behind her.

"What brings you to Vienna?" he asks. "And where is your sister? I so rarely see the two of you apart."

"Lainie is in Dublin, with the circus," Tara says, turning her attention to the contents of the room. "I . . . I wasn't in the mood so I thought I would do some traveling on my own. Visiting far-flung friends seemed a good place to start. I would have sent a telegram but it was all a bit spontaneous. And I wasn't entirely sure if I would be welcome."

"You are always welcome, Tara," Mr. Barris says. He offers her a seat but she does not notice, drifting through the tables covered in highly detailed models of buildings, stopping here and there to investigate a detail further: the arch of a doorway, the spiral of a staircase.

"It becomes difficult to tell the difference between old friends and business associates in cases like ours, I think," Tara says. "Whether we are the kind of people who make polite conversation to cover shared secrets or something more than that. This one is marvelous," she adds, pausing at a model of an elaborate open column with a clock suspended in the center.

"Thank you," Mr. Barris says. "It's quite far from completion. I need to send the finished plans to Friedrick so he can start construction on the clock. I suspect it will be much more impressive when built to scale."

"Do you have the plans for the circus here?" Tara asks, looking over the diagrams pinned to the walls.

"No, I don't, actually. I left them with Marco in London. I meant to keep copies on file but I must have forgotten."

"Did you forget to keep copies of any of your other plans?" Tara asks, running a finger along the line of cabinets fitted with long thin shelves, each one piled with carefully ordered papers.

"No," Mr. Barris says.

"Do you . . . do you find that strange?" Tara asks.

"Not particularly," Mr. Barris says. "Do you think it strange?"

"I think a great many things about the circus strange," Tara says, fidgeting with the lace at the cuff of her sleeve.

Mr. Barris sits at his desk, leaning back in his chair.

"Are we going to discuss whatever it is you are here to discuss instead of dancing around it?" he asks. "I was never a particularly good dancer."

"I know for a fact that is not true," Tara says, settling into the chair opposite, though her gaze continues to wander around the room. "But it would be nice to be direct for a change, I sometimes wonder if any of us remember how. Why did you leave London?"

"I suspect I left London for much the same reasons that you and your sister travel so often," Mr. Barris says. "A few too many curious looks and backhanded compliments. I doubt anyone realized that the day my hair stopped thinning was the same as the opening night of the circus, but they did begin to notice after a time. While our Tante Padva might simply be aging well and anything and everything about Chandresh can be written off as eccentric, we are put under a different kind of scrutiny by being somewhat closer to ordinary."

"It is easier for those who can simply disappear into the circus," Tara says, gazing out the window. "Once in a while Lainie suggests that we follow it around ourselves but I think that would only be a temporary solution, we are too mercurial for our own good."

"You could just let it go," Mr. Barris says quietly.

Tara shakes her head.

"How many years until moving cities becomes insufficient? What is the solution beyond that? Changing our names? I . . . I do not enjoy being forced into such deceptions."

"I don't know," Mr. Barris says.

"There is a great deal more going on than we are privy to, of that I'm quite sure," Tara says with a sigh. "I tried to talk to Chandresh, but it was like we were speaking two different languages. I do not like sitting idly by when something clearly isn't right. I feel . . . not trapped but something like it, and I don't know what to do about it."

"And you are looking for answers," Mr. Barris says.

"I don't know what I'm looking for," Tara responds, and for a moment her face crumples as though she might burst into tears, but then she composes herself. "Ethan, do you sometimes feel like you are dreaming, all the time?"

"No, I can't say that I do."

"I am finding it difficult to discern between asleep and awake," Tara says, tugging at her lace cuffs again. "I do not like being left in the dark. I am not particularly fond of believing in impossible things."

Mr. Barris takes off his spectacles, wiping the lenses with a handkerchief before he replies, holding them up to the light to check for rogue smudges.

"I have seen a great many things that I might once have considered impossible, or unbelievable. I find I no longer have clearly defined parameters for such matters. I choose to do my work to the best of my own abilities, and leave others to their own."

He pulls open a drawer of the desk and after searching for a moment he takes out a business card that contains only a single name. Even looking at it upside down, Tara can easily discern the *A* and the *H* if nothing else. Mr. Barris picks up a pencil and writes a London address beneath the printed name.

"I don't think any of us knew that night precisely what we were getting ourselves into," he says. "If you insist on delving deeper into all of this I think he might be the only one of us that may help, though I cannot guarantee that he will be entirely forthcoming."

He slides the card across the desk to Tara. She regards it carefully before slipping it into her bag, as though she is not entirely sure it is real.

"Thank you, Ethan," she says without looking at him. "I appreciate this, truly."

"You're welcome, my dear," Mr. Barris says. "I . . . I hope you find what you are looking for."

Tara only nods distractedly, and then they discuss other matters of little import while the clock ticks through the afternoon hours and the light beyond the frosted-glass windows fades considerably. Though he asks her to join him for dinner, she declines politely and leaves alone.

Mr. Barris returns to his drafting table, scratching pencil and ticking clock in harmony once more.

The Magician's Umbrella

The sign upon the gates of Le Cirque des Rêves tonight is a large one, hung with braided ribbon that wraps around the bars just above the lock. The letters are tall enough to be read from some ways off, though people still walk right up to it to read it.

Closed Due to Inclement Weather

it says, in a fancy script surrounded by playfully painted grey clouds. People read the sign, sometimes twice, and then look at the setting sun and the clear violet sky and scratch their heads. They stand around, and some wait to see if the sign will be removed and the circus opened, but there is no one in sight and eventually the small crowd disperses to find alternative activities for their evening.

An hour later it starts, sheets of rain pouring down and wind that ripples across the surface of the striped tents. The sign on the gates dances in the wind, shimmering and wet.

*

AT THE OTHER END OF THE CIRCUS, at a part of the fence that looks nothing like a gate but opens nonetheless, Celia Bowen steps out from the shadows of darkened tents and into the rain, opening her umbrella with some difficulty. It is a large umbrella, with a heavy curved handle, and once Celia manages to get it open it provides quite good cover against the rain. Though the lower half of her wine-colored gown is quickly soaked to the point where it appears almost black.

She walks without much notice into the city, though there is not much notice to attract in such a downpour. She passes only a handful of other pedestrians on the cobblestone streets, each partially hidden beneath an umbrella.

Eventually Celia stops at a brightly lit café, crowded and lively despite the weather. She adds her umbrella to the collection gathering in the stands by the door.

There are a few unoccupied tables, but the empty chair that catches Celia's eye is one by the fireplace across from Isobel, where she sits with a cup of tea and her nose buried in a book.

Celia has never been entirely certain what to make of the fortune-teller. Though she has an innate distrust of anyone whose occupation involves telling people what they wish to hear. And Isobel sometimes has the same look in her eye Celia often catches in Tsukiko's glances, that she knows more than she lets on.

Though perhaps that is not unusual for someone in the business of telling other people what their future holds.

"May I join you?" Celia asks. Isobel looks up, the surprise clear in her expression, but the surprise is quickly replaced by a bright smile.

"Of course," Isobel says, marking her page before placing her book aside. "I can't believe you ventured out in the weather, I only just missed the start of it earlier and I thought I'd wait it out. I was meant to be meeting someone but I don't think they'll be coming, considering."

"I can't blame them," Celia says, pulling off her damp gloves. She shakes them gently and they dry instantly. "It's rather like walking through a river out there."

"Are you avoiding the inclement-weather party?"

"I made an appearance before I escaped, I am not in a party mood this evening. Besides, I don't like giving up an opportunity to leave the circus for a change of atmosphere, even if it means practically drowning to do so."

"I like to escape once in a while, myself," Isobel says. "Did you make it rain to have a night off?"

"Of course not," Celia says. "Though if that were true I think I overdid it."

Even as she speaks, Celia's rain-soaked gown is drying, the almost-black color returning to a rich wine, though it is not entirely clear whether this is caused by the nearby fire burning merrily or if it is a subtle transformation she is performing herself.

Celia and Isobel chat about the weather and Prague and books, not purposely avoiding the topic of the circus, but keeping the distance from it alive. Remaining for the moment only two women sitting at a table, rather than a fortune-teller and an illusionist, an opportunity they are not frequently presented with.

The door of the café blows open, sending a gust of rain-spiked wind inside that is met with howls of annoyance from the patrons and the clattering of the umbrellas in their stands.

A harried-looking waitress pauses at their table and Celia requests a mint tea. As the waitress departs, Celia casts a long look around the room, scanning the crowd as though she is looking for someone but not finding a point to focus on.

"Is something the matter?" Isobel asks.

"Oh, it's nothing," Celia says. "A hint of feeling that we're being watched, but it is likely just my imagination."

"Maybe someone has recognized you," Isobel suggests.

"I doubt that," Celia says as she looks at the surrounding patrons, not finding a single eye turned in their direction. "People see what they want to see. I'm sure this place has had more than its share of unusual patrons with the circus in town. That makes it easier for us to blend in."

"I am always amazed that no one recognizes me out of context," Isobel says. "I've read for a handful of people in this very room over the past few nights and not one of them has so much as given me a second glance. Perhaps I do not look so mysterious when not surrounded by candles and velvet. Or perhaps they pay more attention to the cards than they do to me."

"Do you have your cards with you?" Celia asks.

Isobel nods. "Would . . . would you like a reading?" she asks.

"If you do not mind."

"Not once have you ever asked me to read for you."

"I am not usually in the mood to know anything about my future," Celia says. "Tonight I am feeling a tiny bit curious."

Isobel hesitates, glancing around at the clientele, a mostly bohemian crowd sipping absinthe and arguing about art.

"They will not even notice," Celia says. "I promise."

Isobel turns her attention back to Celia, and then she pulls a deck from her bag; not her black-and-white circus cards but her original Marseilles deck, worn and faded.

"Those are lovely," Celia says as Isobel starts to shuffle, watching the shifting blur of cards.

"Thank you."

"But there are only seventy-seven of them."

Isobel's hands falter only momentarily, but a single card falls from the deck onto the table. Celia picks it up, briefly glancing at the two cups upon the surface before handing it back to Isobel, who replaces it in the deck and resumes shuffling, the cards falling seamlessly from one hand to the other.

"One of them is . . . somewhere else," Isobel explains.

Celia does not question her further.

The waitress brings Celia's mint tea, not even glancing at the cards before departing again.

"Did you do that?" Isobel asks.

"I diverted her attention, yes," Celia says after blowing gently on the surface of her steaming tea. It is not exactly what she means, but the invisible veil she has drawn over the table seems too difficult to explain. And the fact that the feeling they are being watched has not faded despite its presence bothers her.

Isobel stops shuffling and places the deck facedown on the table.

Celia cuts the deck in three without waiting for Isobel to instruct her, holding the edges of the cards carefully as she places each pile in a row across the table.

"Which one?" Isobel asks.

Celia regards the three piles of cards thoughtfully while she sips her tea. After a moment she indicates the center pile. Isobel stacks the deck once more, keeping that section of cards on the top.

The cards that she places on the table have no immediate clarity to them. Several cups. The two of swords. *La Papessa*, the enigmatic Priestess.

Isobel only barely manages to contain her involuntary intake of breath as she lays *Le Bateleur* over the already placed cards. She covers it with a cough. Celia appears not to notice anything amiss.

"I'm sorry," Isobel says, after staring silently at the cards for a few moments. "Sometimes it takes awhile for me to translate properly."

"Take your time," Celia says.

Isobel pushes the cards around the table, focusing on one and then another.

"You carry a great many burdens with you. A heavy heart. Things you've lost. But you are moving toward change and discovery. There are outside influences that are propelling you forward."

Celia's expression reveals nothing. She looks at the cards and occasionally up at Isobel, attentive yet guarded.

"You're . . . not fighting, that's not really the right word for it, but there's a conflict with something unseen, something shadowed that's hidden from you."

Celia only smiles.

Isobel places another card on the table.

"But it will be revealed soon," she says.

This catches Celia's attention.

"How soon?"

"The cards do not make for the clearest of timelines, but it is very close. Almost immediate, I would think."

Isobel pulls another card. The two of cups again.

"There's emotion," she says. "Deep emotion but you are only on the shore of it, still near the surface, while it is waiting to pull you under."

"Interesting," Celia remarks.

"It's nothing that I can clearly see as good or bad, but it is . . . intense." Isobel pushes the cards around a bit, *Le Bateleur* and *La Papessa* surrounded by fire-tinged wands and watery cups. The crackle of the fire next to them mingles with the rain pattering against the windows. "It almost contradicts itself," she says after a moment. "It's as if there is love and loss at the same time, together in a kind of beautiful pain."

"Well, that sounds like something to look forward to," Celia says drily, and Isobel smiles, glancing up from the cards but finding little to read in Celia's expression.

"I'm sorry I cannot be more clear," she says. "If anything comes to me later I will let you know, sometimes I need to ruminate on the cards before I can make any real sense of them. These are . . . not unclear, precisely, but they are complex, which makes for a great deal of possibilities to consider."

"No need for apologies. I cannot say I'm terribly surprised. And thank you, I very much appreciate the insight."

Celia changes the subject then, though the cards remain on the table and Isobel does not move to put them away. They discuss less substantial matters until Celia insists that she should be getting back to the circus.

"Do wait until the rain lets up, at least," Isobel protests.

"I have monopolized enough of your time already, and the rain is only rain. I hope the someone you were waiting for turns up."

"I am doubtful about that, but thank you. And thank you for keeping me company."

"It was my pleasure," Celia says, rising from the table as she replaces her gloves. She navigates the crowded café with ease, pulling a dark-handled umbrella from the stand by the door and giving Isobel a parting wave before bracing herself for the walk back to the circus in the pouring rain.

Isobel pushes the tangled path of the cards on the table around a bit.

She did not lie, exactly. She finds it near impossible to lie about the cards.

But the competition is clear, so much so that everything else is tied to it, past and future.

At the same time, it seems to be more of a reading for the circus as a whole than for Celia in particular, but it is so emotional that it overwhelms the details. Isobel piles the cards and shuffles them back into the deck. *Le Bateleur* floats to the top as she shuffles, and she frowns at the card before glancing around the café. While there are a few scattered bowler hats amongst the patrons, there is no sign of the one she is looking for.

She shuffles until the Magician is buried deep within the deck and then she puts her cards away and returns to her book to wait out the rain alone.

*

OUTSIDE, THE RAIN IS HEAVY and the street is dark and almost completely deserted, glowing windows dotting the streets. It is not as cold as Celia had expected, despite the chilling wind.

She cannot read the tarot well herself, there are always too many possibilities, too many meanings. But once Isobel pointed out specific elements, she could see the complicated emotion, the impending revelation. She is unsure what to make of it, though despite her skepticism, she hopes it means she will finally be certain who her opponent is.

She remains distracted as she walks, considering the cards, but she slowly realizes that she is rather warm. At least as warm if not warmer than she had been sitting near the fire with Isobel. More than that, her clothes are still dry. Her jacket, her gloves, even the hem of her gown. There is not a single drop of rain upon her although it continues to pour, the wind causing the rain to fall in several directions beyond the standard gravitational pattern. Drops splatter upward from pond-like puddles and blow in sideways but Celia does not feel any of them. Even her boots are not the slightest bit damp.

Celia stops walking as she reaches the open square, halting next to the towering astronomical clock where carved apostles are making their scheduled hourly appearance despite the weather.

She stands still in the downpour. The rain falls so thickly around her that she can hardly see more than a few paces ahead but she remains both warm and dry. She holds her hand out in front of her, beyond the cover of the umbrella, and regards it carefully but not a single drop of rain falls upon it. Those that come close suddenly change direction before hitting her glove, bouncing off as though she is surrounded by something invisible and impermeable.

It is around this time that Celia becomes certain that the umbrella she is holding is not her own.

"Excuse me, Miss Bowen," a voice calls to her, lifted over the din of the rain and carried down the street. A voice she recognizes even before she turns to find Marco standing behind her, completely drenched in rain, droplets cascading from the brim of his bowler hat. In his hand he holds a closed black umbrella identical to the one she carries.

"I believe you have my umbrella," he says, almost out of breath but wearing a grin that has too much wolf in it to be properly sheepish.

Celia stares up at him in surprise. At first she wonders what on earth Chandresh's assistant is doing in Prague, as she has never seen him outside of London. Then comes the question of how he could possess such an umbrella.

As she stares at him, confused, the pieces of the puzzle begin to shift together. She remembers every encounter she has ever had with the man now standing before her in the rain, recalling the distress he had exhibited at her audition, the years of glances and comments she had read as no more than coy flirtation.

And the constant impression as though he is not really there, blending so well into the background that she would occasionally forget he was in the room.

Before, she thought it was the sign of a very good assistant, never accounting for how deceptive such an appearance might be.

She suddenly feels rather stupid for not once considering the possibility that this could be her opponent.

And then Celia begins to laugh, a buoyant giggle that harmonizes with the din of the rain. Marco's grin wavers as he watches her, blinking water from his eyes.

Once Celia composes herself she gives him a low, perfect curtsey. She hands him his umbrella, gasping as the rain seizes her the moment the handle passes from her fingers. He hands her the identical umbrella.

"My sincere apologies," she says, the amusement still sparkling in her eyes.

"I would very much like to speak with you, if you care to join me for a drink," Marco says. His bowler hat is already dry as he attempts in vain to cover both of them with the open umbrella. The wind whips Celia's dark curls in wet ropes across her face as she considers him, watching his eyes as the raindrops evaporate from his lashes.

For all the years of wondering, being faced with her opponent is not what she had expected.

She had expected it to be someone she knew. Someone inside the bounds of the circus rather than outside, but still involved.

There are so many questions, so many things she longs to discuss despite her father's constant nagging about not concerning herself with her opponent. But at the same time, she feels suddenly exposed, aware that he has always known where each of them stood. Known every time he opened a door for her or took notes for Chandresh. Every time he stared at her as he does now, with those disconcertingly bright-green eyes.

Still, it is a tempting invitation.

Perhaps if she was not nearly drowning from the rain, she would accept it.

"Of course you would," Celia says, returning Marco's grin with one of her own. "Perhaps another time."

She opens her own umbrella with some difficulty, and as she swings the canopy of black silk over her head, she and her umbrella vanish, leaving only drops of water falling onto the empty pavement.

Alone in the rain, Marco regards the space where Celia had been standing for some time before he walks away into the night.

The sign says Hall of Mirrors, but when you enter you find it is more than a simple hall.

You are met not with floor-length unadorned planes of mirrored glass, as you half expected, but hundreds of mirrors of varying sizes and shapes, each in a different frame.

As you move past one mirror reflecting your boots, the mirror next to it shows only empty space and the mirrors on the other side. Your scarf is not present in one mirror and then it returns in the next.

Reflected behind you there is a man in a bowler hat, though he appears in some mirrors and not in others. When you turn you cannot locate him in the room, though there are more patrons walking along with you than you had seen within the glass.

The hall leads to a round room, the light within it bright as you enter. It radiates from a tall lamppost that sits in the center, towering black iron with a frosted-glass lamp that looks as though it would be more at home on a city street corner than in a circus tent.

The walls here are completely mirrored, each long mirror placed to align with the striped ceiling visible above and the floor that is painted to match.

As you walk farther into the room it becomes a field of endless streetlamps, the stripes repeating in fractal patterns, over and over and over.

Cartomancy

As he continues to walk around the circus, Bailey's path leads back to the courtyard. He stops briefly to watch the sparkling bonfire and then at a vendor to purchase a bag of chocolates to make up for his mostly uneaten dinner. The chocolates are shaped like mice, with almond ears and licorice tails. He eats two immediately and puts the rest of the bag in the pocket of his coat, hoping they will not melt.

He chooses another direction to leave the courtyard, circling away from the bonfire again.

He passes several tents with interesting signs, but none that he feels compelled to enter just yet, still playing the illusionist's performance over in his mind. As the path turns, he comes upon a smaller tent, with a lovely elaborate sign:

Fortune-teller

He can read that bit easily, but the rest is a complex swirl of intricate letters, and Bailey has to walk right up to it to read:

Fates Foretold and Darkest Desires Disclosed

Bailey looks around. For a moment, there is no one else in sight in either direction, and the circus feels eerily similar to the way it had when he snuck through the fence in the middle of the day, as though it is empty save for himself and the things (and people) that are always there.

The ongoing argument about his own future echoes in his ears as he enters the tent.

Bailey finds himself in a room that reminds him of his grandmother's parlor, only smelling less like lavender. There are seats, but all of them are unoccupied, and a sparkling chandelier captures Bailey's attention for a moment before he notices the curtain.

It is made up of strings of shiny beads. Bailey has never seen anything like it. It shimmers in the light, and he is not entirely sure whether he should walk through it or wait for some sort of sign or notice. He looks around for an informatively worded sign but finds nothing. He stands, confused, in the empty vestibule, and then a voice calls out from behind the beaded curtain.

"Do come in, please," the voice says. A woman's voice, quiet, and sounding as though she is standing right next to him, though Bailey is sure that the voice came from the next room. Hesitantly he puts a hand out to touch the beads, which are smooth and cold, and he finds that his arm slips through them easily, that they part like water or long grass. The beads clatter as the strands hit one another, and the sound that echoes in the dark space sounds like rain.

The room he is in now is much less like his grandmother's parlor. It is filled with candles, and there is a table in the center, with an empty chair on one side and a lady, dressed in black with a long thin veil over her face, seated on the other. On the table there is a deck of cards and a large glass sphere.

"Have a seat, please, young man," the lady says, and Bailey walks a few steps to the empty chair and sits down. The chair is surprisingly comfortable, not like the stiff chairs at his grandmother's, though they do look remarkably similar. It only now strikes Bailey that, other than the red-haired girl, he has never heard any person in the circus speak. The illusionist was silent for her entire performance, though he had not noticed it at the time.

"I am afraid payment is required before we may begin," she says. Bailey is relieved that he has excess pocket money for the unplanned expense.

"How much is payment?" he asks.

"Whatever you wish to pay for a glimpse of your future," the fortune-teller says. Bailey stops to consider this for a moment. It is strange, but fair. He pulls what he hopes is a suitable amount from his pocket and puts it on the table, and the woman does not pick the money up but passes her hand over it, and it disappears.

"Now what is it you would like to know?" she asks.

"About my future," Bailey says. "My grandmother wants me to go to Harvard, but my father wants me to take over the farm."

"And what do you want?" the fortune-teller asks.

"I don't know," Bailey says.

She laughs in response, but in a friendly way, and it makes Bailey feel more at ease, as though he is just talking to a regular person and not someone mysterious or magical.

"That's fine," she says. "We can see what the cards have to say about the matter."

The fortune-teller picks up the deck and shuffles, shifting the cards from one hand to the other. They fold over and under each other in waves. Then she spreads them across the table in one fluid motion, forming an arc of identical black-and-white-patterned card backs. "Choose a single card," she says. "Take your time. This will be your card, the one that will represent you."

Bailey looks at the arc of cards and frowns. They all look the same. Slivers of pattern, some wider than the others, some not quite as evenly lined up as the rest. He looks back and forth from end to end and then one of them catches his eye. It is more hidden than the rest, almost completely covered by the card above it. Only the edge is visible. He reaches out for it but hesitates just before his hand reaches it.

"I can touch it?" he asks. He feels the same as when he was first allowed to set the table with the nicest dishes, as though he really shouldn't be allowed to touch such things, mixed with an acute fear of breaking something.

But the fortune-teller nods, and Bailey puts a finger on the card and pulls it away from its compatriots so it sits separately on the table.

"You may turn it over," the fortune-teller says, and Bailey flips the card.

On the other side it is not like the black-and-red playing cards he is used to, with hearts and clubs and spades and diamonds. Instead it is a picture, inked in black and white and shades of grey.

The illustration is of a knight on horseback, like a knight from a fairy tale. His horse is white and his armor is grey, there are dark clouds in the background. The horse is mid-gallop, the knight leaning forward in the saddle, with sword drawn as though he is on his way to a great battle of some sort. Bailey stares at the card, wondering where the knight is going and what the card is supposed to mean. *Cavalier d'Épées* it reads in fancy script at the bottom of the card.

"This is supposed to be me?" Bailey asks. The woman smiles as she pushes the arc of cards back into a neat pile.

"It is meant to represent you, in your reading," she says. "It could mean movement or travel. The cards do not always mean the same things every time, they change with each person."

"That must make them hard to read," Bailey says.

The woman laughs again.

"Sometimes," she says. "Shall we give it a try anyway?" Bailey nods and she shuffles the cards again, over and under, and then divides them into three piles and places them in front of him, above the card with the knight. "Pick which pile you are most drawn to," she says. Bailey studies the piles of cards. One is less neat, another larger than the other two. His eyes keep going back to the pile on the right.

"This one," he says, and though it is mostly a guess, it feels like the proper choice. The fortune-teller nods and stacks the three piles of cards back into one deck, leaving Bailey's chosen cards on top. She flips them over, one at a time, laying them faceup in an elaborate pattern across the table, some overlapping and others in rows, until there are about a dozen cards laid out. They are black-and-white pictures, much like the knight, some simpler, some more complicated. Many show people in various settings, and a few have animals, while some of them have cups or coins, and there are more swords. Their reflections catch and stretch in the crystal sphere that sits alongside.

For a few moments the fortune-teller looks at the cards, and Bailey wonders if she is waiting for them to tell her something. And he thinks she is smiling, but trying to hide it just a bit.

"This is interesting," the fortune-teller says. She touches one card, a lady in flowing robes holding a set of scales, and another that Bailey cannot see as well but looks like a crumbling castle.

"What's interesting?" Bailey asks, still confused about the process. He knows no ladies in blindfolds, has been to no crumbling castles. He's not even sure there are any castles in New England.

"You have a journey ahead of you," the fortune-teller says. "There's a lot of movement. A great deal of responsibility." She pushes one card, turns another around, and furrows her brow a bit, though Bailey still thinks she looks like she is trying to hide a smile. It is becoming easier to see her expression through her veil as his eyes adjust to the candlelight. "You are part of a chain of events, though you may not see how your actions will affect the outcome at the time."

"I'm going to do something important, but I have to go somewhere first?" Bailey asks. He had not expected fortune-telling to be so vague. The journey part does seem to favor his grandmother's side, though, even if Cambridge is not very far.

The fortune-teller does not immediately respond. Instead she flips over another card. This time she does not hide her smile.

"You're looking for Poppet," she says.

"What's a poppet?" he asks. The fortune-teller does not answer, and instead looks up from her cards and regards him quizzically. Bailey feels her taking in his entire appearance, or more than that, with her eyes moving over his face from his scarf to his hat. He shifts in his chair.

"Is your name Bailey?" she asks. The color drains from Bailey's cheeks and all the apprehension and nervousness he had felt earlier returns instantly. He has to swallow before he can make himself answer, in barely more than a whisper.

"Yes?" he says. It sounds like a question, as though he is not entirely sure that it is indeed his name. The fortune-teller smiles at him, a bright smile that makes him realize she is not nearly as old as he had previously thought. Perhaps only a few years older than he is.

"Interesting," she says. He wishes she would choose a different word. "We have a mutual acquaintance, Bailey." She looks back down at the cards on the table. "You are here this evening looking for her, I believe. Though I do appreciate that you've chosen to visit my tent as well."

Bailey blinks at her, trying to take in everything she's said, and wondering how on earth she knows the real reason he is at the circus when he has told no one about it and hardly even admits it to himself.

"You know the red-haired girl?" he says, unable to fully believe that this is, indeed, what the fortune-teller means. But she nods.

"I have known her, and her brother, all their lives," she says. "She is a very special girl, with very lovely hair."

"Is . . . is she here still?" Bailey asks. "I only met her once, the last time the circus was here."

"She is here," the fortune-teller says. She pushes the cards around on the table a bit more, touching one and then another, though Bailey is no longer paying attention to which card is which. "You will see her again, Bailey. There's no doubt about that."

Bailey resists the urge to ask her when, and instead waits to see if she has anything else to add about the cards. The fortune-teller moves a card here and there. She picks up the card with the knight from where it sits and places it on top of the crumbling castle.

"Do you like the circus, Bailey?" she asks, looking up at him again.

"It's like no place I've ever been," Bailey says. "Not that I've been many places," he adds quickly. "But I think the circus is wonderful. I like it very much."

"That would help," the fortune-teller says.

"Help with what?" Bailey asks, but the fortune-teller does not answer. Instead, she flips over another card from the deck, placing it over the card with the knight. It is a picture of a lady pouring water into a lake, a bright shining star over her head.

It is still difficult to discern her expressions through her veil, but Bailey is certain that she frowns at the card as she places it on the table, though when she looks back up at him the frown is gone.

"You will be fine," the fortune-teller says. "There may be decisions to make, and surprises in store. Life takes us to unexpected places sometimes. The future is never set in stone, remember that."

"I will," Bailey says. He thinks the fortune-teller looks a bit sad as she begins to gather up the cards on the table, putting them back into a neat pile. She saves the knight for last, placing him on the top of the deck.

"Thank you," Bailey says. He did not receive as clear an answer about his future as he had expected, but somehow the issue does not seem as heavy as it had before. He debates whether to leave, unsure of proper fortune-telling etiquette.

"You're welcome, Bailey," the fortune-teller says. "It was a pleasure to read for you."

Bailey reaches into his pocket and pulls out the bag of chocolate mice and offers it to her.

"Would you like a mouse?" he asks. Before he can mentally berate himself for doing something so silly, the fortune-teller smiles, though for a moment there is something almost sad beneath it.

"Why, yes, I would," she says, pulling one of the chocolate mice out of the bag by its licorice tail. She places it on the top of the crystal sphere. "They're one of my favorites," she confides. "Thank you, Bailey. Enjoy the rest of your time at the circus."

"I will," Bailey says. He stands up and walks back to the beaded curtain. He reaches to part the strings of beads and stops, suddenly, and turns around.

"What's your name?" he asks the fortune-teller.

"You know, I'm not sure any of my querents have ever asked that before," she says. "My name is Isobel."

"It was nice to meet you, Isobel," Bailey says.

"It was nice to meet you, too, Bailey," Isobel says. "And you might want to go down the path to your right when you leave," she adds. Bailey nods and turns back, pushing through the strands of beads into the still-empty vestibule. The beads are not so loud as they settle, and when they quiet, everything is soft and still, as though there is no other room behind them, no fortune-teller sitting at her table.

Bailey feels oddly at ease. As though he is closer to the ground, but taller at the same time. His concerns about his future no longer weigh so heavily on him as he exits the tent, turning right down the curving path that winds between the striped tents.

The Wizard in the Tree

The rooms hidden behind the multitude of tents in Le Cirque des Rêves are a stark contrast to the black and white of the circus. Alive with color. Warm with glowing amber lamps.

The space kept by the Murray twins is particularly vivid. A kaleidoscope of color, blazing with carmine and coral and canary, so much so that the entire room often appears to be on fire, dotted with fluffy kittens dark as soot and bright as sparks.

It is occasionally suggested that the twins should be sent to boarding school to receive a proper education, but their parents insist that they learn more from living with such a diverse company and traveling the globe than they would confined by schoolrooms and books.

The twins remain perfectly pleased with the arrangement, receiving irregular lessons on innumerable subjects and reading every book they can get their hands on, piles of them often ending up in the wrought-iron cradle they would not part with after it was outgrown.

They know every inch of the circus, moving from color to black and white with ease. Equally comfortable in both.

Tonight they sit in a striped tent beneath a rather large tree, its branches black and bare of leaves.

At this late hour there are no patrons lingering in this particular tent, and it is unlikely that any other visitors to the circus will stumble upon it in the remaining hours before dawn.

The Murray twins lean against the massive trunk, sipping steaming cups of mulled cider.

They have finished with their performances for the evening, and the remaining hours before dawn are theirs to spend as they please.

"Do you want to read tonight?" Widget asks his sister. "We could take a walk, it's not that cold." He pulls a pocket watch from his coat to check the time. "It's not that late yet, either," he adds, though their defi-nition of late is what many would consider quite early.

Poppet bites her lip in thought for a moment before answering.

"No," she says. "Last time everything was all red and confusing. I think maybe I should wait a bit before I try again."

"Red and confusing?"

Poppet nods.

"It was a bunch of things overlapping," she explains. "Fire and something red, but not at the same time. A man without a shadow. A feeling like everything was unraveling, or tangling, the way the kittens pull yarn into knots and you can't find the beginning or the end any-more."

"Did you tell Celia about it?" Widget asks.

"Not yet," Poppet says. "I don't like to tell her things that don't make any sense. Most times things make sense eventually."

"That's true," Widget says.

"Oh, and another thing," Poppet says. "We're going to have com-pany. That was in there somewhere, too. I don't know if it was before or after the other things, or sometime in between."

"Can you see who it is?" Widget asks.

"No," Poppet answers simply.

Widget is not surprised.

"What was the red something?" he asks. "Could you tell?"

Poppet closes her eyes, remembering.

"It looks like paint," she says.

Widget turns to look at her.

"Paint?" he asks.

"Like spilled paint, on the ground," Poppet answers. She closes her eyes again, but then opens them quickly. "Dark red. It's all sort of jum-bled and I don't really like the red bit, when I saw it, it hurt my head. The company part is nicer."

"Company would be nice," Widget says. "Do you know when?"

Poppet shakes her head.

"Some of it feels soon. The rest of it feels far away."

They sit quietly sipping their cider for a bit, leaning against the trunk of the tree.

"Tell me a story, please," Poppet says after a while.

"What kind of story?" Widget asks. He always asks her, gives her an opportunity to make a request, even if he has one in mind already. Only preferred or special audiences receive such treatment.

"A story about a tree," Poppet says, looking up through the twisting black branches above them.

Widget pauses before he starts, letting the tent and the tree settle into silent prologue while Poppet waits patiently.

"Secrets have power," Widget begins. "And that power diminishes when they are shared, so they are best kept and kept well. Sharing secrets, real secrets, important ones, with even one other person, will change them. Writing them down is worse, because who can tell how many eyes might see them inscribed on paper, no matter how careful you might be with it. So it's really best to keep your secrets when you have them, for their own good, as well as yours.

"This is, in part, why there is less magic in the world today. Magic is secret and secrets are magic, after all, and years upon years of teaching and sharing magic and worse. Writing it down in fancy books that get all dusty with age has lessened it, removed its power bit by bit. It was inevitable, perhaps, but not unavoidable. Everyone makes mistakes.

"The greatest wizard in history made the mistake of sharing his secrets. And his secrets were both magic and important, so it was a rather serious mistake.

"He told them to a girl. She was young and clever and beautiful—"

Poppet snorts into her cup. Widget stops.

"I'm sorry," she says. "Go on, please, Widge."

"She was young and clever and beautiful," Widget continues. "Because if the girl had not been beautiful and clever, she would have been easier to resist, and then there would be no story at all.

"The wizard was old and quite clever himself, of course, and he had gone a very, very long time without telling his secrets to anyone at all. Maybe over the years he had forgotten about the importance of keeping them, or maybe he was distracted by her youth or beauty or cleverness. Maybe he was just tired, or maybe he had too much wine and didn't realize what he was doing. Whatever the circumstances, he told his deepest secrets to the girl, the hidden keys to all his magic.

"And when the secrets had passed from wizard to girl, they lost bits of their power, the way cats lose bits of fur when you pet them thoroughly. But they were still potent and effective and magical, and the girl used them against the wizard. She tricked him so that she could take his secrets and make them her own. She did not particularly care about keeping them; she probably wrote them down somewhere as well.

"The wizard himself she trapped in a huge old oak tree. A tree like this one. And the magic she used to do so was strong, since it was the wizard's own magic, ancient and powerful, and he could not undo it.

"She left him there, and he could not be rescued since no one else knew he was inside the tree. He was not dead, though. The girl might have killed him if she could, after she had coerced his secrets out of him, but she could not kill him with his own magic. Though maybe she didn't want to at all. She was more concerned with power than with him, but she might have cared about him a little, enough to want to leave him with his life, in a way. She settled for trapping him, and to her mind it served the same purpose.

"Though really she did not succeed quite as well as she liked to think. She was careless in keeping her new magic secret. She flaunted it, and generally did not take very good care of it. Its power faded eventually, and so did she.

"The wizard, on the other hand, became part of the tree. And the tree thrived and grew, its branches spreading up to the sky and its roots reaching farther into the earth. He was part of the leaves and the bark and the sap, and part of the acorns that were carried away by squirrels to become new oak trees in other places. And when those trees grew, he was in those branches and leaves and roots as well.

"So by losing his secrets, the wizard gained immortality. His tree stood long after the clever young girl was old and no longer beautiful, and in a way, he became greater and stronger than he had ever been before. Though if he were given the chance to do it all over again, he likely would have been more careful with his secrets." As Widget finishes, the tent settles into silence again, but the tree feels more alive than it had before he started.

"Thank you," Poppet says. "That was a good one. Kind of sad, though, but kind of not at the same time."

"You're welcome," Widget says. He takes a sip of his cider, now more warm than hot. He holds his cup in his hands and brings it to eye level, staring at it until a soft curl of steam rises from the surface.

"Do mine, too, please," Poppet says, holding out her cup. "I can never do it right."

"Well, I can never levitate anything right, so we're even," Widget says, but he takes her cup without complaint and concentrates until it too is steaming and hot again.

He moves to hand it back to her and it floats from his hand to hers, the surface of the cider wavering with the motion but otherwise moving as smoothly as if it were sliding across a table.

"Show-off," Widget says.

They sit sipping their newly warmed cider, looking up at the twisting black branches reaching toward the top of the tent.

"Widge?" Poppet asks after a long silence.

"Yes?"

"Is it not that bad to be trapped somewhere, then? Depending on where you're trapped?"

"I suppose it depends on how much you like the place you're trapped in," Widget says.

"And how much you like whoever you're stuck there with," Poppet adds, kicking his black boot with her white one.

Her brother laughs and the sound echoes through the tent, carried over the branches that are covered in candles. Each flame flickering and white.

Temporary Places

Tara Burgess does not realize until after she has returned to London that the address on the card given to her by Mr. Barris is not a private residence at all but the Midland Grand Hotel.

She leaves the card sitting out on a table in her parlor for some time, glancing at it whenever she happens to be in the room. Forgetting about it for stretches of time until she remembers it again.

Lainie attempts to persuade Tara to join her for an extended holiday in Italy, but she refuses. Tara tells her sister little about her visit to Vienna, saying only that Ethan asked after her.

Lainie suggests that they might consider moving, and perhaps they should discuss it further when she returns.

Tara only nods, giving her sister a warm embrace before Lainie departs.

Alone in their town house, Tara wanders absently. She abandons half-read novels on chairs and tables.

The invitations from Mme. Padva to join her for tea or accompany her to the ballet are politely declined.

She turns all of the mirrors in the house to face the walls. Those she cannot manage to turn she covers with sheets so they sit like ghosts in empty rooms.

She has trouble sleeping.

One afternoon, after the card has sat patiently gathering dust for months, she picks it up and places it in her pocket, and she is out the door and on her way to the train before she can decide whether or not the idea is a good one.

Tara has never visited the clock-topped hotel attached to St. Pancras Station, but it strikes her immediately as a temporary place. Despite the size and solidity of the building, it feels impermanent, populated by a constant stream of guests and travelers on their way to and from other locations. Stopping only briefly before continuing to other destinations.

She inquires at the desk but they claim they have no such person listed as a guest. She repeats the name several times after the desk clerk keeps mishearing her. She tries more than one variation, as the words on the card from Mr. Barris have been smudged, and she cannot recall the proper pronunciation. The longer she stands there, the more unsure she becomes that she has ever even heard the smudged name on the card pronounced.

The clerk politely asks if she would like to leave a note, if perhaps the gentleman in question were to be arriving later in the day, but Tara declines, thanking the clerk for his time and replacing the card in her pocket.

She wanders the lobby, wondering if the address is incorrect, though it is not like Mr. Barris to provide anything less than exact information.

"Good afternoon, Miss Burgess," a voice next to her says. She has not noticed him approach, but the man whose name she still cannot recall the proper pronunciation of is standing by her shoulder in his distinctive grey suit.

"Good afternoon," she echoes.

"Were you looking for me?" he asks.

"I was, in fact," Tara says. She starts to explain that Mr. Barris sent her. She reaches into her pocket, but there is no card within it and she stops, confused.

"Is something wrong?" the man in the grey suit asks.

"No," Tara says, now unsure if she remembered to bring the card, or if it is still sitting on a table in her parlor. "I wanted to speak with you about the circus."

"Very well," he says. He waits for her to begin, his expression bearing something that could be construed as very mild interest.

She does her best to explain her concern. That there is more going on with the circus than most people are privy to. That there are elements she can find no reasonable explanations for. She repeats some of the things she mentioned to Mr. Barris. The concern of not being able to be certain if anything is real. How disconcerting it is to look in a mirror and see the same face, unchanged for years.

She falters frequently, finding it difficult to articulate precisely what she means.

The expression of very mild interest does not change.

"What is it you would like from me, Miss Burgess?" he asks when she has finished.

"I would like an explanation," she says.

He regards her with the same unchanged expression for some time.

"The circus is simply a circus," he says. "An impressive exhibition, but no more than that. Don't you agree?"

Tara nods before she can properly process the response.

"Do you have a train to catch, Miss Burgess?" he asks.

"Yes," Tara says. She had forgotten about her train. She wonders what time it is, but she cannot find a clock to check.

"I am headed toward the station myself, if you do not mind an escort."

They walk the short distance from the hotel to the train platforms together. He holds doors open for her. He makes empty remarks about the weather.

"I think it may be in your best interest to find something else to occupy your time," he says when they reach the trains. "Something to take your mind off the circus. Don't you agree?"

Tara nods again.

"Good day, Miss Burgess," he says with a tip of his hat.

"Good day," she echoes.

He leaves her on the platform, and when she turns after him to see which way he went, the grey suit is nowhere to be found amongst the crowd.

Tara stands near the edge of the platform, waiting for her train. She cannot recall telling Mr. A. H— which train it was she would be taking, but he has deposited her on the proper platform nonetheless.

She feels as though there was something else she meant to ask, but now she cannot recall what it was. She cannot recall much of anything about the conversation, save for the impression that there is something else she should be spending her time on, somewhere else to be, some other matter that is more deserving of her attention.

She is wondering what that might be when a flash of grey on the opposite platform catches her eye.

Mr. A. H— stands in a shadowy corner, and even with the distance and the shadows Tara can tell that he is arguing with someone she cannot see.

Other people pass by without even glancing in their direction.

When the light from the arching overhead windows shifts, Tara can see who Mr. A. H— is arguing with.

The man is not quite as tall, the top of his hat sits leveled like a step down from the grey one, so much so that at first Tara thinks the man is only a reflection and finds it odd that Mr. A. H— would be arguing with his own reflection in the middle of a train station.

But the other suit is distinctly darker. The reflection's hair is longer, though it is a similar shade of grey.

Through the steam and the crowd, Tara can make out the bright spots of lace at the cuffs of the shirt, the dark eyes that catch the light more than the rest of the man's face. Aspects settle temporarily and then vanish into distorted shadows once more, never remaining steady for more than a moment.

The light filtering in from above shifts again, and the figure quavers as though she were watching through a heat haze, though Mr. A. H— remains comparatively crisp and clear.

Tara takes a step forward, her gaze fixated on the apparition on the opposite platform.

She does not see the train.

Movement

Herr Thiessen is always pleased when the circus arrives in his native Germany, but this time he is particularly delighted that it has arrived quite near Munich, so there is no need for him to secure rooms in another city.

Also, he has been promised a visit from Miss Celia Bowen. He has never met her, though they have been exchanging letters for years, and she expressed an interest in seeing his workshop, if he would not mind.

Friedrick replied that of course he did not mind in the least, and she would be welcome at any time.

Despite so many letters, each carefully filed in his office, he is uncertain what to expect when she arrives.

He is astonished to find the woman he knows as the illusionist standing in his doorway.

She is unmistakable, though she wears a gown of dusty rose rather than the black-and-white creations he is accustomed to seeing her in. Her skin appears warmer, her hair softly curled, and her hat bears no resemblance to the distinctive silk top hat, but he would know her face anywhere.

"This is an honor," he says by way of greeting.

"Most people don't recognize me outside of the circus," Celia says as he takes her hand.

"Then most people are fools," he says, lifting her hand to his lips and lightly kissing the back of her glove. "Though I feel a fool myself for not knowing who you were all this time."

"I should have told you," Celia says. "I do apologize."

"No apology is necessary. I should have guessed you were not merely a *rêveur* from the way you wrote about the circus. You know every corner, better than most."

"I am familiar with a great deal of the corners. Not all of them."

"There remain mysteries in the circus even for its own illusionist? That is impressive."

Celia laughs, and Friedrick takes her on a tour of his workshop.

The workshop is organized so that the front is occupied mostly by blueprints and sketches, moving on to long tables covered in various parts and a great deal of sawdust, drawers full of gears and tools. Celia listens with rapt attention as he describes the entire process, asking questions about the technical aspects as well as the creative ones.

He is surprised to learn that she speaks fluent German, though they have only written each other in English.

"I speak languages with more ease than I read or write them," she explains. "It is something in the feel of the sounds. I could attempt to put them on paper but I am sure the result would be appalling."

Despite his greying hair, Friedrick looks younger when he smiles. Celia cannot keep her eyes from his hands as he shows her the delicate clockwork mechanisms. She pictures the same fingers inscribing each letter she has received and read so many times that she has committed them to memory, finding it strange that she feels shy with someone she knows so well.

He watches her with equal attentiveness as they traverse the shelves of timepieces in varying stages of construction.

"May I ask you something?" he says as she looks at a collection of detailed figurines waiting patiently amongst curls of wood to be housed in their proper clocks.

"Of course," Celia says, though she fears he will ask her how she does her magic, and she dreads having to lie to him.

"You have been in the same city as I on so many occasions, and yet this is the first time you have asked to meet. Why is that?"

Celia looks back at the figurines on the table before she responds. Friedrick reaches out and rights a tiny ballerina that has fallen sideways, returning her to balance on her ribboned slippers.

"Before, I did not want you to know who I was," Celia says. "I thought you might think of me differently if you did. But after so long I felt I was being dishonest. I had wanted to tell you the truth for some time, and I could not resist the chance to see your workshop. I hope you can forgive me."

"You have nothing to be forgiven for," Friedrick says. "A woman

I should like to think I know rather well and a woman I had always considered a mystery are, in fact, the same person. It is surprising, but I do not mind a good surprise. Though I am curious as to why you wrote me that first letter."

"I enjoyed your writings about the circus," Celia says. "It is a perspective that I am not able to view it from properly, because I . . . understand it in a different way. I like being able to see it through your eyes." When she looks up at him, his soft blue eyes are bright in the afternoon sunlight that shines through the windows, illuminating the speckles of sawdust in the air.

"Thank you, Miss Bowen," Friedrick says.

"Celia," she corrects.

He gives her a thoughtful nod before continuing the tour.

The back walls are covered with finished or nearly finished timepieces. Clocks waiting only for final coats of varnish or other minor details. The clocks closest to the windows are already in motion. Each moving in its unique way, but keeping the same harmonious rhythm, a symphony of carefully ordered ticking.

The one that attracts Celia's attention rests on a table rather than hanging on the wall or sitting on a shelf.

It is a beautiful piece, more sculpture than clock. While many of the clocks are wood, this one is predominantly dark, oxidized metal. A large, round cage set on a wooden base that has been carved into swirling white flames. Within, there are overlapping metal hoops marked with numbers and symbols suspended from the top, hanging amongst the visible gears and a series of stars falling from the filigree cap at the top.

But the clock sits quiet, unmoving.

"This one reminds me of the bonfire," Celia says. "Is it not finished?"

"No, it is complete, but broken," Friedrick replies. "It was an experiment, and the components are difficult to balance properly." He turns it so she can see the way the workings extend through the entirety of the cage, stretching in all directions. "The mechanics are complex, as it tracks astronomical movement as well. I shall have to remove the base and dismantle it entirely to get it running again. I have not yet had the time it will require."

"May I?" Celia asks, reaching out to touch it. When he nods, she removes one of her gloves and rests her hand on the metal bars of the cage.

She only watches it thoughtfully, she makes no attempt to move it. To Friedrick, it appears she is gazing through the clock rather than simply looking at it.

Inside, the mechanism begins to turn, the cogs and gears waltzing together as the number-marked hoops spin into place. The hands glide to indicate the proper time, the planetary alignments set themselves in order.

Everything within the cage rotates slowly, the silver stars sparkling as they catch the light.

Once the slow, steady tick begins, Celia removes her hand.

Friedrick does not inquire as to how she managed it.

Instead, he takes her to dinner. They do speak of the circus, but spend most of the meal discussing books and art, wine and favorite cities. The pauses in the conversation are not awkward, though they struggle to find the same rhythm in speaking that was already present in their written exchanges, often switching from one language to another.

"Why haven't you asked me how I do my tricks?" Celia asks, once they have reached the point where she is certain he is not simply being polite about the matter.

Friedrick considers the question thoroughly before he responds.

"Because I do not wish to know," he says. "I prefer to remain unenlightened, to better appreciate the dark."

The sentiment delights Celia so that she cannot properly respond in any of their common languages, and only smiles at him over her wine.

"Besides," Friedrick continues, "you must be asked such things constantly. I find I am more interested in learning about the woman than the magician. I hope that is acceptable."

"It's perfect," Celia says.

They walk together to the circus afterward, past red-roofed buildings glowing in the dying light, going their separate ways only once they reach the courtyard.

Friedrick remains mystified as to why no one seems to recognize her as she walks anonymously amongst the crowd.

When he watches her performance she only catches his eye once with a subtle smile, giving no other hint of recognition.

Later, long after midnight, she appears by his side as he walks, wearing a cream-colored coat and a deep green scarf.

"Your scarf should be red," Friedrick remarks.

"I am not a proper *rêveur*," Celia says. "It would not feel right." But as she speaks, her scarf shifts in hue to a rich, wine-like burgundy. "Is that better?"

"It is perfect," Friedrick says, though his gaze remains fixed on her eyes.

She takes his offered arm and they walk together along the twisting pathways, through the dwindling crowd of patrons.

They repeat this routine in the following evenings, though the circus does not remain in Munich long, once the news arrives from London.

In Loving Memory of Tara Burgess

The funeral is a quiet one, despite the number of mourners present. There are no sobs or flailing handkerchiefs. There is a smattering of color amongst the sea of traditional black. Even the light rain cannot push it down into the realms of despair. It rests instead in a space of thoughtful melancholy.

Perhaps it is because it does not feel as though Tara Burgess is entirely gone, when her sister sits alive and well. One half of the pair still breathing and vibrant.

And at the same time something looks strikingly wrong to everyone who lays eyes on the surviving sister. Something they can't quite put their finger on. Something out of balance.

An occasional tear rolls down Lainie Burgess's cheek but she greets each mourner with a smile and thanks them for attending. She makes jokes that Tara might have quipped were she not inside the polished-wood coffin. There are no other family members present, though some less familiar acquaintances assume that the white-haired woman and bespectacled man who seldom leave Lainie's side are her mother and husband, respectively. While they are incorrect, neither Mme. Padva nor Mr. Barris mind the mistake.

There are countless roses. Red roses, white roses, pink roses. There is even a single black rose amongst the blossoms, though no one knows its origin. Chandresh takes credit only for the white blooms, keeping one pinned to his lapel that he toys with distractedly throughout the service.

When Lainie speaks about her sister her words are met with sighs and laughter and sad smiles.

"I do not mourn the loss of my sister because she will always be with me, in my heart," she says. "I am, however, rather annoyed that my Tara has left me to suffer you lot alone. I do not see as well without her. I do not hear as well without her. I do not feel as well without her. I would be better off without a hand or a leg than without my sister. Then at least she would be here to mock my appearance and claim to be the pretty one for a change. We have all lost our Tara, but I have lost a part of myself as well."

In the cemetery there is a single performer that even some of the mourners who are not part of Le Cirque des Rêves recognize, though the woman bedecked from head to toe in snowiest white has added a pair of feathered wings to her costume. They cascade down her back and flutter gently in the breeze while she remains still as stone. Many of the attendants seem surprised by her presence but they take their cues from Lainie, who is delighted at the sight of the living angel standing over her sister's grave.

It was the Burgess sisters, after all, who originated the tradition of such statues within the circus. Performers standing stock-still with elaborate costumes and painted skin on platforms set up in precarious spaces between tents. If watched for hours, they sometimes change position entirely, but the motion will be agonizingly slow, to the point that many observers insist that they are cleverly crafted automatons and not proper people.

The circus contains several of these performers. The star-speckled Empress of the Night. The coal-dark Black Pirate. The one that now watches over Tara Burgess is most often referred to as the Snow Queen.

There is the softest of sobbing as the coffin is lowered into the ground, but it is difficult to pinpoint who it is coming from, or if it is instead a collective sound of mingled sighs and wind and shifting feet.

The rain increases and umbrellas sprout like mushrooms amongst the graves. The damp dirt turns quickly to mud and the remainder of the burial is hastened to accommodate the weather.

The ceremony fades out rather than ending properly, the mourners shifting from neat rows to mingling crowd without a distinct moment to mark the change. Many linger to pass additional condolences on to Lainie, though some move off to seek shelter from the rain before the last of the dirt has settled.

Isobel and Tsukiko stand side by side some distance from Tara's grave, sharing a large black umbrella that Isobel holds over their heads in one black-gloved hand. Tsukiko insists she does not mind the rain but Isobel shelters her anyway, grateful for the company.

"How did she die?" Tsukiko asks. It is a question that others have asked in hushed whispers throughout the afternoon and has been met with various answers, few of them satisfying. Those who know the details are not forthcoming.

"I was told it was an accident," Isobel says quietly. "She was hit by a train."

Tsukiko nods thoughtfully, pulling a silver cigarette holder and matching lighter from the pocket of her coat.

"How did she really die?" she asks.

"What do you mean?" Isobel says, looking around to see if anyone is close enough to overhear their conversation, but most of the mourners have dissipated into the rain. Only a handful remain, including Celia Bowen with Poppet Murray clinging to her gown, the girl wearing a frown that seems more angry than sad.

Lainie and Mr. Barris stand next to Tara's grave, the angel hovering over them close enough to lay its hands upon their heads.

"You have seen things that defy belief, have you not?" Tsukiko asks. Isobel nods.

"Do you think perhaps those things would be more difficult to reconcile if you were not part of them yourself? Perhaps to the point of driving one mad? The mind is a sensitive thing."

"I don't think she stepped in front of the train on purpose," Isobel says, trying to keep her voice as low as possible.

"Perhaps not," Tsukiko says. "I contend it is a possibility, at the very least." She lights her cigarette, the flame catching easily despite the dampness of the air.

"It could have been an accident," Isobel says.

"Have you had any accidents recently? Any broken bones, burns, any injury at all?" Tsukiko asks.

"No," Isobel says.

"Have you taken ill? Even the slightest of sniffles?"

"No." Isobel racks her brain for the last time she felt under the weather and she can only come up with a head cold she had a decade ago, the winter before she met Marco.

"I do not believe any of us have since the circus started," Tsukiko says. "And no one has died until now. No one has been born, either, not since the Murray twins. Though it is not for lack of trying, given the way some of the acrobats carry on."

"I . . ." Isobel starts but cannot finish. It is too much for her to wrap her mind around, and she is not sure she wants to be able to understand it.

"We are fish in a bowl, dear," Tsukiko tells her, cigarette holder dangling precariously from her lips. "Very carefully monitored fish. Watched from all angles. If one of us floats to the top, it was not accidental. And if it was an accident, I worry that the watchers are not as careful as they should be."

Isobel stays silent. She wishes Marco had accompanied Chandresh, though she doubts he would answer any of her questions, if he consented to speaking to her at all. Every reading she has done privately on the matter has been complicated, but there is always the presence of strong emotion on his part. She knows he cares about the circus, she has never had any reason to doubt that.

"Have you ever read your cards for someone who could not understand what they were dealing with, even though to you it was clear from only a short conversation and pictures on paper?" Tsukiko asks.

"Yes," Isobel says. She has seen them hundreds of times, the querents who could not see things for what they were. Blind to betrayals and heartbreak, and always stubborn, no matter how gently she tried to explain.

"It is difficult to see a situation for what it is when you are in the midst of it," Tsukiko says. "It is too familiar. Too comfortable."

Tsukiko pauses. The curls of smoke from her cigarette slide between the raindrops as they wind around her head and up into the damp air.

"Perhaps the late Miss Burgess was close enough to the edge that she could see it differently," she says.

Isobel frowns, looking back toward Tara's grave. Lainie and Mr. Barris have turned and are walking away slowly, his arm around her shoulders.

"Have you ever been in love, Kiko?" Isobel asks.

Tsukiko's shoulders stiffen as she exhales slowly. For a moment Isobel thinks her question will go unanswered, but then she replies.

"I have had affairs that lasted decades and others that lasted hours. I have loved princesses and peasants. And I suppose they loved me, each in their way."

This is a typical Tsukiko response, one that does not truly answer the question. Isobel does not pry.

"It will come apart," Tsukiko says after a long while. Isobel does not need to ask what she means. "The cracks are beginning to show. Sooner or later it is bound to break." She pauses to take a final drag off her cigarette. "Are you still tempering?"

"Yes," Isobel says. "But I don't think it's helping."

"It is difficult to discern the effect of such things, you know. Your perspective is from the inside, after all. The smallest charms can be the most effective."

"It doesn't seem to be very effective."

"Perhaps it is controlling the chaos within more than the chaos without."

Isobel does not reply. Tsukiko shrugs and says no more.

After a moment they turn to leave together without discussion.

The snow-white angel alone remains, hovering over Tara Burgess's fresh grave, holding a single black rose in one hand. She does not move, does not even bat an eyelash. Her powdered face stays frozen in sorrow.

The increasing rain pulls stray feathers from her wings and pins them to the mud below.

You walk down a hallway papered in playing cards, row upon row of clubs and spades. Lanterns fashioned from additional cards hang above, swinging gently as you pass by.

A door at the end of the hall leads to a spiraling iron staircase.

The stairs go both up and down. You go up, finding a trapdoor in the ceiling.

The room it opens into is full of feathers that flutter downward. When you walk through them, they fall like snow over the door in the floor, obscuring it from sight.

There are six identical doors. You choose one at random, trailing a few feathers with you.

The scent of pine is overwhelming as you enter the next room to find yourself in a forest full of evergreen trees. Only these trees are not green but bright and white, luminous in the darkness surrounding them.

They are difficult to navigate. As soon as you begin walking the walls are lost in shadows and branches.

There is a sound like a woman laughing nearby, or perhaps it is only the rustling of the trees as you push your way forward, searching for the next door, the next room.

You feel the warmth of breath on your neck, but when you turn there is no one there.

Ailuromancy

Leaving the fortune-teller's tent and heading right, as she had suggested, Bailey almost immediately encounters a small crowd watching a performance. He cannot tell what it is at first, there is no raised platform involved. Peering through the space between spectators, he can see a hoop, larger than the one the contortionist used, held in the air. As he moves closer, he glimpses a black kitten leaping through it, landing somewhere out of sight.

A woman in front of him with a large hat turns and then he can see a young man about his own age, but a bit shorter, dressed in a black suit made of all manner of fabrics, and a matching black hat. On his shoulders sits a pair of stark-white kittens. As he lifts his black-gloved hand, palm open, one of the kittens jumps into it and bounces off his palm, leaping through the hoop, executing a rather impressive somersault at the pinnacle of its leap. Several members of the small audience laugh, and a few, including Bailey, applaud. The woman in the large hat steps aside completely, clearing Bailey's line of sight. His hands freeze in mid-clap when he sees the young lady who has just caught the white kitten and is now lifting it to her shoulder where it sits along with the black kitten.

She is older, as he expected, and her red hair is somehow concealed within a white cap. But her costume is similar to the one she had been wearing when he last saw her: a patchwork dress of every fabric imaginable, each in tones of snowy white, a white jacket with lots of buttons, and a pair of bright-white gloves.

She turns her head, Bailey catches her eye, and she smiles at him. Not in the way that one smiles at a random member of the audience when one is in the middle of performing circus tricks with unusually talented kittens but in the way that one smiles when one recognizes someone they have not seen in some time. Bailey can tell the difference, and the fact that she remembers who he is makes him inexplicably and utterly pleased. He feels his ears getting rather hot despite the cold of the night air.

He watches the rest of the act with rapt attention, paying a fair deal more attention to the girl than the kittens, though the kittens are too impressive to ignore, and they steal his attention back periodically. When the act is finished, the girl and boy (and kittens) take a short bow, and the crowd claps and hoots.

Bailey is wondering what he should say, if he should say anything, as the crowd begins to disperse. A man pushes in front of him, another woman blocks his way to the side, and he loses sight of the girl completely. He pushes through the throng of people, and when he is free of them, the girl and the boy and the kittens are nowhere to be seen.

The crowd around him quickly dwindles to only a few people wandering up and down the pathway. There are no other directions to go, as far as he can tell. Only tall striped walls of tents line the area, and he turns around slowly, looking for any possible place they might have disappeared to, some corner or door. He is kicking himself for coming so close only to fail, when there is a tap on his shoulder.

"Hello, Bailey," the girl says. She is standing right behind him. She has taken off her hat, her red hair falling in waves around her shoulders, and she has replaced her white jacket with a heavy black coat and a knit scarf in a vibrant violet. Only the ruffled hem of her dress and her white boots give any indication that she is the same girl who was performing in the same spot moments ago. Otherwise, she looks like any other patron at the circus.

"Hello," Bailey says. "I don't know your name."

"Oh, I'm sorry," she says. "I forgot that we were never properly introduced." She holds out her white-gloved hand, and Bailey notices that it is larger than the glove he was given as proof of a long-ago dare. "I'm Penelope, but no one ever calls me that and I don't really like it anyway, so for all intents and purposes my name is Poppet."

Bailey takes her hand and shakes it. It is warmer than he expected, even through two layers of glove.

"Poppet," Bailey repeats. "The fortune-teller told me that, but I didn't realize it was your name."

The girl smiles at him.

"You saw Isobel?" she asks. Bailey nods. "Isn't she lovely?" Bailey continues to nod, though he's not sure nodding is an appropriate response. "Did she tell you anything good about your future?" Poppet asks, lowering her voice to a dramatic whisper.

"She told me a lot of things I didn't understand," Bailey confesses.

Poppet nods knowingly.

"She does that," Poppet says. "But she means well."

"Are you allowed to be out here like this?" Bailey asks, indicating the steady stream of circus patrons that continues to wander by, completely ignoring them.

"Oh yes," Poppet says, "as long as we're incognito." She indicates her coat. "No one really gives us a second glance. Right, Widget?" She turns to a young man standing nearby, who Bailey had not even recognized as Poppet's performance partner. He has switched his black jacket for a tweedy brown one, and his hair under his matching cap is just as shockingly red as Poppet's.

"People don't pay much attention to anything unless you give them reason to," he says. "Though the hair helps, too, for looking like we don't belong in a black-and-white circus."

"Bailey, this is my brother, Winston," Poppet says.

"Widget," he corrects.

"I was getting to that," Poppet says, sounding a bit cross. "And Widge, this is Bailey."

"Pleased to meet you," Bailey says, offering his hand.

"Likewise," Widget responds in turn. "We were off for a walk, if you'd like to join us."

"Do come, please," Poppet adds. "We hardly ever have company."

"Sure, I'd like that," Bailey says. He cannot think of a single reason to refuse, and is pleased that they both seem remarkably easy to talk to. "Do you not have to do any more, uh, circus things?"

"Not for a few hours, at least," Widget says, as they start off down another pathway through the circus. "The kittens need to nap. Performing makes them sleepy."

"They're very good, how do you make them do all those tricks? I've never seen a cat do a somersault in midair," Bailey says. He notices that all three of them are walking at the same pace, staying easily together as a group. He is much more used to following a few steps behind.

"Most cats will do anything if you ask them nicely," Poppet says. "But it helps to train them early."

"And to give them lots of treats," Widget adds. "Treats always help."

"Have you seen the big cats?" Poppet asks. Bailey shakes his head. "Oh, you should. Our parents do the big-cat show; their tent is down that way." She points in a direction vaguely to the right.

"It's like our performance, only with bigger cats," Widget says.

"Much bigger cats," Poppet elaborates. "Panthers and beautiful spotted snow leopards. They're sweet, really."

"And they have a tent," Widget adds.

"Why don't you have a tent?" Bailey asks.

"We don't really need one," Poppet says. "We can only do a few shows a night, and all we need are the kittens and hoops and strings and things. Anyone who doesn't really need a tent performs wherever there's room."

"It adds to the ambience," Widget says. "So you can see bits of the circus without having to pick a tent to go into, just wandering around."

"That's probably very good for indecisive people," Bailey says, smiling when Poppet and Widget both laugh. "It is hard to choose a tent, you know, when there are so many."

"That's true," Poppet says. They've reached the bonfire courtyard. It is quite crowded and Bailey is still surprised that no one pays them much attention, assuming that they are just the same as any group of young circus patrons visiting for the evening.

"I'm hungry," Widget says.

"You're always hungry," Poppet retorts. "Shall we get something to eat?"

"Yes," Widget says.

Poppet sticks her tongue out at him.

"I was asking Bailey," she says. "Shall we get something to eat, Bailey?"

"Sure," Bailey says. Poppet and Widget seem to get along much better than he and Caroline ever have, and he assumes it is because they are closer to the same age. He wonders if they are twins; they certainly look enough alike to be twins, and he thinks it might be rude to ask.

"Have you tried the cinnamon things?" Poppet asks. "They're rather new. What are they called, Widge?"

"Fantastically delicious cinnamon things?" Widget says, shrugging. "I don't think all of the new things have names yet."

"I haven't, but they sound good," Bailey says.

"They are good," Widget says. "Layers of pastry and cinnamon and sugar all rolled into a twist and covered in icing."

"Wow," Bailey says.

"Exactly," Widget replies. "And we should get some cocoa and some chocolate mice."

"I have chocolate mice," Bailey says, pulling the bag out of his pocket. "I bought them earlier."

"Ah, you think ahead. Very good to be prepared," Widget says. "You were right about him, Poppet."

Bailey looks at Poppet quizzically, but she only smiles at him.

"Shall Bailey and I get cocoa while you get the cinnamon whatnots?" she asks, and Widget nods his approval of this plan.

"Certainly. Meet you at the bonfire?" he asks. Poppet nods, and Widget tips his hat to them both and goes off into the crowd.

Bailey and Poppet continue to walk around the bonfire courtyard. After a few moments of amicable silence, Bailey works up the nerve to ask a question, one he's not sure he'll be comfortable asking once they meet back up with Widget.

"Can I ask you something?" Bailey asks.

"Of course," Poppet says. There is a bit of a line for cocoa, but the vendor notices Poppet who flashes three fingers at him, and he smiles and nods in return.

"When . . . um, when the circus was here last time and I, well . . ." Bailey struggles for words, annoyed that the question seems simpler in his head.

"Yes?" Poppet says.

"How did you know my name?" Bailey asks. "And how did you know I was there?"

"Hmmmm . . ." Poppet says, as though she is having difficulty finding the proper words to respond with. "It's not easy to explain," she starts. "I see things before they happen. I saw you coming, not long before you got there. And I don't always see details well, but when I saw you I knew what your name was, like knowing that your scarf is blue."

They reach the front of the line and the vendor has three cups of cocoa in striped cups waiting for them already, with clouds of extra whipped cream on top. Poppet hands one to Bailey and takes the other two herself, and Bailey notices that the vendor waves them off with no money having changed hands. He assumes that free cocoa is a benefit of being a member of the circus.

"So you see everything before it happens?" Bailey asks. He is not sure Poppet's answer is entirely what he expected, if he expected anything at all.

Poppet shakes her head.

"No, not everything. Sometimes just bits of things like words and pictures in a book, but the book has lots of pages missing and it's been dropped in a pond and some parts are blurry but other parts aren't. Does that make sense?" she asks.

"Not really," Bailey answers.

Poppet laughs. "I know it's strange," she says.

"No, it's not," Bailey says. Poppet turns to look at him, the skepticism at the statement evident on her face. "Well, yes, it is kind of strange. But just odd strange, not bad strange."

"Thank you, Bailey," Poppet says. They circle the courtyard, heading back to the bonfire. Widget is waiting for them, holding a black paper bag and watching the vibrant white flames.

"What took you so long?" Widget asks.

"We had a line," Poppet says, handing him his cocoa. "Didn't you?"

"No. I don't think people have figured out how good these things are yet," Widget says, shaking the bag. "Are we set, then?"

"I think so," Poppet says.

"Where are we going?" Bailey asks.

Poppet and Widget exchange a glance before Poppet answers.

"We're doing rounds," she says. "Circles of the circus. To . . . to keep an eye on things. You do want to come with us, don't you?"

"Of course," Bailey says, relieved that he is not an imposition.

They walk in loops around the circus, sipping their cocoa and munching on chocolate mice and the sugary cinnamon pastry things, which are just as good as promised. Poppet and Widget tell him stories of the circus, pointing out tents as they pass by, and Bailey answers their questions about his town, finding it strange that they seem interested in what he considers very mundane things. They speak with the ease of people who have known each other for years, and the excitement of new friends with new stories.

If Poppet and Widget are keeping an eye on anything beyond their cocoa and himself, Bailey cannot tell what it might be.

"What's the Stargazer?" he asks, catching sight of a sign he has not seen before, as they discard their empty cups and bags.

"Up for gazing, Poppet?" Widget asks his sister. She pauses before she nods. "Poppet reads the stars," he explains to Bailey. "It's the easiest place to see the future."

"It hasn't been all that easy lately," Poppet says quietly. "But we can ride. It's only open on clear nights, so who knows if we'll get another chance while we're here."

They step inside, joining a line that ascends a curving stairway around the perimeter, separated from the interior of the tent by a heavy black curtain. The walls are covered in diagrams, white spots and lines on black paper, framed maps of constellations.

"Is it like the way the fortune-teller reads those cards with pictures on them?" Bailey asks, still trying to wrap his mind around the idea of seeing the future.

"Sort of like that, but different," Poppet says. "I can't read tarot cards at all, but Widget can."

"They're stories on paper," Widget says, shrugging. "You see how the stories in each card go together; it's not really that hard. But with those you have all different possibilities and things, different paths to take. Poppet sees things that actually happen."

"But they're not as clear," Poppet explains. "There isn't context, and most of the time I don't know what things mean until later. Sometimes not until it's too late."

"Disclaimers accepted, 'Pet," Widget says, giving her shoulder a squeeze. "It can just be a ride if you want."

At the top of the stairs they reach a black platform, where everything is endlessly dark save for a circus worker in a white suit who is guiding patrons inside. He smiles at Poppet and Widget, with a curious glance at Bailey, as he escorts them through the darkness into something like a sleigh or a carriage.

They slide onto a cushioned bench with a high back and sides, the door on one side clicking closed as Poppet settles in between Bailey and Widget. It glides forward slowly, and Bailey can see nothing but darkness.

Then something around them clicks softly and the carriage falls just a bit, and at the same time it tilts backward so they are looking up instead of forward.

The tent has no top, Bailey realizes. The upper portion of it is open, with the night sky fully visible.

It is a different sensation than watching the stars while lying in a field, something Bailey has done many times. There are no trees creeping into the edges, and the gentle swaying of the carriage makes him feel almost weightless.

And it is incredibly quiet. As the carriage moves along in what seems to be a circular pattern, Bailey can hear nothing but a soft creak and the sound of Poppet breathing next to him. It is as though the entire circus has faded away into the darkness.

He glances over at Poppet, who is looking at him instead of the sky. She gives him a grin and then turns away.

Bailey wonders if he should ask if she sees anything in the stars.

"You don't have to if you don't want to," Widget says, anticipating the question.

Poppet turns to make a face at him but then focuses her gaze upward, looking into the clear night sky. Bailey watches her carefully. She looks as though she is contemplating a painting or reading a sign from far away, squinting just a little.

She stops suddenly, putting her hands to her face, pressing her white-gloved fingers over her eyes. Widget puts a hand on her shoulder.

"Are you all right?" Bailey asks.

Poppet takes a deep breath before she nods, keeping her hands over her face.

"I'm fine," she says with a muffled voice. "It was very . . . bright. It made my head hurt."

She takes her hands from her face and shakes her head; whatever distress she had been in has apparently passed.

For the remainder of the ride none of them look up at the star-speckled sky.

"I'm sorry," Bailey says quietly as they walk down another curving stairway in order to exit.

"It's not your fault," Poppet says. "I should have known better, the stars have been doing that lately, making no sense and giving me headaches. I should probably stop trying for a while."

"You need some cheering," Widget says as they return to the din of the circus. "Cloud Maze?"

Poppet nods, her shoulders relaxing a bit.

"What's the Cloud Maze?" Bailey asks.

"You haven't found *any* of the best tents yet, have you?" Widget says, shaking his head. "You're going to have to come back, we can't do all of them in one night. Maybe that's why 'Pet got a headache, she saw us having to drag you through every single tent to see what you've been missing."

"Widge can see the past," Poppet says suddenly, diverting the conversation. "It's one of the reasons his stories are always so good."

"The past is easier," Widget says. "It's already there."

"In the stars?" Bailey asks.

"No," Widget says. "On people. The past stays on you the way powdered sugar stays on your fingers. Some people can get rid of it but it's still there, the events and things that pushed you to where you are now. I can . . . well, read isn't the right word, but it's not the right word for what Poppet does with the stars, either."

"So you can see my past on me?" Bailey asks.

"I could," Widget says. "I try not to do it without permission if there's nothing that jumps out automatically. Do you mind?"

Bailey shakes his head. "Not at all."

Widget stares at him for a moment, not quite long enough for Bailey to become uncomfortable under the weight of his eyes, but almost.

"There's a tree," Widget says. "This massive old oak tree that's more home to you than your house but not as much as this is." He gestures around at the tents and the lights. "Feeling like you're alone even when you're with other people. Apples. And your sister seems like a real gem," he adds sarcastically.

"That sounds about right," Bailey says with a laugh.

"What are the apples?" Poppet asks.

"My family has a farm with an orchard," Bailey explains.

"Oh, that sounds lovely," Poppet says. Bailey has never considered the rows of short, twisted trees lovely.

"Here we are," Widget says as they round a turn.

Despite his limited experience with the circus, Bailey is amazed that he has never seen this tent before. It is tall, almost as tall as the acrobat tent but narrower. He stops to read the sign over the door.

The Cloud Maze

An Excursion in Dimension
A Climb Though the Firmament
There Is No Beginning
There Is No End
Enter Where You Please
Leave When You Wish
Have No Fear of Falling

Inside, the tent is dark-walled with an immense, iridescent white structure in the center. Bailey can think of nothing else to call it. It takes up the entirety of the tent save for a raised path along the perimeter, a winding loop that begins at the tent entrance and circles around. The floor beyond the path is covered with white spheres, thousands of them piled like soap bubbles.

The tower itself is a series of platforms swooping in odd, diaphanous shapes, quite similar to clouds. They are layered, like a cake. From what Bailey can see, the space between layers varies from room enough to walk straight through to barely enough to crawl. Here and there parts of it almost float away from the central tower, drifting off into space.

And everywhere, there are people climbing. Hanging on edges, walking through paths, climbing higher or lower. Some platforms move with the weight; others seem strong and sturdy. The whole of it moves constantly, a light movement like breathing.

"Why is it called a maze?" Bailey asks.

"You'll see," Widget says.

They walk along the path and it sways gently, like a dock on water. Bailey struggles to keep his balance while he looks up.

Some platforms are suspended from ropes or chains from above. On lower levels, there are large poles driven through multiple platforms, though Bailey cannot tell if they reach all the way to the top. In some places there are swoops of netting, in others ropes hang like ribbons.

They stop on the far side, where the path swings close enough to jump onto one of the lower platforms.

Bailey picks up one of the white spheres. It is lighter than it looks, and kitten soft. Across the tent, people toss them at each other like snowballs, though instead of breaking they bounce off of their targets, floating gently down. Bailey tosses the one in his hand back and follows Poppet and Widget.

As soon as they have walked a few paces into the structure, Bailey can see why it is called a maze. He had expected walls and turns and dead ends, but this is different. Platforms hang at all levels: some low by his knees or his waist, others stretch high above his head, overlapping in irregular patterns. It is a maze that goes up and down as well as side to side.

"See you later," Widget says, hopping onto a nearby platform and climbing onto the one above it.

"Widge always goes straight to the very top," Poppet says. "He knows all the fastest routes to get there."

Bailey and Poppet take a more leisurely route, choosing platforms to climb at random, crawling up bits of white netting and maneuvering carefully through narrow passages. Bailey cannot tell where the edges are, or how high they have climbed, but he is relieved that Poppet seems much less troubled than she had been on the Stargazer as she laughs, helping him through the more difficult turns.

"How do we get down?" Bailey asks eventually, wondering how they will ever find their way back.

"The easiest way is to jump," Poppet says. She pulls him over to a hidden turn that reveals the edge of the platform.

They are much higher than Bailey had suspected, even though they have not reached the top.

"It's okay," Poppet says. "It's safe."

"This is impossible," Bailey says, peering out over the ledge.

"Nothing's impossible," Poppet responds. She smiles at him and jumps, her red hair trailing out behind her as she falls.

She disappears into the sea of white spheres below, enveloped completely before popping back up, her hair a shock of red against the white as she waves at him.

Bailey only hesitates for a moment, and he resists the urge to close his eyes as he leaps. Instead he laughs as he tumbles through the air.

Reaching the pool of spheres below it is truly like falling into a cloud, soft and light and comforting.

When Bailey climbs out, Poppet and Widget are both waiting on the path nearby, Poppet sitting on the edge with her legs dangling over the side.

"We should be getting back," Widget says, pulling a watch from his pocket. "We have to get the kittens ready for another show and it's nearly midnight."

"Is it really?" Bailey asks. "I didn't know it was that late, I should have been home by now."

"Let us walk you to the gates, Bailey, please?" Poppet asks. "There's something I want to get for you."

They walk together back along the winding paths, making their way across the courtyard toward the gates. Poppet takes Bailey's hand to pull him through the curtained tunnel, navigating the dark turns effortlessly. The field visible beyond the gates when they reach the other side is not crowded at this late hour, though a few scattered patrons coming or going linger nearby.

"Wait here," Poppet says. "I'll be right back." She runs off in the direction of the ticket booth while Bailey watches the clock tick closer to twelve. Within moments, Poppet is back, something silver in her hand.

"Oh, brilliant idea, 'Pet," Widget says when he sees it. Bailey looks back and forth at them, confused. It is a silver piece of paper, about the size of his ticket. Poppet hands it to him.

"It's a special pass," she explains. "For important guests, so you don't have to pay every time you come to the circus. You show it at the booth and they'll let you in."

Bailey stares at it, wide-eyed.

This card entitles the holder to unlimited admission

is imprinted on one side in black ink, and on the reverse it reads:

Le Cirque des Rêves

and in smaller letters beneath that:

Chandresh Christophe Lefèvre, Proprietor

Bailey is dumbstruck, staring at the shiny silver card.

"I thought you might like it," Poppet said, sounding unnerved by his lack of articulate response. "That is, if you want to come back while we're here."

"It's wonderful," Bailey says, looking up from the card. "Thank you very much."

"You're welcome," Poppet says, smiling. "And I told them to tell me and Widget when you arrive, so we'll know when you're here and we can come find you. If that's all right with you."

"That would be great," Bailey says. "Really, thank you."

"So we'll see you soon, then," Widget says, offering his hand.

"Definitely," Bailey answers as he takes it. "I can come back tomorrow night."

"That would be perfect," Poppet says. As Bailey lets go of Widget's hand, she leans forward and kisses him quickly on the cheek, and Bailey can feel his cheeks flush. "Have a good night," she adds as she pulls away.

"Y-you too," Bailey says. "Good night." He waves at them before they slip back through the heavy curtain, and once they disappear he turns to walk home.

It seems a lifetime ago that he walked to the circus, though it was only a few hours. And more than that, it feels as though the Bailey who entered the circus was an entirely different person than the one leaving it now, with a silver ticket in his pocket. He wonders which is the real Bailey, for certainly the Bailey who spent hours in trees alone is not the Bailey who is granted special admission to a spectacular circus, who makes friends with such interesting people without even trying.

By the time he reaches the farm, he is sure that the Bailey he is now is closer to the Bailey he is supposed to be than the Bailey he had been the day before. He may not be certain what any of it means, but for now he does not think that it much matters.

In his dreams, he is a knight on horseback, carrying a silver sword, and it does not really seem that strange after all.

Tête-à-Tête

The Midnight Dinner is rather subdued tonight, despite the number of guests. The circus is preparing for a stretch near London, having recently departed Dublin, so there are a handful of performers present. Mr. Barris is visiting from Vienna as well.

Celia Bowen spends much of the meal talking with Mme. Padva, who is seated to her left, draped in lapis-blue silk.

The gown Celia wears is a Padva design, one that was created for her to perform in but then deemed inappropriate, the silver fabric catching the light at every tuck and curve in such a way that it proved too distracting. The effect was so flattering that Celia could not bear to give it up, and instead kept it for normal wear.

"Someone cannot keep his eyes off of you, my dear," Mme. Padva remarks, subtly tilting her glass in the direction of the door, where Marco is standing quietly to the side, his hands clasped behind his back.

"Perhaps he is admiring your handiwork," Celia says without turning.

"I would wager that he is more interested in the contents than the gown itself."

Celia only laughs, but she knows that Mme. Padva is correct, as she has felt Marco's gaze burning into the back of her neck all evening, and she is finding it increasingly difficult to ignore.

His attention only wavers away from Celia once, when Chandresh knocks over a heavy crystal wineglass that narrowly avoids crashing into one of the candelabras, spilling red wine over the gold brocade of the tablecloth.

But before Marco can react, Celia leaps to her feet from across the table, righting the glass without touching it, a detail only Chandresh has the proper perspective to notice. When she takes her hand away, the glass is filled again, the tablecloth spotless.

"Clumsy, clumsy," Chandresh mutters, looking at Celia warily before turning away to pick up his conversation with Mr. Barris.

"You could have been a ballerina," Mme. Padva remarks to Celia. "You are quite good on your feet."

"I am good off my feet as well," Celia says, and Mr. Barris nearly knocks over his own glass while Mme. Padva cackles.

For the remainder of the dinner, Celia keeps a watchful eye on Chandresh. He spends most of the time discussing some sort of renovation to the house with Mr. Barris, occasionally repeating himself though Mr. Barris pretends not to notice. Chandresh does not touch his wineglass again, and it is still full when it is cleared at the end of the course.

After dinner, Celia is the last to leave. During the exodus, she misplaces her shawl and refuses to let anyone wait for her while she searches for it, waving them away into the night.

It proves difficult, attempting to locate a length of ivory lace in the singular chaos of *la maison* Lefèvre. Though she traces her steps through the library and the dining room it is nowhere to be found.

Eventually, Celia abandons her search and returns to the foyer, where Marco is standing by the door with her shawl folded casually over his arm.

"Are you looking for this, Miss Bowen?" he asks.

He moves to place it on her shoulders but the lace disintegrates between his fingers, falling into dust.

When he looks up at her again she is wearing the shawl, tied perfectly, as though it had never been removed.

"Thank you," Celia says. "Good night." She breezes by him and out the door before he can respond.

"Miss Bowen?" Marco calls, chasing after her as she descends the front stairs.

"Yes?" Celia responds, turning back as she reaches the pavement.

"I was hoping I could trouble you for that drink we did not have in Prague," Marco says. He holds her eyes steadily with his while she considers.

The intensity of his gaze is even stronger than it had been when it was focused on the back of her neck, and while Celia can feel the coercion of it, a technique her father was always fond of, there is something genuine as well, something almost like a plea.

It is that, coupled with curiosity, that causes her to nod her consent.

He smiles and turns, walking back inside the house, leaving the door open.

After a moment, she follows. The door swings shut and locks behind her.

Inside, the dining room has been cleared but the dripping candles still burn in the candelabras.

Two glasses of wine sit on the table.

"Where has Chandresh gone to?" Celia asks, picking up one of the glasses and walking to the opposite side of the table from where Marco stands.

"He has retired to the fifth floor," Marco says, taking the remaining glass for himself. "He had the former servants' quarters renovated to keep as his private rooms because he enjoys the view. He will not be down until the morning. The rest of the staff has departed, so we have the majority of the house to ourselves."

"Do you often entertain your own guests after his have gone?" Celia asks.

"Never."

Celia watches him while she sips her wine. Something about his appearance bothers her, but she cannot identify what, exactly.

"Did Chandresh really insist that all the fire in the circus be white so it would match the color scheme?" she asks after a moment.

"He did indeed," Marco says. "Told me to contact a chemist or something. I opted to take care of it myself." He runs his fingers over the candles on the table and the flames shift from warm gold to cool white, tinged with a silvery blue in the center. He runs his fingers back in the other direction, and they return to normal.

"What do you call it?" Marco asks.

Celia does not need to ask what he means.

"Manipulation. I called it magic when I was younger. It took me quite some time to break that habit, though my father never cared for the term. He'd call it enchanting, or forcibly manipulating the universe when he was not in the mood for brevity."

"Enchanting?" Marco repeats. "I had not thought of it as such before."

"Nonsense," Celia says. "It's precisely what you do. You enchant.

You're clearly good at it. You have so many people in love with you. Isobel. Chandresh. And there must be others."

"How do you know about Isobel?" Marco asks.

"The company of the circus is fairly large but they all talk about each other," Celia says. "She seems utterly devoted to someone whom none of us has ever met. I noticed immediately that she pays particular attention to me, I even wondered at one point if she might be my opponent. After you appeared in Prague when she was waiting for *someone* it was rather simple to figure out the rest. I do not believe anyone else knows. The Murray twins have a theory that she is in love with the dream of someone and not an actual person."

"The Murray twins sound quite clever," Marco says. "If I am *enchanting* in that way it is not always intentional. It was helpful in securing the position with Chandresh, as I had only a single reference and little experience. Though it does not seem to be working quite so effectively on you."

Celia puts down her glass, still not certain what to make of him. The shifting light from the candles enhances the indistinct quality about his face, so she looks away before she replies, turning her attention to the contents of the mantelpiece.

"My father used to do something similar," she says. "That pulling, charming seduction. I spent the first several years of my life watching my mother pine for him, steadfastly. Loving and longing far beyond the time when he had lost what little interest in her he ever held. Until one day when I was five years old and she took her own life. When I was old enough to understand, I promised myself I would not suffer so for anyone. It will take a great deal more than that charming smile of yours to seduce me."

But when she looks back, the charming smile has disappeared.

"I am sorry you lost your mother in such a way," Marco says.

"It was a long time ago," Celia says, surprised by the genuine sympathy. "But thank you."

"Do you remember much about her?" he asks.

"I remember impressions more than actualities. I remember her constant crying. I remember how she looked at me as though I was something to be feared."

"I do not remember my parents," Marco says. "I have no memories before the orphanage that I was plucked out of because I met some unspecified criteria. I was made to read a great deal, I traveled and studied and was generally groomed to play some sort of clandestine game. I've been doing so, along with accounting and bookkeeping and whatever else Chandresh requests of me, for most of my life."

"Why are you being so honest with me?" Celia asks.

"Because it is refreshing to be truly honest with someone for a change," Marco says. "And I suspect you would know if I lied to you outright. I hope I can expect the same from you."

Celia considers this a moment before she nods.

"You remind me a bit of my father," she says.

"How so?" Marco asks.

"The way you manipulate perception. I was never particularly good at that myself, I'm better with tangible things. You don't have to do that with me, by the way," she adds, finally realizing what disconcerts her about his appearance.

"Do what?" Marco asks.

"Look like that. It's very good, but I can tell it's not entirely genuine. It must be terribly annoying to keep it up constantly."

Marco frowns, but then, very slowly, his face begins to change. The goatee fades and disappears. The chiseled features become softer and younger. His striking green eyes fade to a green-tinged grey.

The false face had been handsome, yes, but consciously so. As though he was too aware of his own attractiveness, something Celia found distinctly unappealing.

And there was something else, a hollowness that was likely the result of the illusion, an impression that he was not entirely present in the room.

But now, now there is a different person standing next to her, much more present, as if a barrier has been removed between them. He feels closer, though the distance between them has not changed, and his face is quite handsome, still.

The intensity of his stare increases with these eyes; looking at him now she can see deeper, without being distracted by the color.

Celia can feel the heat rising up her neck and manages to control it enough that the flush is not noticeable in the candlelight.

And then she realizes why there is something familiar there as well.

"I've seen you like this before," she says, placing his true countenance in a location in her memory. "You've watched my show like that."

"Do you remember all of your audiences?" Marco asks.

"Not all of them," Celia says. "But I remember the people who look at me the way you do."

"What way might that be?"

"As though they cannot decide if they are afraid of me or they want to kiss me."

"I am not afraid of you," Marco says.

They stare at each other in silence for a while, the candles flickering around them.

"It seems a great deal of effort for a rather subtle difference," Celia says.

"It has its advantages."

"I think you look better without it," Celia says. Marco looks so surprised that she adds, "I said I would be honest, didn't I?"

"You flatter me, Miss Bowen," he says. "How many times have you been to this house?"

"At least a dozen," Celia says.

"And yet, you have never had a tour."

"I have never been offered one."

"Chandresh does not believe in them. He prefers to let the house remain an enigma. If the guests do not know where the boundaries are, it gives the impression that the house itself goes on forever. It used to be two buildings, so it can be somewhat disorienting."

"I did not know that," Celia says.

"Two adjoining town houses, one a mirror of the other. He bought both and had them renovated into a single dwelling, with a number of enhancements. I do not believe we have the time for the full tour, but I could show you a few of the more obscure rooms, if you would like."

"I would," Celia says, placing her empty wineglass on the table next to his own. "Do you often give forbidden tours of your employer's house?"

"Only once, and that was because Mr. Barris was quite persistent."

*

FROM THE DINING ROOM, they cross under the shadow of the elephant-headed statue in the hall, passing into the library and stopping at the stained-glass sunset that stretches the height of one wall.

"This is the game room," Marco says, pushing the glass and letting it swing open into the next room.

"How appropriate."

Gaming is more theme than function for the room. There are several chessboards with missing pieces, and pieces without boards of their own lined up on windowsills and bookshelves. Dartboards without darts hang alongside backgammon games suspended in mid-play.

The billiard table in the center is covered in bloodred felt.

A selection of weaponry lines one wall, arranged in pairs. Sabres and pistols and fencing foils, each twinned with another, prepared for dozens of potential duels.

"Chandresh has a fondness for antique armament," Marco explains as Celia regards them. "There are pieces in other rooms but this is the majority of the collection."

He watches her closely as she walks around the room. She appears to be attempting not to smile as she looks over the gaming elements artfully arranged around them.

"You smile as though you have a secret," he says.

"I have a lot of secrets," Celia says, glancing at him over her shoulder before turning back to the wall. "When did you know I was your opponent?"

"I did not know until your audition. You were a mystery for years before that. And I'm certain you noticed that you caught me by surprise." He pauses before adding, "I cannot say that it has truly been an advantage. How long have you known?"

"I knew in the rain in Prague, and you know perfectly well that was when I knew," Celia says. "You could have let me go with an umbrella to puzzle over, but instead you chased me down. Why?"

"I wanted it back," Marco says. "I'm quite fond of that umbrella. And I had grown weary of hiding from you."

"I once suspected anyone and everyone," Celia says. "Though I did think it was more likely someone in the circus proper. I should have known it was you."

"And why is that?" Marco asks.

"Because you pretend to be less than you are," she says. "That much is clear as day. I will admit, I never thought to charm my umbrella."

"I have lived most of my life in London," Marco says. "As soon as I learned to charm objects, it was one of the first things I did."

He removes his jacket and tosses it over one of the leather chairs in the corner. He takes a deck of playing cards off of a shelf, unsure if she will be willing to humor him but too curious not to try.

"Do you want to play cards?" Celia asks.

"Not exactly," Marco answers as he shuffles. When he is satisfied, he places the deck on the billiard table.

He flips over a card. The king of spades. He taps the surface and the king of spades becomes the king of hearts. He lifts his hand, pulling it back and unfurling his fingers over the card, welcoming her to make the next move.

Celia smiles. She unties the shawl from her shoulders and drapes it over his discarded jacket. Then she stands with her hands clasped behind her back.

The king of hearts flips up, balancing on its edge. It stands there for a moment before slowly and deliberately ripping in half. The two pieces stay standing, separate, for a moment before they fall, the patterned back facing up.

Mimicking Marco's gesture, Celia taps the card and it snaps back together. She pulls her hand back and the card flips itself over. The queen of diamonds.

Then the entire deck hovers in the air for a moment before collapsing onto the table, cards scattering out over the red felt surface.

"You are better than I am at physical manipulation," Marco admits.

"I have an advantage," Celia says. "What my father calls a natural talent. I find it harder not to influence my surroundings, I was constantly breaking things as a child."

"How much impact can you have on living things?" Marco asks.

"It depends on the thing in question," Celia says. "Objects are easier. It took me years to master anything animate. And I work much better with my own birds than I could with any old pigeon taken off the street."

"What could you do to me?"

"I might be able to change your hair, perhaps your voice," Celia says. "No more than that without your full consent and awareness, and true consent is more difficult to give than you might think. I can't repair injury. I rarely have much more than a temporary, superficial impact. It is easier with people I'm more familiar with, though it is never particularly easy."

"What about with yourself?"

In response, Celia goes to the wall and removes a thin Ottoman dagger with a jade hilt from where it hangs with its partner. Holding it in her right hand, she places her left palm down on the billiard table, over the scattered cards. Without hesitating, she plunges the blade into the back of her hand, piercing through skin and flesh and cards and into the felt underneath.

Marco flinches, but says nothing.

Celia pries the dagger up, her hand and the two of spades still impaled on the blade, blood beginning to drip down to her wrist. She holds out her hand and turns it slowly, presenting it with a certain amount of showmanship so that Marco can see that there is no illusion involved.

With her other hand she removes the dagger, the bloodied playing card fluttering down. Then the droplets of blood begin rolling backward, seeping into the gash in her palm which then shrinks and disappears until there is no more than a sharp red line on her skin, and then nothing.

She taps the card and the blood disappears. The rip left by the blade no longer visible. The card is now the two of hearts.

Marco picks up the card and runs his fingers over the mended surface. Then with a subtle turn of his hand, the card vanishes. He leaves it safely tucked within his pocket.

"I am relieved that we were not challenged to a physical fight," he says. "I think you would have the advantage."

"My father used to slice open the tips of my fingers one by one until I could heal all ten at once," Celia says, returning the dagger to its place on the wall. "So much of it is feeling from the inside how everything is supposed to fit, I have not been able to do it with anyone else."

"I think your lessons were a great deal less academic than mine."

"I would have preferred more reading."

"I think it strange we were prepared in drastically different ways for the same challenge," Marco says. He looks at Celia's hand again, though now there is clearly nothing amiss, no indication that it was stabbed only moments ago.

"I suspect that is part of the point," she says. "Two schools of thought pitted against each other, working within the same environment."

"I confess," Marco says, "I don't fully understand the point, even after all this time."

"Nor do I," Celia admits. "I suspect calling it a challenge or a game is not entirely accurate. I've come to think of it more as a dual exhibition. What else do I get to see on my tour?"

"Would you like to see something in progress?" Marco asks. Knowing that she thinks of the circus as an exhibition comes as a pleasant surprise, as he had stopped considering it antagonistic years ago.

"I would," Celia says. "Especially if it is the project that Mr. Barris was going on about during dinner."

"It is indeed."

Marco escorts her out of the game room through another door, passing briefly through the hall and into the expansive ballroom at the rear of the house, where the moonlight filters in from the glass doors lining the back wall.

*

OUTSIDE, IN THE SPACE the garden formerly occupied beyond the terrace, the area has been excavated to sit a level deeper, sunken into the earth. At the moment it is mostly an arrangement of packed soil and stacks of stone forming tall but rudimentary walls.

Celia carefully descends the stone steps and Marco follows her. Once at the bottom, the walls create a maze, leaving only a small portion of the garden visible at a time.

"I thought it might be beneficial for Chandresh to have a project to occupy himself with," Marco explains. "As he so rarely leaves the house these days, renovating the gardens seemed a good place to start. Would you like to see what it will look like when it is complete?"

"I would," Celia says. "Do you have the plans here?"

In response, Marco lifts one hand and gestures around them.

What had been little more than stacks of rough stone moments before is now set and carved into ornate arches and pathways, covered in crawling vines and speckled with bright, tiny lanterns. Roses hang from curving trellises above them, the night sky visible through the spaces between the blossoms.

Celia puts her hand to her lips to muffle her gasp. The entire scene, from the scent of the roses to the warmth radiating from the lanterns, is astounding. She can hear a fountain bubbling nearby and turns down the now grass-covered path to find it.

Marco follows her as she explores, taking turn after turn through the twisting pathways.

The fountain in the center cascades down a carved stone wall, flowing into a round pond full of koi. Their scales glow in the moonlight, bright splashes of white and orange in the dark water.

Celia puts her hand out, letting the water from the fountain rush over her fingers as she presses against the cold stone below.

"You're doing this in my mind, aren't you?" she asks when she hears Marco behind her.

"You're letting me," he says.

"I could probably stop it, you know," Celia says, turning around to face him. He leans against one of the stone archways, watching her.

"I'm certain you could. If you resisted at all it would not work as well, and it can be blocked almost entirely. And of course, proximity is key for the immersion."

"You cannot do this with the circus," Celia says.

Marco shrugs his shoulders.

"There is too much distance, unfortunately," he says. "It is one of my specialties, yet there is little opportunity to use it. I am not adept at creating this type of illusion to be viewed by more than one person at a time."

"It's amazing," Celia says, watching the koi swimming at her feet. "I could never manage something so intricate, even though they call me the illusionist. You'd wear that title better than I."

"I suppose 'The Beautiful Woman Who Can Manipulate the World with Her Mind' is too unwieldy."

"I don't think that would fit on the sign outside my tent."

His laugh is low and warm and Celia turns away to hide her smile, keeping her attention on the swirling water.

"There is no use for one of my specialties, as well," she says. "I am very good at manipulating fabric, but it seems so unnecessary given what Madame Padva can do." She twirls in her gown, the silver catching the light so she glows as brightly as the lanterns.

"I think she's a witch," Marco says. "And I mean that in the most complimentary manner."

"I think she would take that as a compliment, indeed," Celia says. "You are seeing all this as well, exactly as I see it?"

"More or less," Marco says. "The nuances are richer the closer I am to the viewer."

Celia circles to the opposite side of the pond, nearer to where he stands. She examines the carvings on the stone and the vines twining around them, but her gaze keeps returning to Marco. Any attempt at subtlety is ruined when he repeatedly catches her eyes with his own. Looking away again becomes more difficult each time.

"It was clever of you to use the bonfire as a stimulus," she says, trying to keep her attention on a tiny glowing lantern.

"I'm not surprised you figured that out," Marco says. "I had to come up with some way of staying connected since I am not able to travel with the circus. The lighting seemed a perfect opportunity to establish a lasting hold. I didn't want you to have too much control, after all."

"It had repercussions," Celia says.

"What do you mean?"

"Let's just say there is more that is remarkable about the Murray twins than their hair."

"And you're not going to tell me what that is, are you?" Marco asks.

"A lady cannot reveal all of her secrets," Celia says. She pulls a rose down from a hanging branch, closing her eyes as she inhales the scent, the petals velvet soft against her skin. The sensory details of the illusion are so luscious, it is almost dizzying. "Who thought to sink the garden?" she asks.

"Chandresh. It's inspired by another room in the house, I can show you that one if you'd like."

Celia nods and they retrace their steps through the garden. She stays closer to him as they walk, close enough to touch though he keeps his hands clasped behind his back. When they reach the terrace, Celia glances back at the garden, where the roses and lanterns have reverted to dirt and stone.

*

INSIDE, MARCO LEADS CELIA across the ballroom. He stops at the far wall and slides one of the dark-wood panels open to reveal a curving stairway spiraling downward.

"Is it a dungeon?" Celia asks as they descend.

"Not precisely," Marco says. When they reach the gilded door at the end of the stairs, he opens it for her. "Mind your step."

The room is small but the ceiling is high, a golden chandelier draped with crystals suspended in the center. The rounded walls and ceiling are painted a deep, vibrant blue and ornamented with stars.

A path wraps around the edge of the room like a ledge, though the majority of the floor is sunken and filled with large cushions covered in a rainbow of embellished silk.

"Chandresh claims it is modeled after a room belonging to a courtesan in Bombay," Marco says. "I find it marvelous for reading, myself."

Celia laughs and a curl of her hair falls across her cheek.

Marco tentatively moves to brush it off her face, but before his fingers reach her, she pushes herself off the ledge, her silver gown a billowing cloud as she falls onto the pile of jewel-toned cushions.

He watches her for a moment before copying her action himself, sinking into the center of the room alongside her.

They lie staring up at the chandelier, the light reflecting over the crystals turning it into the night sky without need of any illusion.

"How often are you able to visit the circus?" Celia asks.

"Not as often as I'd like. Whenever it is near London, of course. I try to reach it elsewhere in Europe if I can escape from Chandresh for sufficient periods of time. I sometimes feel like I have one foot on both sides. I am intimately familiar with so much of it, and yet it is always surprising."

"Which is your favorite tent?"

"Truthfully? Yours."

"Why?" she asks, turning to look at him.

"It appeals to my personal taste, I suppose. You do in public things I

217

have been taught in secret. Perhaps I appreciate it on a different level than most. I also very much enjoy the Labyrinth. I had been unsure whether or not you would be willing to collaborate on it."

"I got quite the lecture about that particular collaboration," Celia says. "My father called it debauched juxtaposition, he must have worked for days to come up with a worthy insult. He sees something tawdry in the combining of skills, I have never understood why. I adore the Labyrinth, I have had far too much fun adding rooms. I particularly love that hallway you made where it snows, so you can see the footprints left by other people navigating their way around."

"I had not thought of it in such a lascivious manner before," Marco says. "I look forward to visiting it again with that in mind. Though I had been under the impression that your father was not in the position to be commenting on such matters."

"He's not dead," Celia says, turning back to the ceiling. "It is rather difficult to explain."

Marco decides against asking her to try, returning to the subject of the circus instead.

"Which tent is your favorite?" he asks.

"The Ice Garden," Celia answers, without even pausing to consider.

"Why is that?" Marco asks.

"Because of the way it *feels*," she says. "It's like walking into a dream. As though it is someplace else entirely and not simply another tent. Perhaps I am just fond of snow. However did you come up with it?"

Marco reflects on the process, as he has never been asked to explain the origin of his ideas before.

"I thought it might be interesting to have a conservatory, but of course it necessitated a lack of color," he says. "I pondered a great many options before settling on fabricating everything from ice. I am pleased that you think it like a dream, as that is where the core of the idea came from."

"It's the reason I made the Wishing Tree," Celia says. "I thought a tree covered in fire would make for a proper complement to ones made from ice."

Marco replays in his mind his first encounter with the Wishing Tree. A mixture of annoyance and amazement and wistfulness that seems different in retrospect. He was uncertain he would even be able to light his own candle, his own wish, wondering if it was somehow against the rules.

"Do all of those wishes come true?" he asks.

"I'm not sure," Celia says. "I've not been able to follow up with every person who has wished on it. Have you?"

"Perhaps."

"Did your wish come true?"

"I am not entirely certain yet."

"You shall have to let me know," Celia says. "I hope it does. I suppose in a way, I made the Wishing Tree for you."

"You didn't know who I was then," Marco says, turning to look at her. Her attention remains focused on the chandelier, but that alluring, secret-keeping smile has returned.

"I didn't know your identity, but I had an impression of who my opponent was, being surrounded by things you made. I had thought you might like it."

"I do like it," Marco says.

The silence that falls between them is a comfortable one. He longs to reach over and touch her, but he resists, fearful of destroying the delicate camaraderie they are building. He steals glances instead, watching the way the light falls over her skin. Several times he catches her regarding him in a similar manner, and the moments when she holds his eyes with hers are sublime.

"How are you managing to keep everyone from aging?" Celia asks after a while.

"Very carefully," Marco answers. "And they are aging, albeit extremely slowly. How are you moving the circus?"

"On a train."

"A train?" Marco asks, incredulous. "The entire circus moved by a single train?"

"It's a large train," Celia says. "And it's magic," she adds, making Marco laugh.

"I confess, Miss Bowen, you are not what I had expected."

"I assure you that feeling is mutual."

Marco stands, stepping back up to the ledge by the door.

Celia reaches out her hand to him and he takes it to help her up. It is the first time he has touched her bare skin.

The reaction in the air is immediate. A sudden charge ripples through the room, crisp and bright. The chandelier begins to shake.

The feeling rushing over Marco's skin is intense and intimate, beginning where his palm meets hers but spreading beyond that, farther and deeper.

Celia pulls her hand away after she catches her balance, stepping back and leaning against the wall. The feeling begins to subside as soon as she lets him go.

"I'm sorry," she says quietly, clearly out of breath. "You caught me by surprise."

"My apologies," Marco says, his heartbeat pounding so loudly in his ears that he can barely hear her. "Though I cannot say I'm entirely sure what happened."

"I tend to be particularly sensitive to energy," Celia says. "People who do the sort of things you and I do carry a very palpable type of energy, and I . . . I am not accustomed to yours just yet."

"I only hope that was as pleasurable a sensation for you as it was for me."

Celia does not reply, and to keep himself from reaching for her hand again, he opens the door instead, leading her back up the twisting stairway.

*

THEY WALK THROUGH the moonlit ballroom, their steps echoing together.

"How is Chandresh?" Celia asks, attempting to find a subject to fill the silence, anything to distract herself from her still-shaking hands, and remembering the fallen glass at dinner.

"He wavers," Marco says with a sigh. "Ever since the circus opened, he has been increasingly unfocused. I . . . I do what I can to keep him steady, though I fear it has an adverse effect on his memory. I had not intended to, but after what happened with the late Miss Burgess I thought it the wisest course of action."

"She was in the peculiar position of being involved in all this but not within the circus itself," Celia says. "I am sure it is not the easiest perspective to manage. At least you can observe Chandresh."

"Indeed," Marco says. "I do wish there was a way to protect those outside the circus the way the bonfire protects those within it."

"The bonfire?" Celia asks.

"It serves several purposes. Primarily, it is my connection to the circus, but it also functions as a safeguard of a sort. I neglected the fact that it does not cover those outside the fence."

"I neglected even considering safeguards," Celia says. "I do not think I understood at first how many other people would become involved in our challenge." She stops walking, standing in the middle of the ballroom.

Marco stops as well but says nothing, waiting for her to speak.

"It was not your fault," she says quietly. "What happened to Tara. The circumstances may have played out the same way regardless of anything you or I did. You cannot take away anyone's own free will, that was one of my very first lessons."

Marco nods, and then he takes a step closer to her. He reaches out to take her hand, slowly brushing his fingers against hers.

The feeling is as strong as it had been when he touched her before, but something is different. The air changes, but the chandeliers hanging above them remain steady and still.

"What are you doing?" she asks.

"You mentioned something about energy," Marco says. "I'm focusing yours with mine, so you won't break the chandeliers."

"If I broke anything, I could probably fix it," Celia says, but she does not let go.

Without the concern for the effect she might be having on the surroundings, she is able to relax into the sensation instead of resisting it. It is exquisite. It is the way she has felt in so many of his tents, the thrill of being surrounded by something wondrous and fantastical, only magnified and focused directly on her. The feel of his skin against hers reverberates across her entire body, though his fingers remain entwined in hers. She looks up at him, caught in the haunting greenish-grey of his eyes again, and she does not turn away.

They stand gazing at each other in silence for moments that seem to stretch for hours.

The clock in the hall chimes and Celia jumps, startled. As soon as she releases Marco's hand she wants to take it again, but the whole evening has been too overwhelming already.

"You hide it so well," she says. "I can feel the same energy radiating like heat in each of your tents, but in person it's completely concealed."

"Misdirection is one of my strengths," Marco says.

"It won't be as easy now that you have my attention."

"I like having your attention," he says. "Thank you for this. For staying."

"I forgive you for stealing my shawl."

She smiles as he laughs.

And then she vanishes. A simple trick of distracting his attention long enough to slip out through the hall, despite the lingering temptation to stay.

*

MARCO FINDS HER SHAWL left behind in the game room, still draped over his jacket.

Part III

INTERSECTIONS

I would dearly love to read the reactions, the observations of each and every person who walks through the gates of Le Cirque des Rêves, to know what they see and hear and feel. To see how their experience overlaps with my own and how it differs. I have been fortunate enough to receive letters with such information, to have *rêveurs* share with me writings from journals or thoughts scribbled on scraps of paper.

We add our own stories, each visitor, each visit, each night spent at the circus. I suppose there will never be a lack of things to say, of stories to be told and shared.

—FRIEDRICK THIESSEN, 1895

Standing on the platform in the midst of the crowd, high enough that they can be viewed clearly from all angles, are two figures, still as statues.

The woman wears a dress something akin to a bridal gown constructed for a ballerina, white and frothy and laced with black ribbons that flutter in the night air. Her legs are encased in striped stockings, her feet in tall black button-up boots. Her dark hair is piled in waves upon her head, adorned with sprays of white feathers.

Her companion is a handsome man, somewhat taller than she, in an impeccably tailored black pinstriped suit. His shirt is a crisp white, his tie black and pristinely knotted. A black bowler hat sits upon his head.

They stand entwined but not touching, their heads tilted toward each other. Lips frozen in the moment before (or after) the kiss.

Though you watch them for some time they do not move. No stirring of fingertips or eyelashes. No indication that they are even breathing.

"They cannot be real," someone nearby remarks.

Many patrons only glance at them before moving on, but the longer you watch, the more you can detect the subtlest of motions. The change in the curve of a hand as it hovers near an arm. The shifting angle of a perfectly balanced leg. Each of them always gravitating toward the other.

Yet still they do not touch.

Thirteen

The grand anniversary celebration for Le Cirque des Rêves is not held after ten years, which might have been expected and traditional, but when the circus has been open and traveling for years amounting to thirteen. Some say it is held then because the tenth anniversary had come and gone, and no one thought to have a party for it until after the fact.

The reception is held at Chandresh Christophe Lefèvre's town house on Friday, October 13, 1899. The guest list is exclusive; only members of the circus and some select and special guests are in attendance. It is not publicized, of course, and though some might speculate that the event has something to do with the circus, there is no way to be certain. Besides, no one truly suspects the infamously black-and-white circus would be associated with an event so full of color.

It is extremely colorful, with both the house and the partygoers adorned in a rainbow of shades. The lights in each room are specially treated, greens and blues in one, reds and oranges in another. The tables dotting the dining room are shrouded in vibrant patterned tablecloths. The centerpieces are elaborate floral arrangements with only the brightest of blooms. The members of the ensemble that plays odd but melodic and danceable tunes in the ballroom are bedecked in suits of red velvet. Even the champagne flutes are a deep cobalt-blue glass rather than clear, and the staff wears green rather than black. Chandresh himself wears a suit of vibrant purple with a gold paisley waistcoat, and throughout the evening, he smokes specially made cigars that spout matching violet smoke.

A spectrum of roses ranging in shades from natural to the unimaginable sits in the golden lap of the elephant-headed statue in the foyer, petals cascading down whenever anyone moves by.

Cocktails are poured at the bar in a variety of oddly shaped and colored glasses. There is ruby-red wine and cloudy-green absinthe. Tapestries of vibrant silks hang from walls and are draped over everything that will stay still. Candles glow in stained-glass sconces, casting dancing light over the party and its attendees.

Poppet and Widget are the youngest of the guests, being the same age as the circus. Their bright-red hair is out in full effect, and they wear coordinating outfits the warm blue of a twilight sky, edged in pinks and yellows. As a birthday gift, Chandresh gives them two fluffy orange kittens with blue eyes and striped ribbons around their necks. Poppet and Widget adore them, and promptly dub them Bootes and Pavo, though later they can never quite remember which of the identical kittens is which and refer to them collectively whenever possible.

The original conspirators are there, save for the late Tara Burgess. Lainie Burgess comes dressed in a flowing gown of canary yellow, accompanied by Mr. Ethan Barris in a suit of navy blue that is about as colorful as he can manage, though his tie is a slightly brighter shade, and he pins a yellow rose to his lapel.

Mr. A. H— arrives in his customary grey.

Mme. Padva attends, after some coercion by Chandresh, gloriously adorned in golden silks embroidered with red filigree, crimson feathers in her white hair. She spends most of the evening in one of the chairs by the fire, watching events unfold around her rather than participating in them directly.

Herr Friedrick Thiessen is there by special invitation, under the condition that he is not to write a single public word about the gathering nor mention it to anyone. He promises this gladly, and attends wearing mostly red with a touch of black, a reversal of his usual attire.

He spends the majority of the evening in the company of Celia Bowen, whose elaborate gown changes color, shifting through a rainbow of hues to complement whomever she is closest to.

There are no performers save the band, as it is difficult to hire entertainment to impress a gathering that is comprised predominantly of circus members. Most of the evening is spent in conversation and socializing.

At dinner, which begins promptly at midnight, each course is styled in black or white but bursts with color once pierced with forks or spoons, revealing layer upon layer of flavors. Some dishes are served on small mirrors rather than proper plates.

Poppet and Widget slip tastes of appropriate morsels to the marmalade kittens at their feet, while listening attentively to Mme. Padva's tales of the ballet. Their mother admonishes that the content of said tales may not be entirely appropriate for a pair of just barely thirteen-year-olds, but Mme. Padva continues on unfazed, glossing over only the most sordid of details that Widget can read in the sparkle of her eyes even if she does not speak them aloud.

Dessert consists mainly of a gargantuan tiered cake shaped to resemble circus tents and frosted in stripes, the filling within a bright shock of raspberry cream. There are also miniature chocolate leopards, and strawberries coated in looping patterns of dark and white chocolates.

After dessert has been cleared, Chandresh makes a lengthy speech thanking all the guests for thirteen spectacular years, for the wonderment of the circus that had been nothing but an idea more than a decade ago. It goes on for some time about dreams and family and striving for uniqueness in a world of sameness. Some of it is profound and other bits are rambling and nonsensical, but it is considered a sweet gesture by almost everyone in attendance. Many take the opportunity afterward to thank him personally, for the party and the circus. Several make a point of commenting on his sentiments.

Excepting, of course, for his remark about how none of them seem to age save for the Murray twins, which was followed by an awkward silence broken only by the sound of Mr. Barris coughing. No one dares mention it, and many seem somewhat relieved that Chandresh himself does not recall most of his comments even an hour later.

There is dancing after dinner in the ballroom, where lengths of colorful, gold-embellished silk cascade over the walls and windows, glimmering in the candlelight.

Mr. A. H— moves along the periphery, going mostly unnoticed and speaking with only a few of the other guests, including Mr. Barris, who introduces him to Herr Thiessen. The three men have a brief yet engaging conversation about clocks and the nature of time before Mr. A. H— makes a polite excuse and fades into the background again.

He avoids the ballroom entirely, save for a single waltz when Tsukiko coerces him onto the dance floor. She wears a gown fashioned from a pink kimono, her hair piled in an elaborate knotted style and her eyes rimmed in a striking red.

Their combined grace puts all the other couples to shame.

Isobel, clad in clear sky blue, tries in vain to catch Marco's attention. He avoids her at every turn, and is difficult to spot in the crowd since he is dressed identically to the rest of the staff. Eventually, with the aid of several glasses of champagne, Tsukiko persuades her to abandon the effort, drawing her out into the sunken garden to distract her.

Marco's attention, when he is not being ordered around by Chandresh or hovering over Mme. Padva, who hits him with her cane when he asks her multiple times if she is in need of any assistance, belongs only to Celia.

"It is destroying me that I cannot ask you to dance," Marco whispers as she passes by him in the ballroom, the deep green of his suit seeping across her gown like moss.

"Then you are far too easily destructible," Celia murmurs softly, winking at him as Chandresh sweeps by and offers her his arm. The spreading moss is crushed by deep plum and sparkling gold as he pulls her away.

Chandresh introduces Celia to Mr. A. H——, unable to recall if they have met before. Celia claims that they have not, though she remembers the gentleman who politely takes her hand, as he looks exactly the same as he did when she was six years old. Only his suit has changed, updated to fit the current style.

Several people pester Celia to perform. While at first she refuses, late in the evening she relents, pulling a bemused Tsukiko to the middle of the dance floor and making her disappear in the blink of an eye despite the crowd around them. One moment there are two women in petal-pink gowns and the next Celia is alone.

Seconds later, there are shrieks from the library as Tsukiko reappears in the lantern-festooned sarcophagus propped up in one corner. Tsukiko takes a glass of champagne from a stunned waiter, giving him a beatific smile before returning to the ballroom.

She passes by Poppet and Widget, where Poppet is teaching the marmalade kittens to climb onto her shoulders and Widget is pulling book after book from the library's well-stocked shelves. Eventually Poppet drags him forcibly from the room to prevent him from spending the duration of the party reading.

Guests move in flocks of color from the ballroom through the halls and the library, a constantly shifting rainbow punctuated with laughter and chatter. The mood remains boisterous and bright even into the earliest hours.

As Celia walks alone through the front hall, Marco grabs her hand, pulling her into a shadowed alcove behind the looming golden statue. The rose petals swirl madly with the sudden shift in the air.

"I'm not entirely used to that, you know," Celia says. She takes her hand from his but does not move away, though there is not a great deal of room between the wall and the statue. The color of her gown settles into a deep, solid green.

"You look just as you did the first time I saw you," Marco says.

"I take it you wore that color on purpose?" Celia asks.

"Merely a fortunate coincidence. Chandresh insisted on putting the entire staff in green. And I did not anticipate the ingenuity of your attire."

Celia shrugs her shoulders. "I couldn't decide what to wear."

"You are beautiful," Marco says.

"Thank you," Celia responds, refusing to meet his eyes. "You are too handsome. I prefer your actual face."

His face changes, reverting to the one she recalls in perfect detail from the evening they spent in the same rooms three years ago under much more intimate circumstances. There has been little opportunity since then for anything more than too-brief stolen moments.

"Isn't that a bit risky to wear in this company?" Celia asks.

"I'm only doing it for you," Marco says. "The rest of them will see me as they always have."

They stand watching each other in silence as a laughing group moves through the hall on the other side of the statue. The din echoes through the space though they stay far enough away that Celia and Marco escape any notice, and Celia's gown remains mossy and green.

Marco lifts his hand to brush a stray curl away from Celia's face, tucking it behind her ear and stroking her cheek with his fingertips. Her eyelids flutter closed and the rose petals around their feet begin to stir.

"I've missed you," he whispers softly.

The air between them is electric as he leans in, gently brushing his lips against her neck.

In the next room, the guests complain about the sudden increase in temperature. Fans are drawn from colorful bags, fluttering like tropical birds.

In the shadow of the elephant-headed statue, Celia pulls away suddenly. It is not immediately apparent why until the clouds of grey begin swirling through the green of her gown.

"Hello, Alexander," she says, dipping her head in acknowledgment to the man who has appeared behind them without a sound, not even disturbing the rose petals strewn across the floor.

The man in the grey suit greets her with a polite nod. "Miss Bowen, I would like to speak with your companion privately for a moment, if you do not mind."

"Of course," Celia says. She leaves without even glancing at Marco, her gown shifting from grey dawn to violet sunset as she walks down the hall to where the Murray twins are tempting their marmalade kittens with shiny silver coffee spoons.

"I cannot say I find this behavior appropriate," the man in the grey suit says to Marco.

"You know her," Marco says quietly, his eyes still on Celia as she stops at the entrance to the ballroom, where her gown is cloaked in crimson as Herr Thiessen offers her a glass of champagne.

"I have *met* her. I cannot rightfully say that I know her in any particular fashion."

"You knew exactly who she was before any of this started and you never thought to tell me?"

"I did not think it necessary."

A bevy of guests wanders into the hall from the dining room, sending the cascade of rose petals adrift once more. Marco escorts the man in the grey suit through the library, sliding the stained glass open to access the empty game room and continue their conversation.

"Thirteen years with barely a word and now you wish to speak with me?" Marco asks.

"I did not have anything in particular to speak to you about. I simply wished to interrupt your . . . conversation with Miss Bowen."

"She knows your name."

"She clearly has a very good memory. What is it you would like to discuss?"

"I would like to know if I am doing well," Marco says, his voice low and cold.

"Your progress has been sufficient," his instructor says. "Your employment here is steady, you have a suitable position to work from."

"And yet I cannot be myself. You teach me all these things and then you put me here to pretend to be something I am not, while she is center stage, doing exactly what she does."

"But no one in that room believes it. They think she is deceiving them. They do not see what she is any more than they see what you are, she is simply more noticeable. This is not about having an *audience*. I am proving a point. You can do just as much as she does without passing it off as flamboyant spectacle and trickery. You can maintain your relative anonymity and equal her accomplishments. I suggest you keep your distance from her and concentrate on your own work."

"I'm in love with her."

Never before has anything Marco said or did elicited a visible response from the man in the grey suit, not even when he once accidentally set a table aflame during his lessons, but the expression that crosses the man's face now is unmistakably sad.

"I am sorry to hear that," he says. "It will make the challenge a great deal more difficult for you."

"We have been playing at this for more than a decade, when does it end?"

"It ends when there is a victor."

"And how long does that take?" Marco asks.

"It is difficult to say. The most recent previous challenge lasted thirty-seven years."

"We cannot keep this circus running for thirty-seven years."

"Then you will not have as long a time to wait. You were a fine student, you are a fine competitor."

"How can you know?" Marco asks, his voice rising. "You have not even seen fit to speak to me for years. I have done nothing for you. Everything I have done, every change I have made to that circus, every impossible feat and astounding sight, I have done for her."

"Your motives do not impact the game."

"I am done with playing your game," Marco says. "I quit."

"You cannot quit," his instructor replies. "You are bound to this. To her. The challenge will continue. One of you will lose. You have no choice in the matter."

Marco picks up a ball from the billiard table and hurls it at the man in the grey suit. He steps out of its path easily and it crashes instead into the sunset of stained glass.

Without a word, Marco turns his back on his instructor. He walks out the door at the back of the room, not even noticing Isobel as he passes her in the hall, where she has been close enough to hear the argument.

He goes directly to the ballroom, making his way to the center of the dance floor. He takes Celia's arm, spinning her away from Herr Thiessen.

Marco pulls her to him in an emerald embrace, so close that no distinction remains between where his suit ends and her gown begins.

To Celia, there is suddenly no one else in the room as he holds her in his arms.

But before she can vocalize her surprise, his lips close over hers and she is lost in wordless bliss.

Marco kisses her as though they are the only two people in the world.

The air swirls in a tempest around them, blowing open the glass doors to the garden with a tangle of billowing curtains.

Every eye in the crowded ballroom turns in their direction.

And then he releases her and walks away.

By the time Marco leaves the room, almost everyone has forgotten the incident entirely. It is replaced by a momentary confusion that is blamed on the heat or the excessive amounts of champagne.

Herr Thiessen cannot recall why Celia has suddenly stopped dancing, or when her gown shifted to its current deep green.

"Is something wrong?" he asks, when he realizes that she is trembling.

*

MR. A. H— STORMS THROUGH THE FRONT HALL, somehow avoiding tripping over Poppet and Widget, who are sprawled on the floor teaching Bootes and Pavo how to turn circles on their hind legs.

Widget hands Bootes (or Pavo) to Poppet and follows the man in the grey suit. He watches as he crosses into the foyer, retrieves his grey top hat and silver cane from the butler, and leaves by the front door. After he exits, Widget presses his nose to the nearest window, watching him as he passes beneath the streetlamps before disappearing into the darkness.

Poppet catches up with him then, the kittens perched on her shoulders purring happily. Chandresh follows close behind her, making his way through the crowd in the hall.

"What is it?" Poppet asks. "What's the matter?" Widget turns away from the glass.

"That man has no shadow," he says, as Chandresh leans over the twins to peer out the window at the empty street.

"What did you say?" Chandresh asks, but Poppet and Widget and the orange kittens have already run off down the hall, lost in the colorful crowd.

Bedtime Stories

Bailey spends much of the early part of this evening with Poppet and Widget exploring the Labyrinth. A dizzying network of chambers, interspersed with hallways containing mismatched doors. Rooms that spin and rooms with glowing chessboard floors. One hall is stacked high with suitcases. In another it is snowing.

"How is this possible?" Bailey asks, melting flakes of snow sticking to his coat.

In response, Poppet throws a snowball at him, and Widget only laughs.

While they traverse the Labyrinth, Widget tells the story of the Minotaur in such detail that Bailey keeps expecting to encounter the monster around every turn.

They reach a room resembling a large metal birdcage, with only darkness visible through the bars. The door in the floor that they entered through latches once it falls closed and cannot be opened again. There appears to be no other way to exit.

Widget ceases his narration as they investigate each silver bar, finding no hidden openings or cleverly disguised hinges. Poppet grows visibly distressed.

After a considerable amount of time spent trapped within the room, Bailey finds a key concealed in the seat of the swing in the middle of the cage. When he turns it, the swing itself rises and the top of the cage opens, allowing them to climb out, escaping into a dimly lit temple guarded by an albino Sphinx.

While the temple has at least a dozen doors along its walls, Poppet immediately finds one that leads back out into the circus.

She still seems upset, but before Bailey can ask her if something is the matter, Widget checks his watch and finds they are late for their scheduled performance. The three of them agree to meet up again later, and the twins disappear into the crowd.

Bailey has seen the kittens so many times over the last few nights that he practically has their routine memorized, so he opts to explore by himself while he waits for them to be free again.

The particular path he chooses to wander down has no obvious doors, it is only a passageway between tents, endless stripes illuminated by flickering lights.

He notices an uneven spot in the alternating black and white.

Bailey finds a gap in the side of one of the tents. A split in the fabric, each edge dotted with silver grommets, and a black ribbon hangs just above his head, as though this opening was meant to be laced together to keep the tent firmly closed. He wonders if some circus member forgot to re-lace it.

Then he sees the tag. It is the size of a large postcard, attached to the black ribbon the way one might attach a gift card to a present. The tag hangs loosely a few feet off the ground. Bailey turns it over. The picture side shows a black-and-white etching of a child in a bed covered in fluffy pillows and a checkered quilt, not in a nursery but under a star-sprinkled night sky. The opposite side is white, with elegant calligraphy in black ink that reads:

Bedtime Stories
Eventide Rhapsodies
Anthologies of Memory

Please enter cautiously
and feel free to open what is closed

Bailey cannot tell if the tag refers to the break in the tent, or if it has been misplaced from some other tent. Most of the tents have prominently placed signs in painted wood, and entrances that are clearly defined or marked. This one seems as though it was not meant to be found. Other patrons pass by on their way from one part of the circus to another, too absorbed in their conversations to notice him contemplating a postcard-size tag by the side of a tent.

Tentatively, Bailey pulls the unlaced flaps apart, enough to peek inside to try to discern if this is indeed a separate circus attraction and not the back of the acrobat tent or some sort of storage area. He can make out only several twinkling lights and shapes that could possibly be furniture. Still unsure, he pulls the flaps apart enough to enter, stepping inside carefully per the instructions on the postcard, which proves wise as he walks directly into a table covered in jars and bottles and lidded bowls that rattle against one another. He stops, hoping not to knock anything over.

It is a long room, the size of a formal dining room, or maybe it only resembles a dining room because of the table, which stretches the length of the tent, though there is enough room to maneuver around it carefully. All of the jars and bottles are different. Some jars are simple glass mason jars, others are glazed ceramic jars or ornate frosted glass. Bottles for wine or whiskey or perfume. There are silver-lidded sugar bowls and containers that look rather like urns. They appear to be in no particular pattern or order; they are simply strewn across the table. There are additional jars and bottles around the periphery of the room as well, with some on the ground and some on boxes and tall wooden bookshelves.

The only element that correlates the room with the picture on the tag is the ceiling. It is black and covered with tiny twinkling lights. The effect is almost identical to the upward view of the night sky from outside.

Bailey wonders how all of this might relate to a child in bed, or to bedtime stories, as he walks around the table.

He recalls what the tag said about opening things, wondering what could possibly be inside of all of these jars. Most of the clear-glass ones look empty. As he reaches the opposite side of the table, he picks one at random, a small round ceramic jar, glazed in black with a high shine and a lid topped with a round curl of a handle. He pulls the lid off and looks inside. A small wisp of smoke escapes, but other than that it is empty. As he peers inside he smells the smoke of a roaring fire, and a hint of snow and roasting chestnuts. Curious, he inhales deeply. There is the aroma of mulled wine and sugared candy, peppermint and pipe smoke. The crisp pine scent of a fir tree. The wax of dripping candles. He can almost feel the snow, the excitement, and the anticipation, the sugary taste of a striped candy. It is dizzying and wonderful and disturbing. After a few moments, he replaces the lid and puts the jar carefully back on the table.

He looks around at the jars and bottles, intrigued but hesitant to open another. He picks up a frosted-glass mason jar and unscrews the silver metal lid. This jar is not empty but contains a small amount of white sand which shifts on the bottom. The scent that wafts from it is the unmistakable smell of the ocean, a bright summer day at the seashore. He can hear the sound of waves crashing against the sand, the cry of a seagull. There is something mysterious as well, something fantastical. The flag of a pirate ship on the far horizon, a mermaid's tail flipping out of sight behind a wave. The scent and the feeling are adventurous and exhilarating, with the salty tinge of a sea breeze.

Bailey closes the jar and the scent and the feeling fade, trapped back inside the glass with its handful of sand.

Next he chooses a bottle from a shelf on the wall, wondering if there is any distinction between jars and bottles on the table and the ones that surround it, if there is an indiscernible filing system for these curious containers.

This bottle is tall and thin, with a cork held in place by silver wire. He removes it with some difficulty, and it opens with a popping noise. There is something in the bottom of the bottle, but he cannot tell what it is. The scent wafting from the thin neck is bright and floral. A rosebush full of dew-dripping blossoms, the mossy smell of garden dirt. He feels as though he is walking down a garden path. There is the buzzing of bees and the melody of songbirds in the trees. He inhales more deeply, and there are other flowers along with the roses: lilies and irises and cro-cuses. The leaves of the trees are rustling in the soft warm wind, and the sound of someone else's footsteps falling not far from his own. The sen-sation of a cat brushing past his legs is so genuine that he looks down expecting to see it, but there is nothing on the floor of the tent but more jars and bottles. Bailey puts the cork back in the bottle and returns it to its shelf. Then he chooses another.

Tucked in the back of one of the shelves is a small bottle, rounded with a short neck and closed with a matching glass stopper. He picks it up carefully. It is heavier than he had expected. Removing the stopper, he is confused, for at first the scent and the sensation do not change. Then comes the aroma of caramel, wafting on the crisp breeze of an autumn wind. The scent of wool and sweat makes him feel as though he is wearing a heavy coat, with the warmth of a scarf around his neck. There is the impression of people wearing masks. The smell of a bonfire mixes with the caramel. And then there is a shift, a movement in front of him. Something grey. A sharp pain in his chest. The sensation of falling. A sound like howling wind, or a screaming girl.

Bailey puts the stopper back, disturbed. Not wanting to end on such an experience, he places the strange little bottle back on its shelf and decides to choose one more before leaving to catch up with Poppet and Widget again.

He picks one of the boxes on the table this time, a polished-wood box with a swirling pattern etched into its lid. The inside of the box is lined with white silk. The scent is like incense, deep and spiced, and he can feel smoke curling around his head. It is hot, a dry desert air with pounding sun and powder-soft sand. His cheeks flush from the heat and from something else. The feel and sensation of something as luscious as silk falls across his skin in waves. There is music that he cannot discern. A pipe or a flute. And laughter, a high-pitched laugh that blends harmoniously with the music. The taste of something sweet but spicy on his tongue. The feeling is luxurious and lighthearted, but also secretive and sensual. He feels a hand on his shoulder and jumps in surprise, dropping the lid down on the box.

The sensation ends abruptly. Bailey stands alone in the tent, underneath the twinkling stars.

That is enough, he thinks. He goes back to the flap in the tent wall, careful not to disturb any of the jars or bottles nearby.

He stops to adjust the tag that hangs from the ribbon on the tent flap, so that it is more easily visible, though he is not certain why. The illustration of the child asleep in his bed beneath the stars faces outward, but it is difficult to tell if the child's dreams are peaceful or restless.

He walks back to find Poppet and Widget, wondering if they might want to head to the courtyard for something to eat.

Then the scent of caramel wafts by as he walks, and Bailey finds he is not particularly hungry after all.

Bailey wanders down curving paths, his mind preoccupied with bottles full of mysteries.

As he turns a corner, he encounters a raised platform with a statue-still occupant, but this one is different than the snow-covered woman he had seen before.

This woman's skin is shimmering and pale, her long black hair is tied with dozens of silver ribbons that fall over her shoulders. Her gown is white, covered in what to Bailey looks like looping black embroidery, but as he walks closer he sees that the black marks are actually words written across the fabric. When he is near enough to read parts of the gown, he realizes that they are love letters, inscribed in handwritten text. Words of desire and longing wrapping around her waist, flowing down the train of her gown as it spills over the platform.

The statue herself is still, but her hand is held out, and only then does Bailey notice the young woman with a red scarf standing in front of her, offering the love letter–clad statue a single crimson rose.

The movement is so subtle that it is almost undetectable, but slowly, very, very slowly, the statue reaches to accept the rose. Her fingers open, and the young woman with the rose waits patiently as the statue gradually closes her hand around the stem, releasing it only when it is secure.

And then the young woman bows to the statue, and walks off into the crowd.

The statue continues to hold the rose. The color seems more vibrant against the white and black of her gown.

Bailey is still watching the statue when Poppet taps him on the shoulder.

"She's my favorite," Poppet says, looking up at the statue with him.

"Who is she?" Bailey asks.

"She has a lot of names," Poppet says, "but mostly they call her the Paramour. I'm glad someone gave her a flower tonight. I do it myself, sometimes, if she doesn't have one. I don't think she looks complete without it."

The statue is lifting the rose, gradually, to her face. Her eyelids slowly close.

"What did you do with your time?" Poppet asks as they walk away from the Paramour toward the courtyard.

"I found a tent full of bottles and things that I wasn't sure I was supposed to be in," Bailey says. "It was . . . strange."

To his surprise, Poppet laughs.

"That's Widget's tent," she explains. "Celia made it for him, as a place to practice putting down his stories. He claims it's easier than writing things out. Widge said he wanted to practice reading people, by the way, so we can catch up with him later. He does that sometimes, to pick up bits of stories. He'll probably be in the Hall of Mirrors or the Drawing Room."

"What's the Drawing Room?" Bailey asks, the curiosity about a tent he hasn't heard of winning out over the fleeting thought to ask who Celia is, as he does not recall Poppet mentioning the name before.

"It's a tent that's made up of blank black walls with buckets full of chalk so you can draw everywhere. Some people only sign their names but others draw pictures. Sometimes Widge will write out little stories, but he draws things, too, he's quite good at it."

As they walk around the courtyard, Poppet insists he try a spiced cocoa that is both wonderfully warming and slightly painful. He finds his appetite has returned, so they share a bowl of dumplings and a packet of pieces of edible paper, with detailed illustrations on them that match their respective flavors.

They wander through a tent full of mist, encountering creatures made out of paper. Curling white snakes with flickering black tongues, birds with coal-colored wings flapping through the thick fog.

The dark shadow of an unidentifiable creature scurries across Poppet's boots and out of sight.

She claims there is a fire-breathing paper dragon somewhere in the tent, and though Bailey believes her, he has difficulty reconciling in his head the idea of paper that breathes fire.

"It's getting late," Poppet remarks as they walk from tent to tent. "Do you have to go home?"

"I can stay for a while," Bailey says. He has become something of an expert at sneaking back into his house without waking anyone, so he has been staying at the circus later and later each night.

There are fewer patrons wandering the circus at this hour, and as they walk Bailey notices that many of them are wearing red scarves.

Different types, from heavy cabled wool to fine lace, but each is a deep, scarlet red that looks even redder against all of the black and white.

He asks Poppet about it, once so many flashes of red have passed by that he is sure it is not a coincidence, and recalling that the young woman with the rose had a red scarf as well.

"It's like a uniform," she says. "They're *rêveurs*. Some of them follow the circus around. They always stay later than other people. The red is how they identify each other."

Bailey tries to ask more questions about the *rêveurs* and their scarves, but before he can, Poppet pulls him into another tent and he is immediately silenced by the sight he is met with inside.

The sensation reminds him of the first snow of winter, for those first few hours when everything is blanketed in white, soft and quiet.

Everything in this tent is white. Nothing black, not even stripes visible on the walls. A shimmering, almost blinding white. There are trees and flowers and grass surrounding twisted pebble pathways, every leaf and petal perfectly white.

"What is this?" Bailey asks. He did not have a chance to read the sign outside the door.

"This is the Ice Garden," Poppet says, pulling him down the path. It turns into an open space with a fountain in the middle, bubbling white foam over clear carved ice. Pale trees line the edges of the tent, showers of snowflakes falling from their branches.

There is no one else in the tent, nothing disrupting the surroundings. Bailey peers at a nearby rose, and while it is cold and frozen and white, there is the barest hint of scent as he leans closer. The scent of rose and ice and sugar. It reminds him of the spun-sugar flowers sold by vendors in the courtyard.

"Let's play hide-and-seek," Poppet suggests, and Bailey agrees before she unbuttons her coat and leaves it on a frozen bench, her white costume rendering her all but invisible.

"That's not fair!" he calls as she disappears behind the hanging branches of a willow tree. He follows her around trees and topiaries, through coils of vines and roses, chasing glimpses of her red hair.

Bookkeeping

LONDON, MARCH 1900

Chandresh Christophe Lefèvre sits at the huge mahogany desk in his study, a mostly empty bottle of brandy in front of him. At one point in the evening there was a glass, but he misplaced that hours ago. Wandering from room to room has become a nightly habit fueled by insomnia and boredom. He is also missing his jacket, abandoned in a previously wandered-through room. It will be retrieved without remark by a diplomatic maid in the morning.

In the study, between bottle sips of brandy, he attempts to work. This mainly consists of scribbling with fountain pens on various scraps of paper. He has not genuinely worked in years. No new ideas, no new productions. The cycle of mounting and executing and moving on to the next project has skidded to a halt, and he cannot say why.

It does not make sense to him. Not this night or any other, not at any level of the brandy bottle. This is not how it is supposed to work. A project is started, it is developed and mounted and sent out into the world, and more often than not it becomes self-sufficient. And then he is no longer needed. It is not always a pleasant position to be in, but it is the way of such things, and Chandresh knows this process well. One is proud, one collects one's receipts, and even if one is a bit melancholy, one moves on.

The circus left him behind, sailing forth, and yet he cannot turn away from the shore. More than enough time to mourn the creative process and ignite it again, but there are no sparks of something new. No new endeavors, nothing bigger or better for nearly fourteen years.

Perhaps, he thinks, he has outdone even himself. But it is not a pleasant thought, so he drowns it in brandy and attempts to ignore it.

The circus bothers him.

It bothers him most at times like this, in the bottom of the brandy bottle and the quiet of the night. It is not terribly late, the night is fairly young in circus terms, but the silence is already heavy.

And now, with his bottle and his fountain pen drained, he simply sits, dragging a hand through his hair distractedly, staring across the room at nothing in particular. Flames burn low in the gilded fireplace, the tall bookcases stuffed with curios and relics loom in shadow.

His wandering eyes drift over the open doorway and settle on the door across the hall. The door to Marco's office, tucked discreetly between a pair of Persian columns. Part of a suite of rooms that are Marco's own, the better to keep him at the beck and call, though he is out for the evening.

Chandresh wonders through an alcohol-soaked fog if perhaps Marco keeps the circus documents in his office. And what exactly those documents might contain. He has only seen the paperwork involved with the circus in passing, hasn't bothered to scrutinize the details of the thing in years. Now he is curious.

Empty brandy bottle still in hand, he pulls himself to his feet and stumbles out into the hallway. It will be locked, he thinks, when he reaches the polished dark-wood door, but the silver handle moves easily as he turns it. The door swings open.

Chandresh hesitates in the doorway. The tiny office is dark save for the pool of light spilling in from the hall and the dim haze from the streetlamps seeping in through the single window.

For a moment, Chandresh reconsiders. If there were any brandy left in the bottle he might close the door and wander away. But the bottle is empty, and it is his own house, after all. He fumbles for the switch on the sconce nearest the door and it flickers to life, illuminating the room in front of him.

The office is packed with too much furniture. Cabinets and trunks line the walls, boxes of files are stacked in tidy rows. The desk in the center that takes up nearly half the space is a smaller, more modest version of the one in the study, though its surface holds jars of ink and pens and a pile of notebooks, all in perfect order and not lost in a clutter of figurines and precious stones and antique weaponry.

Chandresh puts the empty brandy bottle down on the desk and begins searching the cabinets and files, opening drawers and flipping through papers without any clear idea of what it is exactly he is looking for. There does not seem to be a particular section for the circus; bits of it are mixed in with books of theater receipts and lists of box-office returns.

He is mildly surprised that there is no discernible filing system. No labels on boxes. The contents of the office are orderly, but not clearly organized.

In a cabinet, Chandresh finds piles of blueprints and sketches. Many bear Mr. Barris's stamps and initials, but there are other diagrams written in different hands that Chandresh does not recognize. In some cases, he cannot even distinguish what language they are inscribed in, though each has "Le Cirque des Rêves" written carefully along the edge of the paper.

Pulling them closer to the light, spreading them out over what little available floor space he can find, he scrutinizes them, sheet after sheet, letting them roll and fall in piles as he moves on to each subsequent piece.

Even the prints that are clearly Mr. Barris's work have been written over. Additions made in different handwriting, layers placed on top of original designs.

Leaving the papers on the floor, Chandresh returns to the desk, to the neat pile of notebooks next to the abandoned brandy bottle. They appear to be bank ledgers, rows upon rows of numbers and calculations with notations and totals and dates. Chandresh tosses these aside.

He turns his attention to the desk itself. He begins pulling open the heavy wooden drawers. Several are empty. One contains dozens of blank notebooks and unopened jars of ink. Another is full of old datebooks, the appointments filling the days written in some sort of shorthand in Marco's neat, delicate handwriting.

The last drawer is locked.

Chandresh makes to turn to another box of files nearby, but something pulls him back to the locked drawer.

There is no key in the desk. There are no locks on the other drawers.

He cannot recall if there was a lock on the desk when it was placed here, years ago, when the office contained only the desk and a single cabinet and seemed almost spacious.

After a few minutes of looking for a key, he grows impatient and returns to his study to retrieve the silver knife that is embedded in the dartboard on the wall.

Lying on the floor behind the desk, he all but destroys the lock in his attempts to pry the mechanism open, but he is rewarded with the satisfying click of the latch as it relents to the blade.

Leaving the knife on the floor, he pulls open the drawer and finds only a book.

It is a large, leather-bound volume. Chandresh takes it from the drawer, startled by the weight of it, and drops it with a thump onto the desk.

The book is old and dusty. The leather is worn and the binding is fraying at the edges.

Hesitating only a moment, Chandresh lifts the cover.

The endpapers are covered in an exquisitely detailed drawing of a tree covered in symbols and markings. It is densely inscribed, more ink than blank page. Chandresh cannot decipher any of it, cannot even tell if the marks are broken into words or simply continuous strings of motifs. Here and there he spots a mark that looks familiar. Some are almost numbers. Some recall the shape of Egyptian hieroglyphs. It reminds him of the contortionist's tattoo.

The pages of the book are covered with similar markings, though predominantly they hold other things. Bits of paper culled from other documents.

It takes Chandresh several pages to realize each bit of paper holds a signature.

It takes longer for him to realize that he knows the names.

Only when he finds the page with the matching, childish scrawls spelling out the names of the Murray twins is he certain that the book contains the names of each and every person involved with the circus.

And only upon closer scrutiny does he notice that they are accompanied by locks of hair.

The later pages hold the names of the original conspirators, though one name is conspicuously absent, and another has been removed.

The final page contains his own signature, a flourish of illegible C's, carefully snipped from a piece of paper that might have been an invoice or a letter. Beneath it there is a single lock of raven hair glued onto the page and surrounded by symbols and letters. Chandresh's hand reaches up to touch the ends of his hair, curling around his collar.

A shadow passes over the desk and Chandresh jumps back in surprise. The book falls closed.

"Sir?"

Marco stands in the doorway, watching Chandresh with a curious expression.

"I . . . I thought you'd left for the evening," Chandresh says. He looks down at the book and then back at Marco.

"I had, sir, but I forgot some of my things." Marco's eyes travel over the papers and blueprints strewn on the floor. "May I ask what you are doing, sir?"

"I might ask you the same question," Chandresh says. "What is all this?" He flips the book open again, the pages fluttering and settling.

"Those are records for the circus," Marco says, without looking at the book.

"What kind of records?" Chandresh presses.

"It's a system of my own devising," Marco says. "There is quite a bit to keep in order with the circus, as you know."

"How long have you been doing this?"

"Doing what, sir?"

"Keeping all this . . . whatever this nonsense is." He flips through the pages of the book, though he finds he does not want to touch it now.

"My system goes back to the inception of the circus," Marco says.

"You're doing something to it, to all of us, aren't you?"

"I am just doing my job, sir," Marco says. There is an edge to his voice now. "And, if I may, I do not appreciate you going through my books without informing me."

Chandresh moves around the desk to face him, stepping over blueprints, stumbling though his voice remains steady.

"You are my employee, I have every right to see what's in my own house, what's being done with my own projects. You're working with him, aren't you? You've been keeping all this from me the entire time, you had no right to go behind my back—"

"Behind your back?" Marco interrupts. "You cannot even begin to comprehend the things that go on behind your back. That have always gone on behind your back before any of this even started."

"That is not what I wanted from this arrangement," Chandresh says.

"You never had a choice about this arrangement," Marco says. "You have no control and you never did. And you never even wanted to know how things were done. You signed receipts without so much as a glance. Money is no object, you said. Nor were any of the details, those were always left up to me."

The papers on the desk ripple as Marco raises his voice and he stops, taking a step away from the desk. The papers settle again into disheveled piles.

"You have been sabotaging this endeavor," Chandresh says. "Lying to my face. Keeping god knows what in these books—"

"What books, sir?" Marco asks. Chandresh looks back at the desk. There are no papers, no pile of ledgers. There is an inkwell next to the lamp, a brass statue of an Egyptian deity, a clock, and the empty brandy bottle. Nothing else remains on the polished-wood surface.

Chandresh stumbles, looking from the desk to Marco and back, unable to focus.

"I will not let you do this to me," Chandresh says, picking up the brandy bottle from the desk and brandishing it in front of him. "You are dismissed from your position. You shall leave immediately."

The brandy bottle vanishes. Chandresh stops, grasping at the empty air.

"I cannot leave," Marco says, his voice calm and controlled. He speaks each word slowly, as though he is explaining something to a small child. "I am not allowed. I must remain here, and I must continue with this *nonsense*, as you so aptly put it. You are going to return to your drinking and your parties and you will not even remember that we had this conversation. Things will continue as they always have. That is what is going to happen."

Chandresh opens his mouth to object and then closes it again, confused. He glances at Marco, then back at the empty desk. He looks at his hand, opening and closing his fingers, trying to grasp something that is no longer there, though he cannot remember what it was.

"I'm sorry," he says, turning back to Marco. "I . . . I've lost my train of thought. What were we discussing?"

"Nothing of import, sir," Marco says. "Just a few minor details about the circus."

"Of course," Chandresh says. "Where is the circus now?"

"Sydney, Australia, sir." His voice wavers but he covers it with a short cough before turning away.

Chandresh only nods absently.

"May I take that for you, sir?" Marco says, indicating the empty bottle that is once again sitting on the desk.

"Oh," Chandresh says. "Yes, yes, of course." He hands the bottle to Marco without looking at it or him, barely registering the action.

"May I get you another, sir?"

"Yes, thank you," Chandresh says, wandering out of Marco's office and back into his own study. He settles into a leather armchair by the window.

In the office, Marco gathers up fallen notebooks and papers with trembling hands. He rolls the blueprints and piles the papers and books.

He takes the silver knife he finds discarded on the floor and returns it to the dartboard in the study, stabbing the blade into the bull's-eye.

Then he empties every drawer in the office, removes each file and document. When everything is properly organized, he locates a set of suitcases in his adjoining rooms and fills them near to bursting, the large leather-bound book cushioned between stacks of paper. He combs through his rooms, removing every personal belonging from the space.

He extinguishes the office lamps and locks the door behind him.

Before he leaves for the night, arms laden with suitcases and rolls of blueprints, Marco places a full bottle of brandy and a glass on the table next to Chandresh's chair. Chandresh does not even acknowledge his presence. He stares out the window into the darkness and the rain. He does not hear the click of the door as Marco leaves.

"He has no shadow," Chandresh says to himself before he pours a glass of brandy.

*

VERY LATE IN THE EVENING, Chandresh has a rather lengthy conversation with the ghost of an old acquaintance he knew only as Prospero the Enchanter. Thoughts that might have drifted away on waves of brandy otherwise remain intact in his head, confirmed and secured by a diaphanous magician.

Three Cups of Tea with Lainie Burgess

Mme. Ana Padva's studio is a remarkable space situated near Highgate Cemetery, with floor-to-ceiling windows providing a panoramic view of London. Dress forms displaying elaborate gowns stand in groups and pairs, giving the impression of a party with a great many headless guests.

Lainie Burgess wanders through a gathering of black-and-white gowns as she waits for Mme. Padva, pausing to admire one in ivory satin delicately covered with black velvet fretwork, like wrought iron in long scrolling lines and curves.

"I can make that in a color if you would like it for yourself," Mme. Padva says as she enters the room, her cane accompanying her with a steady beat against the tile floor.

"It is too grand for me, Tante Padva," Lainie says.

"They are difficult to balance without color," Mme. Padva says, turning the form around and regarding the train with a narrowed eye. "Too much white and people assume they are wedding gowns, too much black and they become heavy and dour. This one may need more black, I think. I would add more of a sleeve but Celia cannot abide them."

Mme. Padva shows Lainie around the rest of her latest work, including a wall of recent sketches, before they sit down for tea at a table by one of the windows.

"You have a new assistant every time I visit," Lainie remarks, after the latest version brings a tray with their tea and quickly disappears again.

"They get bored of waiting for me to die and then they flit off to work for someone else, once they decide shoving me out a window and hoping I might roll down the hill into a mausoleum is too much trouble. I am an old woman with a lot of money and no heir; they are well-coiffed vultures. This one will not last more than a month."

"I had always assumed you would leave everything to Chandresh," Lainie says.

"Chandresh is not in need of any of this financially, and I do not think he would be able to manage the business end of things the way I would prefer. He does not have the eye for it. Not that he has the eye for much of anything, these days."

"Is he that unwell?" Lainie asks, stirring her tea.

"He has lost something of himself," Mme. Padva says. "I have seen him become preoccupied with projects before, but nothing to this degree. It has rendered him a ghost of what he was, though in Chandresh's case, a ghost of his former self is more vibrant than most people. I do what I can. I find avant-garde ballet companies to occupy his theaters. I prop him up at the opera when he should be doing the same for me." She takes a sip of her tea before adding, "And not to bring up a delicate subject, my dear, but I keep him far away from trains."

"That is likely wise," Lainie says.

"I have known him since he was a child, it is the least I can do."

Lainie nods. She has other questions but she decides they are best saved for someone else to whom she has been meaning to pay a visit. For the rest of the afternoon, they discuss no more than fashion and art movements. Mme. Padva insists on making her a less formal version of the ivory-and-black gown in peach and cream, finishing a sketch in a matter of minutes.

"When I do retire, this is all going to you, my dear," Mme. Padva says before Lainie leaves. "I would not trust anyone else with it."

*

THE OFFICE IS LARGE BUT LOOKS SMALLER than it is due to the volume of its contents. While a great deal of its walls are composed of frosted glass, most of it is obscured by cabinets and shelves. The drafting table by the windows is all but hidden in the meticulously ordered chaos of papers and diagrams and blueprints. The bespectacled man seated behind it is almost invisible, blending in with his surroundings. The sound of his pencil scratching against paper is as methodical and precise as the ticking of the clock in the corner.

It is identical to an office that occupied a similar space in London, and then another in Vienna, before it was moved here to Basel.

Mr. Barris puts his pencil down and pours himself a cup of tea. He nearly drops it when he looks up and sees Lainie Burgess standing in his doorway.

"Your assistant appears to be out at the moment," she says. "I did not mean to startle you."

"That's quite all right," Mr. Barris says, putting his teacup down on the desk before rising from his chair. "I was not expecting you until later this evening."

"I took an earlier train," Lainie says. "And I wanted to see you."

"More time spent with you is always a pleasure," Mr. Barris says. "Tea?"

Lainie nods as she navigates her way around the crowded office to the chair on the other side of the desk.

"What is it that you discussed when Tara visited you in Vienna?" she asks before she has even taken her seat.

"I thought you knew," he says without looking at her, keeping his attention on the teapot as he pours.

"We are two different people, Ethan. Just because you could never decide which one of us you were in love with does not make us interchangeable."

He puts down the pot and prepares her tea, knowing how she takes it without having to ask.

"I asked you to marry me and you never gave me an answer," he says as he stirs.

"You asked me after she died," Lainie says. "How could I ever be certain that was a choice you made or one that was made for you?"

He hands her the cup of tea, resting his hand over hers as she takes it.

"I love you," he says. "I loved her as well but it was never the same. You are as dear as family to me, all of you. More dear, in some cases."

He returns to his chair, removing his spectacles to wipe them with his handkerchief.

"I don't know why I wear these things," he says, looking down at them. "I haven't needed them for years."

"You wear them because they suit you," Lainie says.

"Thank you," he says as he replaces them, watching her as she sips her tea. "That offer still stands."

"I know," Lainie says. "I am considering it."

"Take your time," Mr. Barris says. "We appear to have a great deal of it."

Lainie nods, placing her teacup on the desk.

"Tara was always the rational, sensible one," she says. "We balanced each other, that was one of the reasons we excelled at whatever we did. She grounded my imaginative ideas. I saw in details while she saw in scope. Not seeing the scope is why I am here and she is not. I took each element separately and never looked to see that they did not fit together properly."

The clock ticks heavily through the pause that follows.

"I don't want to have this conversation," Mr. Barris says once the ticking becomes insufferable. "I didn't want to have it with her then and I do not want to have it with you now."

"You know what's going on here, don't you?" Lainie asks.

Mr. Barris straightens a pile of papers on his desk while he considers his response.

"Yes," he says after a moment. "I do."

"Did you tell my sister?"

"No."

"Then tell me," Lainie says.

"I cannot. To explain would involve breaking a trust and I am not willing to do that, not even for you."

"How many times have you lied to me?" Lainie asks, rising from her chair.

"I have *never* lied," Mr. Barris counters, standing as well. "I do not share what I am not at liberty to say. I gave my word and I intend to keep it but I have never lied to you. You never even asked me, you assumed I knew nothing."

"Tara asked you," Lainie says.

"Indirectly," Mr. Barris says. "I do not think she knew what to ask and I would not have answered if she did. I was concerned about her and I suggested that she speak with Alexander if she wanted answers. I assume that was why she was at the station. I do not know if she ever spoke to him. I have not asked."

"Alexander knows as well?" Lainie asks.

"I believe there is little, if anything, that he is ignorant about."

Lainie sighs and returns to her chair. She picks up her cup of tea and then without taking a sip puts it down again.

Mr. Barris crosses to the other side of the desk and takes her hands in his, making sure she looks him in the eye before he speaks.

"I would tell you if I could," he says.

"I know that, Ethan," she says. "I do."

She squeezes his hands softly to reassure him.

"I don't mind this, Lainie," Mr. Barris says. "I move my office every few years, I hire a new staff. I keep up with projects through correspondence, it is not a difficult thing to manage considering what I receive in return."

"I understand," she says. "Where is the circus now?"

"I'm not certain. I believe it recently left Budapest, though I do not know where it is en route to. I can find out; Friedrick will know and I owe him a telegram."

"And how will Herr Thiessen know where the circus is headed?"

"Because Celia Bowen tells him."

Lainie does not ask him any further questions.

Mr. Barris is relieved when she accepts the invitation to join him for dinner, and even more so when she agrees to extend her stay in Switzerland before catching up with the circus.

*

LAINIE INVITES CELIA to join her at the Pera Palace Hotel in Constantinople as soon as she reaches the city. She waits in the tea lounge, two lightly steaming, tulip-shaped glasses with matching saucers resting upon the tile table in front of her.

When Celia arrives, they greet each other warmly. Celia inquires about Lainie's journey before they discuss the city and the hotel, including the sweeping height of the room they sit within.

"It's like being in the acrobat tent," Lainie remarks, looking up at the domes that line the ceiling, each one dotted with circles of turquoise-tinted glass.

"You have not been to the circus in far too long," Celia says. "We have your costumes, if you would like to join the statues this evening."

"Thank you, but no," Lainie says. "I am not in the mood to stand so still."

"You are welcome at any time," Celia says.

"I know," Lainie says. "Though truthfully, I am not here for the circus. I am here to speak with you."

"What is it you would like to speak about?" Celia asks, a look of concern falling over her face.

"My sister was killed at St. Pancras Station, after a visit to the Midland Grand Hotel," Lainie says. "Do you know why she went there?"

Celia's grip on her tea glass tightens.

"I know who she went there to see," she says, choosing her words carefully.

"I suppose Ethan told you that," Lainie says.

Celia nods.

"Do you know why she wanted to see him?" Lainie asks.

"No, I do not."

"Because she didn't feel right," Lainie says. "She knew down to her bones that her world had changed and she had received no explanation, nothing to grasp onto, to understand. I believe we have all felt similarly and we are all dealing with it in different ways. Ethan and Tante Padva both have their work to consume their time, to keep their minds occupied. I had not concerned myself with it at all for quite a while. I loved my sister dearly and I always will, but I think she made a mistake."

"I thought it was an accident," Celia says softly, looking down at the patterned tile on the table.

"No, before that. Her mistake was asking the wrong questions of the wrong people. It is not a mistake I plan on repeating."

"That's why you're here."

"That is why I am here," Lainie says. "How long have we known each other, Celia?"

"Over ten years."

"Surely by now you can trust me enough to tell me what it is that's really going on here. I doubt you'd dare to tell me it is nothing, or suggest I not trouble myself with such matters."

Celia places her glass on its saucer. She explains as best she can. She keeps the details vague, covering only the basic concept of the challenge, and how the circus functions as the venue. How certain people know more than others on every level, though she chooses not to name each individual and makes it clear that even she does not have all the answers.

Lainie says nothing, she listens carefully and occasionally sips her tea.

"How long has Ethan known?" she asks when Celia has finished.

"A very long time," Celia says.

Lainie nods and lifts her glass to her lips but instead of sipping her tea, she opens her fingers, releasing her grip.

The cup falls, crashing into the saucer below.

The glass shatters, the sound echoing through the room. The tea spills out over the tiles.

Before anyone turns at the noise, the cup has righted itself. The broken pieces re-form around the liquid and the glass sits intact, the tile surface of the table is dry.

Those who glanced over at their table at the noise assume it was their imagination, and return their attention to their own tea.

"Why didn't you stop it before it broke?" Lainie asks.

"I don't know," Celia says.

"If you ever need anything from me, I would like you to ask," Lainie says as she stands to leave. "I am tired of everyone keeping their secrets so well that they get other people killed. We are all involved in your game, and it seems we are not as easily repaired as teacups."

Celia sits alone for some time after Lainie departs, both cups of tea growing cold.

Stormy Seas

After the illusionist takes her bow and disappears before her rapt audience's eyes, they clap, applauding the empty air. They rise from their seats and some of them chatter with their companions, marveling over this trick or that as they file out the door that has reappeared in the side of the striped tent.

One man, sitting in the outer circle of chairs, remains in his seat as they leave. His eyes, almost hidden in the shadow cast by the brim of his bowler hat, are fixed on the space in the center of the circle that the illusionist occupied only moments before.

The rest of the audience departs.

The man continues to sit.

After a few minutes the door fades into the wall of the tent, invisible once more.

The man's gaze does not waver. He does not so much as glance at the vanishing door.

A moment later, Celia Bowen is sitting in front of him, turned to the side and resting her arms on the back of the chair. She is dressed as she had been during her performance, in a white gown covered in a pattern of unassembled puzzle pieces, falling together into darkness along the hem.

"You came to visit me," she says, unable to hide the pleasure in her voice.

"I had a few days," Marco says. "And you haven't been near London recently."

"We'll be in London in the autumn," Celia says. "It's become somewhat traditional."

"I couldn't wait that long to see you."

"It's good to see you, as well," Celia says softly. She reaches out and straightens the brim of his hat.

"Do you like the Cloud Maze?" he asks. He takes her hand in his as she lowers it.

"I do," she says, her breath catching as his fingers close over hers. "Did you persuade our Mr. Barris to help with that?"

"I did, indeed," Marco says, running his thumb along the inside of her wrist. "I thought I could use some assistance in getting the balance right. Besides, you have your Carousel and we share the Labyrinth, I thought it only fair that I have a Barris original of my own."

The intensity of his eyes and his touch rushes over Celia like a wave and she takes her hand from his before it pulls her under.

"Have you come to show me your own feats of illustrious illusion?" she asks.

"It was not on my agenda for the evening, but if you would like . . ."

"You already watched me, it would only be fair."

"I could watch you all night," he says.

"You have," Celia says. "You've been in every single audience this evening, I noticed."

She stands and walks to the center of the circle, turning so her gown swirls around her.

"I can see every seat," she says. "You are not hidden from me when you sit in the back row."

"I thought I would be too tempted to touch you if I sat in the front," Marco says, moving from his chair to stand at the edge of the circular performance space, just inside the first row of chairs.

"Am I close enough for your illusion?" she asks.

"If I say no, will you come closer?" he retaliates, not bothering to hide his grin.

In response, Celia takes another step toward him, the hem of her gown brushing over his shoes. Close enough for him to lift his arm and gently rest his hand on her waist.

"You didn't have to touch me last time," she remarks, but she does not protest.

"I thought I'd try something special," Marco says.

"Should I close my eyes?" Celia asks playfully, but instead of answering, he spins her around so she faces away from him, keeping his hand on her waist.

"Watch," he whispers in her ear.

The striped canvas sides of the tent stiffen, the soft surface hardening as the fabric changes to paper. Words appear over the walls, typeset letters overlapping handwritten text. Celia can make out snatches of Shakespearean sonnets and fragments of hymns to Greek goddesses as the poetry fills the tent. It covers the walls and the ceiling and spreads out over the floor.

And then the tent begins to open, the paper folding and tearing. The black stripes stretch out into empty space as their white counterparts brighten, reaching upward and breaking apart into branches.

"Do you like it?" Marco asks, once the movement settles and they stand within a darkened forest of softly glowing, poem-covered trees.

Celia can only nod.

He reluctantly releases her, following as she walks through the trees, reading bits of verse on branches and trunks.

"How do you come up with such images?" she asks, placing her hand over the layered paper bark of one of the trees. It is warm and solid beneath her fingers, illuminated from within like a lantern.

"I see things in my mind," Marco says. "In my dreams. I imagine what you might like."

"I don't think you're meant to be imagining how to please your opponent," Celia says.

"I have never fully grasped the rules of the game, so I am following my instincts instead," Marco says.

"My father is still purposefully vague about the rules," Celia says as they walk through the trees. "Particularly when I inquire as to when or how the verdict will be determined."

"Alexander also neglected to provide that information."

"I hope he does not pester you as much as my father does me," Celia says. "Though of course, my father has nothing better to do."

"I have hardly seen him in years," Marco says. "He has always been . . . distant and not terribly forthcoming, but he is the closest thing to family I have. And yet he tells me nothing."

"I'm rather jealous," Celia says. "My father constantly tells me what a disappointment I am."

"I refuse to believe you could ever disappoint anyone," Marco says.

"You never had the pleasure of meeting my father."

"Would you tell me what really happened to him?" Marco asks. "I'm quite curious."

Celia sighs before she begins, pausing beside a tree etched with words of love and longing. She has never told anyone this story, never been given the opportunity to relate it to anyone who would understand.

"My father was always somewhat overambitious," she starts. "What he meant to do, he did not accomplish, not as he intended. He wanted to remove himself from the physical world."

"How would that be possible?" Marco asks. Celia appreciates that he does not immediately dismiss the idea. She can see him trying to work it out in his mind and she struggles with the best way to explain it.

"Suppose I had a glass of wine," she says. A glass of red wine appears in her hand. "Thank you. If I took this wine and poured it into a basin of water, or a lake or even the ocean, would the wine itself be gone?"

"No, it would only be diluted," Marco says.

"Precisely," Celia says. "My father figured out a way to remove his glass." As she speaks, the glass in her hand fades, but the wine remains, floating in the air. "But he went straight for the ocean rather than a basin or even a larger glass. He has trouble pulling himself back together again. He can do it, of course, but with difficulty. Had he been content to haunt a single location, he would likely be more comfortable. Instead, the process left him adrift. He has to cling to things now. He haunts his town house in New York. Theaters he performed in often. He holds to me when he can, though I have learned how to avoid him when I wish to. He hates that, particularly because I am simply amplifying one of his own shielding techniques."

"Could it be done?" Marco asks. "What he was attempting? Properly, I mean."

Celia looks at the wine hovering without its glass. She raises a hand to touch it and it quivers, dividing into droplets and then coming back together.

"I believe it could," she says, "under the right circumstances. It would require a touchstone. A place, a tree, a physical element to hold on to. Something to prevent drifting. I suspect my father simply wanted the world at large to function as his, but I believe it would have to be more localized. To function as a glass but leave more flexibility to move within."

She touches the hovering wine again, pushing it toward the tree she stands beside. The liquid seeps into the paper, slowly saturating it until the entire tree glows a rich crimson in a forest of white.

"You're manipulating my illusion," Marco says, looking curiously at the wine-soaked tree.

"You're letting me," Celia says. "I wasn't certain I'd be able to."

"Could you do it?" Marco asks. "What he was attempting?"

Celia regards the tree thoughtfully for a moment before replying.

"If I had reason to, I think I could," she says. "But I am rather fond of the physical world. I think my father was feeling his age, which was much more advanced than it appeared, and did not relish the idea of rotting in the ground. He may have also wished to control his own destiny, but I cannot be certain, as he did not consult me before he attempted it. Left me with a lot of questions to answer and a funeral to fake. Which is easier than you might suppose."

"But he speaks with you?" Marco asks.

"He does, though not as often as he once did. He looks the same; I think it is an echo, his consciousness retaining the semblance of a physical form. But he lacks solidity and it vexes him terribly. He might have been able to stay more tangible had he done it differently. Though I'm not certain I'd want to be stuck in a tree for the rest of eternity, myself, would you?"

"I think that would depend on the tree," Marco says.

He turns to the crimson tree and it glows brighter, the red of embers shifting to the bright warmth of fire.

The surrounding trees follow suit.

As the light from the trees increases, it becomes so bright that Celia closes her eyes.

The ground beneath her feet shifts, suddenly unsteady, but Marco puts a hand on her waist to keep her upright.

When she opens her eyes, they are standing on the quarterdeck of a ship in the middle of the ocean.

Only the ship is made of books, its sails thousands of overlapping pages, and the sea it floats upon is dark black ink.

Tiny lights hang across the sky, like tightly packed stars bright as sun.

"I thought something vast would be nice after all the talk of confined spaces," Marco says.

Celia walks to the edge of the deck, running her hands along the spines of the books that form the rail. A soft breeze plays with her hair, bringing with it the mingling scent of dusty tomes and damp, rich ink.

Marco comes and stands next to her as she looks at the midnight sea that stretches out into a clear horizon with no land in sight.

"It's beautiful," she says.

She glances down at his right hand resting on the rail, frowning as she regards his bare, unmarked fingers.

"Are you looking for this?" he asks, moving his hand with a flourish. The skin shifts, revealing the scar that wraps around his ring finger. "It was made by a ring when I was fourteen. It said something in Latin, but I don't know what it was."

"*Esse quam videri*," Celia says. "To be, rather than to seem. It's the Bowen family motto. My father was very fond of engraving it on things. I'm not entirely sure he appreciated the irony. That ring was likely something like this one."

She places her right hand next to his, along the adjoining books. The silver band on her finger is engraved with what Marco had thought was an intricate filigree, but is the same phrase in a looping script.

Celia twists the ring, sliding it down her finger so he can see the matching scar.

"It is the only injury I have never been able to fully heal," she says.

"Mine was similar," Marco says, looking at her ring though his eyes keep moving to the scar instead. "Only it was gold. Yours was made by something of Alexander's?"

Celia nods.

"How old were you?" he asks.

"I was six years old. That ring was plain and silver. It was the first time I'd met someone who could do the things that my father did, though he seemed so very different from my father. He told me I was an angel. It was the loveliest thing anyone had ever said to me."

"It is an understatement," Marco says, placing his hand over hers.

A sudden breeze tugs at the layered paper sails. The pages flutter as the surface of the ink ripples below.

"You did that," Marco says.

"I didn't mean to," Celia says, but she does not take her hand away.

"I don't mind," Marco says, entwining his fingers with hers. "I can do that myself, you know."

The wind increases, sending waves of dark ink crashing into the ship. Pages fall from the sails, swirling around them like leaves. The ship begins to tilt and Celia almost loses her footing, but Marco puts his arms around her waist to steady her while she laughs.

"This is quite impressive, Mr. Illusionist," she says.

"Call me by my name," he says. He has never heard her speak his name and holding her in his arms he suddenly craves the sound. "Please," he adds when she hesitates.

"Marco," she says, her voice low and soft. The sound of his name on her tongue is even more intoxicating than he had imagined, and he leans in to taste it.

Just before his lips reach hers, she turns away.

"Celia," Marco sighs against her ear, filling her name with all the desire and frustration she feels herself, his breath hot on her neck.

"I'm sorry," she says. "I . . . I don't want to make this any more complicated than it already is."

He says nothing, keeping his arms around her, but the breeze begins to settle, the waves pounding against the ship become calm.

"I have spent a great deal of my life struggling to keep myself in control," Celia says, leaning her head against his shoulder. "To know myself inside and out, everything kept in perfect order. I lose that when I'm with you. That frightens me, and—"

"I don't want you to be frightened," Marco interrupts.

"It frightens me how much I like it," Celia finishes, turning her face back to his. "How tempting it is to lose myself in you. To let go. To let you keep me from breaking chandeliers rather than constantly worrying about it, myself."

"I could."

"I know."

They stand silently together as the ship drifts toward the endless horizon.

"Come away with me," Marco says. "Anywhere. Away from the circus, away from Alexander and your father."

"We can't," Celia says.

"Of course we can," Marco insists. "You and I together, we could do anything."

"No," Celia says. "We can only do anything here."

"I don't understand."

"Have you ever thought about it, about simply leaving? Really, truly thought about it with the intent to follow through and not as a dream or a passing fancy?" When he does not answer, she continues. "Think about it, right now. Picture us abandoning this place and this game and starting over together somewhere else, and mean it."

Marco closes his eyes and draws it out in his mind, focusing not on the wishful dream but on the practicalities. Planning out the smallest details, from organizing Chandresh's books for a new accountant to packing the suits in his flat, even down to the wedding bands on their fingers.

And then his right hand begins to burn, the pain sharp and searing, beginning at the scar around his finger and racing up his arm, blacking out every thought in his mind. It is the same pain from when the scar was made, increased a thousandfold.

The motion of the ship ceases instantly. The paper crumbles and the ocean of ink fades away, leaving only a circle of chairs inside a striped tent as Marco collapses to the floor.

The pain ebbs slightly when Celia kneels next to him and takes his hand.

"The night of the anniversary party," she says. "The night you kissed me. I thought it that night. I didn't want to play anymore, I only wanted to be with you. I thought I would ask you to run away with me and I meant it. The very moment I convinced myself that we could manage it, I was in so much pain I could barely stand. Friedrick didn't know what to make of me, he sat me in a quiet corner and held my hand and did not pry when I couldn't explain because that's how kind he is."

She looks down at the scar on Marco's hand as he struggles to catch his breath.

"I thought perhaps it was about you," she says. "So once I tried not boarding the train as it departed and that was just as painful. We are well and truly bound."

"You wanted to run away with me," Marco says, smiling despite the lingering pain. "I wasn't sure that kiss would be quite so effective."

"You could have made me forget, taken it out of my memory as easily as you did with everyone else at the party."

"That was not particularly easy," Marco says. "And I did not want you to forget it."

"I couldn't," Celia says. "How are you feeling?"

"Miserable. But the pain itself is fading. I told Alexander I wanted to quit that night. I must not have meant it. I only wanted a reaction from him."

"It is likely meant to make us think we are not caged," Celia says. "We cannot feel the bars unless we push against them. My father says it would be easier if we did not concern ourselves so with each other. Perhaps he is right."

"I've tried," Marco says, cupping her face in his hands. "I have tried to let you go and I cannot. I cannot stop thinking of you. I cannot stop dreaming about you. Do you not feel the same for me?"

"I do," Celia says. "I have you here, all around me. I sit in the Ice Garden to get a hint of this, this way that you make me feel. I felt it even before I knew who you were, and every time I think it could not possibly get any stronger, it does."

"Then what is stopping us from being together now?" he asks. He slides his hands down from her face, following the neckline of her gown.

"I want to," Celia says, gasping as his hands move lower. "Believe me, I want to. This is not only about you and me. There are so many people tangled up in this game. It's becoming more and more difficult to keep everything in order. And this"—she rests her hands over his— "this is extremely distracting. I worry what might happen if I lose my concentration."

"You don't have a power source," he says. She looks at him, confused.

"A power source?" she repeats.

"The way I use the bonfire, as a conduit. Borrowing energy from the fire. You don't have anything like that, you work only with yourself?"

"I don't know any other way," Celia says.

"You are constantly controlling the circus?" Marco asks.

Celia nods. "I am accustomed to it. Most of the time it is manageable."

"I can't imagine how exhausting that must be."

He kisses her softly on the forehead before letting her go, staying as close to her as he can without touching.

And then he tells her stories. Myths he learned from his instructor. Fantasies he created himself, inspired by bits and pieces of others read in archaic books with crackling spines. Circus concepts that would not fit in tents.

She responds with tales from her childhood spent in back rooms of theaters. Adventures in far-flung cities the circus has visited. She recounts events from her spiritualist days, delighted when he finds the endeavor as absurd as she had at the time.

They sit and talk until just before dawn, and he leaves her only when the circus is about to close.

Marco holds Celia to his chest for a moment before he stands, pulling her up with him.

He takes a card from his pocket that contains only the letter *M* and an address.

"I have been spending less time at Chandresh's residence," he says, handing her the card. "When I am not there, this is where you'll find me. You are welcome any time, day or night. Should you ever be in the mood for a distraction."

"Thank you," Celia says. She turns the card over in her fingers and it vanishes.

"When all of this is over, no matter which one of us wins, I will not let you go so easily. Agreed?"

"Agreed."

Marco takes her hand and brings it to his lips, kissing the silver ring that conceals her scar.

Celia traces the line of his jaw with her fingertips. Then she turns, disappearing before he can reach out to pull her back.

An Entreaty

The sheep are in a terrible mood today as Bailey attempts to usher them from one field to another. They have resisted prodding, swearing, and pushing, insisting that the grass in their current field is much nicer than the grass just on the other side of the gate in the low stone wall, no matter how much Bailey tries to persuade them otherwise.

And then there is a voice behind him.

"Hello, Bailey."

Poppet looks wrong, somehow, standing there on the opposite side of the wall. The daylight is too bright, the surroundings too mundane and green. Her clothes, even though they are her incognito-wear and not her circus costume, seem too fancy. Her skirt too ruffled for everyday wear; her boots, though dusty, too dainty and impractical for walking across a farm. She wears no hat, her red hair loose, whipping around her head in the wind.

"Hello, Poppet," he says once he recovers from his surprise. "What are you doing here?"

"I needed to talk to you about something," she says. "Ask you something, I mean."

"It couldn't wait until tonight?" Bailey asks. Meeting up with Poppet and Widget almost as soon as the circus opens each evening has become a nightly routine.

Poppet shakes her head.

"I thought it would be better to give you time to think about it," she says.

"Think about what?"

"Think about coming with us."

Bailey blinks at her. "What?" he manages to ask.

"Tonight is our last night here," she says. "And I want you to come with us when we leave."

"You're joking," Bailey says.

Poppet shakes her head.

"I'm not, I swear I'm not. I wanted to wait until I was sure it was the right thing to ask, the right thing to do, and I'm sure now. It's important."

"What do you mean? Important how?" Bailey asks.

Poppet sighs. She looks up, peering as though she is searching for the stars hidden behind the blue sky dotted with fluffy white clouds.

"I know you're supposed to come with us," she says. "I know that part for certain."

"But why? Why me? What would I do, just tag along? I'm not like you and Widget, I can't do anything special. I don't belong in the circus."

"You do! I'm certain that you do. I don't know why yet, but I'm sure you belong with me. With us, I mean." A scarlet blush creeps into her cheeks.

"I'd like to, I would. I just . . ." Bailey looks around at the sheep, at the house and the barn up on the hill lined with apple trees. It would either solve the argument of Harvard versus farm or make it much, much worse. "I can't just leave," he says, though it is not, he thinks, exactly what he means.

"I know," Poppet says. "I'm sorry. I shouldn't ask you to. But I think . . . No, I don't think, I know. I know that if you don't come with us we won't be back."

"Won't be back here? Why?"

"Won't be back anywhere," Poppet says. She raises her eyes to the sky again, scowling at it before she turns back to Bailey. "If you don't come with us, there won't be any more circus. And don't ask me why, they don't tell me why." She gestures at the sky, at the stars beyond the clouds. "They just say that in order for there to be a circus in the future, you need to be there. You, Bailey. You and me and Widge. I don't know why it's important that it's all three of us, but it is. If not, it will just crumble. It's already starting."

"What do you mean? The circus is fine."

"I'm not sure it's anything that's really noticeable from the outside. It's . . . If one of your sheep was sick, would I notice?"

"Probably not," Bailey says.

"But you would?" Poppet asks.

Bailey nods.

"That's how it is with the circus. I know how it's supposed to feel and it doesn't feel like that right now and it hasn't for a while. I can tell something's wrong and I can feel it crumbling like cake that doesn't have enough icing to hold it together but I don't know what it is. Does that make any sense?"

Bailey only stares at her, and she sighs before she continues.

"Remember the night we were in the Labyrinth? When we got stuck in the birdcage room?"

Bailey nods.

"I've never been stuck anywhere in the Labyrinth before. Never. If we can't find our way out of a room or a hall I can focus and I can feel where the doors are. I can tell what's behind them. I try not to do it because it's not any fun that way, but that night I did when we couldn't figure it out and it didn't work. It's starting to feel unfamiliar and I don't know what to do about it."

"But how can I do anything to help?" Bailey asks.

"You're the one who finally found the key, remember?" Poppet says. "I keep looking for answers, for the right thing to do, and nothing's been clear except for you. I know it's too much to ask to have you leave your home and your family, but the circus is my home and my family and I can't lose them. Not if there's something I can do to prevent it. I'm sorry."

She sits on the rock wall, facing away from him. Bailey sits next to her, still facing the field and the incorrigible sheep. They sit in silence for a while. The sheep wander in lazy circles, nibbling on the grass.

"Do you like it here, Bailey?" Poppet asks, looking out over the farm.

"Not particularly," Bailey says.

"Have you ever wished for someone to come and take you away?"

"Did Widge tell you that?" Bailey asks, wondering if the thought is so strong that it sits on him, evident and readable.

"No," Poppet says. "It was a guess. But Widge did ask me to give you this." She pulls a tiny glass bottle from her pocket and hands it to him.

Bailey knows that though the bottle appears empty it is likely not, and he is too curious not to open it immediately. He pulls out the minuscule stopper, relieved that it remains attached to the bottle with a curl of wire.

The sensation inside is so familiar, so comforting and recognizable and real that Bailey can feel the roughness of the bark, the smell of the acorns, even the chattering of the squirrels.

"He wanted you to be able to keep your tree with you," Poppet says. "If you decide to come with us."

Bailey replaces the stopper in the bottle. Neither of them speaks for some time. The breeze tugs at Poppet's hair.

"How long do I have to think about it?" Bailey asks quietly.

"We're leaving when the circus closes tonight," Poppet says. "The train will be ready before dawn, though it would be better if you could come earlier than that. Leaving can get a bit . . . complicated."

"I'll think about it," Bailey says. "But I can't promise anything."

"Thank you, Bailey," Poppet says. "Can you do me one favor, though? If you're not going to come with us, could you just not come to the circus tonight at all? And let this be goodbye? I think it would be easier."

Bailey stares at her blankly for a moment, her words not quite sinking in. This is even more horrible than the choice to leave. But he nods because it feels like the proper thing to do.

"All right," he says. "I won't come unless I'm going with you. I promise."

"Thank you, Bailey," Poppet says. She smiles, though he cannot tell if the smile is a happy one or not.

And before he can tell her to tell Widget goodbye for him if need be, she leans forward and kisses him, not on the cheek, as she has a handful of times before, but on the lips, and Bailey knows in that moment that he will follow her anywhere.

Poppet turns without a word and walks away. Bailey watches until he can no longer see her hair against the sky and then continues to stare after her, the tiny bottle clutched in his hand, still uncertain of how to feel or what to do and left with only hours to decide.

Behind him, the sheep, left to their own devices, decide to wander through the open gate into the field beyond.

Invitation

When the circus arrives in London, though Celia Bowen is tempted to go immediately to the address of Marco's flat, which is printed on the card she keeps on her person at all times, she goes instead to the Midland Grand Hotel.

She does not make any inquiries at the desk.

She does not speak to anyone.

She stands in the middle of the lobby, going unnoticed by the staff and guests that pass her on their way to other locations, other appointments, and other temporary places.

After she has stood for more than an hour, as still as one of the circus statues, a man in a grey suit approaches her.

He listens without reaction as she speaks, and when she is finished, he only nods.

She executes a perfect curtsey, and then she turns and leaves.

The man in the grey suit stands alone, unnoticed, in the lobby for some time.

Intersections I: The Drop of a Hat

The circus is always particularly festive on All Hallows' Eve. Round paper lanterns hang in the courtyard, the shadows dancing over their white surfaces like silently howling faces. Leather masks in white and black and silver with ribbon ties are set in baskets by the gates and around the circus for patrons to wear, should they wish. It is sometimes difficult to discern performer from patron.

It is an altogether different experience to wander through the circus anonymously. To blend in with the environment, becoming a part of the ambiance. Many patrons enjoy the experience immensely, while others find it disconcerting and prefer to wear their own faces.

Now the crowd has thinned considerably in these hours past midnight as the clock ticks its way into All Hallows' proper.

The remaining masked patrons wander like ghosts.

The line for the fortune-teller has dwindled down to nothing in these hours. Most people seek their fortunes early in the evening. The late of the night is suited for less cerebral pursuits. Earlier the querents filed in almost nonstop, but as October fades into November there is no one waiting in the vestibule, no one waiting behind the beaded curtain to hear what secrets the cards have to tell.

And then the beaded curtain parts, though she heard no one approach.

What Marco comes to tell her should not be a shock. The cards have been telling her as much for years but she refused to listen, choosing to see only the other possibilities, the alternate paths to be taken.

Hearing it from his own lips is another thing entirely. As soon as he speaks the words, a forgotten memory finds its way to the front of her mind. Two green-clad figures in the center of a vibrant ballroom, so undeniably in love that the entire room flushes with heat.

She asks him to draw a single card. The fact that he consents surprises her.

That the card he draws is *La Papessa* does not.

When he leaves, Isobel removes her sign for the evening.

She sometimes removes her sign early, or for periods of time when she is tired from reading or in need of a respite. Often she spends this time with Tsukiko, but instead of seeking out the contortionist this particular evening, she sits alone at her table, shuffling her tarot deck compulsively.

She flips one card faceup, then another and another.

There are only swords. Lines of them in pointed rows. Four. Nine. Ten. The single sharp ace.

She pushes them back into a pile.

She abandons the cards and turns to something else instead.

She keeps the hatbox under her table. It is the safest place she could think of, the easiest for her to access. Often she forgets it is even there, concealed beneath the cascading velvet. Always suspended between her and her querents. A constant unseen presence.

Now she reaches beneath the table and draws it out from velvet shadows into the flickering candlelight.

The hatbox is plain and round, covered in black silk. It has no latch or hinge, its lid kept in place by two ribbons, one black and one white, that are tied in careful knots.

Isobel places the box upon the table and brushes a thick layer of dust off the top, though much of it still sticks to the knotted ribbons. She hesitates, and thinks for a moment that it would be better to leave it alone, to return it to its resting place. But it does not seem to matter any longer.

She unties the ribbons slowly, working the knots out with her fingernails. When they are loosened enough for her to remove the lid, she pulls it off gingerly, as though she fears what she might find inside.

Inside the box is a hat.

It is just as she left it. An old black bowler hat, showing some wear around the brim. It is tied with more black and white ribbons, wrapped like a present in light and dark bows. Beneath the knots of the ribbon there is a single tarot card. Between the hat and the card there is a folded white lace handkerchief, its edges embroidered with looping black vines.

They were such simple things. Knots and intent.

She had laughed through her lessons, much preferring her cards. They seemed so straightforward in comparison, despite their myriad meanings.

It was only a precaution. Precautions are wise in such unpredictable circumstances. No stranger than bringing along an umbrella for a walk on a day that feels like rain, even if the sun is shining brightly.

Though she cannot be certain it is doing much more than gathering dust, not really. She has no way to be sure, no barometer on which to measure such insubstantial things. No thermometer for chaos. At the moment, it feels like she is pushing against an empty void.

Isobel lifts the hat carefully from the box, the long ends of the ribbons spilling in a waterfall around it. It is oddly pretty, for being an old hat and a handkerchief and a card tied up in fraying ribbon. Almost festive.

"The smallest charms can be the most effective," Isobel says, taken aback when her voice catches, almost on the brink of tears.

The hat does not reply.

"I don't think you're having any effect at all," Isobel says.

Again, the hat has no reply.

She had only wanted to keep the circus balanced. To prevent two conflicting sides from causing damage to each other or their surroundings.

To keep the scales from breaking.

Over and over in her mind, she sees them together in the ballroom.

She remembers snatches of an overheard argument. Marco saying he had done everything for *her*, a statement she had not understood at the time and forgotten soon after.

But now it is clear.

All the emotion in the cards when she would try to read about him, it was all for Celia.

The circus itself, all for her. For every beautiful tent he creates, she builds one in return.

And Isobel herself has been helping to keep it balanced. Helping him. Helping them both.

She looks down at the hat in her hands.

White lace caressing black wool, ribbons intertwined. Inseparable.

Isobel tears at the ribbons with her fingers, pulling at the bows in a sudden fury.

The handkerchief floats down like a ghost, the initials C.N.B. legible amongst the embroidered vines.

The tarot card falls to the ground, landing faceup. The image of an angel is emblazoned on it, the word *Tempérance* is lettered beneath.

Isobel stops, holding her breath. Expecting some repercussion, some result from the action. But everything is quiet. The candles flicker around her. The beaded curtain hangs still and calm. She suddenly feels silly and stupid, alone in her tent with a pile of tangled ribbon and an old hat. She thinks herself a fool for believing she could have any impact on such things. That anything she ever did mattered at all.

She reaches down to retrieve the fallen card, but her hand freezes just above it when she hears something. For a split second it sounds like the squealing brakes of a train.

It takes a moment for Isobel to realize that the noise coming from outside the tent is actually the sound of Poppet Murray screaming.

Darkest Before the Dawn

Poppet and Widget stand by the circus gates, just out of the way of the ticket booth, though the line for tickets has waned in the late hour. The star-filled tunnel has already been removed, replaced by a single striped curtain. The *Wunschtraum* clock strikes three times behind them. Widget munches on a bag of chocolate-covered popcorn.

"Wufju fay foo im?" he asks, with his mouth mostly full.

"I tried to explain as much as I could," Poppet says. "I think I made an analogy about cake."

"Well, that must have worked," Widget says. "Who doesn't like a good cake analogy?"

"I'm not sure I made any sense. I think he was most upset that I asked him not to come tonight if he wasn't going to leave with us. I didn't know what else to say, I just tried to make sure he understood it was important." Poppet sighs, leaning against the iron fence. "And I kissed him," she adds.

"I know," Widget says.

Poppet glares at him, her face blushing almost as red as her hair.

"I didn't mean to," Widget says with a shrug. "You're not hiding it well at all. You should practice more if you don't want me to see things. Didn't Celia teach you how to do that?"

"Why is your sight getting better and mine's getting worse?" Poppet asks.

"Luck?"

Poppet rolls her eyes.

"Did you talk to Celia?" she asks.

"I did. I told her you said Bailey was supposed to come with us. All she said was that she wouldn't do anything to prevent it."

"Well, that's something."

"She's distracted," Widget says, shaking his bag of popcorn. "She won't tell me anything, and she barely listened to me when I tried to explain what we were asking. I could have told her we wanted to bring a flying hippopotamus along to keep as a pet and she would have said that was fine. But Bailey's not coming just for fun, is he?"

"I don't know," Poppet says.

"What do you know?"

Poppet looks up at the night sky. Dark clouds cover most of the stars but pockets of them slide into view, twinkling softly.

"Remember when we were on the Stargazer and I saw something bright but I couldn't tell what it was?"

Widget nods.

"It was the courtyard. The entire courtyard, not just the bonfire. Bright and burning and hot. Then . . . I don't know what happened but Bailey was there. That much I'm sure of."

"And this is going to happen soon?" Widget asks.

"Very soon, I think."

"Should we kidnap him?"

"Really, Widge."

"No, really. We could do it. We can sneak into his house and hit him with something heavy and drag him back here as inconspicuously as possible. We can prop him up and people will think he's a town drunk. He'll be on the train before he's conscious, and then he really won't have a choice. Quick and painless. Well, painless for us. Save for the heavy lifting, that is."

"I don't think that's really the best idea, Widge," Poppet says.

"Oh, c'mon, it'll be fun," Widget says.

"I don't think so. I think we already did whatever it was we were supposed to do, and now we have to wait."

"Are you sure about that?" Widget asks.

"No," Poppet says quietly.

After a while Widget goes off in search of something else to eat and Poppet waits by the gates alone, occasionally glancing over her shoulder to check the time on the clock behind her.

Intersections II: Scarlet Furies and Red Destinies

Though any night at the circus can rightfully be called magical," Herr Friedrick Thiessen once wrote, "All Hallows' Eve is something special. The air itself crackles with mystery."

This particular Hallowe'en night is cold and crisp. The boisterous crowd is clothed in heavy coats and scarves. Many of them wear masks, faces lost in swatches of black and silver and white.

The light in the circus is dimmer than usual. The shadows seem to creep from every corner.

Chandresh Christophe Lefèvre enters the circus without notice. He picks up a silver mask from a basket by the gates and slips it over his face. The woman in the ticket booth does not recognize him when he pays his admission in full.

He wanders through the circus like a man in a dream.

The man in the grey suit does not wear a mask. He walks leisurely, with a calm, almost lazy gait. He has no particular destination in mind, wandering from tent to tent. Some he enters, others he passes by. He purchases a cup of tea and stays in the courtyard, watching the bonfire for a while before wandering back into the paths amongst the tents.

He has never attended the circus before, and he appears to be enjoying himself.

Chandresh follows him, every move, every stop. Pursues him through tents and watches him pay for his tea in the courtyard. He stares at the ground near the man in the grey suit's feet, looking for his shadow, though he is thwarted by the ever-shifting light.

Other than Chandresh, no one pays him any notice. Passersby do not look at him, not even a glance is spared despite his height and his pristine grey suit and top hat. Even the girl who sells him tea barely registers him, turning quickly to her next customer. He slides through the circus like a shadow. He carries a silver-tipped cane that he does not use.

Chandresh loses him in the crowd more than once, the grey falling into a blur of black and white dotted with color from the patrons. It never takes him long to spot the grey top hat again, but in the intervals between he becomes nervous to the point of shaking, fidgeting with his coat and the contents of his pockets.

Chandresh mutters to himself. Those that pass by him close enough to hear look at him strangely and make an effort to avoid him.

Following Chandresh is a young man he would not recognize even if he were to look him in the eye, but still the man keeps his distance. Chandresh's attention remains only on the man in the grey suit, and it does not once wander to this other man who bears a passing resemblance to his assistant.

Marco keeps a steady grey-green eye on Chandresh, wearing no mask on a face only Celia would recognize, and the illusionist is otherwise occupied.

This goes on for quite some time. Mr. A. H— tours the circus leisurely. He visits the fortune-teller, who does not recognize him but lays his future out in polite rows of cards, though she admits that bits of it are overlapping and confusing. He watches the illusionist perform. She acknowledges his presence with a single, subtle nod. He tours the Hall of Mirrors, countless figures in matching grey suits and top hats accompanying him. He rides the Carousel. He appears particularly fond of the Ice Garden.

Chandresh follows him from tent to tent, waiting outside the ones he does not enter, drenched in ever-increasing anxiety.

Marco loses track of both of them only briefly, when he takes a few moments to attend to another matter.

The clock by the gates ticks off the minutes later and later, the ornaments upon it twirling and shifting.

October slips into November, a change that goes largely unnoticed other than by those standing closest to the clock.

The crowd grows thinner. Masks are returned to the baskets in the courtyard and by the gates, jumbled piles of empty eyes and ribbons. Children are dragged away with promises that they may return the next evening, though the circus will not be there the next evening and later those children will feel slighted and betrayed.

In a passage near the back of the circus, which is somewhat wide and filled with only a handful of patrons, Mr. A. H— stops. Chandresh watches him from a short distance away, unable to see clearly why he has halted, though he might be conversing with someone. Through his mask, Chandresh sees only the still grey suit, the hovering top hat. He sees an open target with nothing standing in between.

He hears the echo of a voice assuring him that the man is not real. A figment of his imagination. Nothing but a dream.

Then there is a pause. For just a moment, time slows like something falling while fighting with gravity. The chill breeze that has circled through the open paths of the circus stops. In that moment nothing flutters, not the fabric of the tents or the ribbon ties of dozens of masks.

In the tallest tent, one of the acrobats loses her perfect balance, falling some distance before one of her fellow performers catches her, only narrowly avoiding crashing to the ground.

In the courtyard, the bonfire sputters and sparks in a sudden cloud of black smoke, causing those patrons closest to it to jump back, coughing.

The kitten that leaps through the air from Poppet's hands to her brother's suddenly twists in the air, landing on its back rather than its feet and rolling toward Widget with an indignant howl.

The illusionist pauses, her seamless performance halted as she stands frozen, her face suddenly deathly pale. She sways as though she might faint, and several attentive audience members move to assist her but she does not fall.

Marco crumples as though punched in the stomach by an invisible assailant. A passing patron catches his arm to steady him.

And Chandresh Christophe Lefèvre pulls the heavy silver knife from his coat pocket and throws it without hesitation.

The knife flies from Chandresh's hand, blade over handle, spinning in perfect revolutions through the air.

Its aim is precise and steady. As true as such things can be.

Then its target moves.

The tailored grey wool that makes up the back of Mr. A. H—'s suit shifts. He moves ever so slightly to the side. It is a graceful step. An unconscious gesture. A movement of weight in space.

And so the knife brushes by his sleeve, and comes to rest instead in the chest of the man he is speaking with. The blade sliding through his unbuttoned black coat easily, hitting his heart as though it had always been its intended target, the silver handle jutting out just beneath his crimson scarf.

Mr. A. H— catches Herr Friedrick Thiessen as he slumps forward.

Chandresh stares at his empty hand as though he cannot recall what he was holding moments before. He staggers off, wandering back in the direction of the bonfire courtyard. He forgets to remove his mask when he leaves, and when he finds it discarded in his town house the next day, he cannot remember where it came from.

Mr. A. H— lowers Herr Thiessen to the ground, speaking a constant string of words over him in tones too low for anyone to overhear. The scattered patrons around them notice nothing at first, though some are distracted by the fact that the two young performers a few feet away have suddenly ceased their show, the boy in the black suit gathering up the visibly agitated kittens.

After a long moment, Mr. A. H— stops speaking and passes a grey-gloved hand over Herr Friedrick Thiessen's face, gently closing his surprised eyes.

The silence that follows is shattered by Poppet Murray's screaming as the pool of blood on the ground spreads beneath her white boots.

Before the shock turns into chaos, Mr. A. H— gently removes the silver-handled knife from Herr Thiessen's chest and then he stands and walks away.

As he passes by a baffled, still-unsteady Marco, he hands him the blood-covered knife without so much as a word or a glance before disappearing into the crowd.

The handful of patrons who witness the event are ushered quickly away. Later they assume it was a clever stunt. A touch of theatricality for the already festive evening.

THE POOL OF TEARS

The sign outside this tent is accompanied by a small box full of smooth black stones. The text instructs you to take one with you as you enter.

Inside, the tent is dark, the ceiling covered with open black umbrellas, the curving handles hanging down like icicles.

In the center of the room there is a pool. A pond enclosed within a black stone wall that is surrounded by white gravel.

The air carries the salty tinge of the ocean.

You walk over to the edge to look inside. The gravel crunches beneath your feet.

It is shallow, but it is glowing. A shimmering, shifting light cascades up through the surface of the water. A soft radiance, enough to illuminate the pool and the stones that sit at the bottom. Hundreds of stones, each identical to the one you hold in your hand. The light beneath filters through the spaces between the stones.

Reflections ripple around the room, making it appear as though the entire tent is underwater.

You sit on the wall, turning your black stone over and over in your fingers.

The stillness of the tent becomes a quiet melancholy.

Memories begin to creep forward from hidden corners of your mind. Passing disappointments. Lost chances and lost causes. Heartbreaks and pain and desolate, horrible loneliness.

Sorrows you thought long forgotten mingle with still-fresh wounds.

The stone feels heavier in your hand.

When you drop it in the pool to join the rest of the stones, you feel lighter. As though you have released something more than a smooth polished piece of rock.

Farewell

Bailey climbs the oak tree to retrieve his hidden box before sunset, gazing down at the circus that sits bathed in deep orange light, casting long pointed shadows across the field. But when he opens it, he does not find anything he truly wishes to take with him.

He removes only Poppet's white glove, placing it in his coat pocket, and returns the box to the tree.

At home, he counts out his life savings, which is a higher amount than he had expected, and packs a change of clothes and an extra sweater. He considers packing a spare pair of shoes but decides he can likely borrow some from Widget if need be. He shoves everything into a worn leather satchel and waits for his parents and Caroline to go to bed.

While he waits, he unpacks his bag and then packs it again, second-guessing his choices of what to bring and what to leave behind.

He waits an hour after he is certain everyone is asleep, and then another hour for good measure. Though he has become rather proficient at slipping in at abnormal hours, sneaking out is a different matter.

When he finally creeps down the hallway, he is surprised how late it is. His hand is on the door, ready to leave, when he turns around, putting his bag down and quietly searching for a piece of paper.

Once he locates one, he sits down at the table in the kitchen to write a note to his parents. He explains as best he can his reasons for going and hopes they will understand. He does not mention Harvard or anything about the future of the farm.

He remembers when he was very small his mother once said she wished happiness and adventure for him. If this does not count as adventure, he is not sure what does.

"What are you doing?" a voice behind him asks.

Bailey turns to find Caroline standing in the doorway in her nightgown, her hair piled on her head in a spiky mess of pin curls and a knitted blanket pulled around her shoulders.

"Nothing you need to concern yourself with," he says, turning back to his writing. He signs the letter and folds it, leaving it propped upright in the center of the table, next to a wooden bowl full of apples. "Make sure they read that."

"Are you running away?" Caroline asks, glancing at his bag.

"Something like that."

"You can't possibly be serious," she says with a yawn.

"I'm not sure when I'll be back. I'll write when I can. Tell them not to worry about me."

"Bailey, go back to bed."

"Why don't you go back to bed, Caroline? You look like you could use some more beauty rest."

In response, Caroline only twists her face up in a sneer.

"Besides," Bailey continues, "when have you ever cared what I do?"

"You have been acting like a baby all week," Caroline says, raising her voice but keeping it a hissing whisper. "Playing at that stupid circus, staying out all night. Grow up, *Bailey*."

"That is precisely what I'm doing," Bailey says. "I don't care if you don't understand that. Staying here won't make me happy. It will make you happy because you are insipid and boring, and an insipid, boring life is enough for you. It's not enough for me. It will never be enough for me. So I'm leaving. Do me a favor and marry someone who will take decent care of the sheep."

He takes an apple from the bowl and tosses it in the air, catching it and tucking it in his bag before he bids Caroline goodbye with a cheerful wave and nothing more.

He leaves her standing by the table with her mouth opening and closing in silent rage as he closes the door quietly behind him.

Bailey walks away from the house buzzing with energy. He almost expects Caroline to come after him, or to immediately wake their parents and alert them to his departure. But with each step he takes away from the house it becomes more clear that he is truly leaving, with nothing left to stop him.

The walk feels longer in the stillness of the night, no crowds of people heading to the circus along his route as there have been every other evening, when he raced to arrive before the opening of the gates.

The stars are still out when Bailey reaches his oak tree, his bag slung over his shoulder. He is later than he'd wanted to be, though dawn is some time away.

But beneath the starry sky, the field that stretches out below his tree is empty, as though nothing has ever occupied the space but grass and leaves and fog.

Retrospect

The man in the grey suit slips easily through the crowd of circus patrons. They step out of the way without even considering the movement, parting like water as he heads toward the gates.

The figure that blocks his path near the edge of the courtyard is transparent, appearing like a mirage in the glow of the bonfire and the gently swaying paper lanterns. The man in the grey suit halts, though he could easily continue on through his colleague's apparition unimpeded.

"Interesting evening, isn't it?" Hector asks him, drawing curious stares from the nearby patrons.

The man in the grey suit subtly moves the fingers of one gloved hand, as though turning the page of a book, and the staring ceases, curious eyes becoming unfocused, their attention drawn to other sights.

The crowd continues by, moving to and from the gates without noticing either gentleman.

"It's not worth the bother," Hector scoffs. "Half these people expect to see a ghost around every corner."

"This has gotten out of hand," the man in the grey suit says. "This venue was always too exposed."

"That's what makes it *fun*," Hector says, waving an arm over the crowd. His hand passes through a woman's shoulder and she turns, surprised, but continues walking when she sees nothing. "Did you not use enough of your concealment techniques, even after ingratiating yourself with Chandresh to control the venue?"

"I control nothing," the man in the grey suit says. "I established a protocol of secrecy disguised as an air of mystery. My counsel is the reason this venue moves from location to location unannounced. It benefits both players."

"It keeps them apart. If you'd put them together properly from the beginning, she would have broken him years ago."

"Has your current state made you blind? You were a fool to trap yourself like that, and you are a fool if you cannot see that they are each besotted with the other. If they had not been kept apart it simply would have happened sooner."

"You should have been a damned matchmaker," Hector says, his narrowed eyes vanishing and reappearing in the undulating light. "I have trained my player better than that."

"And yet she came to me. She invited me here personally, as you—" He stops, a figure in the crowd catching his eye.

"I thought I told you to choose a player you could tolerate losing," Hector says, watching the way his companion gazes after the distressed young man in the bowler hat who passes by without noticing either of them, pursuing Chandresh through the throng of patrons. "You always grow too attached to your students. Unfortunate how few of them ever realize that."

"And how many of your own students have chosen to end the game themselves?" the man in the grey suit asks, turning back. "Seven? Will your daughter be the eighth?"

"That is not going to happen again," Hector responds, each word sharp and heavy despite his insubstantial form.

"If she wins, she will hate you for it if she does not already."

"She will win. Do not try to avoid the fact that she is a stronger player than yours and always has been."

The man in the grey suit lifts a hand in the direction of the bonfire, amplifying the sound that echoes from beyond the courtyard so that Hector can hear his daughter, repeating Friedrick's name over and over in increasing panic.

"Does that sound like strength to you?" he asks, dropping his hand and letting Celia's voice blend into the din of the crowd.

Hector only scowls, the flames of the bonfire further distorting his expression.

"An innocent man died here tonight," the man in the grey suit continues. "A man your player was quite fond of. If she had not already begun to break, this will do it. Was that what you meant to accomplish here? Have you learned nothing after so many competitions? There is never any way to predict what will come to pass. No guarantees on either side."

"This isn't over yet," Hector says, vanishing in a blur of light and shadow.

The man in the grey suit walks on as though he had not paused, making his way through the curtains of velvet that separate the courtyard from the world outside.

He watches the clock by the gates for some time before he departs the circus.

Beautiful Pain

Marco's flat was once plain and spare but now it is crowded with an assortment of mismatched furniture. Pieces that Chandresh became bored with at one point or another and were adopted into this purgatory instead of being discarded entirely.

There are too many books and not enough shelves to hold them, so they sit piled on antique Chinese chairs and sari-wrapped cushions.

The clock on the mantel is a Herr Thiessen creation, adorned with tiny books flipping through their pages as the seconds tick toward three o'clock in the morning.

The larger books on the desk are moving at a less steady pace as Marco goes back and forth between handwritten volumes, scrawling notes and calculations on loose sheets of paper. Over and over he crosses out symbols and numbers, discards books in favor of others, and then returns to the discarded ones again.

The door of the flat opens of its own volition, locks falling open and hinges swinging wildly. Marco jumps from his desk, spilling a bottle of ink across his papers.

Celia stands in the doorway, stray curls escaping her upswept hair. Her cream-colored coat hangs unbuttoned, too light for the weather.

Only when she moves into the room, the door closing automatically and locking with a series of clicks behind her, does Marco notice that beneath her coat her gown is covered with blood.

"What happened?" he asks, the hand that had been moving to right the bottle of ink halting in midair.

"You know perfectly well what happened," Celia says. Her voice is calm but already the ripples are beginning to form in the dark surface of the ink pooled on the desk.

"Are you all right?" Marco asks, trying to move closer to her.

"I most certainly am not all right," Celia says, and the bottle of ink shatters, raining ink over the papers and splattering Marco's white shirt-sleeves, falling into invisibility on his black vest. His hands are covered in ink but he is still distracted by the blood on her gown, scarlet scream-ing across the ivory satin and vanishing behind the black velvet fretwork that covers it like a cage.

"Celia, what did you do?" he asks.

"I tried," Celia says. Her voice breaks on the word so that she has to repeat herself. "I tried. I thought I might be able to fix it. I've known him so long. That maybe it would be like setting a clock to make it tick again. I knew exactly what was wrong but I couldn't make it right. He was so familiar but it . . . it didn't work."

The sob that has been building in her chest escapes. Tears that she has been holding back for hours fall from her eyes.

Marco rushes across the room to reach her, pulling her close and holding her while she cries.

"I'm sorry," he says, repeating it in a litany over her sobs until she calms, the tension easing in her shoulders as she relaxes into his arms.

"He was my friend," she says quietly.

"I know," Marco says, wiping away her tears and leaving smudges of ink across her cheeks. "I am so sorry. I don't know what happened. Something threw off the balance and I cannot figure out what it was."

"It was Isobel," Celia says.

"What?"

"The charm Isobel put over the circus, over you and me. I knew about it, I could feel it. I didn't think it was doing much of anything but apparently it was. I don't know why she chose tonight to stop."

Marco sighs.

"She chose tonight because I finally told her that I love you," he says. "I should have done it years ago, but I told her tonight instead. I thought she took it well but clearly I was wrong. I haven't the slightest idea what Alexander was doing there."

"He was there because I invited him," Celia says.

"Why would you do that?" Marco asks.

"I wanted a verdict," she says, tears springing to her eyes again. "I wanted this to be over so I could be with you. I thought if he came to see the circus that a winner could be determined. I don't know how else they expect it to be settled. How did Chandresh know he would be there?"

"I don't know. I don't even know what possessed him to go there, and he insisted that I not accompany him so I followed him instead, to keep an eye on him. I only lost track of him for minutes when I went to speak with Isobel and by the time I caught up with him again . . ."

"Did you feel as though you had the ground removed from beneath you as well?" Celia asks.

Marco nods.

"I was trying to protect Chandresh from himself," he says. "I had not even considered he might be a danger to anyone else."

"What is all this?" Celia asks, turning her attention to the books on the desk. They contain endless pages of glyphs and symbols, ringed in text ripped from other sources, affixed to one another and inscribed over and over. In the middle of the desk there is a large leather volume. Pasted inside the front cover, surrounded by an elaborately inscribed tree, Celia can barely make out something that must once have been a newspaper clipping. The only word she can discern is *transcendent*.

"This is how I work," Marco says. "That particular volume is the one which binds everyone in the circus. It's the safeguard, for lack of a better term. I placed a copy of it in the bonfire before the lighting, but I've made adjustments to this one."

Celia turns through the pages of names. She pauses at a page that holds a scrap of paper bearing the looping signature of Lainie Burgess, next to a space where an equal-sized piece has been removed, leaving only a bright blank void.

"I should have put Herr Thiessen in there," Marco says. "I never even thought of it."

"If it had not been him it would have been another patron. There is no way to protect everyone. It's impossible."

"I am sorry," he says again. "I did not know Herr Thiessen as well as you, but I did admire him and his work."

"He showed me the circus in a way I had not been able to see it before," Celia says. "How it looked from the outside. We wrote letters to each other for years."

"I would have written you, myself, if I could put down in words everything I want to say to you. A sea of ink would not be enough."

"But you built me dreams instead," Celia says, looking up at him. "And I built you tents you hardly ever see. I have had so much of you around me always and I have been unable to give you anything in return that you can keep."

"I still have your shawl," Marco says.

She smiles softly while she closes the book. Beside it, the spilled ink seeps back into its jar, the glass fragments reforming around it.

"I think this is what my father would call working from the outside in rather than the inside out," she says. "He was always cautioning against it."

"Then he would despise the other room," Marco says.

"What room?" Celia asks. The bottle of ink settles as though it had never been broken.

Marco beckons her forward, leading her to the adjoining room. He opens the door but does not step through it, and when Celia follows him she can see why.

It may once have been a study or a parlor, not a large room, but perhaps it could be referred to as cozy were it not for the layers of paper and string that hang from every available surface.

Strings hang from the chandelier and loop over to the tops of shelves. They tie back upon each other like a web cascading from the ceiling.

On every surface, tables and desks and armchairs, there are meticulously constructed models of tents. Some made from newsprint, others from fabric. Bits of blueprints and novels and stationery, folded and cut and shaped into a flock of striped tents, all tied together with more string in black and white and red. They are bound to bits of clockwork, pieces of mirror, stumps of dripping candles.

In the center of the room, on a round wooden table that is painted black but inlaid with light stripes of mother-of-pearl, there is a small iron cauldron. Inside it a fire burns merrily, the flames bright and white, casting long shadows across the space.

Celia takes a step into the room, ducking to avoid the strings that hang from the ceiling. The sensation is identical to entering the circus, even down to the scent of caramel lingering in the air, but there is something deeper beneath it, something heavy and ancient underlying the paper and string.

Marco stays in the doorway as Celia navigates carefully around the room, mindful of the sweep of her gown as she peers into the tiny tents and runs her fingers delicately over the bits of string and clockwork.

"This is very old magic, isn't it?" she asks.

"It's the only kind I know," Marco responds. He tugs a string by the doorway and the movement reverberates throughout the room, the entire model circus sparkling as bits of metal catch the firelight. "Though I doubt it was ever meant for this purpose."

Celia pauses at a tent containing a tree branch covered in candle wax. Orienting herself from there, she locates another, gently pushing open the paper door to find a ring of tiny chairs representing her own performance space.

The pages that comprise it are printed with Shakespearean sonnets.

Celia lets the paper door swing closed.

She finishes her tentative tour around the room and rejoins Marco in the doorway, pulling the door closed softly behind her.

The sensation of being within the circus fades as soon as she has crossed the threshold, and she is suddenly acutely aware of everything in the adjoining room. The warmth of the fire fighting against the draft from the windows. The scent of Marco's skin beneath the ink and his cologne.

"Thank you for showing me that," she says.

"I take it your father would not approve?" Marco asks.

"I don't particularly care what my father approves of any longer."

Celia wanders past the desk and stops in front of the fireplace, watching the miniature pages turning through time on the clock upon the mantel.

Next to the clock there sits a solitary playing card. The two of hearts. It bears no sign that it was once pierced with an Ottoman dagger. No evidence that Celia's blood has ever marred its surface, but she knows that it is the same card.

"I could speak with Alexander," Marco suggests. "Perhaps he saw enough to provide a verdict, or this will result in some sort of disqualification. I'm certain he thinks me a disappointment at this point, he could declare you the win—"

"Stop," Celia says without turning. "Please, stop talking. I don't want to talk about this damned game."

Marco attempts to protest but his voice catches in his throat. He struggles against it but finds he is unable to speak.

His shoulders fall in a silent sigh.

"I am tired of trying to hold things together that cannot be held," Celia says when he approaches her. "Trying to control what cannot be controlled. I am tired of denying myself what I want for fear of breaking things I cannot fix. They will break no matter what we do."

She leans against his chest and he wraps his arms around her, gently stroking the back of her neck with an ink-stained hand. They stay like this for some time, alongside the crackling of the fire and the ticking of the clock.

When she lifts her head, he keeps his eyes locked on hers as he slides her coat from her shoulders, resting his hands on her bare arms.

The familiar passion that always accompanies the touch of his skin against hers washes over Celia and she can no longer resist it, no longer wants to.

"Marco," she says, her fingers fumbling with the buttons on his vest. "Marco, I—"

His lips are on hers, hot and demanding, before she can finish.

While she undoes button after button, he pulls blindly at fastenings and ribbons, refusing to take his lips from hers.

The meticulously constructed gown collapses into a puddle around her feet.

Wrapping the unbound laces of her corset around his wrists, Marco pulls her down to the floor with him.

They continue to remove layer after layer until nothing separates them.

Trapped in silence, Marco traces apologies and adorations across Celia's body with his tongue. Mutely expressing all the things he cannot speak aloud.

He finds other ways to tell her, his fingers leaving faint trails of ink in their wake. He savors every sound he elicits from her.

The entire room trembles as they come together.

And though there are a great many fragile objects contained within it, nothing breaks.

Above them, the clock continues to turn its pages, pushing stories too minuscule to read ever onward.

*

MARCO DOES NOT REMEMBER FALLING ASLEEP. One moment Celia is curled in his arms, her head resting against his chest as she listens to his heart beating, and the next he is alone.

The fire has died down to smoldering embers. The grey dawn creeps in through the windows, casting soft shadows.

Upon the two of hearts on the mantel, there sits a silver band engraved in Latin. Marco smiles, slipping Celia's ring onto his pinkie, alongside the scar on his ring finger.

He does not notice until later that the leather-bound safeguard that had been on his desk is gone.

Part IV

INCENDIARY

There are tents, I am certain, that I have not discovered in my many visits to the circus. Though I have seen a great deal of the sights, traveled a number of the available paths, there are always corners that remain unexplored, doors that remain unopened.

—FRIEDRICK THIESSEN, 1896

Technicalities

Celia wishes she could freeze time as she listens to the steady beat of Marco's heart against the ticking of the clock. To stay forever within this moment, curled in his arms, his hands softly stroking her back. To not have to leave.

She only succeeds in slowing Marco's heartbeat enough that he falls deeply asleep.

She could wake him, but already the sky outside is brightening, and she dreads the thought of saying goodbye.

Instead, she kisses him gently on the lips and quietly dresses as he sleeps. She takes her ring from her finger and leaves it on the mantel, resting between the two hearts emblazoned on the playing card.

She pauses as she puts on her coat, looking at the books scattered across the desk.

Perhaps if she better understood his systems, she could use them to make the circus more independent. To take some of the weight off of herself. Allowing them to be together for more than a few stolen hours, without challenging the rules of the game.

It is the best gift she can think to give him, if they are unable to force a verdict from either of their instructors.

She picks up the volume filled with names. It seems a good place to start as she understands the basis of what it is meant to accomplish.

She takes it with her as she leaves.

Celia closes the door to Marco's flat as quietly as she can after she slips out into the darkened hall, the leather-bound book tucked under her arm. The locks slide into place behind her with a series of soft, muffled clicks.

She does not notice the figure concealed in the nearby shadows until he speaks.

"You deceitful little slut," her father says.

Celia shuts her eyes, attempting to concentrate, but it has always been difficult to push him away once he has grabbed ahold of her, and she cannot manage it.

"I'm surprised you waited in the hall to call me that, Papa," she says.

"This place is so well protected it's downright absurd," Hector says, waving at the door. "Nothing could get in without that boy explicitly wanting it there."

"Good," Celia says. "You can stay away from him, and you can stay away from me."

"What are you doing with that?" he asks, gesturing at the book under her arm.

"Nothing to concern yourself with," Celia says.

"You cannot interfere with his work," Hector says.

"I know, interference is one of the very few things that is apparently against the rules. I do not intend to interfere, I intend to learn his systems so I can stop having to constantly manage so much of the circus."

"His systems. *Alexander's* systems are nothing you should be bothering with. You have no idea what you're doing. I overestimated your ability to handle this challenge."

"This is the game, isn't it?" Celia asks. "It's about how we deal with the repercussions of magic when placed in a public venue, in a world that does not believe in such things. It's a test of stamina and control, not skill."

"It is a test of strength," Hector says. "And you are weak. Weaker than I'd thought."

"Then let me lose," she says. "I'm exhausted, Papa. I cannot do this any longer. It's not as though you can gloat over a bottle of whiskey once a winner is declared."

"A winner is not *declared*," her father says. "The game is played out, not stopped. You should have figured that much out by now. You used to be somewhat clever."

Celia glares at him, but at the same time she begins turning over his words in her mind, collecting the obscure non-answers about the rules he has given her over the years. Suddenly the shape of the elements he has always avoided becomes more distinct, the key unknown factor clear.

"The victor is the one left standing after the other can no longer endure," Celia says, the scope of it finally making devastating sense.

"That is a gross generalization but I suppose it will suffice."

Celia turns back to Marco's flat, pressing her hand against the door.

"Stop behaving as though you love that boy," Hector says. "You are above such mundane things."

"You are willing to sacrifice me for this," she says quietly. "To let me destroy myself just so you can attempt to prove a point. You tied me into this game knowing the stakes, and you let me think it was nothing but a simple challenge of skill."

"Don't look at me like that," he says, "as if you think me inhuman."

"I can see through you," Celia snaps. "It is not particularly trying on my imagination."

"It would not be any different if I were still as I was when this started."

"And what happens to the circus after the game?" Celia asks.

"The circus is merely a venue," he says. "A stadium. A very festive coliseum. You could continue on with it after you win, though without the game it serves no purpose."

"I suppose the other people involved serve no purpose as well, then?" Celia asks. "Their fates are only a matter of consequence?"

"All actions have repercussions," Hector says. "That's part of the challenge."

"Why are you telling me all this now when you have never mentioned it before?"

"Before, I had not thought you were in the position to be the one to lose."

"You mean the one to die," Celia says.

"A technicality," her father says. "A game is completed only when there is a single player left. There is no other way to end it. You can abandon any misguided dreams of continuing to play whore to that *nobody* Alexander plucked out of a London gutter after this is over."

"Who is left, then?" Celia asks, ignoring his comment. "You said Alexander's student won the last challenge, what happened to him?"

A derisive laugh shudders through the shadows before Hector replies.

"*She* is bending herself into knots in your precious circus."

The only illumination in this tent comes from the fire. The flames are a radiant, flickering white, like the bonfire in the courtyard.

You pass a fire-eater elevated on a striped platform. He keeps small bits of flame dancing atop long sticks while he prepares to swallow them whole.

On another platform, a woman holds two long chains, with a ball of flame at the end of each. She swings them in loops and circles, leaving glowing trails of white light in their paths, moving so quickly that they look like strings of fire rather than single flames on lengths of chain.

Performers on multiple platforms juggle torches, spinning them high into the air. Occasionally, they toss these flaming torches to each other in a shower of sparks.

Elsewhere, there are flaming hoops perched at different levels that performers slip in and out of with ease, as though the hoops were only metal and not encased in flickering flames.

The artist on this platform holds pieces of flame in her bare hands, and she forms them into snakes and flowers and all manner of shapes. Sparks fly from shooting stars, birds flame and disappear like miniature phoenixes in her hands.

She smiles at you as you watch the white flames in her hand become, with the deft movement of her fingers, a boat. A book. A heart of fire.

月子

The train is unremarkable as it chugs across the countryside, puffing clouds of grey smoke into the air. The engine is almost entirely black. The cars it pulls are equally as monochromatic. Those with windows have glass that is tinted and shadowed; those without are dark as coal.

It is silent as it travels, no whistles or horns. The wheels on the track are not screeching but gliding smoothly and quietly. It passes almost unnoticed along its route, making no stops.

From the exterior, it appears to be a coal train, or something similar. It is utterly unremarkable.

The interior is a different story.

Inside, the train is opulent, gilded, and warm. Most of the passenger cars are lined with thick patterned carpets, upholstered in velvets in burgundies and violets and creams, as though they have been dipped in a sunset, hovering at twilight and holding on to the colors before they fade to midnight and stars.

There are lights in sconces lining the corridors, cascades of crystals falling from them and swaying with the motion of the train. Soothing and serene.

Shortly after its departure, Celia places the leather-bound book safely away, camouflaged in plain sight amongst her own volumes.

She changes from her bloodstained gown to a flowing one in moonlight grey, bound with ribbons in black, white, and charcoal, which had been one of Friedrick's particular favorites.

The ribbons drift behind her as she makes her way down the train.

She stops at the only door that has two calligraphed characters as well as a handwritten name on the tag next to it.

Her polite knock is answered immediately, inviting her inside.

While most of the train compartments are saturated with color, Tsukiko's private car is almost completely neutral. A bare space surrounded by paper screens and curtains of raw silk, perfumed with the scent of ginger and cream.

Tsukiko sits on the floor in the center of the room, wearing a red kimono. A beating crimson heart in the pale chamber.

And she is not alone. Isobel lies on the floor with her head in Tsukiko's lap, sobbing softly.

"I did not mean to interrupt," Celia says. She hesitates in the doorway, ready to slide the door closed again.

"You are not interrupting," Tsukiko says, beckoning her inside. "Perhaps you will be able to help me convince Isobel that she is in need of some rest."

Celia says nothing, but Isobel wipes her eyes, nodding as she stands.

"Thank you, Kiko," she says, smoothing out the wrinkles in her gown. Tsukiko remains seated, her attention on Celia.

Isobel stops next to Celia as she makes her way to the door.

"I am sorry about Herr Thiessen," she says.

"I am as well."

For a moment, Celia thinks Isobel means to embrace her, but instead she only nods before leaving, sliding the door closed behind her.

"The last hours have been long for all of us," Tsukiko says after Isobel has departed. "You need tea," she adds before Celia can explain why she is there. Tsukiko sits her down on a cushion and walks silently to the end of the car, fetching her tea supplies from behind one of the tall screens.

It is not the full tea ceremony that she has performed on several occasions over the years, but as Tsukiko slowly prepares two bowls of green matcha, it is beautiful and calming nonetheless.

"Why did you never tell me?" Celia asks when Tsukiko has settled herself across from her.

"Tell you what?" Tsukiko asks, smiling over her tea.

Celia sighs. She wonders if Lainie Burgess felt a similar frustration over two different cups of tea in Constantinople. She has half a mind to break Tsukiko's tea bowl, just to see what she would do.

"Did you injure yourself?" Tsukiko asks, nodding at the scar on Celia's finger.

"I was bound into a challenge almost thirty years ago," Celia says. She sips her tea before adding, "Are you going to show me your scar, now that you have seen mine?"

Tsukiko smiles and places her tea on the floor in front of her. Then she turns and lowers the neck of her kimono.

At the nape of her neck, in the space between a shower of tattooed symbols, nestled in the curve of a crescent moon, there is a faded scar about the size and shape of a ring.

"The scars last longer than the game, you see," Tsukiko says, straightening her kimono around her shoulders.

"It was one of my father's rings that did that," Celia says, but Tsukiko does not confirm or deny the statement.

"How is your tea?" she asks.

"Why are you here?" Celia counters.

"I was hired to be a contortionist."

Celia puts down her tea.

"I am not in the mood for this, Tsukiko," she says.

"Should you choose your questions more carefully, you may receive more satisfying answers."

"Why did you never tell me you knew about the challenge?" Celia asks. "That you had played before yourself?"

"I made an agreement that I would not reveal myself unless approached directly," Tsukiko says. "I keep my word."

"Why did you come here, in the beginning?"

"I was curious. There has not been a challenge of this sort since the one I participated in. I did not intend to stay."

"Why did you stay?"

"I liked Monsieur Lefèvre. The venue for my challenge was a more intimate one, and this seemed unique. It is rare to discover places that are truly unique. I stayed to observe."

"You've been watching us," Celia says.

Tsukiko nods.

"Tell me about the game," Celia says, hoping to get a response to an open-ended inquiry now that Tsukiko is more forthcoming.

"There is more to it than you think," Tsukiko says. "I did not understand the rules myself, in my time. It is not only about what you call magic. You believe adding a new tent to the circus is a move? It is more than that. Everything you do, every moment of the day and night is a move. You carry your chessboard with you, it is not contained within canvas and stripes. Though you and your opponent do not have the luxury of polite squares to stay upon."

Celia considers this while she sips her tea. Attempting to reconcile the fact that everything that has happened with the circus, with Marco, has been part of the game.

"Do you love him?" Tsukiko asks, watching her with thoughtful eyes and the hint of a smile that might be sympathetic, but Celia has always found Tsukiko's expressions difficult to decipher.

Celia sighs. There seems no good reason to deny it.

"I do," she says.

"Do you believe he loves you?"

Celia does not answer. The phrasing of the question bothers her. Only hours ago, she was certain. Now, sitting in this cave of lightly perfumed silk, what had seemed constant and unquestionable feels as delicate as the steam floating over her tea. As fragile as an illusion.

"Love is fickle and fleeting," Tsukiko continues. "It is rarely a solid foundation for decisions to be made upon, in any game."

Celia closes her eyes to keep her hands from shaking.

It takes longer for her to regain her control than she would like.

"Isobel once thought he loved her," Tsukiko continues. "She was certain of it. That is why she came here, to assist him."

"He does love me," Celia says, though the words do not sound as strong when they fall from her lips as they did inside her head.

"Perhaps," Tsukiko replies. "He is quite skilled at manipulation. Did you not once lie to people yourself, telling them only what they wished to hear?"

Celia is not certain which is worse. The knowledge that for the game to end, one of them will have to die, or the possibility that she means nothing to him. That she is only a piece across a board. Waiting to be toppled and checkmated.

"It is a matter of perspective, the difference between opponent and partner," Tsukiko says. "You step to the side and the same person can be either or both or something else entirely. It is difficult to know which face is true. And you have a great many factors to deal with beyond your opponent."

"Did you not?" Celia asks.

"My venue was not as grand. It involved fewer people, less movement. Without the challenge within it, there was nothing to salvage. Most of it is now a tea garden, I believe. I have not returned to that place since the challenge concluded."

"The circus could continue, after this challenge is . . . concluded," Celia says.

"That would be nice," Tsukiko says. "A proper tribute to your Herr Thiessen. Though it would be complicated, making it completely independent from you and your opponent. You have taken on a great deal of responsibility for all of this. You are vital to its operation. If I stabbed a knife in your heart right now, this train would crash."

Celia puts down her tea, watching as the smooth motion of the train sends soft ripples through the surface of the liquid. In her head, she calculates how long it would take to halt the train, how long she might be able to keep her heart beating. She decides it would likely depend on the knife.

"Possibly," she says.

"If I were to extinguish the bonfire, or its keeper, that would also be problematic, yes?"

Celia nods.

"You have work to do if you expect this circus to endure," Tsukiko says.

"Are you offering to help?" Celia asks, hoping she will be able to aid in translating Marco's systems, as they shared the same instructor.

"No," Tsukiko says with a polite shake of her head, her smile softening the harshness of the word. "If you are unable to manage it properly yourself, I will step in. This has gone on too long already, but I shall give you some time."

"How much time?" Celia asks.

Tsukiko sips her tea.

"Time is something I cannot control," she says. "We shall see."

They sit in meditative silence for some of that uncontrollable time, the motion of the train gently billowing the silk curtains, the scent of ginger and cream enveloping them.

"What happened to your opponent?" Celia asks.

Tsukiko looks not at Celia but down at her tea as she responds.

"My opponent is now a pillar of ash standing in a field in Kyoto," she says. "Unless wind and time have taken her away."

Escapement

Bailey walks circles around the empty field for some time before he can convince himself that the circus is well and truly gone. There is nothing at all, not so much as a bent blade of grass, to indicate that anything had occupied the space hours before.

He sits down on the ground, holding his head in his hands and feeling utterly lost though he has played in these very fields ever since he was little.

He recalls Poppet mentioning a train.

A train would have to travel to Boston in order to reach any far-flung destination.

Within moments of the thought crossing his mind, Bailey is on his feet, running as fast as he can toward the depot.

There are no trains to be seen when he gets there, out of breath and aching from where his bag has been hitting against his back. He had been hoping that somehow the circus train he was not even entirely certain existed would still be there, waiting.

But instead the depot is all but deserted; only two figures sit on one of the benches on the platform, a man and a woman in black coats.

It takes Bailey a moment to realize that they are both wearing red scarves.

"Are you all right?" the woman asks as he runs up to the platform. Bailey cannot quite place her accent.

"Are you here for the circus?" Bailey says, gasping for breath.

"Indeed we are," the man says with a similar lilting accent. "Though it has departed, I trust you have noticed."

"Closed early as well, but that is not unusual," the woman adds.

"Do you know Poppet and Widget?" Bailey asks.

"Who?" the man asks. The woman tilts her head as though she did not catch the meaning of the question.

"They're twins, they do a show with kittens," Bailey explains. "They're my friends."

"The twins!" the woman exclaims. "And their wonderful cats! However did you come to be friends with them?"

"It's a long story," Bailey says.

"Then you should tell it to us while we wait," she says with a smile. "You are off to Boston as well, yes?"

"I don't know," Bailey says. "I was trying to follow the circus."

"That is precisely what we are doing," the man says. "Though we cannot follow Le Cirque until we know where it has gone. That should take about a day."

"I do hope it turns up somewhere manageable," the woman says.

"How will you know where it is?" Bailey asks, in a state of mild disbelief.

"We *rêveurs* have our methods," the woman says, smiling. "We have awhile yet to wait, that should be plenty of time to exchange stories."

The man's name is Victor, his sister is Lorena. They are on what they call an extended circus holiday, following Le Cirque des Rêves around to as many locations as they can manage. They normally do this only within Europe, but for this particular holiday they have decided to chase it around the other side of the Atlantic. They had been in Canada previously.

Bailey tells them a shortened version of how he came to be friends with Poppet and Widget, leaving out the more curious details.

As it creeps closer to dawn they are joined by another *rêveur*, a woman named Elizabeth who had been staying at the local inn and is headed to Boston as well now that the circus has departed. She is greeted warmly, and they appear to be old friends though Lorena says they only met her a few days ago. While they wait for the train Elizabeth takes out her knitting needles and a skein of deep red wool.

Lorena introduces Bailey to her as a scarf-less young *rêveur*.

"I'm not a *rêveur*, really," Bailey says. He is still not entirely sure he grasps the meaning of the term.

Elizabeth looks at him over her knitting, sizing him up with narrowed eyes that remind him of his sternest teachers, though he stands much taller than she does. She leans forward in a conspiratorial manner.

"Do you adore Le Cirque des Rêves?" she asks him.

"Yes," he says without hesitation.

"More than anything in the world?" she adds.

"Yes," Bailey says. He cannot keep himself from smiling despite her serious tone and the nerves that are still keeping his heart from beating at a steady rate.

"Then you are a *rêveur*," Elizabeth pronounces. "No matter what you wear."

They tell him stories of the circus and of other *rêveurs*. How there is a society of sorts that keeps track of the movement of the circus, notifying other *rêveurs* so they might travel from destination to destination. Victor and Lorena have followed the circus as often as their schedules allow for years, while Elizabeth typically only makes excursions closer to New York and this trip is an extended one for her, though there is an informal club of *rêveurs* based in the city that holds gatherings from time to time, to keep in touch while the circus is away.

The train arrives shortly after the sun has fully risen, and on the way to Boston the stories continue, while Elizabeth knits and Lorena props her head up sleepily on her arm.

"Where are you staying in town?" Elizabeth inquires.

Bailey has not considered this, as he has been taking this endeavor one step at a time, attempting not to worry about what might happen once they reach Boston.

"I'm not entirely sure," he says. "I'll probably stay at the station until I know where to go next."

"Nonsense," Victor says. "You shall stay with us. We have nearly an entire floor at the Parker House. You can have August's room, he went back to New York yesterday and I never bothered to alert the management that we have an unoccupied room."

Bailey attempts to argue but Lorena stops him.

"He is terribly stubborn," she whispers. "He will not take no for an answer once he has set his mind to something."

And indeed, Bailey is swept into their carriage almost as soon as they step off the train. His bag is taken along with Elizabeth's luggage when they reach the hotel.

"Is something wrong?" Lorena asks as he openly stares around the opulent lobby.

"I feel like one of those girls in fairy tales, the ones who don't even have shoes and then somehow get to attend a ball at the castle," Bailey whispers, and she laughs so loudly that several people turn and stare.

Bailey is escorted to a room half the size of his entire house but he finds he cannot sleep, despite the heavy curtains blocking out the sunlight. He paces the room until he begins worrying about damaging the carpet, and then he sits in the window instead, watching the people below.

He is relieved when there is a knock at the door midafternoon.

"Do you know where the circus is yet?" he asks, before Victor can even speak.

"Not yet, dear boy," he says. "We sometimes have advance notice of where it is headed but not as of late. I imagine we will have word by the end of the day, and if our luck holds we will depart first thing in the morning. Do you have a suit?"

"Not with me," Bailey says, remembering the suit packed in a trunk at home that was only ever pulled out for special occasions. He guesses he has likely outgrown it in the interim, unable to recall exactly what the last suit-worthy occasion was.

"We shall get you one, then," Victor says, as though this is as simple a thing as picking up a newspaper.

They meet Lorena in the lobby and the two of them drag him around town on a number of errands, including a stop at a tailor for his suit.

"No, no," Lorena says while they look at samples. "These are entirely wrong for his coloring. He needs a grey. A nice deep grey."

After a great deal of pinning and measuring, Bailey ends up with a nicer suit than he has ever owned in his life, nicer even than his father's best suit, in a charcoal grey. Despite his protestations Victor also buys him very shiny shoes and a new hat.

The reflection in the mirror looks so different from the one he is accustomed to that Bailey has difficulty believing it is really him.

They return to the Parker House with a multitude of packages in tow, stopping by their rooms for hardly enough time to sit before Elizabeth comes to take them down to dinner.

To Bailey's surprise, there are almost a dozen *rêveurs* waiting in the restaurant downstairs, some who will be following the circus and others who are remaining in Boston. His anxiety at the fanciness of the restaurant is eased by the casual, boisterous manner of the group. True to form, they are clad almost entirely in black and white and grey with bright touches of red on ties or handkerchiefs.

When Lorena realizes that Bailey has no red, she surreptitiously removes a rose from a nearby floral arrangement to tuck in his lapel.

There are endless stories from the circus related over each course, mentions of tents Bailey has never seen and countries he has never even heard of. Bailey mostly listens, still rather astounded that he has stumbled upon a group of people who love the circus as much as he does.

"Do you . . . do you think anything is wrong with the circus?" Bailey asks quietly, when the table has fallen into separate conversations. "Recently, I mean?"

Victor and Lorena glance at each other as though gauging who should respond, but it is Elizabeth who answers first.

"It has not been the same since Herr Thiessen died," she says. Victor frowns suddenly while Lorena nods in agreement.

"Who is Herr Thiessen?" Bailey asks. The three of them look somewhat surprised by his ignorance.

"Friedrick Thiessen was the first of the *rêveurs*," Elizabeth says. "He was a clockmaker. He made the clock inside the gates."

"That clock was made by someone outside the circus? Really?" Bailey asks. It is not something he had ever thought to ask Poppet and Widget about. He had assumed it was a thing born of the circus itself. Elizabeth nods.

"He was a writer as well," Victor says. "That is how we met him, years and years ago. Read an article he wrote about the circus and sent him a letter and he wrote back and so on. That was before we were even called *rêveurs*."

"He made me a clock that looks like the Carousel," Lorena says, looking wistful. "With little creatures that loop through clouds and silver gears. It is a wonderful thing, I wish I could carry it around with me. Though it is nice to have a reminder of the circus I can keep at home."

"I heard he had a secret romance with the illusionist," Elizabeth remarks, smiling over her glass of wine.

"Gossip and nonsense," Victor scoffs.

"He did always sound very fond of her in his writing," Lorena says, as though she is considering the possibility.

"How could anyone not be fond of her?" Victor asks. Lorena turns to look at him curiously. "She is extremely talented," he mumbles, and Bailey catches Elizabeth trying not to laugh.

"And the circus isn't the same without this Herr Thiessen?" Bailey asks, wondering if this has something to do with what Poppet had told him.

"It is different without him, for us, of course," Lorena says. She pauses thoughtfully before she continues. "The circus itself seems a bit different as well. Nothing in particular, only something . . ."

"Something off-kilter," Victor interjects. "Like a clock that is not oscillating properly."

"When did he die?" Bailey asks. He cannot bring himself to ask how.

"A year ago tonight, as a matter of fact," Victor says.

"Oh, I had not realized that," Lorena says.

"A toast to Herr Thiessen," Victor proposes, loud enough for the entire table to hear, and he raises his glass. Glasses are lifted all around the table, and Bailey raises his as well.

The stories of Herr Thiessen continue through dessert, interrupted only by a discussion about why the cake is called a pie when it is clearly cake. Victor excuses himself after finishing his coffee, refusing to weigh in on the cake issue.

When he returns to the table, he has a telegram in his hand.

"We are headed to New York, my friends."

Impasse

After the illusionist takes her bow and disappears before her rapt audience's eyes, they clap, applauding the empty air. They rise from their seats and some of them chatter with their companions, marveling over this trick or that as they file out the door that has reappeared in the side of the striped tent.

One man, sitting in the inner circle of chairs, remains in his seat as they leave. His eyes, almost hidden in the shadow cast by the brim of his bowler hat, are fixed on the space in the center of the circle that the illusionist occupied only moments before.

The rest of the audience departs.

The man continues to sit.

After a few minutes, the door fades into the wall of the tent, invisible once more.

The man's gaze does not waver. He does not so much as glance at the vanishing door.

A moment later, Celia is sitting in a chair across the circle from him, still dressed as she had been during her performance, in a black gown covered with delicate white lace.

"You usually sit in the back," she says.

"I wanted a better view," Marco says.

"You came quite a ways to be here."

"I had to take a holiday."

Celia looks down at her hands.

"You didn't expect me to come all this way, did you?" Marco asks.

"No, I did not."

"It's difficult to hide when you travel with an entire circus, you know."

"I have not been hiding," Celia says.

"You have," Marco says. "I tried to speak with you at Herr Thiessen's funeral, but you left before I could find you, and then you took the circus across the ocean. You've been avoiding me."

"It was not entirely intentional," Celia says. "I needed some time to think. Thank you for the Pool of Tears," she adds.

"I wanted you to have a place where you felt safe enough to cry if I could not be with you."

She closes her eyes and does not reply.

"You stole my book," Marco says after a moment.

"I'm sorry," she says.

"As long as it is somewhere safe it does not matter whether I keep it or you do. You could have asked. You could have said goodbye."

Celia nods.

"I know," she says.

Neither of them speaks for some time.

"I am trying to make the circus independent," Celia says. "To untie it from the challenge, from us. From me. I needed to learn your system to make it work properly. I cannot let a place that is so important to so many people fade away. Something that is wonder and comfort and mystery all together that they have nowhere else. If you had that, wouldn't you want to keep it?"

"I have that whenever I'm with you," Marco says. "Let me help you."

"I don't need your help."

"You cannot do this alone."

"I have Ethan Barris and Lainie Burgess," Celia says. "They have agreed to assume management for the basic operation. With a little more training, Poppet and Widget should be able to handle the manipulation aspects that Ethan and Lainie cannot manage. I . . . I do not need you."

She cannot look him in the eye.

"You don't trust me," he says.

"Isobel trusted you," Celia says, looking at the ground. "So did Chandresh. How can I believe that you are honest with me and not with them, when I am the one you have the most reason to deceive?"

"I never once told Isobel that I loved her," Marco says. "I was young and I was desperately lonely, and I should not have let her think I felt more strongly than I did, but what I felt for her is nothing compared to what I feel for you. This is not a tactic to deceive you; do you think me that cruel?"

Celia rises from her chair.

"Good night, Mr. Alisdair," she says.

"Celia, wait," Marco says, standing but not moving closer to her. "You are breaking my heart. You told me once that I reminded you of your father. That you never wanted to suffer the way your mother did for him, but you are doing exactly that to me. You keep leaving me. You leave me longing for you again and again when I would give anything for you to stay, and it is killing me."

"It has to kill one of us," Celia says quietly.

"What?" Marco asks.

"The one who survives is the victor," she says. "The winner lives, the loser dies. That's how the game ends."

"That—" Marco stops, shaking his head. "That cannot be the intent of this."

"It is," Celia says. "It is a test of endurance, not skill. I'm attempting to make the circus self-sufficient before . . ."

She cannot say the words, still barely able to look at him.

"You're going to do what your father did," Marco says. "You're going to take yourself off the board."

"Not precisely," she says. "I suppose I was always more my mother's daughter."

"No," Marco says. "You cannot mean that."

"It's the only way to stop the game."

"Then we'll continue playing."

"I can't," she says. "I can't keep holding on. Every night it becomes more difficult. And I . . . I have to let you win."

"I don't want to *win*," Marco says. "I want *you*. Truly, Celia, do you not understand that?"

Celia says nothing, but tears begin to roll down her cheeks. She does not wipe them away.

"How can you think that I don't love you?" Marco asks. "Celia, you are everything to me. I don't know who is trying to convince you otherwise, but you must believe me, please."

She only looks at him with tear-soaked eyes, the first time she has held his gaze steadily.

"This is when I knew I loved you," he says.

They stand on opposite sides of a small, round room painted a rich blue and dotted with stars, on a ledge around a pool of jewel-toned cushions. A shimmering chandelier hangs above them.

"I was enchanted from the moment I first saw you," Marco says, "but this is when I knew."

The room around them changes again, expanding into an empty ballroom. Moonlight filters in through the windows.

"This is when I knew," Celia says, her voice a whisper echoing softly through the room.

Marco moves to close the distance between them, kissing away her tears before catching her lips with his own.

As he kisses her, the bonfire glows brighter. The acrobats catch the light perfectly as they spin. The entire circus sparkles, dazzling every patron.

And then the immaculate cohesion stops as Celia reluctantly breaks away.

"I'm sorry," she says.

"Please," Marco says, refusing to let her go, his fingers holding tightly to the lace of her gown. "Please don't leave me."

"It's too late," she says. "It was too late by the time I arrived in London to turn your notebook into a dove; there were too many people already involved. Anything either of us does has an effect on everyone here, on every patron who walks through those gates. Hundreds if not thousands of people. All flies in a spiderweb that was spun when I was six years old and now I can barely move for fear of losing someone else."

She looks up at him, lifting her hand to stroke his cheek.

"Will you do something for me?" she asks.

"Anything," Marco says.

"Don't come back," she says, her voice breaking.

She vanishes before Marco can protest, as simply and elegantly as at the end of her act, her gown fading beneath his hands. Only her perfume lingers in the space she occupied moments before.

Marco stands alone in an empty tent with nothing but two rings of chairs and an open door, waiting for him to leave.

Before he departs, he takes a single playing card from his pocket and places it on her chair.

Visitations

C elia Bowen sits at a desk surrounded by piles of books. She ran out of space for her library some time ago, but instead of making the room larger she has opted to let the books become the room. Piles of them function as tables, others hang suspended from the ceiling, along with large golden cages holding several live white doves.

Another round cage, sitting on a table rather than hanging from above, contains an elaborate clock. It marks both time and astrological movements as it ticks steadily through the afternoon.

A large black raven sleeps uncaged alongside the complete works of Shakespeare.

Mismatched candles in silver candelabras, burning in sets of three, surround the desk in the center of the room. Upon the desk itself there is a slowly cooling cup of tea, a scarf that has been partially unraveled into a ball of crimson yarn, a framed photograph of a deceased clockmaker, a solitary playing card long separated from its deck, and an open book filled with signs and symbols and signatures procured from other pieces of paper.

Celia sits with a notebook and pen, attempting to decipher the system the book is written in.

She tries to think the way she imagines Marco might have as he wrote it, picturing him inscribing each page, rendering the delicate ink branches of the tree that winds throughout the book.

She reads each signature over and over, checking how securely each lock of hair is pasted, scrutinizing each symbol.

She has spent so much time repeating this process that she could recreate the book from memory, but she still does not fully comprehend how the system works.

The raven stirs and caws at something in the shadows.

"You're bothering Huginn," Celia says, without looking up.

The candlelight catches only the edges of her father's form as he hovers nearby. Highlighting the creases of his jacket, the collar of his shirt. Glinting in the hollows of his dark eyes.

"You should really get another one," he says, peering at the agitated raven. "A Muninn to complete the set."

"I prefer thought to memory, Papa," Celia says.

"Hrmph" is the only response.

Celia ignores him as he leans over her shoulder, watching her flip through the inscribed pages.

"This is a god-awful mess," he says.

"A language you cannot speak yourself is not necessarily a god-awful mess," Celia says, transcribing a line of symbols into her notebook.

"This is messy work, bindings and charms," Hector says, floating to the other side of the desk to get a better look. "Very much Alexander's style, overly complicated and covert."

"Yet with enough study anyone could do it. Quite the contrast to all your lectures about how I was special."

"You are special. You are beyond this"—he waves a transparent hand over the pile of books—"this use of tools and constructs. There is so much more you could accomplish with your talents. So much more to explore."

"'There are more things in heaven and earth, Horatio, than are dreamt of in your philosophy,'" Celia quotes at him.

"Please, no Shakespeare."

"I am haunted by the ghost of my father, I think that should allow me to quote *Hamlet* as much as I please. You used to be quite fond of Shakespeare, Prospero."

"You are too intelligent for this behavior. I expected more of you."

"I apologize for not living up to your absurd expectations, Papa. Don't you have anyone else to bother?"

"There are very few people I can converse with in this state. Alexander is dreadfully boring, as always. Chandresh was interesting enough but that boy has altered his memory so many times that it's not much better than talking to myself. Though it might be nice for a change of scenery."

"You talk to Chandresh?" Celia asks.

"Occasionally," Hector says, inspecting the clock as it turns within its cage.

"You told Chandresh that Alexander was going to be at the circus that night. You sent him there."

"I made a suggestion to a drunk. Drunks are highly suggestible. And nicely accepting of conversations with dead people."

"You must have known he could do nothing to Alexander," Celia says. The reasoning makes no sense, not that her father's reasoning often does.

"I thought the old man could use a knife in the back for a change. That student of his was practically screaming to do it himself, so much so that the idea of it was already in Chandresh's head, all of that rage sneaking into his subconscious from being exposed to it over time. All I had to do was give him a push in the right direction."

"You said there was a rule about interference," Celia says, placing down her pen.

"Interfering with you or your opponent," her father clarifies. "I can interfere with anyone else as much as I please."

"Your *interfering* got Friedrick killed!"

"There are other clockmakers in the world," Hector says. "You could find a new one if you are in need of additional timepieces."

Celia's hands are shaking as she picks up a volume from the pile of Shakespeare and hurls it at him. *As You Like It* passes through his chest without pause, hitting the wall of the tent beyond and falling to the ground. The raven caws, ruffling its feathers.

The cages around the doves and the clock begin to quiver. The glass over the framed photograph cracks.

"Go away, Papa," Celia says through clenched teeth, trying to control herself.

"You cannot keep pushing me away," he says.

Celia turns her attention to the candles on the desk, concentrating on a single dancing flame.

"You think you are making personal connections with these people?" Hector continues. "You think you mean anything to them? They are all going to die eventually. You are letting your emotions trump your power."

"You are a coward," Celia says. "You are both cowards. You fight by proxy because you are too cowardly to challenge each other directly. Afraid that you will fail and have nothing to blame except yourselves."

"That is not true," Hector protests.

"I hate you," Celia says, still staring at the candle flame.

The shadow of her father shudders and vanishes.

*

THERE IS NO FROST UPON THE WINDOWS of Marco's flat, so he inscribes lines of symbols in the shape of a letter *A* with ink, pressing his darkened fingers against the panes. The ink drips down over the glass like rain.

He sits staring at the door, twisting the silver ring around his finger in anxious circles until the knock comes early the next morning.

The man in the grey suit does not admonish him for calling. He stands in the hall outside the door with his hands on his cane and waits for Marco to speak.

"She thinks one of us has to die in order for the game to end," Marco says.

"She is correct."

Having the confirmation is worse than Marco had expected. The small glimmer of hope he had held that she might be mistaken is crushed in three simple words.

"To win would be worse than losing," he says.

"I did inform you that your feelings for Miss Bowen would make the challenge more difficult for you," his instructor replies.

"Why would you do this to me?" Marco asks. "Why would you spend all that time training me for such a thing?"

The pause before the response is heavy.

"I thought it preferable to the life you might have had otherwise, regardless of the consequences."

Marco closes and locks the door.

The man in the grey suit lifts his hand to knock again, but then lowers it and walks away instead.

You follow the sound of a flute into a hidden corner, the hypnotic melody beckoning you closer.

Seated on the ground, nestled in an alcove on striped silk pillows, are two women. One plays the flute you heard. A burning coil of incense sits between them, along with a large black-lidded basket.

A small audience is gathering. The other woman carefully removes the lid from the basket before taking out a flute of her own and adding a countermelody to the first.

Two white cobras coil around each other as they rise from the woven basket, in perfect time with the music. For a moment they seem to be one snake and not two, and then they separate again, moving down along the sides of the basket, gliding onto the ground quite close to your feet.

The snakes move back and forth together in motions resembling a strikingly formal dance. Elegant and graceful.

The music increases in tempo, and now there is something harsher about the way the snakes move. Waltz morphs into battle. They circle each other, and you watch for one or the other to strike.

One of them hisses, softly, and the other responds in kind. They continue to circle as the music and the incense rise into the starry sky above.

You cannot tell which snake strikes first. They are identical, after all. As they rear and hiss and jump at each other you are distracted by the fact that they are both no longer stark white but a perfect ebony black.

Precognition

Most of the train's passengers have settled into their respective cars and compartments to read or sleep or otherwise pass the journey. Corridors that were bustling with people at departure time are now nearly empty as Poppet and Widget make their way from car to car, quiet as cats.

Tags hang by each compartment door, marked with handwritten names. They stop at the one that reads "C. Bowen" and Widget lifts his hand to knock softly on the frosted glass.

"Come in," calls a voice from inside, and Poppet slides the door open.

"Are we interrupting anything?" she asks.

"No," Celia says. "Do come in." She closes the symbol-filled book she has been reading and places it on a table. The entire compartment looks like an explosion in a library, piles of books and paper amongst the velvet-covered benches and polished-wood tables. The light dances around the room with the motion of the train, bouncing off the crystal chandeliers.

Widget slides the door closed behind them and latches it.

"Would you like some tea?" Celia asks.

"No, thank you," Poppet says. She looks nervously at Widget, who only nods.

Celia watches both of them, Poppet biting her lip and refusing to meet Celia's eyes, while Widget leans against the door.

"Out with it," she says.

"We . . ." Poppet starts. "We have a problem."

"What kind of problem?" Celia asks, moving piles of books so they can sit on the violet benches but the twins both remain where they are.

"I think something that was supposed to happen didn't happen," Poppet says.

"And what might that be?" Celia asks.

"Our friend Bailey was supposed to come with us."

"Ah yes, Widget mentioned something about that," Celia says. "I take it he did not?"

"No," Poppet says. "We waited for him but he didn't come, but I don't know if that's because he didn't want to or because we left early."

"I see," Celia says. "It seems a very big decision to me, deciding whether or not to run away and join the circus. Perhaps he did not have enough time to properly consider it."

"But he was supposed to come," Poppet says. "I know he was supposed to come."

"Did you see something?" Celia asks.

"Sort of."

"How does one sort of see something?"

"It's not as clear as it was before," Poppet says. "I can't see anything as clearly as I used to. It's all bits and pieces that don't make sense. Nothing here has made any sense for a year and you know it."

"I think that is an exaggeration, but I understand how it can seem that way," Celia says.

"It is not an exaggeration," Poppet says, raising her voice.

The chandeliers begin to shudder and Celia closes her eyes, taking a deep breath and waiting for them to return to a gentle sway before she speaks.

"Poppet, there is no one here who is more upset by what happened last year than I am. And I have told you before it is not your fault, and there is nothing that could have been done to prevent it. Not by you, not by me, not by anyone else. Do you understand that?"

"Yes," Poppet says. "But what's the use in seeing the future if I can't do anything to stop it?"

"You cannot stop things," Celia says. "You can only be prepared for them to happen."

"You could stop them," Poppet mumbles, looking around at the multitude of books. Celia puts a finger under Poppet's chin and turns her head to look her in the eye.

"Only a handful of people on this train have any idea how integral I am to the running of the circus," she says. "And as much as you two are

amongst them and you are both extremely clever, you do not comprehend the scope of what goes on here and you wouldn't particularly like it
if you did. Now, tell me what you *sort of* saw."

Poppet closes her eyes, trying to concentrate. "I don't know," she
says. "It was bright, everything was on fire, and Bailey was there."

"You're going to have to do better than that," Celia says.

"I can't," Poppet says. "I haven't seen anything clearly since
before—"

"And that's likely because you don't want to see anything clearly
after that, and I can't say I blame you. But if you want me to do something to prevent whatever this is, I am going to need more information."

She unclasps the long silver chain that hangs around her neck, checking the time on the pocket watch that hangs from it before she holds it up
in front of Poppet's eyes.

"Please, Poppet," Celia says. "You don't need the stars for this. Just
focus. Even if you don't want to."

Poppet frowns, then turns her attention to the dangling silver watch
as it sways in the warm light.

Her eyes narrow, focusing on the reflections in the curve of the
watch, and then they soften, looking at something beyond the watch,
beyond the train.

She starts to sway as her eyes flutter closed, and she falls backward.
Widget leaps forward to catch her before she hits the floor.

Celia helps him move Poppet to one of the velvet benches by the
table, while on a nearby shelf a cup of tea pours itself, steaming and
brewing instantly in a flowered china cup.

Poppet blinks, looking up at the chandeliers as though seeing them
for the first time, before turning back to Celia to accept the cup of tea.

"That hurt," Poppet says.

"I'm sorry, dearest," Celia says. "I think your sight is getting stronger,
which makes it even more troublesome for you to be suppressing it."

Poppet nods, rubbing her temples.

"Tell me everything you saw," Celia says. "Everything. I don't care
if it doesn't make any sense. Try to describe it."

Poppet looks into her tea before she starts.

"There's a fire," she says. "It starts with the bonfire but . . . bigger and there's nothing containing it. Like the whole courtyard is on fire, there's a loud noise and this heat and . . ." Poppet pauses, closing her eyes as she attempts to concentrate on the images in her head. She opens her eyes and looks back at Celia. "You're there. You're with someone else and I think it's raining, and then you're not there anymore but you still are, I can't explain it. And then Bailey is there, not during the fire but after it, I think."

"What did the someone else look like?" Celia asks.

"A man. He was tall. In a suit, with a bowler hat, I think. It was hard to tell."

Celia rests her head in her hands for a moment before she speaks.

"If that is who I think it is, I know for a fact he is in London at the moment, so perhaps this is not as immediate as you think."

"But it is, I'm sure of it," Poppet protests.

"Timing has never been your strong point. You said yourself that this friend of yours is also present for this incident, and your first complaint was that he is not here. This might not happen for weeks or months or years, 'Pet."

"But we have to *do* something," Poppet says, slamming her teacup down on the table. The tea stops before it splashes onto an open book as though there is an invisible wall surrounding it. "To be prepared, like you said."

"I will do what I can to prevent the circus from going up in smoke. I shall fireproof it as much as possible. Is that enough for now?"

After a moment, Poppet nods.

"Good," Celia says. "We'll be off the train in a matter of hours, we can discuss this more later."

"Wait," Widget says. He has been sitting on the back of one of the velvet benches, staying out of the conversation. Now he turns to Celia. "I have a question before you shoo us away."

"What is it?" she asks.

"You said we don't comprehend the scope of what goes on here," he says.

"That was likely not the best choice of words."

"It's a game, isn't it?" Widget asks.

Celia looks at him, a slow, sad smile tugging at her lips.

"It took you sixteen years to figure that one out," she says. "I expected more from you, Widge."

"I'd guessed as much for a while," he says. "It's not easy to see things you don't want me to know, but I've been picking up bits of it lately. You haven't been as guarded as usual."

"A game?" Poppet asks, looking back and forth between her brother and Celia.

"Like a chess game," Widget says. "The circus is the board."

"Not exactly," Celia says. "It's not as straightforward as chess."

"We're all playing a game?" Poppet asks.

"Not us," Widget says. "Her and someone else. The rest of us are, what, extra pieces?"

"It's not like that," Celia says.

"Then what is it like?" Widget asks.

In response, Celia only looks at him, staring directly into his eyes without wavering.

Widget returns her gaze silently for some time while Poppet watches them curiously. Eventually, Widget blinks, the surprise evident on his face. Then he looks down at his shoes.

Celia sighs, and when she speaks she addresses them both.

"If I have not been completely honest with you, it is only because I know a great deal of things that you do not want to know. I am going to ask that you trust me when I tell you I am trying to make things better. It is an extremely delicate balance and there are a great many factors involved. The best we can do right now is take everything as it comes, and not worry ourselves over things that have happened, or things that are to come. Agreed?"

Widget nods and Poppet reluctantly follows suit.

"Thank you," Celia says. "Now please go and try to get some rest."

Poppet gives her an embrace before slipping out the door back into the hall.

Widget lingers a moment.

"I'm sorry," he says.

"You have nothing to be sorry about," Celia tells him.

"I'm sorry anyway."

He kisses her on the cheek before he leaves, not waiting for her to reply.

"What was that about?" Poppet asks when Widget joins her in the hall.

"She let me read her," Widget says. "All of her, without concealing anything. She's never done that before." He refuses to elaborate as they walk quietly back down the length of the train.

"What do you think we should do?" Poppet asks once they have reached their car, a marmalade cat crawling onto her lap.

"I think we should wait," Widget says. "I think that's all we can do right now."

*

ALONE IN HER BOOK-FILLED CHAMBER, Celia begins tearing her handkerchief into strips. One at a time she drops each scrap of silk and lace into an empty teacup and lights it on fire. She repeats this process over and over, working until the cloth burns without charring, remaining bright and white within the flame.

Pursuit

It is a cold morning, and Bailey's faded grey coat does not look particularly elegant paired with his new charcoal suit, and he is not entirely certain the two shades are complementary, but the streets and the train station are too busy for him to worry much about his appearance.

There are other *rêveurs* headed to New York, but they end up getting tickets for a later train, so there is a round of farewells and the confusion of sorting dozens of bags before they manage to board.

The journey is slow, and Bailey sits staring out the window at the changing landscape, absently gnawing at his fingernails.

Victor comes to sit by him, a red leather-bound book in his hands.

"I thought you might like something to read to pass the time," he says as he gives the book to Bailey.

Bailey opens the cover and glances through the book, which he is surprised to see is a meticulously organized scrapbook. Most of the black pages are filled with articles clipped from newspapers, but there are also handwritten letters, the dates ranging from only a few years previous to more than a decade ago.

"Not all of it is in English," Victor explains, "but you should be able to read most of the articles, at least."

"Thank you," Bailey says.

Victor nods and returns to his seat across the car.

As the train chugs on, Bailey forgets the landscape entirely. He reads and rereads the words of Herr Friedrick Thiessen, finding them both familiar and entrancing.

"I have never seen you take such a sudden interest in a new *rêveur*," he overhears Lorena remark to her brother. "Especially not to the point of sharing your books."

"He reminds me of Friedrick" is Victor's only reply.

They are almost to New York when Elizabeth takes the empty seat opposite him. Bailey notes his place in the middle of an article that is comparing the interplay of light and shadow in a particular tent to Indonesian puppet theater before putting the book down.

"We lead strange lives, chasing our dreams around from place to place," Elizabeth says quietly, looking out the window. "I have never met so young a *rêveur* who clearly feels as strongly toward the circus as those of us who have been following it for years. I want you to have this."

She hands him a red wool scarf, the one she has been knitting on and off. It is longer than Bailey expected from watching her knit, with intricate patterns of knotted cables at each end.

"I can't accept this," he says, part of him deeply honored and the other part wishing people would stop giving him things.

"Nonsense," Elizabeth says. "I make them all the time, I am at no loss for yarn. I started this one with no particular *rêveur* in mind to wear it, so clearly it is meant for you."

"Thank you," Bailey says, wrapping the scarf around his neck despite the warmth of the train.

"You are quite welcome," Elizabeth says. "We should be arriving soon enough, and then it will only be a matter of waiting for the sun to set."

She leaves him in his seat by the window. Bailey stares out at the grey sky with a mixture of comfort and excitement and nervousness that he cannot reconcile.

When they arrive in New York, Bailey is immediately struck by how strange everything looks. Though it is not that different from Boston, Boston had some passing familiarity. Now, without the comforting lull of the train, it strikes him how very far he is from home.

Victor and Lorena seem equally discombobulated, but Elizabeth is on familiar ground. She ushers them through intersections and herds them onto streetcars until Bailey begins to feel like one of his sheep. But it does not take long for them to reach their destination, a spot outside the city proper where they are to meet up with another local *rêveur* named August, the same whose room Bailey had inherited in Boston, who has graciously invited them to stay with him at his home until they can find rooms elsewhere.

August turns out to be a pleasant, heavyset fellow and Bailey's first impression is that he resembles his house: a squat sort of building with a porch wrapping around the front, warm and welcoming. He practically lifts Elizabeth off the ground in greeting and shakes hands so enthusiastically while being introduced to Bailey that his fingers are sore afterward.

"I have good news and bad news," August says as he helps them lift their bags onto the porch. "Which should come first?"

"The good," Elizabeth answers before Bailey has time to consider which would be preferable. "We have traveled too long to be met with bad news straight off."

"The good news," August says, "is that I was indeed correct in predicting the exact location and Le Cirque has set up less than a mile away. You can see the tents from the end of the porch if you lean properly." He points down the left side of the porch from where he stands on the stairs.

Bailey rushes to the end of the porch with Lorena close on his heels. The tops of the striped tents are visible through the trees some distance away, a bright punch of white against grey sky and brown trees.

"Wonderful," Elizabeth says, laughing at Lorena and Bailey as they lean over the railing. "And what is the bad news, then?"

"I'm not certain it is bad news, precisely," August says, as though he is not sure how to explain. "Perhaps more disappointing, really. Regarding the circus."

Bailey steps down from the railing and turns back to the conversation, all the elation he had felt moments before draining away.

"Disappointing?" Victor asks.

"Well, the weather is not ideal, as I'm certain you've noticed," August says, gesturing up at the heavy grey clouds. "We had quite a storm last night. The circus was closed, of course, which was odd to begin with as in all my time I have never seen it set up only to be closed the first night for inclement weather. Regardless, there was some sort of, I don't even know what to call it, a noise of some sort around midnight. A crashing sound that practically shook the house. I thought perhaps something had been struck by lightning. There was a great deal of smoke over the circus, and one of the neighbors swears he saw a flash of light bright as day. I took a walk down there this morning and nothing appears to be amiss, though the closure sign is still up on the gates."

"How strange," Lorena remarks.

Without a word Bailey leaps over the porch railing and takes off in a full run through the trees. He heads toward the striped tents as fast as he can, his red scarf trailing out behind him.

Old Ghosts

LONDON, OCTOBER 31, 1902

It is late and the pavement is dark despite the streetlamps dotting the line of grey stone buildings. Isobel stands near the shadowed stairs of the one she called home for almost a year, what now seems like a lifetime ago. She waits outside for Marco to return, a pale blue shawl pulled around her shoulders like a patch of day-bright sky in the night.

Hours pass before Marco appears at the corner. His grip on his briefcase tightens when he sees her.

"What are you doing here?" he asks. "You're supposed to be in the States."

"I left the circus," Isobel said. "I walked away. Celia said I could."

She takes a faded scrap of paper from her pocket, bearing her name, her real name that he coaxed from her years ago and asked her to write in one of his notebooks.

"Of course she did," Marco says.

"May I come upstairs?" she asks, fidgeting with the edge of her shawl.

"No," Marco says, glancing up at the windows. A dim, flickering light illuminates the glass. "Please, just say whatever it is you're here to say."

Isobel frowns. She looks around the street but it is dark and empty, only a crisp breeze blowing through, rustling the leaves in the gutter.

"I wanted to say that I was sorry," she says quietly. "For not telling you that I was tempering. I know what happened last year was partly my fault."

"You should apologize to Celia, not to me."

"I already have," Isobel says. "I knew she was in love with someone, but I thought it was Herr Thiessen. I didn't realize until that night that it was you. But she loved him as well, and she lost him and I was the cause."

"It was not your fault," Marco says. "There were a great many factors involved."

"There have always been a great many factors involved," Isobel says. "I didn't mean to get so tangled up in this. I only wanted to be helpful. I wanted to get through . . . *this* and go back to the way things were, before."

"We cannot go backward," Marco says. "A great deal is not how it used to be."

"I know," Isobel says. "I cannot hate her. I have tried. I cannot even dislike her. She let me carry on for years, clearly suspicious of her, but she was always kind to me. And I loved the circus. I felt like I finally had a home, a place I could belong. After a while I didn't feel like I needed to protect you from her, I felt I should protect everyone else from both of you, and both of you from each other. I started after you came to see me in Paris, when you were so upset about the Wishing Tree, but I knew I had to continue after I read Celia's cards."

"When was this?" Marco asks.

"That night in Prague when you were supposed to meet me," Isobel says. "You never let me read for you, not even a single card before last year. I had not realized that before. I wonder if I would have let this go on so long if I'd had the opportunity. It took ages for me to truly understand what her cards were saying. I could not see what was right in front of me. I wasted so much time. This was always about the two of you, even before you met. I was only a diversion."

"You were not a diversion," Marco says.

"Did you ever love me?" Isobel asks.

"No," Marco admits. "I thought perhaps I could, but . . ."

Isobel nods.

"I thought you did," she says. "I was so certain that you did, even though you never said it. I couldn't tell the difference between what was real and what I wanted to be real. I thought this was going to be temporary, even when it kept dragging on and on. But it's not. It never was. I was the one who was temporary. I used to think that if she were gone, you would come back to me."

"If she were gone, I would be nothing," Marco says. "You should think better of yourself than to settle for that."

They stand in silence on the empty street, the chill of the night air falling between them.

"Good night, Miss Martin," Marco says, starting up the stairs.

"The most difficult thing to read is time," Isobel says, and Marco stops, turning back to her. "Maybe because it changes so many things. I have read for countless people on innumerable subjects and the most difficult thing to understand within the cards is always the timing. I knew that, and still it surprised me. How long I was willing to wait for something that was only a possibility. I always thought it was just a matter of time, but I was wrong."

"I did not expect this to go on as long as——" Marco begins, but Isobel interrupts him.

"It was all a matter of timing," she says. "My train was late that day. The day I saw you drop your notebook. Had it been on schedule we never would have met. Maybe we were never meant to. It was a possibility, one of thousands, and not inevitable, the way some things are."

"Isobel, I am sorry," Marco says. "I am sorry that I involved you in all of this. I am sorry that I did not tell you sooner how I feel for Celia. I do not know what else you want from me that I can give you."

Isobel nods, pulling her shawl tighter around her shoulders.

"I read for someone a week ago," she says. "He was young, younger than I was when I met you. Tall in the way of someone who is not yet used to being tall. He was genuine and sweet. He even asked me my name. And everything was in his cards. Everything. It was like reading for the circus, and that has only happened to me once before, when I read for Celia."

"Why are you telling me this?" Marco asks.

"Because I thought he could have saved you. I didn't know how to feel about that; I still don't. It was there in his cards along with everything else, as plain as anything I have ever seen. I thought then that this was going to end differently. I was wrong. I seem to be wrong quite frequently. Perhaps it is time for me to find a new occupation."

Marco stops, his face going pale in the lamplight.

"What are you saying?" he asks.

"I am saying that you had a chance," Isobel says. "A chance to be with her. A chance for everything to resolve itself in a favorable manner. I almost wanted that for you, truly, in spite of everything. I still want you to be happy. And the possibility was there." She gives him a small, sad smile as she slides her hand into her pocket. "But the timing isn't right."

She removes her hand from her pocket and uncurls her fingers. In her palm sits a pile of sparkling black crystals, silt as fine as ash.

"What is that?" Marco asks as she lifts her palm to her lips.

In response, Isobel blows softly, and the ash flies at Marco in a stinging black cloud.

When the dust clears, Marco's briefcase sits abandoned on the pavement by her feet. Isobel takes it with her as she leaves.

Aftermath

Though the surroundings have changed, the circus looks exactly the same as it did in his own fields, Bailey thinks when he finally reaches the fence, holding a stitch in his side and breathing heavily from running through an area that is more woods than fields.

But something more than that is different. It takes him a moment of trying to catch his breath by the side of the gates, staring at the sign that reads:

Closed Due to Inclement Weather

hanging over the normal sign denoting the hours of operation.

It is the smell, he realizes. It is not the smell of caramel blended perfectly with the woody smoke of a warming fire. Instead it is the heavy scent of something burned and wet, with a sickly sweet undertone.

It makes him nauseous.

There is no sound within the bounds of the curling iron fence. The tents are perfectly still. Only the clock beyond the gates makes any motion, slowly ticking by the afternoon hours.

Bailey discovers quickly that he is not able to slip through the bars of the fence as easily as he did when he was ten. The space is too narrow, no matter how he tries to shift his shoulders. He half expected Poppet to be there waiting for him, but there is not a soul in sight.

The fence is too high to climb, and Bailey is considering simply sitting in front of the gates until sundown when he spots a curving tree branch that does not quite reach the fence but comes close, hanging above the twisting iron spikes at the top.

From there he could jump. If he got the angle right he would land in a path between tents. If he got the angle wrong he'd likely break his leg, but that would be only a minor problem that could be dealt with, and then at least he would be inside the circus.

The tree is easy enough to climb, and the limb closest to the circus wide enough to manage until he gets closer to the fence. But he is unable to balance well and while he attempts a graceful leap, it ends up being something closer to a planned fall. He lands heavily in the path, rolling into the side of the tent and taking a large amount of the white powder on the ground with him.

His legs hurt but seem to be in working order, though his shoulder feels badly bruised and the palms of his hands are a mess of scrapes and dirt and powder. The powder brushes off his hands easily enough, but sticks like paint to his coat and the legs of his new suit. And now he stands alone inside the circus again.

"Truth or dare," he mutters to himself.

Dry, fragile leaves dance around his feet, drawn in through the fence by the wind. Spots of muted autumn color disrupting the black and white.

Bailey is not certain where to go. He wanders through paths expecting to see Poppet around every corner, but he is met with only stripes and emptiness. Finally, he heads toward the courtyard, toward the bonfire.

As he turns a corner that opens up into the wide space of the bonfire courtyard, he is more surprised by the fact that the fire is not burning than he is to find that there is indeed someone waiting for him.

But the figure standing by the cauldron of curling iron is not Poppet. This woman is too short, her hair too dark. When she turns she has a long silver cigarette holder at her lips, and the smoke curls around her head like snakes.

It takes him a moment to recognize the contortionist, having only ever seen her upon a platform bending herself into impossible shapes.

"You are Bailey, yes?" she says.

"Yes," Bailey answers, wondering if absolutely everyone in the circus knows who he is.

"You are late," the contortionist tells him.

"Late for what?" Bailey asks, confused.

"I doubt she will be able to hold on much longer."

"Who?" Bailey asks, though the thought pops into his head that the contortionist might be referring to the circus itself.

"And of course," she continues, "had you arrived earlier it might have played out differently. Timing is a sensitive thing."

"Where's Poppet?" Bailey asks.

"Miss Penelope is indisposed at the moment."

"How can she not know that I'm here?" he asks.

"She might very well know you are here, but that does not change the fact that she is, as I have mentioned, indisposed at the moment."

"Who are you?" Bailey asks. His shoulder is throbbing now and he cannot quite pinpoint when everything stopped making sense.

"You may call me Tsukiko," the contortionist says. She takes a long drag on her cigarette.

Beyond her, the monstrous bowl of wrought-iron curls sits hollow and still. The ground around it, usually painted in a spiral pattern of black and white, is now nothing but darkness, as though it has been swallowed up by empty space.

"I thought the fire never went out," Bailey says, walking closer to it.

"It never has before," Tsukiko says.

Reaching the edge of the still-hot iron curls, Bailey stands on his toes to peer inside. It is almost filled with rainwater, the dark surface rippling in the breeze. The ground beneath his feet is black and muddy, and when he steps back he accidentally kicks a black bowler hat.

"What happened?" Bailey asks.

"That is somewhat difficult to explain," Tsukiko answers. "It is a long and complicated story."

"And you're not going to tell it to me, are you?"

She tilts her head a bit, and Bailey can see the hint of a smile playing around her lips.

"No, I am not," she says.

"Great," Bailey mutters under his breath.

"I see you have taken up the banner," Tsukiko says, pointing her cigarette at his red scarf. Bailey is unsure how to respond to this, but she continues without waiting for an answer. "I suppose you could call it an explosion."

"The bonfire exploded? How?"

"Remember when I said it was difficult to explain? That has not changed."

"Why didn't the tents burn?" Bailey asks, looking around at the seemingly never-ending stripes. Some of the closer tents are splattered with mud, but none are burned despite the charred ground surrounding them.

"That was Miss Bowen's doing," Tsukiko says. "I suspect without that precaution there would have been more extensive damage."

"Who is Miss Bowen?" Bailey asks.

"You ask a lot of questions," Tsukiko responds.

"You don't answer very many of them," Bailey retaliates.

The smile appears in full then, curling up in a manner Bailey finds almost disturbingly friendly.

"I am only an emissary," Tsukiko says. "I am here to act as convoy to escort you to a meeting, for a discussion of such matters, I suppose, because at the moment I am the only living person who has any idea of what has transpired, and why you are here. Your questions are better saved for someone else."

"And who might that be?" Bailey asks.

"You shall see," Tsukiko says. "Come this way."

She beckons him forward, leading him around the bonfire to the other side of the courtyard. They walk a short way down an adjoining passageway, layers of mud sticking to Bailey's formerly shiny shoes.

"Here we are." Tsukiko stops at a tent entrance, and Bailey moves closer to check the sign, knowing which tent it is as soon as he glances at the words upon it.

Fearsome Beasts and Strange Creatures
Wonders in Paper and Mist

"Are you coming with me?" Bailey asks.

"No," Tsukiko says. "Only an emissary, remember? I shall be in the courtyard if you need me."

With that she gives him a polite nod and walks back the way they came, and as Bailey watches her go he notices that the mud is not sticking to her boots.

After she disappears around a corner, Bailey enters the tent.

Incendiary

Marco's back slams against the ground as though he has been roughly pushed, leaving him coughing both from the impact and the cloud of black ash surrounding him.

A light rain is falling as he pulls himself up, and as the air around him clears he sees a row of tiny trees and stars, surrounded by silver gears and black-and-white chess pieces.

It takes him a moment to realize he is standing next to the *Wunschtraum* clock.

The clock is ticking toward midnight, the harlequin juggler at the top balancing eleven balls amongst the twinkling stars and moving pieces.

The sign announcing the circus's closure due to inclement weather clatters in the wind. Though for the moment, the rain is not much more than a heavy mist.

Marco rubs the shimmering powder from his face, which has reverted to its true form and he is too disoriented to change it. He tries to get a better look at the dark ash on his suit but it is already fading away.

The striped curtain beyond the ticket booth hangs open, and through the haze, Marco can see a figure standing in the shadows, illuminated by the sharp spark of light from a cigarette lighter.

"*Bonsoir*," Tsukiko says cheerfully as he approaches, tucking her lighter back in her pocket as she balances her cigarette in its long silver holder. A rush of wind howls across the space, rattling the circus gates.

"How . . . how did she do this?" Marco asks.

"Isobel, you mean?" Tsukiko replies. "I taught her that particular trick. I do not think she understood the nuances of it, but it appears she performed fine regardless. Do you feel unsteady at all?"

"I'm fine," Marco says, though his back is aching from the fall and his eyes still sting. He watches Tsukiko curiously. He has never spoken at any great length with the contortionist, and her presence is almost as confusing as the fact that moments ago he had been somewhere else entirely.

"Here, come out of the wind at least." Tsukiko motions him into the curtained tunnel with her cigarette-free hand. "That is a better face than the other one," she says, scrutinizing his appearance through mist and smoke. "It suits you." She lets the curtain fall once he has entered, leaving them enclosed in darkness studded with dimly sparkling lights, the glowing tip of her cigarette the one spot of color amongst the dots of white.

"Where is everyone?" Marco asks, shaking the rain from his bowler hat.

"Inclement-weather party," Tsukiko explains. "Traditionally held in the acrobats' tent, as it is the largest. But you would not know that, as you are not truly a member of the company, are you?"

He cannot see her expression well enough to read it, though he can tell that she is grinning brightly.

"No, I suppose I am not," he says. He follows her as she walks through the mazelike tunnel, moving deeper into the circus. "Why am I here?" he asks.

"We will get to that in due time," she says. "How much did Isobel tell you?"

The conversation with Isobel outside his building is almost lost in Marco's memory, despite occurring only moments ago. He recalls fleeting pieces of it. Nothing coherent enough to articulate.

"No matter," Tsukiko says when he does not respond immediately. "It is sometimes difficult to gather one's senses after such a journey. Did she tell you that we have something in common?"

Marco recalls Isobel mentioning Celia and someone else, but not who, exactly.

"No," he says.

"We are both former students of the same instructor," Tsukiko says. The end of her cigarette glows brighter as she inhales in the near darkness. "Temporary cover only, I am afraid," she adds as they reach another curtain. She pulls it back and the space is flooded with glowing light from the courtyard. She gestures for Marco to step out into the rain, taking a drag from her cigarette as he obediently walks through the open curtain, trying to make sense of her last statement.

The lights that adorn the tents are dark, but in the center of the courtyard the bonfire burns brightly, glowing and white. The soft rain falling around it glistens.

"It is lovely," Tsukiko says, stepping into the courtyard with him. "I will grant you that."

"You were a former student of Alexander's?" Marco asks, not certain he has understood.

Tsukiko nods.

"I tired of writing things in books, so I began inscribing them on my body instead. I am not fond of getting my hands dirty," she says, indicating his ink-stained fingers. "I am surprised he agreed to such an open venue for this challenge. He always preferred seclusion. I suspect he is not pleased with the way it has progressed."

As he listens to her, Marco notices that the contortionist is completely dry. Every drop of rain that falls on her evaporates instantly, sizzling into steam as soon as it touches her.

"You won the last game," he says.

"I survived the last game," Tsukiko corrects.

"When?" Marco asks as they walk toward the bonfire.

"It ended eighty-three years, six months, and twenty-one days ago. It was a cherry-blossom day."

Tsukiko takes a long drag from her cigarette before she continues.

"Our instructors do not understand how it is," she says. "To be bound to someone in such a way. They are too old, too out of touch with their emotions. They no longer remember what it is to live and breathe within the world. They think it simple to pit any two people against each other. It is never simple. The other person becomes how you define your life, how you define yourself. They become as necessary as breathing. Then they expect the victor to continue on without that. It would be like pulling the Murray twins apart and expecting them to be the same. They would be whole but not complete. You love her, do you not?"

"More than anything in the world," Marco says.

Tsukiko nods thoughtfully.

"My opponent's name was Hinata," she says. "Her skin smelled of ginger and cream. I loved her more than anything in the world, as well. On that cherry-blossom day, she set herself on fire. Ignited a pillar of flame and stepped into it as though it were water."

"I'm sorry," Marco says.

"Thank you," Tsukiko says, with a shadow of her normally bright smile. "It is what Miss Bowen is planning to do for you. To let you win."

"I know."

"I would not wish such pain on anyone. To be the victor. Hinata would have adored this," she says as they reach the bonfire, watching the flames dance in the increasing rain. "She was quite fond of fire. Water was always my element. Before."

She holds out her hand and watches as the raindrops refuse to reach her skin.

"Do you know the story of the wizard in the tree?" she asks.

"The Merlin story?" Marco asks. "I know several versions."

"There are many," Tsukiko says with a nod. "Old stories have a habit of being told and retold and changed. Each subsequent storyteller puts his or her mark upon it. Whatever truth the story once had is buried in bias and embellishment. The reasons do not matter as much as the story itself."

The rain continues to increase, falling heavily as she continues.

"Sometimes it is a cave, but I like the version with the tree. Perhaps a tree is more romantic."

She takes the still-glowing cigarette from its holder, balancing it gently between her graceful fingers.

"While there are a number of trees here that could be used for this purpose," she says, "I thought this might be more appropriate."

Marco turns his attention to the bonfire. It illuminates the rain falling over it in such a way that the droplets of water sparkle like snow.

All of the versions of the Merlin story he knows involve the magician being imprisoned. In a tree or a cave or a rock.

Always as a punishment, the consequence of a foolish love.

He looks back at Tsukiko.

"You understand," she says, before he can speak.

Marco nods.

"I knew you would," she says. The light from the white flames brightens her smile through the rain.

"What are you doing, Tsukiko?" a voice calls from behind her. When Tsukiko turns, Marco can see Celia standing at the edge of the courtyard. Her moonlight gown is soaked to a dull grey, its crisscrossing ribbons stream out behind her in trails of black and white and charcoal, tangling with her hair in the wind.

"Go back to the party, dear," Tsukiko says, tucking the silver cigarette holder in her pocket. "You will not want to be here for this."

"For what?" Celia says, staring at Marco.

When Tsukiko speaks, she addresses them both.

"I have been surrounded by love letters you two have built each other for years, encased in tents. It reminds me of what it was to be with her. It is wonderful and it is terrible. I am not yet prepared to give it up, but you are letting it fade."

"You told me love was fickle and fleeting," Celia says, confused.

"I lied," Tsukiko says, rolling her cigarette between her fingers. "I thought it might be easier if you doubted him. And I gave you a year to find a way for the circus to continue without you. You have not. I am stepping in."

"I am try—" Celia starts, but Tsukiko cuts her off.

"You continue to overlook a simple fact," she says. "You carry this circus within yourself. He uses the fire as a tool. You are the greater loss, but too selfish to admit it. You believe you could not live with the pain. Such pain is not lived with. It is only endured. I am sorry."

"Kiko, please," Celia says. "I need more time."

Tsukiko shakes her head.

"I told you before," she says, "time is not something I can control."

Marco has not taken his eyes from Celia since she appeared in the courtyard, but now he turns away.

"Go ahead," he says to Tsukiko, shouting over the growing din of the rain. "Do it! I would rather burn by her side than live without her."

What might have been a simple cry of the word "No" is distorted into something greater by the wind as Celia screams. The agony in her voice cuts through Marco like every blade in Chandresh's collection combined, but he keeps his attention on the contortionist.

"It will end the game, yes?" he asks. "It will end the game even if I am trapped in the fire and not dead."

"You will be unable to continue," Tsukiko says. "That is all that matters."

"Then do it," Marco says.

Tsukiko smiles at him. She places her palms together, curls of smoke from her cigarette rising over her fingers.

She gives him a low, respectful bow.

Neither of them are watching as Celia runs toward them through the rain.

Tsukiko flicks her still-glowing cigarette toward the fire.

It is still in the air when Marco cries out for Celia to stop.

It has barely touched the flickering white flames of the bonfire when she leaps into his arms.

Marco knows he does not have the time to push her away, so he pulls her close, burying his face in her hair, his bowler hat torn from his head by the wind.

And then the pain starts. Sharp, ripping pain as though he is being pulled apart.

"Trust me," Celia whispers in his ear, and he stops fighting it, forgetting everything but her.

In the moment before the explosion, before the white light becomes too blinding to discern precisely what is happening, they dissolve into the air. One moment they are there, Celia's dress fluttering in the wind and the rain, Marco's hands pressed against her back, and the next they are only a blur of light and shadow.

Then both of them are gone and the circus is ablaze, flames licking against the tents, twisting up into the rain.

Alone in the courtyard, Tsukiko sighs. The flames pass by her without touching, swirling around in a vortex. Illuminating her with impossible brightness.

Then, as quickly as they came, the flames die down to nothing.

The bonfire's curling cage sits empty, not even a smoldering ember remains. The rain patters in a hollow echo against the metal, drops evaporating into steam where the iron is still hot.

Tsukiko pulls another cigarette from her coat, flicking open her lighter with a lazy, practiced gesture.

The flame catches easily, despite the rain.

She watches the cauldron fill with water while she waits.

Transmutation

If Celia could open her mouth, she would scream.

But there is too much to control between the heat and the rain and Marco in her arms.

She focuses only on him, pulling everything that he is with her as she breaks herself apart. Holding to the memory of every touch of his skin against hers, every moment she has spent with him. Carrying him with her.

Suddenly, there is nothing. No rain. No fire. A stretch of calm white nothingness.

Somewhere in the nothingness, a clock begins to strike midnight.

Stop, she thinks.

The clock continues to chime, but she feels the stillness fall.

The breaking is the easy part, Celia realizes.

The pulling back together is the problem.

It is like healing her sliced-open fingertips as a child, taken to an extreme.

There is so much to balance, trying to find the edges again.

It would be so simple to let go.

It would be so much easier to let go.

So much less painful.

She fights against the temptation, against the pain and the chaos. Struggling for control with herself and her surroundings.

She picks a location to focus on, the most familiar place she can think of.

And slowly, agonizingly slowly, she pulls herself safely together.

Until she is standing in her own tent, in the center of a circle of empty chairs.

She feels lighter. Diluted. Slightly dizzy.

But she is not an echo of her former self. She is whole again, breathing. She can feel her heart beating, fast but steady. Even her gown feels the same as it did, cascading around her and no longer wet from the rain.

She spins in a circle and it flares out around her.

The dizziness begins to fade as she collects herself, still amazed at the accomplishment.

Then she notices that everything in the tent around her is transparent. The chairs, the lights hanging above her head, even the stripes on the walls seem insubstantial.

And she is alone.

*

FOR MARCO, THE MOMENT of the explosion lasts much longer.

The heat and the light stretch endlessly as he clings to Celia through the pain.

And then she is gone.

Nothing remains. No fire. No rain. No ground beneath his feet.

His sight begins to shift continuously from shadow to light, darkness replaced by expansive white only to be consumed by darkness again. Never settling.

*

THE CIRCUS SHIFTS AROUND CELIA, as fluid as one of Marco's illusions.

She pictures where she wishes to be within it, and she is there. She cannot even tell if she is moving herself or manipulating the circus around her.

The Ice Garden is silent and still, nothing but crisp, cool whiteness in every direction.

Only a fraction of the Hall of Mirrors reflects her own countenance, and some contain only a shimmering blur of pale-grey gown, or the motion of the billowing ribbons as they float behind her.

She thinks she catches glimpses of Marco in the glass, the edge of his jacket or the bright flash of his collar, but she cannot be certain.

Many of the mirrors sit hollow and empty within their ornate frames.

The mist in the Menagerie slowly dissipates as she searches the tent, finding nothing concealed within it but paper.

The Pool of Tears does not even ripple, the surface calm and smooth, and she is unable to grasp a stone to drop within it. She cannot light a candle on the Wishing Tree, though the wishes that hang on its branches continue to burn.

She moves through room after room in the Labyrinth. Rooms she created leading to ones he made and back again.

She can feel him. Close enough that she expects him around each turn, behind each door.

But there are only softly drifting feathers and fluttering playing cards. Silver statues with unseeing eyes. Chessboard-painted floors with vacant squares.

There are traces of him everywhere, but nothing for her to focus on. Nothing to hold on to.

The hallway lined with mismatched doors and covered in fallen snow bears traces of what could be footprints, or might only be shadows.

And Celia cannot tell where they lead.

*

MARCO GASPS AS AIR FILLS HIS LUNGS, as though he had been underwater and unaware of it.

And his first coherent thought is that he did not expect being trapped in a fire to feel so cold.

The cool air is sharp and stinging, and he can see only white in all directions.

As his eyes adjust, he can discern the shadow of a tree. The hanging branches of a frosty white willow tree cascading around him.

He takes a step forward, the ground disconcertingly soft beneath his feet.

He stands in the middle of the Ice Garden.

The fountain in the center has halted, the normally bubbling water quiet and still.

And the whiteness makes the effect difficult to see, but the entire garden is transparent.

He looks down at his hands. They are shaking slightly but they appear to be solid. His suit remains dark and opaque.

Marco lifts his hand to a nearby rose and his fingers pass through its petals with only a soft resistance, as though they are made of water rather than ice.

He is still looking at the rose when he hears a gasp behind him.

*

CELIA HOLDS HER HANDS TO HER LIPS, not quite believing her eyes. The sight of Marco standing in the Ice Garden is one she has imagined so many times before while alone in the icy expanse of flowers, it does not seem real despite the darkness of his suit against a bower of pale roses.

Then he turns and looks at her. As soon as she sees his eyes all her doubts vanish.

For a moment, he looks so young that she can see the boy he was, years before she met him, when they were already connected but still so far apart.

There are so many things she wants to say, things she feared she would never have the opportunity to tell him again. Only one seems truly important.

"I love you," she says.

The words echo throughout the tent, softly rustling the frozen leaves.

*

MARCO ONLY STARES at her as she approaches, thinking her a dream.

"I thought I'd lost you," she says when she reaches him, her voice a tremulous whisper.

She seems to be as substantial as he is, not transparent like the garden. She appears rich and vibrant against a background of white, a bright flush in her cheeks, her dark eyes brimming with tears.

He brings his hand to her face, petrified that his fingers will pass through her as easily as they had with the rose.

The relief when she is solid and warm and alive to his touch is overwhelming.

He pulls her into his arms, his tears falling onto her hair.

"I love you," he says when he finds his voice.

*

THEY STAND ENTWINED, each unwilling to release the other.

"I couldn't let you do it," Celia says. "I couldn't let you go."

"What did you do?" Marco asks. He is still not entirely certain he understands what has happened.

"I used the circus as a touchstone," Celia says. "I didn't know if it would work but I couldn't let you go, I had to try. I tried to take you with me and then I couldn't find you and I thought I'd lost you."

"I'm here," Marco says, stroking her hair. "I'm here."

It is not what he expected, being liberated from the world and reinstated in a confined location. He does not feel confined, only separate, as though he and Celia are overlapping the circus, rather than contained within it.

He looks around at the trees, the long frosted willow branches cascading down, the topiaries that line the nearby path like ghosts.

Only then does he notice that the garden is melting.

"The bonfire went out," Marco says. He can feel it now, the emptiness. He can feel the circus all around him, as though it hangs on him like mist, like he could reach out and touch the iron fence despite the distance from it. Detecting the fence, how far it is in every direction, where every tent sits, even the darkened courtyard and Tsukiko standing within it, is almost effortless. He can feel the entirety of the circus as easily as feeling his shirt against his skin.

And the only thing burning brightly within it is Celia.

But it is a flickering brightness. As fragile as a candle flame.

"You're holding the circus together," he says.

Celia nods. It is only beginning to weigh on her, but it is much more difficult to manage without the bonfire. She cannot focus enough to keep the details intact. Elements are already slipping away, dripping like the flowers around them.

And she knows that if it breaks, she will not be able to put it back together again.

She is shaking, and though she steadies when Marco holds her tighter, she continues to tremble in his arms.

352

"Let go of it, Celia."

"I can't," she says. "If I let go it will collapse."

"What will happen to us if it collapses?" Marco asks.

"I don't know," Celia says. "I suspended it. It can't be self-sufficient without us. It needs a caretaker."

Suspended

The last time Bailey entered this particular tent, Poppet was with him, and it was filled with a dense white fog.

Then, and Bailey has difficulty believing it was only days ago, the tent had seemed endless. But now without the cover of mist, Bailey can see the white walls of the tent and all the creatures within it, but none of them are moving.

Birds and bats and butterflies hang throughout the space as if held by strings, completely still. No rustling of paper wings. No motion at all.

Other creatures sit on the ground near Bailey's feet, including a black cat crouched pre-pounce near a silver-tipped white fox. There are larger animals, as well. A zebra with perfectly contrasting stripes. A reclining lion with a snowy mane. A white stag with tall antlers.

Standing next to the stag is a man in a dark suit.

He is almost transparent, like a ghost, or a reflection in glass. Parts of his suit are no more than shadows. Bailey can see the stag clearly through the sleeve of his jacket.

Bailey is debating whether or not it is a figment of his imagination when the man looks over at him, his eyes surprisingly bright, though Bailey cannot discern their color.

"I asked her not to send you this way," he says. "Though it is the most direct."

"Who are you?" Bailey asks.

"My name is Marco," the man says. "You must be Bailey."

Bailey nods.

"I wish you were not so young," Marco says. Something in his voice sounds profoundly sad, but Bailey is still distracted by his ghostlike appearance.

"Are you dead?" he asks, walking closer. With the changing angle, Marco appears almost solid one moment, and transparent again the next.

"Not precisely," Marco says.

"Tsukiko said she was the only living person here who knew what happened."

"I suspect Miss Tsukiko is not always entirely truthful."

"You look like a ghost," Bailey says. He can think of no better way to describe it.

"You appear the same way to me, so which of us is real?"

Bailey has no idea how to answer that question, so he asks the first one of his own that comes to mind instead.

"Is that your bowler hat in the courtyard?"

To his surprise, Marco smiles.

"It is, indeed," he says. "I lost it before everything happened, so it got left behind."

"What happened?" Bailey asks.

Marco pauses before he answers.

"That is a rather long story."

"That's what Tsukiko said," Bailey says. He wonders if he can find Widget, so he can do the storytelling properly.

"She was truthful on that point, then," Marco says. "Tsukiko intended to imprison me in the bonfire, the reasons for which are a longer story than we have time for, and there was a change of plan that resulted in the current situation. I was pulled apart and put back together again in a less concentrated state."

Marco holds out his hand and Bailey reaches to touch it. His fingers move through without stopping, but there is a soft resistance, the impression that there is something occupying the space, even if it is not completely solid.

"It is not an illusion or a trick," Marco says.

Bailey's brow furrows in thought, but after a moment he nods. Poppet said nothing is impossible, and he finds he is beginning to agree.

"I am not interacting with the surroundings as directly as you are," Marco continues. "You and everything here appear equally insubstantial from my perspective. Perhaps we will be able to discuss it at greater

355

length another time. Come with me." He turns and begins walking toward the back of the tent.

Bailey follows, taking a winding path around the animals. It is difficult to find places to step, though Marco glides ahead of him with much less difficulty.

Bailey loses his balance stepping around the prone figure of a polar bear. His shoulder knocks into a raven hanging in the air. The raven falls to the ground, its wings bent and broken.

Before Bailey can say anything, Marco reaches down and picks up the raven, turning it over in his hands. He moves the broken wings and reaches inside, twisting something with a clicking noise. The raven turns its head and lets out a sharp, metallic caw.

"How can you touch them?" Bailey asks.

"I am still figuring out the logistics of interacting with physical things," Marco says, flattening the raven's wings and letting it limp down the length of his arm. It flaps its paper feathers but cannot fly. "It likely has something to do with the fact that I made them. Elements of the circus I had a hand in creating seem to be more tangible."

The raven hops off by a mountainous pile of paper scales with a curling tail that looks as though it might once have been a dragon.

"They're amazing," Bailey says.

"They are paper and clockwork wrapped up in fairly simple charms. You could do the same with a bit of study."

It has never crossed Bailey's mind that he could do such things himself, but having been told as much so simply and directly, it seems strangely achievable.

"Where are we going?" Bailey asks as they approach the far side of the tent.

"Someone would like to speak with you," Marco says. "She's waiting at the Wishing Tree; it seemed to be the most stable."

"I don't think I've seen the Wishing Tree," Bailey says, mindful of each step as they approach the other side of the tent.

"It is not a tent that is stumbled upon," Marco says. "It is found when it is needed, instead. It is one of my favorite tents. You take a candle from the box at the entrance and light it from one that already burns on the tree. Your wish is ignited by someone else's wish." They have reached the wall of the tent, and Marco indicates a break in the fabric, a barely visible row of ribbon ties that reminds Bailey of the entrance to Widget's tent with all the strange bottles. "If you go out here you will see the entrance to the acrobat tent across the way. I'll be right behind you, though you might not be able to see me until we're inside again. Be . . . be careful."

Bailey unties the bows and slips out of the tent easily, finding himself in a winding path between tents. The sky above is grey but bright, despite the soft rain that is beginning to fall.

The acrobat tent looms higher than the tents surrounding it and the sign that reads DEFIANCE OF GRAVITY swings over the entrance only a few paces away.

Bailey has been in this tent several times, he knows the open floor with the performers hanging above it well.

But when he steps through the door he is not met with the wide-open space he expects.

He walks into a party. A celebration that has been frozen in place, suspended the same way the paper birds had been in the air.

There are dozens of performers throughout the tent, bathed with light from glowing round lamps that hang high above amongst ropes and chairs and round cages. Some are standing in groups and pairs, others sit on pillows and boxes and chairs that add flashes of color to the predominantly black-and-white crowd.

And each figure is perfectly still. So motionless that it seems they are not even breathing. Like statues.

One near Bailey has a flute at his lips, the instrument silent in his fingers.

Another is pouring a bottle of wine, the liquid hovering above the glass.

"We should have gone around," Marco says, appearing like a shadow by his side. "I've been keeping an eye on them for hours and they haven't gotten any less disturbing."

"What's wrong with them?" Bailey asks.

"Nothing, as far as I can tell," Marco answers. "The entirety of the circus has been suspended to give us more time, so . . ." He lifts a hand and waves it over the party.

"Tsukiko's part of the circus and she's not like this," Bailey says, confused.

"I believe she plays by her own rules," Marco says. "This way," he adds, moving into the crowd of figures.

Navigating the party proves more difficult than walking around the paper animals, and Bailey takes every step with extreme caution, afraid of what might happen if he accidentally hits someone the way he knocked down the raven.

"Almost there," Marco says as they maneuver their way around a cluster of people grouped in a broken circle.

But Bailey stops, staring at the figure the group is facing.

Widget wears his performance costume but his patchwork jacket has been discarded, his vest hanging open over his black shirt. His hands are lifted in the air, gesturing in such a familiar way that Bailey can tell he has been stopped mid-story.

Poppet stands next to him. Her head is turned in the direction of the courtyard, as though something pulled her attention away from her brother at the precise moment the party was halted. Her hair spills out behind her, waves of red floating in the air as if she were suspended in water.

Bailey walks around to face her, reaching out tentatively to touch her hair. It ripples beneath his fingers, undulating slowly before settling back into its frozen state.

"Can she see me?" Bailey asks. Poppet's eyes are still yet bright. He expects her to blink at any moment, but she does not.

"I don't know," Marco says. "Perhaps, but—"

Before he can conclude the thought, one of the chairs hanging above them falls, its ribbons snapping. It comes close to hitting Widget as it crashes to the ground, splintering into pieces.

"Bloody hell," Marco says as Bailey jumps back, almost colliding with Poppet and sending her hair into another brief wave of motion. "Through there," Marco says, indicating the side of the tent that is some distance away. Then he vanishes.

Bailey looks back at Poppet and Widget. Poppet's hair settles again, unmoving. Fragments of the fallen chair rest on Widget's boots.

Turning away, Bailey moves carefully around stationary figures to reach the edge of the tent. He casts nervous glances upward at the additional chairs and the round iron cages suspended by nothing but fraying ribbon.

His fingers shake as he undoes the ties in the wall.

As soon as he passes through, he feels as though he has walked into a dream.

Inside the adjoining tent there is a towering tree. As large as his old oak tree, growing right out of the ground. The branches are bare and black but they are covered with dripping white candles, translucent layers of wax frosting over the bark.

Only a fraction of the candles are burning, but the sight is no less resplendent as they illuminate the twisting black branches, casting dancing shadows over the striped walls.

Beneath it, Marco stands with his arms around a woman Bailey recognizes instantly as the illusionist.

She appears as transparent as Marco does. Her gown looks like mist in the candlelight.

"Hello, Bailey," she says as he approaches. Her voice echoes around him, softly, as close as if she were standing next to him, whispering in his ear. "I like your scarf," she adds when he does not immediately reply. The words in his ears are warm and strangely comforting. "I'm Celia. I don't believe we were ever properly introduced."

"Nice to meet you," Bailey says.

Celia smiles, and Bailey is struck by how different she seems from the way she did when he watched her perform, even beyond the fact that he can look through her at the dark tree branches.

"How did you know I was coming here?" he asks.

"Poppet mentioned you as part of the series of events that occurred earlier, so I hoped you would arrive eventually."

At the mention of Poppet's name, Bailey glances over his shoulder at the wall of the tent. The suspended party seems farther away than just beyond the canvas stripes.

"We need your help with something," Celia continues as he turns back. "We need you to take over the circus."

"What?" Bailey asks. He is not sure what he was expecting, but it was not this.

"Right now the circus is in need of a new caretaker," Marco says. "It is drifting, like a ship without an anchor. It needs someone to anchor it."

"And that someone is me?" Bailey asks.

"We would like it to be, yes," Celia says. "If you are willing to make the commitment. We should be able to assist you, and Poppet and Widget would be able to help, as well, but the true responsibility would be yours."

"But I'm not . . . special," Bailey says. "Not the way they are. I'm not anyone important."

"I know," Celia says. "You're not destined or chosen, I wish I could tell you that you were if that would make it easier, but it's not true. You're in the right place at the right time, and you care enough to do what needs to be done. Sometimes that's enough."

As he watches her in the flickering light, it strikes Bailey suddenly that she is a fair deal older than she appears, and that the same is likely true of Marco. It is like realizing someone in a photograph is no longer the same age as they were when it was taken, and they seem farther away because of it. The circus itself feels far away, even though he stands within it. As though it is falling away from him.

"All right," Bailey says, but Celia holds up a transparent hand to stop him before he agrees.

"Wait," Celia says. "This is important. I want you to have something neither of us truly had. I want you to have a choice. You can agree to this or you can walk away. You are not obliged to help, and I don't want you to feel that you are."

"What happens if I walk away?" Bailey asks. Celia looks at Marco before she answers.

They only look at each other without speaking, but the gesture is so intimate that Bailey glances away, looking up at the twisting branches of the tree.

"It won't last," Celia says after a moment. She does not elaborate, turning back to Bailey as she continues. "I know this is a great deal to request from you, but I do not have anyone else to ask."

Suddenly the candles on the tree begin to spark. Some of them darken, curls of smoke replacing the bright flames only momentarily before disappearing themselves.

Celia wavers, and for a moment Bailey thinks she might faint, but Marco steadies her.

"Celia, love," Marco says, running his hand over her hair. "You are the strongest person I have ever known. You can hold on for a while longer, I know you can."

"I'm sorry," Celia says.

Bailey cannot tell which one of them she is speaking to.

"You have nothing to be sorry about," Marco says.

Celia holds tightly to his hand.

"What would happen to the two of you, if the circus . . . stopped?" Bailey asks.

"Truthfully, I'm not entirely certain," Celia says.

"Nothing good," Marco mutters.

"What would you need me to do?" Bailey asks.

"I need you to finish something I started," Celia says. "I . . . I acted rather impulsively and played my cards out of order. And now there is the matter of the bonfire as well."

"The bonfire?" Bailey asks.

"Think of the circus as a machine," Marco says. "The bonfire is one of the things that powers it."

"There are two things that need to happen," Celia says. "First, the bonfire needs to be lit. That will . . . power half the circus."

"What about the other half?" Bailey asks.

"That's more complicated," Celia says. "I carry that with me. And I would have to give that to you."

"Oh."

"You would then carry it with you," Celia says. "All of the time. You'd be tied very tightly to the circus itself. You could leave, but not for extended periods of time. I do not know if you would be able to give it to someone else. It would be yours. Always."

It is only then that Bailey realizes the scope of the commitment he is being asked for.

It is not the handful of years committed to Harvard. It is, he thinks, an even greater commitment than inheriting responsibility for the family farm.

He looks from Marco to Celia, and knows from the look in her eyes that she will let him go if he asks to leave, no matter what that might mean for them or for the circus.

He thinks of a litany of questions but none of them truly matter.

He knows his answer already.

His choice was made when he was ten years old, under a different tree, bound up in acorns and dares and a single white glove.

He will always choose the circus.

"I'll do it," he says. "I'll stay. I'll do whatever it is you need me to do."

"Thank you, Bailey," Celia says softly. The words resonating in his ears soothe the last of his nerves.

"Indeed," Marco says. "I think we should make this official."

"Do you think that's absolutely necessary?" Celia asks.

"At this point I'm not about to settle for a verbal contract," Marco says. Celia frowns for a moment but then nods her consent, and Marco carefully lets go of her hand. She stays steady and her appearance does not waver.

"Do you want me to sign something?" Bailey asks.

"Not exactly," Marco says. He takes a silver ring from his right hand, it is engraved with something Bailey cannot discern in the light. Marco reaches up to a branch above his head and passes the ring through one of the burning candles until it glows, white and hot.

Bailey wonders whose wish that particular flame might be.

"I made a wish on this tree years ago," Marco says, as though he knows what Bailey is thinking.

"What did you wish for?" Bailey asks, hoping it is not too forward a question, but Marco does not answer.

Instead, he folds the glowing ring into his palm, and then he offers his hand to Bailey.

Bailey hesitantly reaches out, expecting his fingers to pass through Marco's hand as easily as they did before.

But instead they stop, and Marco's hand in his is almost solid. Marco leans forward and whispers into Bailey's ear.

"I wished for her," he says.

Then Bailey's hand begins to hurt. The pain is bright and hot as the ring burns into his skin.

"What are you doing?" he manages to ask when he can gasp for enough air. The pain is sharp and searing, coursing through his entire body, and he is barely able to keep his knees from buckling beneath him.

"Binding," Marco says. "It's one of my specialties."

He releases Bailey's hand. The pain vanishes instantly but Bailey's legs continue to tremble.

"Are you all right?" Celia asks.

Bailey nods, looking down at his palm. The ring is gone, but there is a bright red circle burned into his skin. Bailey is certain without having to ask that it will be a scar he carries with him always. He closes his hand and looks back at Marco and Celia.

"Tell me what I need to do now," he says.

The Second Lighting of the Bonfire

Bailey finds the tiny, book-filled room without much difficulty. The large black raven sitting in the corner blinks at him curiously as he sorts through the contents of the desk.

He flips anxiously through the large leather book until he finds the page with Poppet's and Widget's signatures. He tears the page from the binding carefully, removing it completely.

He finds a pen in a drawer and writes his own name across the page as he has been instructed. While the ink dries he gathers up the rest of the things he will need, running through the list over and over in his head so he does not forget anything.

The yarn is easily found, a ball of it sits precariously on a pile of books.

The two cards, one a familiar playing card and the other a tarot card emblazoned with an angel, are amongst the papers on the desk. He tucks these into the front cover of the book.

The doves in the cage above him stir with a soft fluttering of feathers.

The pocket watch on its long silver chain proves most difficult to locate. He finds it on the ground beside the desk, and when he attempts to dust it off a bit he can see the initials H.B. engraved on the back. The watch no longer ticks.

Bailey places the loose page on top of the book and tucks it under his arm. The watch and the yarn he puts in his pockets with the candle he pulled from the Wishing Tree.

The raven cocks its head at him as he leaves. The doves remain asleep.

Bailey crosses the adjoining tent, walking around the double circle of chairs as passing directly through it does not seem appropriate.

Outside the light rain is still falling.

He hurries back to the courtyard, where he finds Tsukiko waiting for him.

"Celia says I need to borrow your lighter," he says.

Tsukiko tilts her head curiously, looking oddly like a bird with a cat-like grin.

"I suppose that is acceptable," she says after a moment. She pulls the silver lighter from her coat pocket and tosses it to him.

It is heavier than he had expected, a complicated mechanism of gears partially encased in worn and tarnished silver, with symbols he cannot distinguish etched into the surface.

"Be careful with that," Tsukiko says.

"Is it magic?" Bailey asks, turning it over in his hand.

"No, but it is old, and it was constructed by someone very dear to me. I take it you are attempting to light that again?" She gestures at the towering bowl of twisted metal that once held the bonfire.

Bailey nods.

"Do you want any help?"

"Are you offering?"

Tsukiko shrugs.

"I am not terribly invested in the outcome," she says, but something about the way she looks around at the tents and the mud makes Bailey doubt her words.

"I don't believe you," he says. "But I am, and I think I should do this on my own."

Tsukiko smiles at him, the first smile he has seen from her that seems genuine.

"I shall leave you to it, then," she says. She runs a hand along the iron cauldron and most of the rainwater within it turns to steam, rising in a soft cloud that dissipates into the fog.

With no further advice or instruction she walks off down a black-and-white striped path, a thin curl of smoke trailing behind her, leaving Bailey alone in the courtyard.

He remembers Widget telling him the story of the lighting of the bonfire, the first lighting. Though he only now realizes that it was also the night that Widget was born. He had told the story in such detail that Bailey assumed he had witnessed it firsthand. The archers, the colors, the spectacle.

And now here Bailey stands, trying to accomplish the same feat with only a book and some yarn and a borrowed cigarette lighter. Alone. In the rain.

He mumbles to himself what he can remember of Celia's instructions, the ones that are more complicated than finding books and tying strings. Things about focus and intent that he does not entirely understand.

He wraps the book with a length of fine wool yarn dyed a deep crimson, bits of it stained darker with something dried and brown.

He knots it three times, binding the book closed with the loose page against the cover, the cards securely pressed inside.

The pocket watch he hangs around it, looping the chain as best he can.

He throws it in the empty cauldron where it lands with a dull wet thud, the watch clattering against the metal.

Marco's bowler hat sits in the mud by his feet. He throws that in as well.

He glances back in the direction of the acrobat tent, he can see the top of it from the courtyard, rising taller than the surrounding tents.

And then, impulsively, he takes out the remaining contents of his pockets and adds them to the collection in the cauldron. His silver ticket. The dried rose that he had worn in his lapel at dinner with the *réveurs*. Poppet's white glove.

He hesitates, turning the tiny glass bottle with Widget's version of his tree trapped inside over in his hand, but then he adds it as well, flinching as it shatters against the iron.

He takes the single white candle in one hand and Tsukiko's lighter in the other.

He fumbles with the lighter before it consents to spark.

Then he ignites the candle with the bright orange flame.

He throws the burning candle into the cauldron.

Nothing happens.

I choose this, Bailey thinks. *I want this. I need this. Please. Please let this work.*

He wishes it, harder than he has ever wished for anything over birthday candles or on shooting stars. Wishing for himself. For the *réveurs* in their red scarves. For a clockmaker he never met. For Celia and Marco and Poppet and Widget and even for Tsukiko, though she claims she does not care.

Bailey closes his eyes.

For a moment, everything is still. Even the light rain suddenly stops.

He feels a pair of hands resting on his shoulders.

A heaviness in his chest.

Something within the twisted iron cauldron begins to spark.

When the flames catch they are bright and crimson.

When they turn to white they are blinding, and the shower of sparks falls like stars.

The force of the heat pushes Bailey backward, moving through him like a wave, the air burning hot in his lungs. He falls onto ground that is no longer charred and muddy, but firm and dry and patterned in a spiral of black and white.

All around him, lights are popping to life along the tents, flickering like fireflies.

*

MARCO STANDS BENEATH THE WISHING TREE, watching as the candles come alight along the branches.

A moment later, Celia reappears at his side.

"Did it work?" he asks. "Please, tell me that it worked."

In response, she kisses him the way he once kissed her in the middle of a crowded ballroom.

As though they are the only two people in the world.

Part V

DIVINATION

I find I think of myself not as a writer so much as
someone who provides a gateway, a tangential route
for readers to reach the circus. To visit the circus again,
if only in their minds, when they are unable to attend it
physically. I relay it through printed words on crumpled
newsprint, words that they can read again and again,
returning to the circus whenever they wish, regardless
of time of day or physical location. Transporting them
at will.

When put that way, it sounds rather like magic,
doesn't it?

—FRIEDRICK THIESSEN, 1898

Our revels now are ended. These our actors,
As I foretold you, were all spirits, and
Are melted into air, into thin air:
And, like the baseless fabric of this vision,
The cloud-capp'd tow'rs, the gorgeous palaces,
The solemn temples, the great globe itself,
Yea, all which it inherit, shall dissolve,
And, like this insubstantial pageant faded,
Leave not a rack behind. We are such stuff
As dreams are made on; and our little life
Is rounded with a sleep.

—PROSPERO, *THE TEMPEST*, ACT IV, SCENE I

It is late, so there is no line for the fortune-teller.

While outside the cool night air is scented with caramel and smoke, this tent is warm and smells of incense and roses and beeswax.

You do not wait long in the antechamber before passing through the beaded curtain.

It makes a sound like rain as the beads collide. The room beyond is lined with candles.

You sit down at the table in the center of the room. Your chair is surprisingly comfortable.

The fortune-teller's face is hidden behind a fine black veil, but the light catches her eyes as she smiles.

She has no crystal ball. No deck of cards.

Only a handful of sparkling silver stars that she scatters across the velvet-covered table, reading them like runes.

She refers to things she could not know with uncanny specificity.

She tells you facts you already knew. Information you might have guessed. Possibilities you cannot fathom.

The stars on the table almost seem to move in the undulating candlelight. Shifting and changing before your eyes.

Before you leave, the fortune-teller reminds you that the future is never set in stone.

Blueprints

Poppet Murray stands on the front steps of *la maison* Lefèvre, a leather briefcase in hand and a large satchel sitting by her feet. She rings the doorbell a dozen times, alternating with a series of loud knocks, though she can hear the bell echoing within the house.

When the door finally swings open, Chandresh himself stands behind it, his violet shirt untucked and a crumpled piece of paper in his hand.

"You were smaller last time I saw you," he says, looking Poppet over from her boots to her upswept red hair. "And there were two of you."

"My brother is in France," Poppet says, picking up the satchel and following Chandresh inside.

The golden elephant-headed statue in the hall is in need of polishing. The house is in a state of disarray, or as much disarray as a house crammed from floor to ceiling with antiques and books and objets d'art can be in its inherent cozy, cluttered way. It does not shine as brightly as it had when she ran through the halls with Widget what seems like more than a few years ago, chasing marmalade kittens through a rainbow of guests.

"What happened to your staff?" she asks as they ascend the stairs.

"I dismissed the lot of them," Chandresh says. "They were useless, could not keep a single thing in order. I retained only the cooks. Haven't had a dinner in quite some time, but at least they know what they're doing."

Poppet follows him down the column-lined hall to his study. She has never been in this particular room before, but she doubts it was always so covered with blueprints and sketches and empty brandy bottles.

Chandresh wanders across the room, adding the crumpled piece of paper in his hand to a stack on a chair, and staring idly at a set of blueprints hanging over the windows.

Poppet clears a space on the desk to put the briefcase down, moving books and antlers and carved jade turtles. She leaves the satchel on the floor nearby.

"Why are you here?" Chandresh says, turning and looking at Poppet as though he has only just noticed her presence.

Poppet snaps open the briefcase on the desk, pulling out a dense pile of paper.

"I need you to do a favor for me, Chandresh," she says.

"What might that be?"

"I would like you to sign over ownership of the circus." Poppet finds a fountain pen amongst the clutter on the desk and tests it on a scrap of paper to see if it is properly inked.

"The circus was never mine to begin with," Chandresh mutters.

"Of course it was," Poppet says, drawing a swirling letter *P*. "It was your idea. But I know you don't have time for it, and I thought it might be best if you relinquished your position as proprietor."

Chandresh considers this for a moment, but then he nods and walks over to the desk to read through the contract.

"You have Ethan and Lainie listed here, but not Tante Padva," he says as he peruses it.

"I've spoken with all of them already," Poppet says. "Madame Padva wished not to be involved any longer, but she is confident that Miss Burgess can handle her responsibilities."

"Who is this Mr. Clarke?" Chandresh asks.

"He is a very dear friend of mine," Poppet says, a soft blush warming her cheeks. "And he will take excellent care of the circus."

When Chandresh reaches the end of the document, she hands him the pen.

He signs his name with a wobbling flourish, letting the pen drop onto the desk.

"I appreciate this more than I can say." Poppet blows on the ink to dry it before she returns the contract to the briefcase. Chandresh brushes her words away with a lazy wave of his hand, walking back to the window and staring at the expanse of blue papers hanging over it.

"What are the blueprints for?" Poppet asks after she closes the briefcase.

"I have all of these . . . *plans* from Ethan and I don't know what to do with them," Chandresh says, waving an arm around at the multitudes of paper.

Poppet removes her coat, leaving it draped over the back of the desk chair, and takes a closer look at the blueprints and sketches hanging from shelves and tacked to mirrors and paintings and windows. Some are complete rooms, others are bits of exterior architecture or elaborate archways and halls.

She stops when she reaches a dartboard with a silver knife embedded in the patterned cork, its blade marred with dark stains. The knife vanishes as Poppet continues walking, though Chandresh does not notice.

"They are meant to be renovations to the house," he says as she tours the room, "but they do not fit together properly."

"It's a museum," Poppet says, overlaying the pieces in her mind and seeing where they match up with the building she has already seen in the stars. They are completely out of order, but it is unmistakable. She pulls down a set of blueprints and switches it with another, arranging them story by story. "It's not this building," she explains as Chandresh watches her curiously. "It's a new one." She takes a series of doors, alternate versions of the same possible entrance, and lays them side by side along the floor, letting each lead to a different room.

Chandresh watches as she rearranges the plans, a grin spreading across his face as he begins to see what she is doing.

He makes adjustments to the flood of Prussian blue paper himself, responding to her arrangements, surrounding replicas of ancient Egyptian temples with columns of curving bookshelves. They sit together on the floor, combining rooms and halls and stairs.

Chandresh starts to call for Marco, but catches himself.

"I keep forgetting that he's gone," he says to Poppet. "Left one day and did not come back. Didn't even leave a note. You would think someone who was constantly writing notes would leave one."

"I believe his departure was unplanned," Poppet says. "And I know he regrets not being able to properly settle his responsibilities here."

"Do you know why he left?" Chandresh asks, looking up at her.

"He left to be with Celia Bowen," Poppet says, unable to keep from smiling.

"Ha!" Chandresh exclaims. "Didn't think he had it in him. Good for them. Let's have a toast."

"A toast?"

"You're right, there's no champagne," Chandresh says, pushing aside a pile of empty brandy bottles as he lays out another string of sketches along the floor. "We'll dedicate a room to them, which one do you think they would like?"

Poppet looks over the blueprints and sketches. There are several that she thinks either or both of them might like. She stops at a drawing of a round, windowless room illuminated only by light that filters through the koi pond enclosed in glass above it. Serene and enchanting.

"This one," she says.

Chandresh takes a pencil and writes "Dedicate to M. Alisdair and C. Bowen" along the edge of the paper.

"I could help you find a new assistant," Poppet offers. "I can stay in London for a while."

"I would appreciate that, my dear."

The large satchel that Poppet had placed on the floor nearby suddenly falls to its side with a soft thump.

"What's in that bag?" Chandresh asks, eyeing it with a certain amount of trepidation.

"I brought you a present," Poppet says brightly.

She rights the bag, opening it carefully and pulling out a small black kitten with splotches of white along its legs and tail. It looks as though it has been dipped in cream.

"Her name is Ara," Poppet tells him. "She'll come when she's called and she knows a few tricks but mostly she likes attention and sitting in windows. I thought you might like the company."

She puts the kitten gently on the floor and holds her hand above it. The kitten stretches up on its hind legs with a soft mew and licks Poppet's fingers before turning its attention to Chandresh.

"Hello, Ara," he says.

"I'm not going to give you your memory back," Poppet says, watching Chandresh as the kitten attempts to crawl onto his lap. "I don't know if I could even if I tried, though Widge could probably manage it. At this point, I don't think you need that weight on you. I think looking forward will be better than looking back."

"Whatever are you talking about?" Chandresh asks, picking up the kitten and scratching it behind the ears as it purrs.

"Nothing," Poppet says. "Thank you, Chandresh."

She leans over and kisses him on the cheek.

As soon as her lips touch his skin, Chandresh feels better than he has in years, as though the last of a fog has been lifted from him. His mind is clear, the plans for the museum becoming cohesive, ideas for future projects aligning themselves in ways that seem completely manageable.

Chandresh and Poppet spend hours arranging and adding to the blueprints, creating a new space to be filled with antiques and art and visions of the future.

The black-and-white kitten paws playfully at the curling paper as they work.

Stories

Stories have changed, my dear boy," the man in the grey suit says, his voice almost imperceptibly sad. "There are no more battles between good and evil, no monsters to slay, no maidens in need of rescue. Most maidens are perfectly capable of rescuing themselves in my experience, at least the ones worth something, in any case. There are no longer simple tales with quests and beasts and happy endings. The quests lack clarity of goal or path. The beasts take different forms and are difficult to recognize for what they are. And there are never really endings, happy or otherwise. Things keep going on, they overlap and blur, your story is part of your sister's story is part of many other stories, and there is no telling where any of them may lead. Good and evil are a great deal more complex than a princess and a dragon, or a wolf and a scarlet-clad little girl. And is not the dragon the hero of his own story? Is not the wolf simply acting as a wolf should act? Though perhaps it is a singular wolf who goes to such lengths as to dress as a grandmother to toy with its prey."

Widget sips his glass of wine, considering the words before he replies.

"But wouldn't that mean there were never any simple tales at all?" he asks.

The man in the grey suit shrugs, then lifts the bottle of wine from the table to refill his own glass.

"That is a complicated matter. The heart of the tale and the ideas behind it are simple. Time has altered and condensed their nuances, made them more than story, greater than the sums of their parts. But that requires time. The truest tales require time and familiarity to become what they are."

Their waiter stops at their table and converses briefly with Widget, paying no notice to the man in the grey suit.

"How many languages do you speak?" the man asks once the waiter has departed.

"I've never stopped to count," Widget says. "I can speak anything once I have heard enough to grasp the basis."

"Impressive."

"I picked up bits and pieces naturally, and Celia taught me how to find the patterns, to put the sounds together in complete sets."

"I hope she was a better teacher than her father."

"From what I know of her father they are quite different. She never forced Poppet or me into playing complicated games, for one thing."

"Do you even know what the challenge you are alluding to was?" the man in the grey suit asks.

"Do *you*?" Widget asks. "It seems to me it was not entirely clear-cut."

"Few things in this world are clear-cut. A very long time ago—I suppose you could say *once upon a time* if you wished it to sound a grander tale than it is—one of my first students and I had a disagreement about the ways of the world, about permanence and endurance and time. He thought my systems outdated. He developed methods of his own that he thought superior. I am of the opinion that no methodology is worthwhile unless it can be taught, so he began teaching. The pitting of our respective students against each other began as simple tests, though over time they became more complex. They were always, at the heart, challenges of chaos and control to see which technique was strongest. It is one thing to put two competitors alone in a ring and wait for one to hit the ground. It is another to see how they fare when there are other factors in the ring along with them. When there are repercussions with every action taken. This final challenge was particularly interesting. I will admit that Miss Bowen found a very clever way out. Though I do regret losing a student of my own in the process." He takes a sip of his wine. "He was possibly the best student I ever taught."

"You believe he's dead?" Widget asks.

The man puts down his glass.

"You believe he is not?" he counters after a significant pause.

"I know he's not. Just as I know that Celia's father, who is also not dead, precisely, is standing by that window." Widget lifts his glass, tilting it toward the darkened window by the door.

The image in the glass, which could be a grey-haired man in a finely tailored coat, or could be an amalgamation of reflections from customers and waiters and bent and broken light from the street, ripples slightly before becoming completely indistinguishable.

"Neither of them are dead," Widget continues. "But they're not that, either." He nods at the window. "They're in the circus. They *are* the circus. You can hear his footsteps in the Labyrinth. You can smell her perfume in the Cloud Maze. It's marvelous."

"You think being imprisoned marvelous?"

"It's a matter of perspective," Widget says. "They have each other. They are confined within a space that is remarkable, one that can, and will, grow and change around them. In a way, they have the world, bound only by his imagination. Marco has been teaching his illusion technique to me, but I've not yet mastered it. So yes, I think it marvelous. He thought of you as his father, you know."

"Did he tell you that?" the man in the grey suit asks.

"Not in words," Widget says. "He let me read him. I see people's pasts, sometimes in great detail if the person in question trusts me. He trusts me because Celia does. I do not think he blames you any longer. Because of you, he has her."

"I chose him to contrast her, and to complement. Perhaps I chose too well." The man in the grey suit leans into the table, as though he might whisper his words conspiratorially, but the tenor of his voice does not change. "That was the mistake, you realize. They were too well matched. Too taken with each other to be competitive. And now they can never be separated. Pity."

"I take it you are not a romantic," Widget says, picking up the bottle to refill his glass.

"I was in my youth. Which was a very, very long time ago."

"I can tell," Widget says as he replaces the bottle on the table. The man in the grey suit's past stretches back a long, long time. Longer than anyone Widget has ever met. He can only read parts of it, so much of it is worn and faded. The parts connected to the circus are clearest, the easiest for him to grasp.

"Do I look that old?"

"You have no shadow."

The man in the grey suit cracks a smile, the only noticeable change his expression has displayed the entire evening.

"You are quite perceptive," he says. "Not one person in a hundred, perhaps even a thousand, notices as much. Yes, my age is quite advanced. I have seen a great many things in my time. Some I would prefer to forget. It takes a toll on a person, after all. Everything does, in its way. Just as everything fades with time. I am no exception to that rule."

"Are you going to end up like him?" Widget nods at the window.

"I certainly hope not. I am content to accept inevitabilities, even if I have ways of putting them off. He was seeking immortality, which is a terrible thing to seek. It is not seeking anything, but rather avoiding the unavoidable. He will grow to despise that state if he does not already. I hope my student and your teacher are more fortunate."

"You mean . . . you hope they can die?" Widget asks.

"I mean only that I hope they find darkness or paradise without fear of it, if they can." He pauses before adding, "I hope that for you and your compatriots as well."

"Thank you," Widget says, though he is not entirely certain he understands the sentiment.

"I sent your cradle when you were born to welcome you and your sister to this world, the least I can do is wish you a pleasant exit from it, as I highly doubt I will be there to see you off in person. I hope not to be, in fact."

"Is magic not enough to live for?" Widget asks.

"Magic," the man in the grey suit repeats, turning the word into a laugh. "This is not magic. This is the way the world is, only very few people take the time to stop and note it. Look around you," he says, waving a hand at the surrounding tables. "Not a one of them even has an inkling of the things that are possible in this world, and what's worse is that none of them would listen if you attempted to enlighten them. They want to believe that magic is nothing but clever deception, because to think it real would keep them up at night, afraid of their own existence."

"But some people can be enlightened," Widget says.

"Indeed, such things can be taught. It is easier with minds that are younger than these. There are tricks, of course. None of this rabbits-in-hats nonsense, but ways of making the universe more accessible. Very, very few people take the time to learn them nowadays, unfortunately, and even fewer have natural access. You and your sister do, as an unforeseen effect of the *opening* of your circus. What is it you do with that talent? What purpose does it serve?"

Widget considers this before he answers. Beyond the confines of the circus there seems to be little place for such things, though perhaps that is part of the man's point. "I tell stories," he says. It is the most truthful answer he has.

"You tell stories?" the man asks, the piquing of his interest almost palpable.

"Stories, tales, bardic chronicles," Widget says. "Whatever you care to call them. The things we were discussing earlier that are more complicated than they used to be. I take pieces of the past that I see and I combine them into narratives. It's not that important, and this isn't why I'm here—"

"It is important," the man in the grey suit interrupts. "Someone needs to tell those tales. When the battles are fought and won and lost, when the pirates find their treasures and the dragons eat their foes for breakfast with a nice cup of Lapsang souchong, someone needs to tell their bits of overlapping narrative. There's magic in that. It's in the listener, and for each and every ear it will be different, and it will affect them in ways they can never predict. From the mundane to the profound. You may tell a tale that takes up residence in someone's soul, becomes their blood and self and purpose. That tale will move them and drive them and who knows what they might do because of it, because of your words. That is your role, your gift. Your sister may be able to see the future, but you yourself can shape it, boy. Do not forget that." He takes another sip of his wine. "There are many kinds of magic, after all."

Widget pauses, considering the change in the way the man in the grey suit watches him. He wonders if all the grand words earlier about stories no longer being what they once were was all for show, something that the man does not truly believe.

While before his interest level bordered on indifferent, now he looks at Widget as a child might look at a new toy, or the way a wolf would regard a particularly interesting piece of prey, scarlet-clad or otherwise.

"You're trying to distract me," Widget says.

The man in the grey suit only sips his wine, regarding Widget over the rim of his glass.

"Is the game finished, then?" Widget asks.

"Yes and no." He puts down his glass before continuing. "Technically, it has fallen into an unforeseen loophole. It has not been properly completed."

"And what of the circus?"

"I suppose that is why you wished to speak with me?"

Widget nods. "Bailey has inherited his position from your players. My sister has settled the business end of things with Chandresh. On paper and in principle, we own and operate the circus already. I volunteered to handle the remainder of the transition."

"I am not fond of loose ends, but I am afraid it is not that simple."

"I did not mean to suggest that it was," Widget says.

In the pause that follows, a gale of laughter rises from a few tables over, rippling through the air before settling back down, disappearing into the low, steady hum of conversations and clinking glasses.

"You have no idea what you're getting into, my boy," the man in the grey suit says quietly. "How fragile an enterprise it all is. How uncertain the consequences are. What would your Bailey be, had he not been so adopted into your circus? Nothing but a dreamer, longing for something he does not even understand."

"I don't think there's anything wrong with being a dreamer."

"There is not. But dreams have ways of turning into nightmares. I suspect Monsieur Lefèvre knows something of that. You'd be better off letting the whole endeavor fade away into myth and oblivion. All empires fall eventually. It is the way of things. Perhaps it is time to let this one go."

"I'm afraid I'm unwilling to do that," Widget says.

"You are very young."

"I would wager that combined, even beyond the fact that Bailey and my sister and myself are comparatively, as you say, very young, if I calculated the ages of everyone I have behind this proposition, the total might trump your own age."

"Perhaps."

"And I do not know exactly what kind of rules your game had, but I suspect that you owe us this much, if we were all put at risk for your wager."

The man in the grey suit sighs. He casts a quick glance toward the window, but the shadow of Hector Bowen is nowhere to be seen.

If Prospero the Enchanter has an opinion on the matter, he chooses not to voice it.

"I suppose that is a valid argument," the man in the grey suit says after some consideration. "But I owe you nothing, young man."

"Then why are you here?" Widget asks.

The man smiles, but he says nothing.

"I am negotiating for what is, essentially, a used playing field," Widget continues. "It is of no further use to you. It holds a great deal of importance to me. I will not be dissuaded. Name your price."

The man in the grey suit's smile brightens considerably.

"I want a story," he says.

"A story?"

"I want this story. Your story. The tale of what brought us to this place, in these chairs, with this wine. I don't want a story you create from here"—he taps his temple with his finger—"I want one that is here." He lets his hand hover over his heart for a moment before sitting back in his chair.

Widget considers this offer for a moment.

"And if I tell you this story, you will give me the circus?" he asks.

"I will pass on to you what little of it remains for me to give. When we leave this table I will have no claim over your circus, no connection to it whatsoever. When that bottle of wine is empty, a challenge that started before you were even born will be over, officially declared a stalemate. That should suffice. Do we have an agreement, Mr. Murray?"

"We have an agreement," Widget says.

The man in the grey suit pours the last of the wine. The candlelight catches and bends in the empty bottle as he places it on the table.

Widget swirls his wine around his glass. *Wine is bottled poetry*, he thinks. It is a sentiment he first heard from Herr Thiessen, but he knows it is properly attributed to another writer, though at the moment he cannot recall who, exactly.

There are so many places to begin.

So many elements to consider.

He wonders if the poem of the circus could possibly be bottled.

Widget takes a sip of his wine and puts his glass down on the table. He sits back in his chair and steadily returns the stare aimed at him. Taking his time as though he has all of it in the world, in the universe, from the days when tales meant more than they do now, but perhaps less than they will someday, he draws a breath that releases the tangled knot of words in his heart, and they fall from his lips effortlessly.

"The circus arrives without warning."

There are very few people wandering through Le Cirque des Rêves with you in these predawn hours. Some are wearing red scarves that are particularly vibrant against the black and white.

You do not have much time before the sun inevitably rises. You are faced with the conundrum of how to fill the remaining minutes of the night. Should you visit one last tent? One that you have already entered and particularly enjoyed, or an unexplored tent that remains a mystery? Or should you seek out one last prebreakfast caramel apple? The night that seemed endless hours before is now slipping from your fingers, ticking by as it falls into the past and pushes you toward the future.

You spend your last moments at the circus as you wish, for it is your time and yours alone. But before long, it is time for Le Cirque des Rêves to close, at least for the time being.

The star-filled tunnel has been removed, only a single curtain separates the courtyard from the entrance now.

When it closes behind you, the distance feels greater than a few steps divided by a striped curtain.

You hesitate before you exit, pausing to watch the intricate, dancing clock as it ticks down the seconds, pieces moving seamlessly. You are able to watch it more closely than you had when you entered, as there is no longer a crowd obscuring it.

Beneath the clock, there is an unobtrusive silver plaque. You have to bend down to make out the inscription engraved onto the polished metal.

it reads across the top, with names and dates below in a smaller font.

FRIEDRICK STEFAN THIESSEN
September 9, 1846–November 1, 1901

and

CHANDRESH CHRISTOPHE LEFÈVRE
August 3, 1847–February 15, 1932

Someone is watching you as you read the memorial plaque. You sense their eyes on you before you realize where the unexpected gaze is coming from. The ticket booth is still occupied. The woman stationed inside is watching, and smiling at you. You are not entirely sure what to do. She waves at you, a small but friendly wave as if to assure you that everything is fine. That visitors often stop before they depart Le Cirque des Rêves to stare at the clockwork wonder that sits by the gates. That some even read the inscribed memorial for two men who died so many years ago. That you stand in a position that many have stood in before, under already fading stars and sparkling lights.

The woman beckons you over to the ticket booth. While you walk toward her, she sorts through piles of paper and tickets. There is a spray of silver-and-black feathers in her hair that flutters around her head as she moves. When she finds what she is seeking, she hands it to you, and you take the business card from her black-gloved hand. One side is black and the other is white.

Le Cirque des Rêves

is printed in shimmering silver letters on the black side. On the reverse, in black ink on white, it reads:

Mr. Bailey Alden Clarke, Proprietor
bailey@nightcircus.com

You turn it over in your hand, wondering what you might write to Mr. Clarke. Perhaps you will thank him for his very singular circus, and perhaps that will suffice.

You thank the woman for the card, and she only smiles in response.

You walk toward the gates, reading the card in your hand again. Before you pass through the gates to the field beyond, you turn back to the ticket booth, but it is empty, a black grate pulled down over it.

You tuck the card carefully in your pocket.

The step through the gates that takes you from painted ground to bare grass feels heavy.

You think, as you walk away from Le Cirque des Rêves and into the creeping dawn, that you felt more awake within the confines of the circus.

You are no longer quite certain which side of the fence is the dream.

Acknowledgments

There were a number of associates and conspirators behind this book, and I owe them a great deal of gratitude.

First and foremost, my agent, Richard Pine, who saw potential in something that was once truly a god-awful mess and believed in me every step of the way. He earned his red scarf a thousand times over.

My editor, Alison Callahan, is a dream come true, and everyone at Doubleday deserves more chocolate mice than I can possibly provide.

I am grateful to all who gave their time and insight to revision after revision, particularly Kaari Busick, Elizabeth M. Thurmond, Diana Fox, and Jennifer Weltz.

I raise a glass to the denizens of Purgatory. You are strange, wonderful, talented people, and I would not be here without you.

Kyle Cassidy unknowingly prompted me to buy the vintage fountain pen that was used to compose a significant portion of Part IV, so I said I would put him in the acknowledgments. He probably thought I was kidding.

The circus itself has many influences, but two that should have special recognition are the olfactory geniuses of Black Phoenix Alchemy Lab and the immersive experience of Punchdrunk, which I was lucky enough to fall into thanks to the American Repertory Theater of Cambridge, Massachusetts.

Finally, my eternal thanks to Peter and Clovia. This book simply would not exist without one, and it is better than I'd ever thought possible because of the other. I adore you both.